THE TAKEN

A.J. SCUDIERE

GRIFFYN INK

1

"She's what?" Joule felt her whole body go into shock. Surely, she'd heard Deveron wrong. The phone had cut out or . . .

"Sarah is missing."

No, she'd heard it right.

"Since Monday morning . . . her roommates don't know if she went to work or not. No one who knows her has seen her since then," Deveron told Joule, the worry evident in his tone.

"Hold on." Joule frantically waved Cage over, grabbing his attention as well as that of Ivy and Kayla.

Joule had stepped into the dining room to have a private conversation, but that wasn't happening now. The movie had been paused and three concerned faces crowded around her. Joule worried most about Cage. He knew Sarah. Ivy and Kayla had only heard of her through the stories the twins had told.

Still holding the phone up, she put it on speaker, then looked him in the eyes. "It's Sarah, she's missing."

His face instantly changed from curious to horrified. "How long?"

It was Deveron who answered. "They think almost forty-eight hours now."

Joule's heart hammered. It wasn't like Sarah to disappear or to even casually not pay attention to what she told those around her. If she was intending to miss work and be hard to get a hold of, she would have alerted someone.

Not again.

She watched her brother freeze. They couldn't lose anyone else. The last death had hit her hard, and Joule could feel her muscles tightening, trying to protect her from loss. It never worked.

But Sarah wasn't dead, just gone—at least as far as they knew. So, Joule asked the pertinent questions. "Are the police involved?"

"Yes." Dev's answer was clean. "They notified the local PD just after noon yesterday. When she was a half day late and not answering her phone." There was a pause. "Someone suggested she was just hung over and missing work."

Joule felt her eyes flick up to meet her brother's. A tight shake of his head told her he thought the same thing. *No way.*

"Her car was gone, she didn't answer the door." A sigh. "But what do I know? I'm not there."

He was an engineer, not an investigator. Joule knew the feeling. She'd become so many things—so many that she'd never intended to become—over the past few years.

"What did the police do?" Cage finally jumped into the conversation.

"They agreed with me, then questioned the neighbors and her roommates."

There was a concerning pause. Then he added, "They said they weren't sure if she had come home the night before."

"*What?*" Joule practically yelped it. "And they didn't call the police then? Or the next morning?"

Dev answered, "They didn't know. Thought maybe she'd

stayed out late and left early . . . It wasn't like when we were rooming together."

Apparently not. She hated the thought.

She and Cage had left the job, floated a little aimlessly, grieved Dr. Brett. But it hurt that Sarah had suffered for not having them as roommates. They would have been calling around as soon as Sarah wasn't there for bedtime. *Wouldn't they?*

It was so easy for Joule to believe *she* would have done the right thing. But she hadn't been there. Maybe there was a reason the roommates hadn't thought much of it. "Had her behavior changed since we were there?"

"A little. The last time we talked she said she wanted a new place and a fresh start. She always said she was busy, but I didn't get the impression that she'd made some whole new group of friends or anything. I don't know."

"Is there any word yet from the police?" Cage asked.

Kayla and Ivy hung back, clearly concerned but not part of the conversation.

"They have a BOLO on her car but haven't found it yet." It was clear from his tone that he was worried, very worried.

The conversation—as it were—lagged. Joule felt her ribs caving in on themselves. Cage had hit this point a few apocalypses ago. She'd held it together, but now? She couldn't lose Sarah. She couldn't sit back.

Cage looked at her and mouthed the words, "Are we going?"

Joule nodded. *Of course they were.*

2

    "**A**re you sure you don't want to fly? It would be faster," Cage pointed out as he stood next to the packed car. He knew his argument was already too late.

Joule was shaking her head. "I don't know that it is faster, given layovers, delays, or just getting a rental car once we get there."

"True. And we won't be able to take as much." He accepted that they were driving down to Texas. They'd tried to think of everything they might possibly need, and they had no idea what that would be.

The job Sarah had disappeared from was just outside El Indio, a small town just east of the border in Texas. Helio Systems Tech was installing a solar panel array and, this time, adding a water power plant. It would take advantage of a small tributary of the Rio Grande.

Cage loved HST's forward thinking and that he and Joule had gotten to be a part of it—that they were helping add new, sustainable technologies all the time. Change had happened a little slower than he'd expected, but he gave them credit: They were doing it.

None of that mattered if his friend was gone, though.

Joule climbed into the passenger seat, leaving him to slide behind the wheel. As they pulled down the long driveway— once again having locked up their childhood home to a feeling of a vast emptiness—the words kept ringing in his head, *It wasn't supposed to be this way.*

His parents should have still been alive. The house should have been warm and vibrant even as he and Joule left. They shouldn't be looking for a missing friend.

The twins had been constantly checking in with Deveron as he seemed the most reliable source, but no new information had turned up about Sarah, other than the fact that the police didn't consider her case a high priority.

That had disturbed Cage maybe more than anything. A woman who didn't ever miss work had missed work. A woman whom all her friends said would never do anything like this, had seemingly done something like this. A woman who always answered her phone wasn't answering.

Or, more likely, something had made her do those things. But, because there was no blood and no sign of a struggle and her car hadn't been found, the police saw no reason to treat it as a priority. Given that her purse had not turned up, nor her wallet or any other identifying items, they were operating under the assumption that she'd willingly taken them all with her and that there wasn't much they could do.

Cage turned on the engine. The first portion of the drive was the easiest. They only went three houses down and pulled up to the garage. As they climbed out, Ivy came out the front door with a long hug and a reminder to stay safe and check in often. Kayla shoved a bag of snacks at them, which he knew would be packed Tetris-style from both the weight of the bag and the person handing it to him.

Ivy eventually let go of him and turned to Joule, who somehow managed to look as if they were going on vacation. Kayla came to him next. Her arms wrapped around him tight, not even lasting a full second before she stepped back. But given that when they'd first met several years ago, she had blatantly said, "I don't hug," this was a huge gesture. It was over too soon.

Then, once again, the twins drove away from what little safety and normalcy seemed to exist in their life.

He still hadn't gotten over the stunning blow of losing Dr. Brett, he didn't think Joule had either. That was maybe why they jumped into action so quickly. Action was easier to deal with than the slow, steady thrum of grief.

Cage couldn't lose anyone else, but he had a sinking feeling he was going to.

It seemed to be the way the world went these days. No one emerged unscathed. His college friends had lost family, parents, and often homes. Whole neighborhoods were sometimes abandoned, and no one thought it was odd anymore. No one asked "why?" because no one wanted to hear the answers. It was always a different version of the same story, anyway—something had gone horribly wrong, and the place had become uninhabitable.

He drove on, Joule mostly staying quiet, his brain locked on the droning of tires on pavement and the whir of passing trucks. For a while, the roads were familiar and then they were simply long. He traded the wheel to Joule and slept for a while as she cut through another state on their way.

They stuck to the major highways as best they could. The road changed beneath their tires multiple times. The gas prices increased. The billboards changed and so did the food offerings.

His stomach felt terrible. Was it anxiety or his diet? Probably both.

Cage kept waiting for word that Sarah had been found. Though he hadn't asked his sister if there was a plan for that, he'd already decided that they would simply continue the trip. Hug their friends, tell Sarah how happy they were that it wasn't anything major, just a misunderstanding. They could stay for a few days and call it some kind of vacation.

Not that they'd been doing much of anything productive when Dev's call had come in. Still, breathing was productive, he knew—productive in the necessary sense.

They had new cell phones because the last set they'd had were cloned by the Sheriff's Department. For obvious reasons, the twins didn't feel like running around with a law enforcement tracker in their pockets anymore. They also had burners —one of which belonged to Dr. Brett. Life had taught them to have every possible layer of communication.

They had clothing for all kinds of weather. Beyond that, there wasn't much more to plan for. He had no idea what they would find. And—as Dev said—they weren't investigators.

Just over the Texas border, the phone rang while he was driving. Joule fumbled for it, her eyebrows rising as she whispered "Dev!"

Hitting buttons, she answered without any formal greeting, just, "Any news?"

"Not really." Dev's voice came over the speaker she'd put on automatically. "No one seems to know anything."

"I don't understand." Joule looked at Cage and he saw the confusion there. "She has so many friends. How did she not tell anyone?"

"She and I are the only ones on this job who already knew each other. At least well enough to talk regularly."

Cage felt his eyes squeeze shut at the thought. Then he purposely opened them, reminding himself to keep his gaze on the road. Of course, the call came in while it was his turn to drive. Long drives always felt like it was his turn the whole time.

"What did you find out today?" He leaned a little closer to the phone, the road long and straight and not requiring much effort.

"They all went to work," Dev answered, a bite in his tone.

Joule frowned, her expression carrying through to Cage. He knew they were thinking the same thing. *Was no one looking for Sarah?*

"I called everybody I could once I got home tonight, including her parents. I was hoping, you know, maybe she just had a breakdown and had gone home."

That was wishful thinking. Cage was about to ask what they said, but Dev was filling it all in.

"That call sucked ass, by the way. Her parents didn't know she was missing."

"*No?*" Joule's voice echoed the surprise that gripped Cage's limbs.

"No one had told them!" Dev sounded frantic.

"The team didn't take the day off to look for her?" Joule finally asked what Cage had been thinking.

"They *can't*." The bite in the tone was back. "Unlike you, the rest of us don't have trust funds. Dr. Murasawa is working to get time to do a search, but she's not the top of the food chain. And the police report isn't helping her case."

An interesting term, Cage thought, but said, "I'm sorry, Dev."

Like his sister, he hadn't thought that through. He also didn't correct his friend. The twins didn't have trust funds. Their family hadn't been wealthy enough for that kind of thing. His parents had simply set up good life insurance. Unlike many others, the twins had been in a position to collect it.

"I'm sorry. It's okay." Dev's voice was softer, weary. He'd been doing what he could, Cage knew.

That was why they were coming down here. Because no one else had the opportunity to drop everything and spend all day looking for someone the police declared "not a concern."

"We're still a good handful of hours away," Cage told him. "We won't be there until dark, but we're going."

"Thank you, man."

They said their goodbyes and ended the call. It occurred to Cage for the first time that they might be Sarah's only defense.

3

J oule had managed to get a small rental home set up
during the drive down. It was twenty minutes away from
Sarah's, but it was the best she could do.

No one was renting houses just outside El Indio,
Texas. Any place that was available, Helio Systems Tech had
already snapped up for their employees. Apparently, they'd
taken over almost half of a nearby hotel. Joule couldn't imagine
living and working from a hotel bed with only a small bathroom, a mini fridge, and one window.

They would simply put more miles on the car every day.
Joule just didn't care. They should have run a rental into the
ground, but she loved this car. Even though this one hadn't
been with them as long as it should have; their first car had
been lost in the flood at Stanford.

She grew attached to things and she didn't take lightly to
just getting something different. She was confident she should
hang on to what she could as long as she could. The world
would snatch things away soon enough.

She wanted to begin looking through Sarah's things immediately. But Cage had warned her about that. This was similar

to the arrangement they'd had in Alabama, with several room-mates living in the house—roommates who might not like being barged in on . . . or searched.

They'd learned from Dev that people were looking for Sarah, but no one was walking away from work to do it. It wasn't that they didn't care, it was just that no one could steal the time and they didn't even know where to look.

Joule texted Dr. Murasawa hoping any friendliness that lingered between them would help. The text came back imme-diately.

— You're here to look for Sarah?

— Yes.

— Thank God. I'm driving around in my spare time, but the higher ups won't give me a day to have everyone look. Meet on site in the morning?

That at least made sense, Joule thought. She got directions from her old boss thinking this was the best news they'd gotten. People were doing more than it appeared.

As they'd gotten close, they'd hit a grocery store for a gallon of milk, cereal, and crackers, enough to see them through in the morning. They'd already eaten most of the bag of snacks that Kayla had sent.

Entering the small vacation home, Joule found the decor just a little too cheerful for the circumstances. But there was a full kitchen, which made her wonder if it was possible that there would be enough time to cook a meal. She might have to force it.

By the morning, she was rolling awake before the alarm went off. While she would love to believe she'd gotten a good night's sleep, it hadn't happened. She'd thought that—espe-cially after going off to college—she'd gotten skilled at sleeping anywhere, on any strange mattress, but it wasn't true.

Unfortunately, Joule had logged just enough hours to know better than to crawl back under the covers. There was enough anxiety to roll out of bed and start moving. The phone had dinged all night because Joule had been unwilling to set it to 'do not disturb.' A spam call had excitedly woken her at 3a.m. only to be nothing.

Now, all the lines of communication she'd hoped would yield good news were empty. She showered, got dressed, and found her brother already in the kitchen, his spoon hovering over a bowl of Cheerios. He looked at her as if to say *I see it happened to you, too.*

They were off before even discussing it, hoping to get to the apartment where Sarah lived with her three roommates. Joule prayed one of them would be on hand and be generous enough to let them in to look around.

Though they followed the directions for Sarah's address, neither twin had any familiarity with the area. The land was open and arid, patchy brush sprouting up on either side of a road that periodically turned to rough-trod gravel rather than pavement. Luckily, the apartments were the only two-story building in the whole area. Once a cream-colored stucco, the sides now showed evidence of storms, dirt, and time.

As Cage put the car in park, Joule asked, "Should we watch and see if anyone is home first?"

"And look like stalkers?" he immediately replied, already stepping out of the car into the hot morning air. "I'm sure everyone here will notice us."

He was right. She joined him, the heat assaulting her despite the fact that she'd dressed for it.

She was placated by the movement she saw in one of the windows of the unit she was certain belonged to Sarah and her co-workers. Joule turned to motion to Cage, but had to follow him as he was already across the lot, heading up the metal staircase to knock on the door.

Even as she arrived on the landing and thought it was

already too hot to run upstairs, a petite Hispanic woman opened the door.

"Hello?" She was wary and something in her look let them know it wasn't quite her natural state.

Though Joule was opening her mouth, Cage beat her to it. "My name is Cage Mazur. This is my sister Joule. We're friends of Sarah's."

That didn't quite wipe the suspicious look off her face. "What do you want? She's not here."

"We know. We were hoping to look around and find anything that might help find her."

Joule added, "Deveron told us that the police aren't really looking for her."

Maybe it was the mention of another co-worker or perhaps the fact that the police weren't doing enough to find her room-mate that led her to open the door all the way. Her tone wasn't warm, but she tried. "I'm Gisela, Gisela Lima. This is Brooklyn Cox and Amber Rivera."

She motioned to Brooklyn as she said her name. Amber however was behind a closed door. She'd ducked out to see what was happening but disappeared quickly, clearly not fully dressed.

Gisela pushed the front door shut behind them, something Joule appreciated. Her anxiety pushed at the edges and she wanted to tell the others to keep the mosquitoes and bugs out. But it wasn't her place and being weird wouldn't help. Sarah was likely the only one here who would know to close the doors and douse herself in bug spray.

Gisele looked at them oddly, but luckily, Amber came out and motioned to the room she'd just vacated. Clearly, she'd heard everything, because she said, "That's Sarah's side of the room. You can look at anything on *that side*."

She was clear on the last two words, but Joule nodded that she understood.

Amber quickly added a solemn, "I hope you can find her. We've tried calling, and some of us drove around looking for her car, but ..." She waved her hand at the empty room.

Joule understood. "Thank you."

She and Cage ducked into the now empty room. They might have only a few minutes to see what they could find before the women left for work.

Outside, in the small dining room and kitchen area, she heard an argument between the roommates, but she couldn't afford to pay attention. As Cage rifled through the closet, Joule began opening drawers.

They needed to find *anything* that could help.

4

Joule jerked upright at the sound of a rough cough. She was acting as if she'd been caught in some bad act, but she was sticking to Sarah's side of the room.

In the doorway, the three roommates crowded, looking in at the twins' handiwork.

It was Gisela who spoke. "We called Dev. We thought he might know something we didn't."

Her voice sounded almost accusatory, and Joule stilled, waiting. Her fingers still holding the pair of pants she'd pulled from the bottom drawer. The drawer of long sleeves and pants looked unused, and given the heat, that made sense.

She wasn't surprised when Gisela added, "Dev said you were in town."

Cage nodded. "Checking was smart."

Gisela's strict expression stayed in place. Clearly, she was not quite done. "Can we see your IDs?"

"Of course!" Joule replied, reaching for the small backpack now slung across one shoulder and out of the way. Cage quickly pulled his from his pocket, though Gisela frowned and held it right back out after one glance. "It says Nathaniel Mazur."

"Oh, that's my dad's."

Joule tried to hide how her heart clenched. Cage was still carrying it, right there next to his own ID. He scrambled to switch the two.

The three women passed the driver's licenses around while Joule stayed mostly motionless, though she tried to hold her chin up so they could see her face clearly.

Then the IDs were back in Gisela's hands and she was holding them out. "We have to go to work—"

"We *have* to," Brooklyn added, emphasizing the same argument everyone else had given.

Joule nodded, not quite sure where this was leading, until Brooklyn added, "We're glad someone's looking for Sarah."

"Someone needs to be. The police aren't. And so far, they won't let us off work, in part because we don't even know where to go." Amber crossed her arms and looked away, clearly upset at the situation.

Joule wondered just how much they had looked for their missing roommate. Was it everything they could do? Or enough to assuage their own guilt at losing her? At not knowing Sarah better than they apparently did?

Joule added, "They seem to think she left of her own accord."

Gisela nodded somberly and added, "I didn't know her very well, but she didn't seem like someone who would do this."

"She wasn't." Joule said it staunchly . . . until she realized what she'd said. "She *isn't*."

It had been three days. They were already well outside the golden forty-eight-hour window. *Had they already lost their chance to find Sarah alive?*

She felt the cold squeeze in her heart—the one that said something bad was coming. Joule ignored it like a champ.

Gisela looked at Joule first, meeting her eyes before turning to Cage. "You can stay, but you have to lock the front door when you leave. I want to tell you not to look through our things—"

Amber looked quickly to the floor then. Amber had been very clear they were not supposed to look through her things. Maybe that was what the argument was about. Gisela added, "But if it helps you find Sarah . . . then look wherever you need to. Just don't toss the place like an FBI raid!"

"Of course not," Cage told them. He shook his head and waved his hand around as if to reassure the women the twins knew what they were doing.

They didn't.

He had that way about him that put people at ease, even when he didn't deserve it. He asked, "Is there a number we can reach you at?"

Smart. Joule thought, she hadn't thought of that.

"That way we can text you when we lock up. We can send pictures of anything we find. Maybe even ask you if we find something—if it was Sarah's or if it means anything to you."

"That would be great," Amber said as she handed over her phone number. She was now fully dressed and clearly ready for a day on a solar farm or building a small dam. Joule couldn't tell which.

Joule quickly recorded all the data. "We'll stay in touch. Thank you so much."

With that, they were left alone in a stranger's apartment.

She turned to her brother. "We need to photograph everything. Because we don't know what's important. Not yet."

"Good point."

About an hour later, her phone was full of pictures. Her head was full of nothing. She asked her brother, "Any ideas?"

He only shrugged. "It looks like she went somewhere. But I can't tell if she went to work, or if she went out with friends. Everything seems to be here. You would know better than me."

Joule had roomed with Sarah on several of the jobs they'd done for Helio Systems Tech. "This just looks like *Sarah*. It's neat, reasonably well organized. She always seemed to leave a few things on the end of the bed. This is all typical for her."

It had been a while. "I don't know what her favorite shoes are. Or if this pair of boots—" she pointed to a neat row of shoes just beyond the dresser, "—are her only work boots. Does that mean she wasn't going to work? Or maybe it's a second pair and she disappeared right after a day on site."

Cage didn't have an answer.

"Maybe this isn't where we find anything," Joule conceded. "She took her car. She seems very much to have left *here* of her own free will."

"But none of the roommates have any idea where she could have gone." Cage clearly felt the same frustration.

"According to Dev," Joule pointed out. She remembered her own interrogation at the hands of the sheriff's deputies. They'd asked the same questions repeatedly, hoping for a change in answers or a different wording that gave something away or revealed a gap in memory. "We need to ask again."

"Right now, the roommates are at work. But we can check with the neighbors." He closed Amber's closet door, having found nothing there either.

They didn't lock the door behind them as they headed out onto the front landing that ran the entire length of the upper story. They knocked politely at first, then pounded on doors, though most yielded nothing. One woman seemed angry about "those kids and their noise," though Joule suspected from the woman's demeanor that she was just mostly angry in general.

The door next to hers yielded nothing, and they headed downstairs as Joule made a mental note to make sure they locked the apartment before they drove off.

The first two doors were answered, but neither the harried

young father nor the old man recognized Sarah's picture. But at the third door, they found an older woman.

"Yeah, I know her. I mean I saw her a lot." She handed Cage's phone back to him after putting her glasses on to check the picture. "I don't know her name or anything, but she walked by my window plenty."

The upstairs had a small landing. The lower floor had a short patio that ran the length of the building. Not enough for chairs or any kind of patio, it was barely big enough for the twins to walk along. But the gravel bed with scrub planted in it meant this was the only path to the other apartments unless someone walked through the weeds at the end of the building.

Joule leaned in. "Do you know where she was going?"

"I think she was visiting the guy next door."

"Often?"

"I don't know. I don't keep track!" The woman was getting irritated, but Joule figured a person was missing and they could all suck it up. Or did she think maybe they were blaming her for something?

"We're trying to find her. She's missing." People could be so frustrating, and Joule tried not to heave a sigh.

"Oh. Maybe twice a week?"

"Do you remember what time of day?" Cage added, maybe stepping in and smoothing things over.

"Evenings?"

She'd said it as a question, but it was an answer, Joule thought. Probably something Sarah had done after work. Someone she saw regularly. Did he also work for Helio Systems Tech? Several of the units were supposed to house the workers. But Murasawa would have questioned the person then, wouldn't she?

Cage thanked the older woman profusely, his kindness outweighing her sourness—a skill Joule would have liked to master. She tended to respond to sour with more sour.

The woman was clearly done with them. She'd done her diligence and needed to get back to the iced tea warming on the coffee table behind her or the TV that had been running the whole time.

As the door clicked, the twins looked to each other. Without a word, they headed next door to apartment 104.

5

———————

Cage took stock of the man who'd opened the door. They'd banged on it to get his attention . . . maybe a little too harshly.

"We're friends of Sarah's," Joule said immediately when the man opened the door and offered only a cautious, "Hello?"

He was probably in his late twenties or early thirties, his expression giving away nothing. That was what told Cage immediately that he did know Sarah . . . and that there was something about his relationship to her that he didn't want them to know.

"Have you seen her recently?" Joule asked, barging straight ahead.

Cage watched again as the man simply withheld all comments. In fact, aside from the "hello" when he'd opened the door, he'd said nothing else.

Without stepping up beside his sister—though he had only an inch on her in height—Cage spoke from where he was. He tried an introduction for the second time today.

"My name is Cage Mazur. This is my sister Joule. We've

known Sarah for several years. No one has seen her for several days."

Still, the man's expression didn't change at all.

It should have. If they were asking about a stranger, he would have been saying he didn't know her. He would have said he was sorry their friend was missing, that he would keep an eye out. Not this non-reaction.

Instead, his dark eyes watched them, taking in as much as Cage's were. His nearly-black hair hung in waves to just below his chin, the white tank top and jeans were clean, but nothing special. His bare feet said he was in for the day.

Cage noted all of it.

If this person wasn't going to respond to the basic niceties, then he would play a higher level card. "She's missing. No one has seen her since Tuesday night."

That got a reaction.

His facial hair twitched, revealing the slightest reaction on the face underneath. His dark eyes flashed. What Cage had said wasn't even true. *Tuesday night* was a bit of a stretch. It was more like late Sunday afternoon.

Cage was playing on a bet. Wondering if Tuesday evening or night meant anything to this man. "How often do you see her?"

While he was still slow to answer, this time the man stepped out, his bare feet landing on the cement sidewalk as he pulled the door closed behind him. "She's missing, your friend?"

The slight hint of an accent told Cage that the man wasn't a native to the area, but Cage couldn't distinguish where he was from. Another country. Somewhere farther away than Texas.

Joule nodded in answer. "Her roommates filed the report two days ago." Then she was opening her mouth to say more.

Cage reached out with the back of his hand tapping at her where the man hopefully couldn't see the signal. Joule quickly snapped her teeth together and Cage watched as the dark eyes had flitted up and to his right.

The man knew where she lived. Sarah wasn't just somebody who walked by the row of apartments periodically. She came down here and knocked on his door. He knew which unit was hers.

Though his expressions were still slight, Cage got the impression that he was troubled at the idea that Sarah was missing. But he still wasn't giving them any information.

Cage decided to back off. Even from where he stood behind her, he could practically see the gears turning in Joule's head, too. He hoped the man standing in front of them couldn't.

They would need to form a real plan, not just one based on the basic twin signals they'd developed.

In the past, they'd managed—sometimes just barely—to keep themselves alive. *Could they do the same for Sarah?*

"Can I leave my number with you?" Cage asked. "In case you see her, you can let us know that she's okay."

The man nodded and held out his hand. Certainly, he didn't want Cage to grab a pen and write the number on his palm. So, he searched his pockets for a scrap of paper, but it was Joule who produced a receipt. That backpack was tiny, but she managed to Mary Poppins it.

Cage quickly jotted down both their names and their numbers and handed the faded paper over.

"If I hear anything . . ." the man said. As he motioned with the receipt in one hand the other reached behind him, expertly grabbing for the knob he couldn't see. Then he was gone, the door closed in their faces.

Again, with a subtle tap of his hand, Cage motioned for his sister to get out of the way before they began talking. It would be best not to have this conversation on the man's doorstep where he might overhear.

Joule led the way, even as she looked back at him over her

shoulder, her eyes wide as if to say *that was a bizarre conversation.*

They let themselves back into the roommates' apartment upstairs and closed the door before either of them spoke.

"He clearly knows her," Joule started.

"And he's concerned that she's missing but he doesn't want to give us any information." Cage sighed. "I want to say it's the first good lead that we have. But he's all we've got."

"Maybe it's enough to get some information on him." Joule was looking around the living room as if she might find a desktop computer set up. Cage didn't think so.

"I'm going to run back down to the car and grab our laptops." He motioned toward the door. "Can you message the roommates and ask if it's okay if we hang out here today? I'd like to keep an eye on the neighbor. See if we can figure out which car is his if he goes anywhere."

Not that the front window to the apartment was going to be big enough to watch the parking lot. He couldn't see the man's front door at all from here. But Cage was going to try.

Trying to look nonchalant, he went to the car and opened the door, constantly aware of his surroundings. The door to apartment 104 didn't budge, the curtains didn't flutter. He returned with bag in hand, but no further information. He was glad that he didn't look like he was carrying a couple of laptops —just in case whatever-his-name-was was watching out his own window. The twins used an old duffle bag to carry equipment, to make is seem less like something someone would want to steal.

Joule quickly pulled her computer out and set him up with the Wi Fi password even as she claimed space at the small dining table. He, however, put a cutting board over the sink and set his laptop on that. He hoped he could see all the cars in the parking lot from there.

An hour later, Joule had found out quite a bit about the

apartment complex and had even done a reverse address search, getting the name of the resident in 104. But searching the name brought up a much older man.

She sighed and spun her laptop around to show him.

"That's definitely not our guy." Cage agreed.

No one had come or gone from the parking lot. So, unless the man had left on foot behind the building—which Cage had searched from overhead map footage and seen there wasn't anywhere he could plausibly go that direction—he hadn't left yet.

Turning to his sister, Cage hit her up to trade places so he could sit for a while. He still wanted someone watching the parking lot. Just as he started to move out of the way, a car careened around the corner, and would have squealed into the center of the lot had it not been for the packed gravel. Dust spun up from the tires and the car looked too shiny and high-end to belong here.

Mesmerized, Cage watched as an older couple got out, frantic expressions lining their faces. They dashed under the walkway and Cage lost sight of them for a moment, but then he heard their footsteps ringing on the stairs.

It was all the warning the twins got before the pounding came at the front door.

6

"What the hell?" Joule ran toward the door but stopped short as the loud banging came again.

She'd been happy to set up shop here and wait out the neighbor, but what was this?

Cage stayed where he was, peering out the window over the kitchen sink as if he might be able to see who was on the other side of the door. But from where she stood—looking back and forth between her brother and the angry door—the angle looked wrong.

Pressing her face to the peephole, she saw an older man and woman. The man's tight black curls were cropped close to his head and graying. Lines on his face made the woman next to him look noticeably younger. Her hair was pulled back into a low poof of a ponytail, her edges neat. The deep brown eyes and wide mouth triggered a memory in Joule.

She threw the door open, but she didn't get a word out.

"Sarah!" the man yelled into the empty space of the apartment behind her.

The woman, however, stopped and looked Joule up and down. "Do you know where Sarah is?"

Joule shook her head.

"Are you *Brooklyn*?" the woman asked as if she knew she had the wrong name already.

"Joule," she said, holding her hand out, but the woman didn't grab it.

As her husband pressed by, barging his way into the apartment, she exclaimed "Joule!" and engulfed her in a huge hug. When she finally stepped back, she said, "I'm so glad you're here. You're not *here* though, are you?"

She seemed to realize right away that she had asked a ridiculous question and tried again. "I thought you and your brother weren't working on this job."

"We aren't. Dev told us Sarah was missing and we came right down."

The woman braced her hands on Joule's shoulders, holding her at arm's length as if to inspect a child. "Of course, you did. Where are my manners? I'm Aurora Walker. This is—that *was*—my husband, Malcolm."

"This is Cage." Joule stepped back and motioned to him through the open doorway into the kitchen. "These are Sarah's parents."

At least the woman was still there to greet him. Sarah's father had disappeared into the unit, banging through every door and calling out as though Sarah might simply be under the bed or hiding in a closet like a wayward child.

"We just spoke with the police," Aurora told her.

"Oh, good!" Cage entered the conversation as he held his hand out to say hello. But he, too, was engulfed in a super-human hug.

As Joule watched, he accepted it more gracefully than she did. He hugged the woman back, a fierce tight hold that told her that her brother needed it as much as Aurora did.

"What did you find out from the police?" he asked when he was finally let go.

"A whole bunch of bullshit!" The voice boomed from behind them.

Joule and Cage turned to look at Malcolm as he stood with his hands braced on his hips as if to say *she's not here*. As if he were the only one who didn't already believe that.

But he continued, "They can't find her car, but they aren't putting any manpower on it. They've issued a BOLO, but I'm not sure what good that is. They said they're going to come interview people, but they haven't done it yet—"

"It's been three days!" Joule cried out. She hadn't meant to interrupt but, *what about the golden forty-eight-hour window?* Was it just a myth? Or did they truly not care that a woman had gone missing?

Aurora tipped her head, hands on her own hips, as if to say, *isn't that the way it always is?* though her words spoke a different story. "They said they're a small station. They don't have the manpower to look for someone without evidence that she's missing against her will."

That, Joule knew, was the problem: They didn't know if Sarah had gone off on her own volition or not. None of them did.

Was she safe? Was she in trouble? *Was she already dead?*

The last one put a shiver in Joule's bones.

"Then it's up to us," Cage said, "to find something that will make them have to look."

Tears fell from Aurora's eyes. Her tight smile stretched from one side of her face to the other, conveying all her conflicting emotions at once. "I'm so glad you're here. Thank you."

Joule hadn't realized how much Sarah must have told her parents about her roommates. For a moment a rush of sadness swept through her that she didn't have that option herself. Aurora hadn't even asked who Dev was, she already knew.

The good news was that their little team had just doubled.

"We have the slightest tremor of a lead," Cage told them.

As Malcolm's eyes snapped to him, hope shined in the deep brown of his irises.

"There's a guy downstairs who's not answering our questions. I want to see if we can get his license plate and figure out who he is."

Joule jumped in. "Sarah was apparently walking down to his apartment to see him a couple of times a week—"

"She didn't have a boyfriend," Aurora said suddenly, firm in her knowledge that if Sarah had had a boyfriend, she would know.

Joule didn't comment. She didn't know if that would be true or not. But she didn't get to think about it.

"I'm hoping he'll leave soon, and we can follow him to get whatever that will tell us." Cage looked between them. Now there were four to make the decisions.

"Like that?" Malcolm asked as he pushed past them, stepping up to the kitchen window and pointing at an old sedan as it pulled out of the parking lot and turned onto the dusty road.

7

T hey bolted out the door and down the stairs, trying to see where the sedan had gone.

Only Aurora waited, calling out, "I'll stay here . . . in case someone calls or . . ."

Looking back, Cage watched her shrug and heard what she didn't say, *In case Sarah comes home.*

Malcolm looked like he would have turned back to give her a quick peck on the mouth, but there wasn't time. Joule was already at the bottom of the stairs; Cage lingered at the back of the little brigade.

Joule was clicking the button on her keys as he heard the telltale sound of it unlocking. Then she was sliding in behind the wheel and pulling out. He barely made it into the back passenger seat, his foot leaving the gravel of the parking lot even as the wheels rolled beneath him. Cage tugged the still-open door, holding on against the forces of her turn as he finally managed to pull it shut.

"Slow down!" he cautioned her. "If he realizes we're following him, we're in trouble."

"It's worse than that," she said her hand clenched on the

wheel as she kept the car straight on the narrow road. "If this isn't one-oh-four, then he's probably watching from his window. He saw us peel out after someone else."

She let the idea hang as Cage swore a blue streak in his own head. He hadn't counted on that possibility. They should have stayed and waited. If this was him, they could have caught him when he came home, seen his license plate, maybe his face again.

His brain churned with possibilities. They could talk to the building manager, maybe cajole some names of people in the rental units. They should definitely figure out how to do a reverse search on a license plate.

But all those ideas were moot. They were following the sedan at what he hoped was a reasonable pace. As always, when he was a passenger, he was simultaneously convinced that he was going to die, and that Joule was going too slow.

The car got further and further in front of them. It had once been white, but time and dust had mottled the color until it almost disappeared into the desert road. Only the chrome of the bumpers and the black of the tires kept them paced behind it.

"Stay closer," Malcolm said.

"I'm trying not to let him know we're following him," Joule replied softly, as though the man might hear them from the car in front. Her knuckles were still white. Had she even put her seatbelt on?

Cage looked over and saw that, of course, she had. She'd probably done it from rote habit. Same as him.

Up ahead, the car took a turn onto a road he couldn't see. It looked as though it had just turned right into the scrub brush and decided to drive that way. But his barely fourteen hours in town had told him there were roads like that here . . . or paths . . . or even just ruts.

Cage wished he had binoculars, so he could see who the driver was, see if anyone else was in the car with him.

Had anyone else been in the apartment?

The man had clearly known Sarah, but maybe other people lived there and knew her, too.

Though there were trees in the area that grew almost the height of a one-story building, most of what was out here was low, scraggly brush. It covered the ground but lacked the bushy greenery he was used to from home. There were no hedges a person could hide behind. Even from a distance, they would likely be seen. The better bet was to stay still, rather than to crouch behind something. Cage tucked the thought away for later.

He watched up ahead, making more mental notes. The car was from the eighties or even seventies, with its rounded edges and silver trim. Maybe an old Chevy Malibu or such. It was dirty enough now that it threatened to disappear into the landscape.

He'd once driven a blue grey car that, in the evening, he couldn't distinguish the hood from the road in front of him. Now he saw the miracle of camouflage ahead of him and he had to wonder if it had been done on purpose.

Were they even chasing the right person? Though the man knew Sarah, he hadn't left immediately after Cage and Joule had shown up at his door. He'd waited a good hour or so. Likely, wherever he was going right now, it didn't have anything to do with them or Sarah.

"I'm going to try to get close enough to see his license plate," Joule announced.

Luckily, she had excellent vision, and it wouldn't have to be too close. Then she asked back over her shoulder. "Can you set up a hotspot out here?"

"Good thought." Cage pulled out his tech and struggled a bit for the connection as they slowly gained ground on the car in front of them. No one else was out here, they were obvious in the landscape and likely obviously trailing him.

Joule was having the same thoughts . . . "I think once we get the plate, we should take a turn and let him go, pretend that we're not actually following him."

"Really? Just the plate?" Malcolm asked. He could have taken over, but Cage was glad he was trying to be part of the team, understanding that it wasn't his car being driven and his car someone might target if they'd followed the wrong kind of person—even if it was his daughter that was missing.

"The license plate should give us a lot of information," Cage assured him. "And if he knows he's being followed, I don't think he's going to take us to the right place, anyway."

"We've got a general direction." Joule added, though she was leaning forward, and rattled off the first three letters.

She squinted. "I can't tell if the next one is an eight or a B."

It was clear Malcolm didn't like the plan, but he stayed quiet, leaned forward like it might get him farther down the road, one hand braced on the dash as if ready for impact.

For a moment, Cage thought he couldn't imagine what it must be like to have his child go missing. But then he realized to a certain extent, he absolutely could. Not a child but a parent. He thought of the ID that he still carried for his dad. About the death certificate they'd finally gotten, and the small ember of hope that burned in him. He knew it burned in Joule, too, that they might one day find their father alive.

If anyone could survive, Nathaniel Mazur was at the top of the list. But if anyone was ever going to voluntarily leave their children behind, Nathaniel Mazur was at the bottom of that list. That was one of the things that convinced Cage his father was dead.

It was that same reasoning that convinced him now that Sarah had not left of her own accord.

He knew her well enough to believe that she would not do

this—not even to her roommates, let alone them or her parents. He searched for information frantically. They had to find Sarah.

"The first three spaces on a Texas plate are letters," he announced to the front seat. "The last four are numbers."

"Then it's an eight," Joule declared before rattling off the string of four numbers.

He typed them onto a blank note in his phone just to hold onto them until he could get some information. Even with the hotspot, connection out here seemed sketchy. Things loaded slower and slower the farther they got from the very tiny town of El Indio.

Joule took the next left turn, heading away from the car they had been tailing and hopefully convincing the driver that they had not been followed.

"Are we headed toward the worksite?" he asked her. They hadn't been initially, but if they were close enough, they could just head over and finally talk to Dr. Murasawa.

They'd planned on checking in that morning but had messaged her when they decided to stay at the apartment.

"I don't know. Let's get farther away, somewhere with a real road, then we can check." Her fists still clenched the wheel fiercely, the driving bumpy on the non-road.

Next to her, Mr. Walker finally leaned back in his seat, the lead they'd followed played out for now.

Cage continued to check what he could. Though the internet was sketchy, it slowly pulled up information. He managed to find a site that offered him the make and model of the car. "It's a Chevy Laguna."

They didn't respond from the front seat. But what he was seeing meant the plate matched the car. *So, it probably wasn't stolen.*

From there he began searching furiously, trying to figure

out who it was registered to as his fingers mistyped and jolted around until Joule managed to get them back onto a real road.

This still wasn't paved, but at least was hard packed which made it sturdier. They passed three low, one-story houses, two with metal roofs, one caved in and appearing unlivable, despite the car parked out front.

"Anything about the owner?" Joule asked.

"Not yet."

But then he got an idea.

8

"Kayla!" Cage heard her voice over the phone, relief sweeping through him.

They'd managed to speak to Dr. Murasawa who only had a few minutes. Still, she took their information and said she would once again petition for at least half a day off so the employees could search for Sarah.

She sounded as frustrated as he felt. "I've argued that's what they would want us to do if it was their child missing or *them*."

Cage had always liked the people he worked with. Maybe the higher ups in the company weren't quite as progressive or pro-worker as they thought they were.

The three of them returned to the apartment, Mr. Walker having already explained to Aurora how the chase had gone. He didn't disagree about the decisions made as a unit, but he did seem frustrated by how it had turned out.

Even Cage had hoped—stupidly, he knew—that they would follow the car and the man would get out and meet Sarah. That she would be okay, and they would hug her and say she gave them quite a scare.

That hadn't even been close.

"How is everything going?" Kayla asked him now.

"It's just going," he told her then brought her and Ivy, who was listening in, up to speed on what little investigation they'd managed to do so far.

"And you need me to what?" Kayla asked, always clarifying, especially on the phone.

"We can't find any open source websites that will tell us who a car is registered to. Everything we found wants a payment—and we don't trust the payment system—or that they'll tell us who the car is registered to."

"That makes sense. You're talking about state records." There was a small sigh at the other end. Cage knew what he was asking might be a little bit illegal—or maybe a lot.

Kayla asked next, "How confident are you that the driver is the person you need?"

It was an interesting and important question. He'd considered simply asking Kayla, "Can you . . .?" She would have answered yes, because she *could* do it. But when he then asked her *to* do it, she would have said no.

Her moral objections would be strong, but she also understood a good argument. Cage looked up at Joule, who rolled her eyes and tipped her head at him. Cage agreed.

She told Kayla, "We don't really have the answer to that."

"We feel we need this information to get to the answer," he added.

"Then give me the plate," Kayla told them, "and let me see what I can find. Maybe I know somebody."

Kayla—his kind neighbor who often hung back in conversations—turned out to know all kinds of people. She had made friends at various jobs she'd held. She'd helped her family rehabilitate an old property. While there she'd met a number of people with dubious connections, though Cage hadn't quite figured out how the two went together.

At one point, she and Ivy had alluded to a connection with

an insanely wealthy philanthropist who would have their backs if ever they truly needed it. Cage and Joule had never quite pressed that one further. But sometimes they called and asked for favors.

Ivy got on the line then, too, and caught up a little bit with the details.

"We're probably going to stay here—" he'd almost said *until Sarah is found* but realized that might be an indefinite timeframe. "For a while."

The acid hit the back of his throat as he thought about Mr. and Mrs. Walker maybe having to make the decision to go back to their own home if they hadn't found Sarah and what that timeframe might look like.

"What's next?" Joule asked after they hung up.

"Lunch," Mrs. Walker announced as she put her hands on her knees to stand. "I attempted to order delivery while you were out."

Cage felt his eyebrows climb at the thought of finding delivery to the edge of town that had once had a high population under four hundred.

She looked at him now, the corner of her mouth pulling up as she nodded at him. "You would be right, young man. One of us is going to have to get out and get food. We will not be eating the food in these nice young ladies' fridge." She waved toward the kitchen then. "How about Malcolm and I go out and get food for everybody?"

Suddenly, they were all hungry and Cage and Joule were placing orders. The Walkers refused to take any money for it, grateful that the twins had felt strongly enough to come down here to look for Sarah.

Once the door clicked shut behind them, Joule opened her laptop again. "It was nice of them to feed us."

"I think maybe they needed to speak in private," Cage told her, "and this was their chance."

"Oh." So maybe Joule hadn't caught that. "I don't begrudge them that though. I don't begrudge them any of the decisions they're having to make right now."

He didn't either.

When he'd been younger and looked at his own family, he'd imagined growing up and being much like his father. He'd wondered if he and his future partner would have twins, too. Now so much had changed. The thought of having a child in this world had already been relegated to a distant *someday*— someday when the world was better. Someday when he wasn't waiting for the other shoe to drop. Someday when the other shoe wasn't a hockey skate with a razor-sharp blade attached.

Now, watching as Mr. and Mrs. Walker held it together as best as anyone could in this situation, he began to think *maybe never*.

The twins worked during the wait, trying to find whatever they could, constantly asking questions and mostly writing down notes so they could get the answers from someone else later.

"Does Sarah have an app on her phone that tracks it?"

"Can anyone find that app if she does?"

"Has anyone pulled her cell phone data?"

"Did the police tell the Walkers anything else?"

Then, just as Cage was once again asking Joule if she would take over the spot in the window, he watched as the white car pulled back into the parking lot.

He froze where he stood, as if the car were a dinosaur and he were the prey. If he didn't move, he might not get noticed. But he shifted his eyes and altered his focus. The driver was the man from apartment 104.

They had been following the right person.

Just then, his phone rang.

9

Everything happened at once. Joule heard her email ding just as she watched her brother freeze at the window. Then her phone let her know with an incoming text that the Walkers were about five minutes away.

She quickly tapped a message back to them.

— The car we followed returned and it's definitely the man from 104.

— That's good.

The two words came back quickly and didn't need any more explanation.

Joule felt as if she were pulling at threads on a sweater. Pull for a little while and more things came to light, then suddenly, it would tangle. The police should be helping . . . but nothing. The man from 104 wasn't on any documents, but he was driving out into the desert. What did it even mean?

Another knot had to be untied or another thread found that could be pulled. She was determined to unravel it. They had to find Sarah—Joule couldn't even entertain the thought that they might never know what had happened. She fought back the base level of fear that thrummed through her blood.

What if it had been her?

What if it had been Cage?

Her brother had asked her to trade places, but now that the white car had returned and lunch was coming, that didn't seem like the thing to do.

He headed over to the table to sit next to her, but he didn't open his laptop. "We should clear this off so we can sit down and eat. Maybe have a discussion as we go."

Joule agreed, but there were a few minutes left and she wasn't quite ready to close up. She pointed to her screen. "Look."

The email had been addressed to both of them, but Cage seemed to have not spotted it in his own inbox yet. Clicking it open, she saw Ivy had sent them the information they requested. Probably Kayla had found it, but Ivy was in charge of communication.

Joule read out loud, so her brother didn't have to lean over. "The car was registered last year to one Salvador Torres." She looked up at him. "That's the same last name as the one on the lease."

"Do you think it's his father on the lease?"

Joule had checked out the first name as best she could. "Grandfather, likely. There are almost fifty years between them. And—if I've got everything right—the lease was last signed three years ago. Hard to tell if it changed hands or not. But the grandfather, Pablo Torres, died two years ago."

She had no idea if Salvador was the legal renter on the apartment now. Judging from the looks of the building itself and the surrounding lot, she wouldn't be surprised if they were still signing paper documents that were kept in a metal file drawer in a garage. If they were kept at all . . .

"Here's a picture of Salvador." She pushed her laptop around. They'd have to clear the table in a minute.

Cage leaned over and nodded along. "That's definitely our guy."

His hair was longer and tied back in the picture.

Joule mused out loud, "So Salvador Torres in apartment 104 knew Sarah. He saw her on a semi-regular basis and no one else seems to know about it."

"That just doesn't sound like Sarah." Cage said.

Joule agreed, but a second thought flitted through her mind. She and her brother knew Sarah from work. They'd lived with Sarah in the same unit on more than one job. The first time had been Sarah and Joule in one room and Cage and Deveron in the other in Alabama. But the four had remained friends.

Or had they?

Were they just "work friends"? Having a twin that she'd consistently gotten along with as a child had maybe spoiled her or altered her understanding of how normal friendships worked. She knew that people were often grouped into friend categories, like friend-friends, family, coworkers. And that there were coworkers you liked and coworkers you didn't. Most coworkers weren't roommates, too.

Maybe Sarah had only considered Cage and her as "work friends," and had simply not included other parts of herself when she spoke to them.

Joule wondered now what else might exist in the person that she knew was hard working and loyal? Sarah was very much one who followed the rule of "when you know better, do better" in both her life and her work. But what else might she have been involved in?

As the front door opened, the Walkers headed into the small apartment that belonged to none of them. Joule didn't want to touch things or mess anything up—not any more than she already had. But it was now past two o'clock and she felt her stomach rumble. She'd barely made it since her paltry breakfast. She'd been so upset this morning that she simply pushed a handful of crackers into her face to say she'd done it.

The twins showed the Walkers the new information that had come in while the older couple set bags of fast food out on the table. They plopped tall, sweating sodas next to them, both of theirs already partially drunk.

The room was quiet as tiny packs of ketchup were handed out, along with little cardboard boxes of fries, and paper wrapped burgers. The logo on the food wasn't even a name that Joule recognized, maybe not even a chain. The town was small like that.

Hardly waiting for everyone to sit down, Joule began asking the questions they'd stockpiled. "Are the police tracking Sarah's phone?"

Mr. Walker nodded, but Mrs. Walker quickly filled in. "However, they said it's going to take several days to get all the paperwork through to get that information out of the phone company—"

"*Several days?*" Joule cried out, once again startled and upset by the speed with which the system failed to work. "Can you go directly to the phone company and ask them?"

The two frowned at each other but Mr. Walker said, "I pay the bill. We've always thought of it as her phone, but it was cheaper to put it on a family plan."

For a moment, Joules' heart twisted at the idea. She and Cage had been in high school when they'd lost their parents. They'd never made it to an adult phase where their parents might still simply pay their phone bill because it was cheaper to have it all together.

Then Cage next asked about Sarah having any tracking apps on her phone.

The Walkers didn't know.

"You can maybe find that out from the phone company, too." Joule wasn't sure but it was worth asking.

The twins went through their list, still none of the answers were completely satisfying. However, building a to do list made Joule feel more comfortable. She might not get what she needed, but she needed to know what to do next, who she should talk to, something besides wandering off to bed tonight, waiting for a friend who might not come back.

When the questions ran out, the table grew silent.

Aurora looked to Malcolm, and he gave a small nod.

Joule looked between them, but she didn't have to wait.

With a deep breath, the woman started talking. "Sarah told me a while ago that she'd taken up a volunteer position a couple of nights a week."

That was news to Joule. When she glanced at Cage, she saw he hadn't heard about it either. Though, why would they? She was just glad Sarah had told her mother.

"She said she was volunteering at the local Y."

For a moment, Joule thought nothing of that. It seemed perfectly reasonable. But then she caught the question in Mrs. Walker's eyes.

There was no local YMCA. The town was hardly big enough for a drive-through burger place.

So, why had Sarah lied?

10

_____

Cage stood next to a car that wasn't his, flashlight heavy in his hand as he listened to instructions. The group was bigger than he'd anticipated, and for that, he was happy. But the Texas night had not cooled off. The heat was oppressive, or maybe that was just his fear.

The Helio Systems Tech workers gathered in a circle. Their ages ranged from the youngest being around his and Joule's age, up to about forty or fifty years old. The Walkers were clearly the oldest here.

Dr. Murasawa stood in the center handing out instructions. This was clearly organized through work, though not sanctioned by it. They still hadn't been given official time off.

The lack of outsiders told Cage that the community hadn't rallied to find their missing member either. Though Helio Tech workers often breezed into a place and altered it, they also quickly left. They didn't quite become members of the place, despite living there for months on end.

"Every pair will go together in one car," Dr. Murasawa was announcing. All around him, heads nodded.

A few faces he recognized—people he and Joule had said

hello to as they arrived and a few who had offered hugs of return. But most he didn't know. The Walkers stood next to him holding hands. It was clear they had designated they would be a pair.

Joule glanced sideways at him, shaking her head slightly and he caught the implication they should go separate directions. People were pairing up.

"I'm dividing up the map. We'll drive the roads and look for Sarah's car." Dr. Murasawa spread a huge paper map out on the hood of her car, already having marked some of it up with the green highlighter she was gesturing with.

She didn't say they would look for Sarah.

"What about the border?" Brooklyn asked.

All three of Sarah's roommates were here, ready to put in the time. That made him happy because he hadn't been sure about the reception they'd received that morning. Then again, he and his sister had simply knocked on their door and announced they wanted to come in and search Sarah's things.

Now the group crowded around the map, claiming various sections to search. Since he didn't know his way around, none of it mattered to him.

"Don't cross the border," Dr. Murasawa admonished them. "You may be able to see across in certain places. You're welcome to look, but please stay in United States territory." The tone of her voice told him she meant exactly what she was saying. It wasn't a hidden directive, but a genuine plea.

"Be sure you have a valid, unexpired driver's license or legal ID on you." One of the older men cut in as he scanned the group to see if they understood.

Cage hadn't understood before, but he was starting to. He wondered what might be expected on the other side. He made a mental note to look into it tomorrow.

Dr. Murasawa began counting the people again, then she divided by two and announced the number of teams. After she had done that, she began drawing additional search sections—these were farther out on the map and larger.

Mr. Walker stepped forward, snapping a picture of one of the divisions on his phone, then he and his wife were off in their car. Preset pairs started to leave, but others simply hung back and waited for assignments.

When half of them were gone, Dr. Murasawa marked the already chosen sections and then looked up to say, "I need a partner. I can drive. Who wants to ride with me?"

The bump at the back of his elbow told Cage that Joule wanted him to volunteer. So, he stepped forward. "I will."

It would be a great time to get to talk to her again, see if she knew anything about Sarah that they didn't. Which was probably what Joule had been smart enough to think of first.

"Everyone else needs to pair up," their leader announced.

Cage watched as his sister cleanly inserted herself as the fourth between the roommates and said, "I have a car if one of you wants to come with me, then we can be two teams."

The three looked to each other back and forth before Gisela moved to Joule's side.

With the decision made, he was climbing into the gold, four-door sedan next to his boss, surprised to see a car seat in the middle of the backseat. But now wasn't the time to ask.

As his door clicked shut, she began talking. "It's good to see you and your sister again. Really good. I've been wondering if you were going to come back and work for us." She paused. "We currently have you on indefinite leave."

He appreciated that but didn't have an answer.

She wasn't waiting for one. "But I'm really concerned about the circumstances under which you both came back."

"Me too."

She'd kept the big map, handing it over to him to navigate. She'd allowed the other pairs to choose the area they wanted to search, leaving herself and Cage to search the last unwanted area.

It was a large, open space away from the border and farther away from the town. There were no roads listed, so he opened his phone and tried to direct her along the faint lines that indicated these were not highways or even well populated paths— and mostly not paved.

It would be a while before they even reached the edge of their area. Cage began asking questions and he was surprised to find Dr. Murasawa knew more than he expected.

11

"Sarah was hanging out with the group less on this job," Dr. Murasawa said. She was keeping her hands at "ten" and "two" on the steering wheel before taking a turn cleanly hand over hand, as if she were a driving instructor.

It didn't surprise Cage that his old boss knew this about Sarah. Dr. Chithra Murasawa always seemed to keep track of her employees—she'd even taken a bullet for one once.

"I got the impression she fit in well on every site." Cage was looking out the passenger window and then back at the GPS for directions.

"She did." Dr. Murasawa glanced at him sideways with a shrug. "I didn't get the feeling that she didn't get on well here, she just seemed not interested in the usual group dinners or whatever. More that she had other things to do this time."

"Is it the location?" he asked. "Did she already know people here?"

"Not that I'm aware of."

They both remembered Sarah's cousin protesting the solar array back in Alabama. But apparently nothing similar was at stake here. At least not that Dr. Murasawa knew.

"She drove a couple hours out and saw a friend once, but that was on another job near Denver. I didn't get that same impression about what was going on with this site."

Cage pointed in front of them. "It looks like we're hitting the edge of our territory."

He would have asked what they were looking for, but Dr. Murasawa had made it as clear as possible: Anything. Anything that might be Sarah's—her purse, her wallet, her phone. Her car would be the easiest thing to spot if it was out here somewhere.

But why would it be? he wondered. As Cage looked around, he saw virtually nothing of importance to finding his friend.

They passed a house and a shed that seemed to have been abandoned. In other places, he would have expected a lawn mower in the front yard but there were no lawns to mow here. No crops to harvest, so no tractors. The landscaping—when there was any—was gravel and low indigenous shrub.

So instead, an old fluffy recliner sat in the front lawn next to a VW bug left up on blocks. Cage wasn't even sure there was enough moisture in the air here to make it rust. Maybe it would just mummify.

Having entered their territory, Dr. Murasawa slowed down so they could begin scanning the road and surrounding areas. The conversation lagged as they looked. Cage wondered what the chances were that something important was just out of sight or buried in the bushes. Something they wouldn't find without a real crime scene tech.

The silence only lasted a few minutes of spotting absolutely nothing other than the scurry of one odd small animal Cage couldn't identify.

Dr. Murasawa kept looking out her window, but added, "The problem is I'm completely going by what I feel. I don't *know* anything, it's all *impressions* that I get from what she said. Thinking back, I can't remember if she said anything specific about what was different here. I can tell you there were a couple of times that we went out for dinner and Sarah didn't join us. But I'm not sure what that means."

Cage just kept his eyes on the landscape. Luckily, the moon was up and bright. They would have seen nothing if it had been a darker night, and he could only assume that Dr. Murasawa knew this and had planned accordingly.

She kept talking as if something might pop up if she said everything she knew. "A few times, Sarah even asked off work, not early, but just making a point that she would need to go directly at five or six, that she had somewhere she needed to be."

Cage had to ask. "You didn't think that was odd?"

"Yes and no." Dr. Murasawa shrugged and took the next turn. "I mean, it was unusual for Sarah, but not an odd request in itself. And she didn't do this in most places she went, but we had gone places where she knew people before. We've also been places where she would say, Oh, I found this bookstore. Or, I found this shop or this event that people might like to visit. So, it wasn't the norm but it didn't worry me."

Clearly, she was beating herself up now for not having known.

The road—if it could be called that—came to a perfect 90-degree intersection.

"Go right," Cage told her, hoping that the majority of these little side roads were on his map in some way. Perhaps some car had come out and driven them and left a trail on the GPS service.

Again, motion caught his eye, and he snapped his gaze to the side to see a small cluster of bats ducking and diving near one of the distant trees. Hopefully, the road would loop and they could cover their territory this way.

He had to admit that he didn't expect to find anything. Cage could think of no reason for Sarah to be out in the middle of nowhere, not even related to the job site.

In the distance, a pair of eyes gathered light and reflected it back to him. Likely a rabbit or a raccoon. Slowly, the car rolled to a stop.

"There's motion out there." Dr. Murasawa had seen it, too and pointed the headlights that way. They still only helped to a certain number of feet in front of the car. After that, something in the dusty night air seem to make the light dissipate and disappear.

If he were in a horror film, Cage would take it as a sign. But as he turned and looked, he saw something once again begin to move.

"It could be a large cat," she said. "They have them out here."

And snakes. It hadn't occurred to him to look up the native animal population, but Dr. Murasawa had told them that if they got out of their cars, they needed to be very careful. Raccoons and squirrels would likely scatter, but the snakes could be a problem.

He was about to ask, "should we get out and check it out?" But Dr. Murasawa's words preempted him.

"What if it's Sarah?"

He was already opening the door, heavy flashlight once again in his grip. This time, his finger only hovered over the button, ready to aim the light as he walked forward a little bit. The two of them, by unspoken agreement, leaving the lights off until they left the range provided by the car.

Everything seemed to fade at about fifteen feet out. The darkness rolled in around them, only the moon overhead kept him from feeling blind. But if something came at him suddenly, would he be able to even duck to avoid it?

A flashback to the Night Hunters brought a chill to his

heart. But Cage shoved it aside with one thought. *What if it was Sarah?*

They'd been having the same thoughts then, about the horror of maybe driving right past her, of not seeing the clue they needed. Cage scanned the area, focus sharply trained, desperate for anything that would help.

Dr. Murasawa had smartly left the lights on in the car. And he'd wondered now, if she hadn't done that would they even be able to find it once they made it a few feet away and it disappeared?

Quickly, they reached the edge of the available light. Despite the fact that his eyes were adjusting, he clicked the flashlight on and once again caught movement in the distance.

Dr. Murasawa's light clicked on barely a second later. A handful of startled eyes looked back at him.

Next to Cage, his former boss whispered, "Holy shit."

—————

12

"I can't think of his name." Gisela sighed, clearly a bit frustrated with herself.

Joule understood. The name of someone Sarah had talked to a couple of times wouldn't mean anything to a work roommate. Not, of course, until said roommate had gone missing for several days. Then suddenly it became important, but no one remembered.

"She went out with him a handful of times."

"A boyfriend?" Joule nudged, hoping if she asked other things Gisela then might remember the name.

"I don't think so. They didn't go out on weekends, not like a date. And she never dressed up, I guess if anything she dressed down. I got the idea that it wasn't just the two of them—Here!" Gisela pointed to a turn as Joule hit the brakes and made it.

She had set Gisela in charge of weaving them through their territory. She'd watched as Cage and Dr. Murasawa wound up checking out open space heading in toward the center of Texas. Others had made their way toward the border. But she and Gisela had taken a portion of the small town.

They drove small sparsely paved streets, often the only car

out here. It wasn't as if there were enough people to produce actual traffic. Each time a car came from the other direction, both slowed as if understanding some kind of small road protocol.

The two women were trying to cover every street, wondering if Sarah had maybe parked at one of the houses. Joule drove slowly enough so they could check each car in each driveway. They hoped against hope to identify Sarah's. And they drove impossibly slow, enough to probably make the neighbors nervous.

"I want to say she went out mostly on Mondays and Thursdays." Gisela huffed lightly again, clearly frustrated by her own lack of clean memory. "She would come home right from work. Sometimes one of us would catch a ride with her."

Joule understood, they all lived together, and they worked together, so they often carpooled. She'd done it herself. "I'll see if Dev knows anything about him."

"Sarah would just change clothes and head right out the door—" Then Gisela interrupted herself. "Is that her car?"

It looked like it. Older and dustier, more beat up than Joule remembered, but it absolutely could be. Joule slowed to a stop and backed up so they could check it out. But she didn't even get out of the car. "It's a Texas state plate. Absolutely not Sarah's."

Disappointment washed through her. She hadn't expected it, hadn't realized how excited she'd gotten even when she knew it likely wasn't Sarah's. Hope was resilient, even when it shouldn't be.

"It's the right kind of car, though," Joule added. "Even the right year or close to it. Let's make a note of where it is."

"Even though it's not hers?" Gisela asked, but then answered her own question even as she marked the location on her phone. "You think she swapped out the plates like a criminal?"

No, Joule thought, *it would be worse than that.* "I'm thinking if someone stole her car, *they* might have swapped the plates to cover for it."

Gisela only nodded slowly, clearly not having thought like a criminal element about this before. Neither of them liked where the thought of Sarah's car being stolen would lead them, given that Sarah had not reported it and still had not reported in.

"Got it," Gisela noted quietly.

"So, she was seeing the guy downstairs?" Joule asked. She didn't like to inject extra information hoping to get whatever Gisela might give her and put it together for herself. But since her companion seemed to have run out of things to tell her, she'd added the bit about 104.

"I don't know. Maybe. I think she did a couple of times." They both continued looking out the windows, checking for cars or anyone or anything that might help. Gisela continued. "It didn't seem odd, you know? I just didn't think anything of it at the time. I haven't roomed with Sarah before. This is the first job I've worked with her, so I didn't know. Then she disappeared and everybody showed up and said this wasn't normal for her!"

A slight tremor under her voice revealed that the cold welcome of the early morning had not revealed the roommates' true feelings about Sarah being missing. Gisela sniffed slightly. "Turn here. We'll zigzag these ones back and forth."

Joule nodded, hanging a right onto the next street and then another right onto the next. Small houses divided the area, the space between them decent enough to indicate that the property values here were low.

Gisela offered more. Maybe, like Joule, she thought if she told everything, some tiny important detail might shake out. "She kept talking to one guy on the phone, and I think it's the person she was meeting. I mean, I can't say for sure. But he had a short, one-syllable name." For a moment she turned and looked at Joule, as if to ask *Did it mean anything to her?*

Joule tried not to respond, not wanting to push anything but a one syllable name didn't mean anything to her. But wait. "Dev?"

"No, we know Dev. If it was Dev, I would have remembered. It was a different sound. Mal? Val?"

Something clicked, and Joule asked, "Sal?"

13

Gisela didn't even answer as their phones lit up simultaneously with incoming texts.

Group text, Joule thought but as the driver she didn't look. "Read it to me?"

"Ohhellohhell!" Gisela seemed excited or flustered Joule didn't know her quite well enough to read her.

She wanted to yell, "Tell me something I can use!" but instead she took a deep breath. "Is it good? Is it bad?"

"They found Sarah's car."

Not thinking, Joule slammed on the brakes. Luckily, there was no traffic, no one behind her to run into her. Only maybe someone in one of these houses wondering why someone was running their car at a crawl down their street. "Where?"

"I don't know. It was Amber and Brooklyn, though."

Joule thought about that for a moment. The other two roomies had picked a territory closer to the border. South, closer to La Escondida and La Mision.

Gisela nodded along as if she, too, was remembering information. "Let me check the map."

Both had taken a photo before they left. However, Gisela's

phone screen was small, and it took a moment for her to scroll around noting individual territories and enlarging them enough to read.

"Yeah, they are down closer to here." She held the phone up and pointed. "Should we go there?"

Joule was already hitting the gas and turning the wheel, making a three-point U-turn on the tiny street. Not only did she think they should go, but it was possible everyone would converge there. Whatever happened, she wanted to be there.

Joule simply didn't like relying on secondhand information. She preferred her own senses.

At least now Gisela's initial *oh hell oh hell* made sense, not being either excited or sad or upset. There was still no telling what the news meant. They might be very close to finding Sarah. They might be very close to finding information that indicated Sarah was dead or hurt. They might be very close to finding out nothing except the location of Sarah's car.

Joule hated the uncertainty. She'd lived with so much of it. Maybe it was anxiety, but she preferred to have a plan for every possible outcome—and it was so hard to plan when there were so many. So many outcomes that she couldn't anticipate or get ahead of. Though her family had once made plans for what to do if one of the Night Hunters had actually gotten through one of the windows, it hadn't gone down that way.

No plan survives contact with the enemy.

Yet still she clung to her plans and hated being adrift without them.

The twins' had found their mother's body sometime later. The details of her mother's death making it clear that she'd saved them all. Now, Joule wondered what the details surrounding Sarah's car would reveal. Without knowing them, she had no idea how to handle it. She stayed on the road, taking the turns Gisela indicated, her heart tight, her muscles clenching as they got closer.

Another car pulled onto the small road in front of them, seeming to be headed the same way. Though she didn't recognize it, she could only assume it was one of their group. Behind them, another car pulled onto the road. It pulled off a few blocks later, going a different direction, but another quickly took its place. The area out here wasn't populated enough for this to be anything other than members of their group converging.

Going back to the earlier conversation that had been interrupted by the incoming text, Joule decided to distract them both. She asked again, "Could that have been the name? Sal?"

"That was it!"

Salvador Torres. Apartment 104. Joule couldn't decide if she liked or disliked that the information was starting to come together. What would Salvador Torres have to do with the location of Sarah's missing car? She had no idea.

Was it possible she'd come face to face with Sarah's killer already?

The thought chilled her, and she had to admit she was surprised she hadn't thought of it before. He had not come across that way. Then again, any good killer didn't. They wouldn't last very long if they drew suspicion from the people they interacted with.

Other, darker thoughts passed through Joule's mind.

"You're going to turn right up here," Gisela told her. Sure enough, the car in front of them took the same turn. After a few moments, the headlights behind them followed.

Where was Cage? she wondered. He and Dr. Murasawa would surely be on their way, too. But they were coming from further back.

The car behind them pulled up closer, the old sedan clean and shiny. Compared to the local car she'd just been scoping, it stuck out. Her heart sank as she recognized it. Aurora and Malcolm Walker were right behind her.

Though Amber and Brooklyn might be checking it out already, the Walkers would get the information about their daughter about the same time Joule and Gisela did.

The phones lit up again, this time Joule could see hers. She wasn't trying to read anything, though she quickly recognized a series of photographs popping up in the text chain.

Amber and Brooklyn had gotten into Sarah's car.

14

They were people. A group of them out here in the . . . nowhere.

Cage froze as the eyes stared back at him.

Crouched low, they also froze.

Their position had made him think they were animals when he only saw the reflection in their eyes. He must have thought they were smaller or maybe closer than they were. Beside him, he felt Dr. Chithra Murasawa cease all movement herself.

Was she even breathing? He wasn't sure he was.

What were people doing out here at night?

The town of El Indio was too small to see people out on the edges. Nothing was out here. No houses, no businesses. Not even Sarah's car.

In his pocket, his phone buzzed, but he didn't dare reach for it in front of the people. They were dusty, dirty, and several of them carried full jugs of water. A backpack graced each back, some heavier than others. Some looked like elementary school bags that had been pulled from Goodwill. One of the smaller kids toward the back—oh God, there were kids in the group—even had a stuffed penguin that Cage thought he might have recognized the cartoon character. Or he would have had it not been so dusty and dirty.

Without moving anything other than his eyes, he looked down. The only thing between him and Dr. Murasawa and the group was a handful of scrub brushes and one stunted looking twisted tree between.

His eyes had adjusted and he looked at the people again as they began to slowly move. Several wore sturdy shoes, but a few were just in thin flip flops. Not out for a hike.

Next to him, Dr. Murasawa at last moved, tipping her head downward and looking at the ground. She then angled it slightly to the side and motioned for him to do the same. Slowly, she began to step backward.

Were these people dangerous? Cage had thought nothing of the sort from his own assessment, but Dr. Murasawa was clearly thinking something different.

The two of them edged cautiously backward. As she tipped her light toward the ground and away from the people, Cage did the same, making the people they'd spotted seem to disappear into the darkness.

The shuffling noises told him they were now moving quickly beyond where the two might sweep their light and find them again. He suspected if he shone his light in the place that he'd seen them, it would now be empty. And he would have to question whether he had seen them at all in the first place.

"Keep moving backwards," Dr. Murasawa whispered, her tone low and cautious. Moreso than he would have expected given the scene in front of him.

He wondered again, *Were they dangerous?* They had seemed just as scared of him as he could possibly be of them.

It took forever, one cautious step backward at a time,

wondering if he should be more concerned about the people in front of him—who were likely long gone now—or the snake he might step on.

When he was convinced the people were no longer there, and too anxious about the other dangers around them, Cage turned. Sweeping his light at his feet he found only ground. A sigh of relief escaped until he remembered he had no training in spotting camouflaged things in this desert-scape.

He swept a glowing circle, checking where he intended to step. Dr. Murasawa followed him, their pace picking up slightly, though she stayed facing behind them. Each time Cage looked back, he caught her gaze sweeping one side to the other. The concerned expression on her face conveyed more than he would have expected of the situation.

Finally, in the car, he slammed the door and immediately asked, "What was that?"

She didn't answer, instead turning the key. But she didn't roll the engine, only turned all the lights off, plunging him into utter darkness for a moment before he found the moon again. She jerked her hand up, tapping rapidly against the ceiling, and clicking at the dash. It took a confused second for him to figure out what she was doing.

When she finally did turn the engine on, nothing in the car lit up.

How were they going to get out of here without any lights?

But he found his own vision had adjusted just enough. Hers must be better, or she was desperate enough, because she turned the car confidently. Slowly they rolled away, crunching gravel beneath tires and not answering his question as she headed back the way they came.

It wasn't until they turned on to a road that was fully paved, then she answered. "They had to have been crossing the border illegally."

He'd already gathered that much. "But you acted like they were dangerous."

"I'm confident that most of them weren't. *Most of them.* But it's entirely possible that the man toward the front of the group—"

The one with the black backpack, Cage remembered. He had good shoes and the backpack looked like it was made for hiking.

"He may have been a coyote."

Something Cage had not yet thought of. And yes, a human coyote might very well have been dangerous.

Though everyone knew where Cage and Dr. Murasawa were headed, they'd been out of the car. The keys had been in the ignition to keep the headlights on. All anyone would have to do was move their bodies and drive the car further into the desert. The two of them could have disappeared just as easily as Sarah did.

His throat clenched at the thought.

Was that what had happened to his friend?

"It was stupid of me," Dr. Murasawa was saying, "to send everyone out here like this, when it's entirely possible that there is illegal activity going on along the border."

"I didn't get the impression that we were in any danger." He hadn't, though her explanation was concerning.

"We might not have been in any. It might have just been a group walking across on their own. But others in our search party might have run into other groups, or even individual people, and it might not have been safe." She banged a palm on the steering wheel in frustration at a mistake he didn't blame her for.

Only then, did he watch as another car on the road flashed its headlights at them. She banged on the wheel again but sighed and turned her own lights on. They'd been driving like a ghost—as she'd intended initially.

His phone buzzed again in his pocket, the chime dinging loudly in the silence of the night. As he pulled it out, he saw that they had missed a number of messages in the group.

15

C age gave directions as he and Dr. Murasawa raced to find where the others had gathered.

Examining the photographs on his phone, he found Amber and Brooklyn had opened Sarah's car. They'd been checking out the interior and were photographing what they pulled out. His irritation rose, but there was nothing he could do, the damage was already done.

There might have been fingerprints on the car doors, maybe on the trunk. Maybe even blood . . . Pulling things out of Sara's car could have destroyed evidence!

He tried to remind himself, it might have seemed like a good idea at the time if he'd been the one who found her car. Also, some of these things he hadn't known until Dr. Achebe had been murdered and he'd been accused of the crime.

Beside him, he watched as his old boss cranked the wheel into the turn. Pulling up next to the other cars she swung a sharp arc. Had they been on pavement the tires would have squealed. Using the centripetal force, Cage opened his door and practically tumbled out, running toward the car. He was anxious to see what they had found, because clearly, it wasn't Sarah. Unfortunately, there was nothing in the pictures he'd been scrolling through—wishing he could make them larger on his phone—that told him where she might be.

"Any luck?" he asked into the crowd in general. But it was Malcolm and Aurora Walker, standing back, holding hands tightly, who turned to him with sad faces, shaking their heads *No*.

Everyone stood around watching as Amber and Brooklyn went about their work as if it was all okay. It didn't seem to bother anyone that they were simply destroying evidence, that they might be losing the very thing that could lead them to Sarah.

But Joule's hand reached out, grabbing his wrist and holding him back when he would have lunged forward yelling angrily.

"Look," she told him pointing at the car with her free hand.

Only then did he see. Both girls wore blue non-latex gloves. Though Amber worked her way slowly through the car, Brooklyn had her phone out and was taking pictures from every possible angle before anything was moved. She motioned to a third member of the work party, telling him where and how to aim his light so she could get the best images.

"They shone the lights on the car door handles looking for fingerprints," Joule told him, her voice catching Amber's attention, and the woman looked up at Cage.

Her dark caramel colored hair was pulled back in a hasty ponytail. As she worked, she offered him what she could. "We worked very hard not to destroy evidence. We entered through the passenger rear door—" she pointed, "—the only handle that didn't have any fingerprints. And even then—"

Brooklyn turned around then, "We used Amber's belt."

She pointed one blue gloved finger at her friend's waist

where the belt had clearly been returned. "We did our best not to mess up anything that we couldn't see."

Smart, he thought. Smarter than he'd given them credit for. He'd had no right to be angry. If he'd been thinking at all he would have realized that. He was used to Sarah and her overalls and hiking boots. Amber and Brooklyn and Gisela looked a little more like they were going to the mall, but they were still Helio Systems Tech employees—smart, well vetted, and able to think on their feet.

"Also, my sister is a forensic scientist," Brooklyn told him as she turned back to her work of photographing the things in the trunk. "I can lift these prints if we need to, if the police won't do it themselves."

Not only had they likely done better than he would have, they thought ahead to a point he hadn't arrived at yet. He'd simply been excited and scared to find the car. They'd reasoned through notifying the police. Even as he realized that, Cage heard the wail of sirens in the distance, likely coming here.

"Hurry up!" Gisela rushed her two roommates.

Ah. They'd done the work themselves on purpose. If any of the group trusted the police around here to gather everything, they were in the minority apparently. Even as all the pieces clicked together for him, Brooklyn mumbled, "I wish I had a plaster kit for these tire tracks."

With his wrist now free from his sister's grasp, Cage tapped her with the back of his hand, reaching for his own phone. "We've got it."

The tracks that Brooklyn had pointed to led from Sarah's tires back toward the rutted path. He walked over, careful not to bother anything as he took pictures, motioning Joule to shine the flashlight from her phone.

"Some with flash on and some with it off," Brooklyn called out to him, but she didn't look up from her work. Sound must travel far out here on flat land, he thought. The sirens were still getting closer, but he couldn't see them yet.

He nodded, now following her lead. He clicked a handful of pictures, right up to the shifting of the tracks as Sarah had parked the car—or when whoever had driven it last had parked it. But looking where Brooklyn pointed revealed a wide berth. He and Joule realized quickly that another car had pulled up alongside Sarah's. A car that was no longer here.

Had Sarah's car been here the entire time she had been missing? The dust made it look like it had. The other car had possibly come with her. Which would make the tracks likely days old. Though the tracks themselves were for different tires, the depth and the way they'd worn a little looked the same to his untrained eye. Later, he could ask Brooklyn what she thought, or maybe her sister could analyze it for them.

The desert appeared to have degraded the indentations only very slightly. There'd been very little wind over the past few days, keeping the heat oppressive. But suddenly he was grateful.

The sirens were growing louder.

"Look," Joule pointed out. "It seems the car stopped right next to Sarah's."

As he looked up, he saw Brooklyn and Amber nod. They'd been first on the scene and likely had been talking their way through this ever since. Amber told them, "We're guessing they both arrived at the same time. Then, when Sarah disappeared, whoever was in the other car came back and drove it away. But it's hard to say for—"

She was cut off by flashing lights and the sound of slamming doors. Authoritative voices called out, telling them to step back.

Glancing every direction, Cage snapped one last picture of the tire tracks. Noticing as he looked up that Amber and

Brooklyn had carefully peeled their gloves and stuffed them surreptitiously into their pockets.

Interesting, he thought.

But it was Joule's gaze that caught his as she motioned to the tires and whispered, "You know whose tires we have to test these against."

16

J oule had slept hard and woken up worse. She felt as if she were crawling out of a deep crevice in the earth, fingers clenching at the dirt that kept giving way. She slid back down into restless sleep more than once.

The fog above her cleared in stages and she felt groggy, achy. Sucking in a breath, she finally came fully awake, if not fully alert. Her memories replayed the nightmares she'd had the night before.

She dreamed of the Night Hunters following her down the street—not so much the kind of dream that an analyst could ask her about, but more a distinct, straightforward, terrifying memory.

In another snippet, she'd dreamed of being in the car with Sarah, then Sarah disappearing from behind the wheel, vaporizing like dust in the wind. Joule dreamed of getting lost in the streets of El Indio, somehow managing to take four right hand turns and not winding up back where she'd started. Each time she saw a street she recognized and headed that direction, only to find out it wasn't at all what she'd expected.

It didn't take a therapist to tell her what it all meant.

She rolled over slowly, the ache in her upper back making her feel older than she was. This rental bed wasn't her favorite. How long until she turned thirty? How long until her father had been gone for a decade? That one was closer on her calendar.

The back of her jaw ached, like when she ate sugar too quickly. Joule wondered again if perhaps she and Cage should have worked harder to find their father. She'd been the one who argued and argued that Nate was dead. Even now, she hated the idea that he might be alive even though she would love to have him back more than anything. She simply couldn't fathom how he could have left his children for so long.

Nathaniel Mazur would not have left the twins to do this on their own. She knew that in her heart. So once again, this morning, she convinced herself that her father was dead.

She could not convince herself the same of Sarah. And she refused to entertain the thought that Sarah might remain missing forever.

The sound of voices from elsewhere in the tiny house had her getting dressed in a hurry. As she exited the bedroom heading for the small bath, she saw the barstools at the high table were occupied. Cage, Malcolm, and Aurora all looked over their shoulders at her. The Walkers must have shown up early.

"Good morning," she told them realizing after the words had tumbled out of her mouth that it wasn't good. And it might not even be morning.

No, it still was. She'd seen the number eight on the alarm clock provided with the bedroom when she'd rolled over. Or at least she was pretty sure it was an eight; it had been fuzzy from the blur of her gaze.

Still, she headed into the bathroom. She needed to brush

her teeth, splash water on her face and wake up before she went out to have any intelligent conversation. She arrived at the table a few minutes later, a plate of toaster waffles waiting on her.

With just the first bite down, her stomach began to settle. She turned to the Walkers. "Did you get any sleep last night?"

Aurora only offered a sad smile. "I don't think I've slept in days."

Joule nodded. If not for nightmares, she wouldn't have known that she had gotten any either. She certainly hadn't gotten any rest.

"Did the police tell you anything useful?" she asked between bites. But the couple shook their heads again.

"They told us what they're going to do." Joule waited. "They're going to send the car to San Antonio, where the evidence team can look it over. They were mad that the two young ladies had taken it apart."

Joule understood that. But Brooklyn and Amber offered to hand over their photographs as evidence.

"I think the police actually took the one girl's phone," Malcolm Walker said, shrugging. He didn't seem that mad about it.

The good news, Joule thought, was that Amber and Brooklyn reported that there were no obvious bloodstains. No signs of a struggle. They'd found and photographed Sarah's purse, which had been pushed up under the driver's seat. But there was no cash in the wallet, no driver's license. Her health insurance card was also missing.

Joule had seen the photographs Brooklyn had offered up after the police left and she logged into her online repository.

In Sarah's wallet—Joule remembered seeing it before—there were slots for each of those things. Given the arrangement of the other cards, receipts, and such that were still left inside, it appeared Sarah had plucked them before she went wherever she went.

"There were fingerprints on the door handles," Aurora said. "They told us that just from looking. But that's the same as the two young ladies said."

Brooklyn and Amber had even commented that there were more on the trunk that they'd been able to see with just the flashlights. Joule hoped the car was crawling with prints and that some would turn up useful. She took several more bites of her waffle.

In the silence that prevailed around the table, she sat uncomfortably, the only one eating. But she knew she needed to. She missed tasting food. Missed Ivy's chili. Missed Kayla's secret formula cookies. She missed that she hadn't really tasted them yet after Dr. Brett had died and now here she was, eating dust again.

"We should be getting the records from the phone company today," Malcolm Walker told them, breaking into her melancholy thoughts. "Do you two want to see them?"

"Absolutely," Joule answered, swallowing the bite of waffle. With each subsequent bite, it had become more and more of a chore to chew. It settled in the back of her throat and she tried again to get it down.

"I'm going to call Dr. Murasawa," Cage announced. "Now that we know where Sarah's car is, we have a new central point to look from. And that point isn't at her apartment, like we thought." He paused a moment. "Also," he added "we need drones. I'm hoping Helio Systems Tech has some we can borrow."

It was a good idea, Joule thought.

Malcolm Walker pulled out his phone as it beeped and buzzed at him. He put on his glasses to check the screen, a move that would have been Hallmark-movie worthy had this situation meant anything other than what it did. He tapped at the image, his finger briskly landing on something before he jumped back, almost as though it might bite him.

A good number of taps later, he announced to the room at large, "It's the phone company . . . they said they moved our request to a priority because she's officially a missing person now. But we have Sarah's phone records."

17

The drive was solemn, and Cage felt the weight of it. It had taken a while to get all of them into the Walkers' car.

The phone company had provided a map of where Sarah's cellphone had gone and Malcolm—being his old school self— had printed all of it out.

At first, the exercise had been academic. It was easy enough to look and say *this is where Sarah's phone had been,* without tying it to the fact that Sarah remained missing. But the first startling information was that the phone had been off since Sunday night just after eight—the night she'd disappeared.

What "volunteering" had she been doing that she'd lied to her mother about?

None of them knew at this point.

The phone had moved well past the spot where her car had been discovered, but they already knew that it wasn't with the vehicle. Had Sarah traveled further out along a road or a walking path?

Now he sat in the back of the Walkers' nice Buick, his sister next to him, usually the one to ask questions. Even Joule was quiet, this morning. Maybe everyone was on the same page. They all understood there was a possibility that they were following this map to a set of coordinates where they would find Sarah's cell phone . . . and that they would find it on Sarah's body.

No one had spoken those words out loud, though. No one had to.

Cage admired Malcolm Walker's too steady hands on the steering wheel, as he accomplished such a horrific task calmly. They were all likely assuming that the others wanted the same outcome: It would be best if they didn't find anything at all.

Then they could wish that the phone had been turned off, or the battery had run out, and Sarah was still out somewhere with it, trying to make contact.

Even though it was a harsh outcome, he and Joule had discussed the possibilities the night before. After the police had let the search party go, they'd headed back toward the rental house, ready to crash.

"What if she's lost in the desert?" Cage had asked last night, but Joule had just shaken her head.

"It's been too long."

Joule was right. It had been days, and Sarah hadn't taken the week off work, so she almost definitely had not expected to be out this long. She wouldn't have been prepared, and even he knew that being in the desert unprepared could easily mean death.

The car turned off the main road and Cage imagined it was relatively easy for Mr. Walker to trace the route from the night before back to where Sarah's car had been. Cage had no doubt the location was forever seared in his mind. Only this time, crime scene tape hung, dead and heavy in the too-still air.

Sarah's car was already gone. Other deeper, fresher tracks lined the area, almost definitely indicating where a tow truck had come in. Her car had been hauled to San Antonio as promised. Cage could only hope that they'd done their job and preserved all the evidence they could. They didn't seem to be out here scouring the area now.

Brooklyn had had no issues handing over her phone because she checked her service and found all her pictures were uploading to the cloud and that she would retain access. Dr. Murasawa had given the group a two-hour later start at work the next morning, but it was the best she had been able to do.

Looking at his watch now, Cage was relatively confident that the Helio Systems Tech people would only just now be rolling into the job site, ready for another day in the heat—but with heavier hearts. Finding the car, and not finding any real evidence of Sarah, hadn't helped anyone. Though maybe, he thought, *maybe* some of them had found hope. Because there hadn't been any signs of a struggle, they could still believe she was out there somewhere waiting to be found.

"I guess we just drive around it," Cage said, as he craned his head to look out the front window, looking for some semblance of a path.

It had been easy enough up to this point, particularly in the daylight, to follow the ruts that had been worn when someone else had cut their way through here. But now, with everything blocked off, it became more difficult.

Conversation suddenly bloomed in the car, with Aurora suggesting they go right and Cage suggesting they try to drive around it on the left.

Joule began tapping on her phone. "There's nothing really out here. There aren't even GPS trails left by other cars who came before us. Not past this point anyway."

That, Cage thought, was odd. He pulled up his own phone and checked the map. Let the others figure out how to get around the blockade.

When enough people drove the same track, the GPS system

they used added it as a trail. But why did the lines come here and then stop? They all came to the same point where they'd found Sarah's car and never went any further. When he actually looked at the ground, he could see the ruts in the distance. People did drive through here, more than one of them had to.

Did people not come out past here in GPS capable cars? The systems didn't forget that a person had driven on a road, they cataloged location and even speed to report things like traffic jams and find new roads that hadn't yet been uploaded by mapping companies. But the trails didn't extend beyond here . . . so had the drivers all stopped here?

Or had they turned off the tracking, not wanting their movements traced? And what would be the purpose for that?

The car rocked and bumped as Mr. Walker finally uttered "Fuck it." A phrase Cage had not expected to come from the older man's mouth.

He'd simply pulled around to the side, letting the tires and the undercarriage of the nice blue Buick take the brunt of the damage as they bumped up and over the shrubs and rocks. Cage held on, but a few minutes later they were back on the tracks.

Mrs. Walker continued navigating and Joule and Cage leaned back and went quiet again. It took another twenty minutes to go what felt like only a hundred feet. Between the information that the phone company had offered them in coordinates, their own GPS, and the Buick that was not suited to this kind of terrain, the going was slow. Honestly, it was entirely possible no one actually wanted to arrive at their destination.

Then, suddenly, they were stopping. They had arrived but there was nothing obvious, nothing anyone could see from their seat in the car. No movement grabbed their attention, even in the distance, just the hot sun beating down.

The four of them turned inside the car and faced each

other. Mr. Walker seemed to have taken it upon himself to lead the group, and Cage was more than willing to let him.

"Now we get out and we look on foot. We try not to mess up anything that might be evidence."

Cage nodded, trying to keep his expression neutral though his heart cracked at the idea of this man talking about his daughter's things as "evidence."

It was Joule who said, "We each go out our respective doors, then we trace an outward spiral in a counterclockwise path . . . So we don't miss anything, we keep each other in sight . . ."

His sister trailed off as if she'd been ready to tell them when they should stop but couldn't quite bring herself to do it.

Aurora, braver than anyone should have to be, simply said, "Yes," and opened her door, the first to put her foot down into the harsh desert sand.

The four each began their slow careful steps, marking their pace off the three others as they wound their way outward from the car in a ring.

Keeping their eyes on the ground, they searched. Cage saw nothing, just felt the hot air filling his lungs and stealing the water he'd drunk that morning.

Though he walked farther and farther, he found nothing but small scrubs and the occasional prints left by tiny desert animals he couldn't identify.

Then Joule began shouting. "Over here! Over here!"

18

_____

J oule stopped where she stood, her heart pounding. She had to be wrong. But she wasn't.

Her brain moved without her permission as she looked down at the indentation in the ground. There it was, between the shrubs. Was the faint smell creosote? Or mesquite? Were those native to the area? Would the scent be forever burned into her brain along with the fear at what she'd found?

At first, she'd been startled, before she processed what she'd found. She'd been excited at the find. Now she wondered what it might mean.

Though the wind had been fairly mild, it was still covered in dust. Little twigs sat across the top. She'd almost not seen it.

Unthinking, she'd reached down, but Cage put a hand out to hold her arm. "No. We have to preserve any evidence."

He was right. She was running on adrenaline rather than logic.

Joule watched as he pulled out his phone and began taking pictures from every angle. He'd been the closest to her, or maybe the fastest. Did the Walkers move more slowly because they were older or because they didn't want to see evidence of their daughter's disappearance?

The sneaker sat before her, obviously having been there for some time.

"I think this is Sarah's," Joule said to Aurora as the older woman came close.

"Looks like it," Aurora agreed. Still, it made sense that none of them would be quite sure exactly what sneakers their grown daughter and ex roommate might be wearing.

Joule remembered the white shoes with shocks of pink on the side. Or she believed she did.

"It's exactly the kind of thing Sarah would buy." Malcolm Walker looked down at the shoe, then off into the distance. "She likes the colors. More than that, look how well it's built."

The thick sole was clearly well padded and reasonably worn.

It could absolutely have been one of the shoes that lived on the other side of the room in Alabama when Joule had roomed with Sarah.

"Do you have enough pictures?" she asked Cage, but she didn't wait for his answer. Moving around, she searched for a few clean, relatively straight sticks.

They were hard to come by. As she reached down to break a branch off one of the little scrubby bushes, it pricked her finger. She wouldn't have been able to see the spot if the blood hadn't welled up. Whatever had stuck her was simply that small and that sharp. She ignored it.

Winning the fight with the small bush and claiming two bent and twisted sticks, she stuck them into the body of the shoe and rolled it over. Using one, she pushed up the tongue and revealed the little tag underneath.

"That's Sarah's size," her mother nodded solemnly.

There would likely be DNA on it from whoever wore it. But

more concerning than that, Joule figured, was that it was out here alone.

Being without your shoes in the desert was dangerous at best. But to be out and have only one? *That was odd.* Almost definitely something Sarah had not chosen to do.

Joule scanned her eyes across the horizon, hoping against hope to see something more. Her brain still turned over what she'd found—only one shoe? She had no explanation.

"Do we bag it and take it to the police?" Aurora asked.

Joule was about to answer but Malcolm beat her to it. Shaking his head, he calmly said, "We call them, and we stay here. We make them get the crime scene team to check it out."

Just the words "crime scene team" had to hurt his heart, but he was holding it together remarkably well. It didn't escape Joule's notice though, that he always spoke of Sarah in the present tense.

It was closing in on a week now. It was past four days, going on five, and no one had seen or heard from Sarah at all.

While the four of them waited for the police, they stood watching it in the heat, as if the shoe might disappear if they left it. As if they might not be able to find the one thing they had if someone didn't keep an eye on it.

They chugged water from bottles going warm in the morning air. Cage crushed the plastic after emptying his just before Joule ran out. They'd been prepared to be out for a while, but not to simply be standing and doing nothing waiting for the police to come check out a shoe. It would be hours at a minimum.

Malcolm pulled out the phone records he'd printed, and they bowed their heads over the papers in the bright light for something to keep them occupied.

"Look," Joule pointed to one line. "The phone has been off since Sunday night—" she didn't have to say, *when Sarah was last seen* "—but the battery didn't run out."

In fact, it had been just over 40% charged when it went off.

Had Sarah turned it off and taken it with her? Had someone else turned it off and taken it with them?

"That could have happened if it was broken," Cage offered.

That made Joule look up. She hadn't thought to look beyond the one shoe. But the phone was last traced to this direct area and it might have been broken.

She stood silent for a moment, but there was no sound of sirens, no hint of the police officers arriving to help. "Shall we start from here?"

The Walkers turned and looked to the twins as if they just didn't have it in them to answer anything else right now.

Cage took care of it. "You should stay here with the shoe. Joule and I will look for the phone."

Malcolm nodded at them, always the stoic. Joule once again began fanning outward in a spiral pattern, her eyes on the ground at her feet.

19

———————

Joule leaned back in the passenger seat as she and her brother headed into San Antonio. It was a haul, definitely.

After the police and the crime tech had taken the shoe, the Walkers had needed a break. Cage and Joule agreed, but first they'd driven by Sarah's apartment, to see about the white sedan. It wasn't there. So, they'd headed to their little rental house and crashed hard.

Now she was running her fingers through her hair, pulling a ponytail holder from her pocket, and thinking how she needed to cut it much shorter than this. Though she was grateful that the sleep had been hard and dreamless this time, she couldn't say she'd woken up refreshed. Joule had to wonder if she ever would again.

Then her brother had suggested the trip, and she'd seen no reason to say no. They could ask around in the city and see if anyone recognized Sarah's picture. They could try to find out if she was involved in some organization—which was more likely in San Antonio than in El Indio. The other nearest option was

Piedras Negras, but it also wasn't big enough to have what they needed.

"We'll get some decent food," Cage said into the air of the car and Joule found herself looking forward to a lunch that wasn't from the same lone drive thru. Or crackers and cheese from the limited variety at the small chain grocery in El Indio. It was disturbing to Joule that the mom and pops hadn't even survived out in the middle of nowhere.

Their car rattled as a huge semi rolled past them. Joule found herself wondering what was in it. It was unmarked. The cab was red with swirls inexpertly painted down the side. The trailer was white, battered, dirty and dented in spots. But nothing suggested what it was carrying, packages or produce?

She remembered a story from a few years earlier, when a truck had had an accident and had been left on the side of the road. Fifty people had been stuck in the back of it, most of whom had died from the impact or right after.

Had that happened here, or had it been somewhere else along another freeway? She didn't remember and she couldn't. She felt drained, so much of her effort going into looking for Sarah. They lived in a near constant state of panic, using every ounce of food she could force herself to consume just to stay alert.

"I wonder if they have an all you can eat buffet," she asked. Even though she knew she could put food away sometimes, she couldn't remember the last time she'd done it. Only that at one point she'd been able to take out an entire pizza or return to a buffet line multiple times.

Cage shook his head, knowing that she wasn't actually suggesting that. After their stint with the disease scientists, food that was available to the collective public was not high on their list.

"We do need a salad, though." She meant that part and watched as her brother's lip curled. But he didn't deny the fact.

Now that she was talking, it was easier to continue to do so. "The other night when you were out with Dr. Murasawa—"

"Last night?" he asked.

Jesus, she felt her fingers rake through her hair again. Only this time it was held back with the ponytail holder. She shook her head and looked out the window. She'd slept twice since then. If it could be called *sleeping.* "Yes, *last* night. You said you ran into people, and you think they were migrants crossing the border."

"I didn't think anything. That's what Dr. Murasawa said."

"You just ran into them?"

"Not really. We had our lights aimed down. I guess I heard a little bit of rustling, and I thought it was an animal. But there were lots of eyes." He seemed to be thinking now. He rested one hand in his lap, the other at the bottom of the steering wheel. Hardly any effort was needed as the car followed the straight line of the road almost by itself. "Their eyes didn't reflect like animals. But I didn't really process it until we shone the light on them, and they all froze."

"What did they look like?" Joule asked, wishing that she'd been there to see for herself.

"They had backpacks, all kinds. The guy in the front had a pretty good pack and good shoes. Some of the others were in flip flops."

"Flip flops? In the desert at night?" Dr. Murasawa had warned them about snakes and even scorpions.

"They definitely weren't casual night hikers."

Who would be? she thought.

"I mean, what do I know?" he said. "I have no ability to identify any nationality on sight. They were people, out in the desert. That's all I know."

Joule nodded. "Which way were they headed?"

He paused for a moment, and she could tell he had not thought of that before.

"This way." He lifted one finger pointing down the road. "If I have my orientation right from where we were, they were headed towards San Antonio."

"So why would they cross the border? In a group at night?" she asked, "when you can present yourself at the checkpoints and ask for asylum?"

Cage shrugged, his lone hand still on the wheel. "I don't know much, but I want to say that asylum isn't that easy to get. You might need it, but you still might not qualify. If you don't get it you get sent back to die. For a lot of people, it's safer not to hit the checkpoints."

That was a harsh reality, she knew. Joule quoted a line from one of her favorite poems about the water being safer than the land.

Her brother nodded. Whatever had brought those people there, she didn't know. And maybe, *maybe,* they were just a group of ill-prepared local night hikers.

Then her brother asked a question, "Do you think Sarah might have run into someone out in the middle of the desert? I'm guessing her shoe didn't come off by itself."

"It almost couldn't have." Then Joule said the words out loud for the first time. "Sarah ran into someone."

The question was, *who?*

20

"It's here." It disturbed Cage how excited he felt to see the dirty white car.

Unfortunately, it was parked directly in front of unit 104. Had it been on the other side of the small lot it might have been easier to surreptitiously check out the tires. *But no.*

He pulled into a spot far away from it, grateful that late lunch in San Antonio had been good. A much needed break, not that either twin had actually managed to stop thinking about Sarah being gone. But they did hit up a store and had each gotten a pair of good, comfortable walking sneakers. Though neither of them said anything, it was clear now that Sarah had made it further than the car had.

Though they'd looked and looked, no one had found her phone, even the crime scene techs. Cage didn't know if they ever would, but looking for it remained high on the list.

Dr. Murasawa had called and said, "Look, we have four drones and they're going to be left just inside the trailer. I believe you still may have a key?"

It would be the same trailer from their previous jobs, a portable classroom that Helio brought with them to the job site. Because he and his sister were on leave—and not gone from the company—they'd not been asked to give back any of their shirts, keys, or any Helio Systems equipment.

Dr. Murasawa continued. "I can't officially give them to you, I'm not *authorizing* the use. But if you return them before Monday morning, likely no one will notice and there won't be anything anyone can or likely will do."

Hence the phone call. Cage understood that she had to tell them this information directly, that she didn't want any of it in writing. So, they could get drones to do aerial surveillance. It wasn't completely on the up and up, but it shouldn't get any of them in too much trouble. And if he was the one missing, Cage would want Sarah to take the chance.

The twins had swung by the job site on the way back—the long drive had put them plenty past when everyone had left for the weekend—and now there were four drones sitting across the backseat of the car. Joule had buckled them in, suggesting they didn't want to explain any damage from a sudden stop.

Stepping out of the car now, Cage had his phone in hand, ready to get pictures of the tires on Salvador Torres' car.

"Where are you going?" Joule slammed her door behind him.

He motioned with one hand, as if to ask *why was she even asking?*

"No. Like this." She pulled her phone out and went to the opposite side of the parking lot. Crouching down, she obviously got a horizon shot. Then she stood at the front of the building, snapping pictures of that next.

Smart. She'd work her way around the entire lot, and Salvador Torres might not figure out that they were here specifically to ID his tires. Also, it wouldn't hurt the twins at all to have a full spate of pictures from here. Maybe there was something they would spot later or need to know and these "extra" pictures would help.

Three minutes later, Joule stood up from where she'd once again crouched at the edge of the lot and walked back to her brother. "I've got it."

Cage turned a full three-sixty, though they'd come here to find the white car, the stop made him realize there was value in more information.

Was there anything about the building that was an issue? Maybe there were other cars in the lot that they hadn't paid attention to, and they should have.

Sarah hadn't disappeared from here, but something was definitely going on.

Climbing back into their own car, he found himself once again at the wheel after a long day of driving. At least it was near the end. He'd make Joule drive next time.

As he backed out, she sat in the passenger seat, her head down as she cycled through the shots she'd just taken.

"Wait until we get home," He admonished. The phone was too small, the road too bumpy, the day too long.

She nodded, neither of them questioning that he just referred to a little rental house that they'd barely been in for a few days as *home*. Had they gotten so nomadic?

The answer was *yes*.

They moved from place to place with Helio Systems Tech. And they didn't tend to stay in hotel rooms. Usually, they were housed in small apartments, rental homes, or temporary housing. Likely a place they would live for anywhere from six weeks to six months.

Home hadn't felt like home for some time. He didn't mean their house, where they'd lived since moving to Rowena Heights from Curie. That feeling changed the day their mother had died.

Now, when they'd tried to go back, to actually make it a home again, it was all derailed. The whole point of the leave of absence from their jobs had been to go home to grieve their losses. To settle in.

The twins had talked about furniture, paint, rearranging things. Joule might even take over the largest bedroom that their parents had once occupied. They'd thought that even a small investment into the tasks would help them. But they hadn't gotten past the first few weeks of getting over Dr. Brett being gone.

Now having Sarah disappear was too much. Cage was getting whiplash from it all. The only thing that would stop this would be finding Sarah. And he wasn't even sure that was possible anymore.

Every day that passed was an exponential drop in the likelihood of finding her. Beyond even finding her was the now very slim chance of finding her *alive*.

He pulled into the little gravel driveway. The pale blue house was not really to his liking, but nothing about this had been to his liking. None of the homes they'd lived in had really been what he wanted. They'd all been rentals, places he'd stayed where he lived out of a suitcase, sometimes for months on end.

He usually roomed with his sister. Though he should have grown up and become more independent, he'd become less and less willing to let her out of his sight. They'd been through too much. He'd learned more than once or twice that lives could change in a heartbeat.

Their lives had been more and more threatened each time they encountered something dangerous. Now Joule walked into the little house as though nothing were bothering her. As though this were just another job, this time the task was "finding Sarah."

But Cage knew that her feelings ran stronger and deeper than that. She simply kept them locked up better than he did.

Evidence of her driving need to quell her own fears was

that she had her laptop open in a moment. She was seated at the table, pictures loaded, ready to work, even before he'd made it fully through the door.

He had other work. Cage headed into the kitchen, grabbing a bag of carrots and a plastic container of hummus. They needed something to eat. It had already been hours since they'd had lunch and he could hear his mother's voice telling him to eat a vegetable.

He put the food in front of her and even motioned for her to eat it.

But two bites later, she pointed at the screen. "Look."

21

W as this going to be a waste of a whole day? Joule thought on Saturday afternoon.

Then she mentally talked herself down. It was not a complete waste.

The twins and the Walkers had gone out to the desert again, this time in separate cars, covering close but different territories. They all kept the cars in sight of each other as they searched the desert again.

Heading back to where they'd found the shoe—the one they still didn't have confirmation was Sarah's—they pulled out the drones and tried to bring their best into the oppressive heat.

Mr. Walker had never quite gotten the hang of controlling his equipment, while Aurora turned out to be the best of them. She took to the task as though the drone were an extension of her own body.

The twins had played with drones some in high school and these weren't that different. Neither of them had been tasked with using them for Helio systems tech work, so they weren't familiar with these exact machines. In fact, Joule couldn't remember if they'd used them on any of the jobs she'd been on.

Now, she looked at the ground and then looked at the image on the screen on the handheld device. They'd have to watch the footage later for details, right now she was just trying to spot anything.

The local police, the ones who'd come out to claim the shoe, hadn't even put crime scene tape around the spot. If Joule hadn't marked the coordinates on her phone the day before, they wouldn't have been able to find it. The marks where the crime scene techs had dug it out, taking the sand with them, wouldn't have been clear enough if they hadn't had directions back to this exact spot. Then they wouldn't have known that they were in the right place at all.

Was that bad? she wondered. She hadn't asked it out loud, not in front of the Walkers, when they'd all started at the site and fanned out. But if the site where the shoe was wasn't worth being marked, then the police certainly didn't expect to find any other evidence here.

Next to her, Cage commented softly, "It doesn't look like they took anything besides the shoe."

Though they could see the Walkers, they were now only tiny dots on the horizon, searching their own area, not in earshot of the conversation.

She shook her head. That meant Cage didn't think there was any other evidence besides the shoe, either.

"What if it's not hers?" Joule had to ask. She had to have a plan in case it wasn't.

"I've wondered that myself. It'll basically be DNA testing, right?"

"Which could be negative or even inconclusive." Joule shrugged hating that thought, but then her drone dipped wildly, until she jerked and brought it back under control.

"Or they could tell us it's hers. But either way, I'm afraid it's going to take weeks to get it back."

They didn't have weeks.

He softened his tone, even though she was the only one who could hear, except for the slim-headed snake nearby she'd deemed not a threat. "I wonder if the Walkers can expedite it."

Cage looked down at the ground and his feet again, took a few more steps, looked at the screen and then looked up at the drone in the distance. Even though it was relaying images, letting each of them know that it was doing its job, he still didn't seem to trust the data. He kept looking up to spot the dot in the sky.

They also needed to be sure they didn't run into each other's drones midair or something else. Joule followed his lead and found her own black dot in the air. She didn't know what else might be that high up out here, but she wasn't going to ruin a Helio Systems Tech drone that they hadn't quite legally borrowed.

"I don't know if they can expedite it now," she told her brother. "It's already in the hands of the crime scene team. If they've done their job, they've already swabbed it and sent the sample off. If they've done their job."

Cage nodded along. Though they stood close to each other, they worked to keep the drones far apart. "And who would the Walkers know around here who could speed it up?"

It was a valid question. She certainly didn't know anyone who could be considered a contact. Her brother didn't either.

This time when he spoke, he was more frustrated. "She's a missing person! Can't we get the FBI involved?"

She'd thought through that one every night and still hadn't figured out how to do it. "I don't think so. Not until we have evidence of a crime. She's an adult."

The conversation lulled, both of them watching their drones. So far, all Joule had discovered were a couple of crushed water bottles, empty jugs, two flip flops, and scrub brush. She'd seen a jack rabbit hop away, startled by the drone. While she and Cage both loved lizards, she'd seen enough for a lifetime now, especially once she'd learned to spot them. They could camouflage into the desert sand so well that she hadn't realized they were everywhere.

She waited another beat, watching one bush rattle for a moment, then a small, lean rabbit burst out. The heat was getting to her. She'd drunk enough water. Or had she?

"Do we need to tell them," Joule asked, breaking the silence, "that Salvador Torres' tires match the prints of the car next to Sarah's?"

The twins had this same conversation last night, but it hadn't been resolved. Cage stayed almost where he was, didn't even turn toward her to answer that. "But the police must know that? They took those tire prints. They've been to Sarah's home. Surely, they've checked it out already."

Joule didn't know.

He continued. "I don't think we should interfere with the police investigation. They have so many more tools than we have. And it's not like a fingerprint."

"True," Joule replied, her thumbs on the joysticks.

Though Cage wasn't quite pulling an Aurora Walker over here, he did seem to be getting better and better at the controls with each passing minute. Joule still felt klutzy with hers. She didn't look up. "The police also thought we were murderers."

Cage nodded, remembering what she was referring to. They'd been hauled in and questioned. They'd had their phones confiscated and eventually duplicated for evidence. All over what both the twins felt was pretty clearly nothing. The only thing pointing at them was that they'd found the body.

Joule had another thought. "Do the police here even have the resources to check out the parking lot? To look at all the tires there and see what matches?"

"There was more than just the one other set of tracks," Cage pointed out.

There had been the tire prints leading up to where Sarah's

car had been parked. A dead end, those were hers. There were the big truck tires, more recent and thus more obvious, from when her car had been towed. But there had been other tire tracks of a car that seemingly parked next to hers. Those were the ones that matched to Salvador Torres.

Those tracks pulled up even with Sarah's and had eventually backed up, turned around, and driven out of the desert. But the group had found several other sets of tire prints, not quite at the same location but nearby.

"Maybe they *don't* have the resources. Maybe they haven't looked in the parking lot."

Cage shrugged. No one knew. The local police weren't sharing much information even with the Walkers. They only assured them that they were doing everything they legally could.

But did that mean they were hard at work, not letting anything leak while they diligently searched for Sarah and tested every bit of evidence linked to her disappearance? Or did it mean that the things the Walkers heard back were all that was happening?

Joule didn't want to think later that maybe something had been missed. "We should tell them. If they already have the information, we only wasted a little time." She felt she was wasting a lot of time out here today. Nothing popped. The Walkers hadn't shouted that they'd found anything. She'd just managed to drink way more water than she'd thought possible, and somehow still be dry despite the fact that she was actively sweating. Wasn't she?

Joule looked to Cage. "I got pictures of everything in the parking lot yesterday evening. Let's check all of those out first."

Finally turning to look at her, Cage nodded. "Maybe there's another match."

22

"My eyes are crossing." Cage leaned back in the chair at the table.

He would have liked to have sat on the couch and sunk into the plush cushions. The one here was relatively comfy. But he couldn't. Four drones sat across it, like invited guests. There was no room for an exhausted, nearly cross-eyed, and ready-to-tap out human.

The twins had downloaded the footage from all four of the drones. Though they had all watched the tiny screens and looked at the ground they covered as they worked, it wasn't enough. The point of the drones was to go farther than they could cover on foot. So, they were watching it all again.

They'd watched all their own footage already. Even at a faster speed, it took forever. Now they'd moved onto the footage from the Walkers' drones.

"I need a drink." Joule's tone let him know she meant alcohol, and not just something liquid. That wasn't her usual.

"But if I do," she continued, "the footage from Malcolm's drone will make it all come back up."

Cage agreed. The man's footage had been shaky at best. It was part of what was making him cross-eyed.

Joule's surreptitious pictures of the entire parking lot at Sarah's apartment building had already paid off. There had been ten other cars in the lot besides theirs. It was evening and a weekend day and many of the residents had been home.

Joule had pictures of all their cars. Matching tire tracks was not in his normal job description and after watching shaky drone footage for several hours then trying to match imprints to tires, the tension at the back of his eyeballs was beginning to get to him.

Dr. Murasawa had called another search that night. Though Cage had wanted to go, he voted against it.

"They'll send us pictures," he'd argued.

Joule replied, "Pictures suck."

He agreed. "But we're about dead on our feet."

Just having to wait for the police to provide results or the phone company to give them the phone data alone was exhausting. And that didn't count yesterday's trip to San Antonio. The shopping for supplies, and playing detective in the parking lot. Then today, they'd spent the day out in the desert, in the heat.

He'd gone through more bottles of water than he imagined possible. The fact that he'd only peed a normal amount told him he'd been losing it at a high rate. They couldn't afford to go back into the heat tonight.

Joule sighed heavily, but she must have agreed, even though she didn't say all of it out loud. Because she didn't argue back.

He went back to trying to watch the image on the screen and scan it for any small detail in the endless scape of monotone color. Even the bright white and pink shoe hadn't popped when they'd found it. The focus that was required was more than he had to give right now.

He couldn't maintain this level of fight or flight much

longer. It was wearing him down, even though he'd lived with it off and on for a long, long time now.

Closing his eyes, he took a deep breath and stood in the middle of the living room. He stretched and turned, wondering if he was old enough to be feeling his joints pop the way he did.

The chairs at the table weren't really made for relaxing, more for eating or working. But the twisting and jumping didn't help much. He couldn't shake the tension from his shoulders or the back of his neck. He couldn't stop the clenching of his throat every time he thought about Sarah.

And when he tried to stop thinking about Sarah, it only worked partly.

The evening wore on and he tried to focus. The search started without them, and he tried to remind himself that he wasn't responsible for it, and he was allowed to take a break. He had to take a break. So did Joule.

But part of his argument to his sister was that they had to return the drones before they were discovered missing. Which was best done at night, when no one would be at the job site to catch them. He didn't want anyone to see them and be put in the position of keeping the secret, small though it might be.

Another task wasn't a win. It wasn't rest.

He turned and faced Joule, whose eyes were still glued to her screen. "When we get back, we'll get out the microwave popcorn and get some drinks and watch a movie."

Another screen, but in the distance and one that wouldn't matter if he cataloged every lizard and every piece of trash.

It would be late, but there wasn't anywhere they had to be in the morning. Only that they had agreed they should call the police and explain that they had matched Salvador Torres' tires to the tracks in the desert. And that another car in the lot had matched to another set of prints a little farther away.

He hoped they could sleep in a little bit. Though he desperately wanted to keep going to find Sarah and do everything he could, and he knew it would hurt for the rest of his life if they found her body. He couldn't keep going.

What if they missed her by only a day? Or even a couple of hours?

What if Sarah was still alive now, but they weren't fast enough to save her?

He pushed the thoughts away, unable to even process them now.

"All right," Joule agreed from where she still sat at the table. "I think we have about thirty more minutes of this drone footage. Can we just get through it? Then we'll return them."

He would have taken a break now even despite the fact that there was so little left. His eyes and his brain were done. "Fine, but I get to watch Aurora's footage. I can't watch Malcolm's anymore."

She shook her head and moved her shoulders. Not a shrug. Not a yes. Not a no. But she quietly got up and shifted into his seat, looking at his computer where the footage was pulled up, and began tapping at it. "Shit, there's more than an hour left."

Joule agreed to take the break now. He was grateful, his body letting go of more tension than he'd known he was holding.

Closing both the laptops, she headed to the couch and began loading up the drones. They'd carried them in cloth grocery bags, so it didn't appear they had contraband evidence. Not that anyone should really see them, but hauling them in and out of the cars might be an issue. Did this little house have cameras outside? He hadn't found any, and he'd looked, but that didn't mean they weren't there. Just that they weren't obvious.

They put them into the backseat this time, putting the bags down into the footwells. If they got pulled over, or somehow anyone looked in, they wouldn't look like they were running around with a pile of drones.

In a short while they were out of town, though El Indio hardly even qualified as that. They pulled up the long gravel road that he could see had been laid by the Helio front team that cleared the site for construction. The gravel was too new, too clean, too thick to be the same as what existed in town.

Though he'd only been on this particular job site a couple of times, it still looked like all the other Helio System Tech sites. The twins put the drones in a neat row on the table across the back of the room, trying to leave them exactly as they'd found them. The footage was erased, fingerprints wiped down, double-checked, and then they were out.

The dark night and the still air seemed to cover for them when there were no trees, woods, or anything to take up the view. Anyone who showed up would see their car. Technically, they were still employees, so he didn't think they could be prosecuted in any way other than internally.

But then they were back home, despite not speaking the whole way back. That alone told him how much this was wearing on them. They talked constantly. He and his sister argued. They tried to outdo each other. But only sometimes were they silent, and it usually meant something.

He punched in the code to the front door and thought again how much he did not want to watch the last of the drone footage. He wanted a movie, but he was even beginning to question the sanity of that.

He wanted popcorn and to pop the lid on a hard lemonade that he didn't really like the taste of but he almost *needed* the buzz from. It said something that he and Joule had even bought them in the first place.

"You have to watch it." Joule was reading his thoughts. "We have to finish this."

He nodded, glad that he bartered for Aurora's footage. The room was quiet for twenty minutes as he checked his watch and the time stamps on the video consistently, hoping it would soon be over.

"Hey!" Joule suddenly tapped at the table beside him. "Hey, look at this!"

She pointed at her screen. His eyes focused.

Did Mr. Walker catch this, too?

Cage didn't think he had.

23

Joule stared at the officer, not able to believe what she was hearing.

Cage had insisted that she drive here; apparently, he'd had enough the past few days. That much she could understand. But she'd done it. Then she'd trekked across the parking lot that felt like a frying pan on the stove. They'd sat here for an hour and a half, the AC too cold and spotty at best.

And this was what they'd waited for?

"Yes, six weeks will be a good turn around time." The officer looked at them with a blank expression that both conveyed he was bored with their questions and also thought they were crazy.

Cage nodded, but Joule was about to lose it. "Sarah will be dead by then."

"Or not." The counter answer was as ridiculously controlled as everything else the man had said.

Joule bit her tongue, not adding, *if she isn't dead already*. Because if Sarah was still alive right now, the police and their slow investigation were going to make sure that she was dead before she was found.

The man had already told them that he could not and would not put any kind of "rush" on the order. That standard tracking and timeframes were all that was available to the police for an adult woman whose family still was unable to produce evidence of a struggle or harm or anything indicating that she'd left in any way other than voluntarily. The police would step up the investigation when that happened.

They had just given them the shoe, too. Since testing was—like this—six to eight weeks away, they were practically guaranteeing they would never put effort into the case. She tried to hold her frustration in check even as her fingers twitched. "What about the jacket?"

He tapped his pencil, even his answers were as slow as his work. "What makes you think it's hers?"

"It looks exactly like her jacket." Joule was about to grind her teeth. Beside her, Cage was silent and she suspected he was saving himself for when she finally blew up.

"Lots of jackets look the same." He could not have cared less, and Joule was approaching boiling. "Do you have proof that it's hers?"

The lightweight jacket was still out there, partially buried in the sand. Something they never would have found without the drones. They hadn't touched it, so no, they didn't have proof.

Before Joule could tell him that it was his job to get that proof, he asked, "Do you even know she was wearing it the night she disappeared? Because none of her roommates specifically watched her walk out the door so there's no record *from the people who were there* of what she was wearing."

He was jabbing at her, suggesting she had no clue what she was talking about because she hadn't noted what Sarah wore each time she left the apartment. He knew Cage and Joule had come here to find their friend and he seemed irritated that he wasn't able to simply ignore the case entirely.

This time he asked, "Do you know how many items of discarded clothing are out in the desert?"

She didn't, but he only tapped the pencil again and his expression changed. "When was the last time you saw her before she disappeared?"

She almost spat out "Fuck you." Because it had been a month. He knew that. She and her brother had sat down with him and given him all their information before, when she'd still believed he cared about the case. She used that now.

"Oh, my brother and I talked to you and your partner before. I would have thought you'd be smart enough to remember the answers and not ask the same things twice."

With that, she gave up. Being decent wasn't getting her anywhere so she might as well say what she wanted. She stood up and stalked out of the room, muttering "Have a ball sucking day, you complete fucknugget."

Cage could offer any pleasantries he wanted, and it might be the better thing to do, but she was sheer out of fucks.

She nearly stomped down the hallway, pushing open doors with no concern who might be on the other side, until she emerged onto the creamy concrete that made a small patio at the front of the low, drab station. The heat assaulted her, but the change was welcome.

She could only say that Sarah had a jacket exactly like that and shoes exactly like what had been found and neither was in her room now. But she was all out of faith that it would mean anything to this asshat.

It didn't help that the jacket appeared to have maybe blown around a little bit, maybe hadn't originally landed where they'd found it. It was certainly caught on a shrub now. Or at least yesterday, she could only hope that it was still there.

Between the coloring and the way it was partially under the

sand, Joule was pretty sure that Mr. Walker hadn't seen it. Surely if he had recognized it as something belonging to his daughter, he would have called out yesterday.

With the drones connected into satellite feeds, Joule and Cage had come in and given the officer a set of coordinates of a ten foot by ten foot square where the jacket was. They'd done everything they could to make it easy, and she almost cried. No one cared.

The easy explanation was that Sarah had simply parked her car in the middle of nowhere and just walked away from her old life. But where would *anyone* go from that location? The officer had even suggested one of the other cars belonged to some man she was running away with. Joule could still almost bark out a laugh at the thought of Sarah doing that. She'd told them as much, but her word meant nothing to them. Less than nothing.

Cage came out next to her.

"Anything good?"

He shook his head. "He actually told me that the very fact that 'we're testing the shoe shows that we're going above and beyond in this case'."

Just when she thought she couldn't be any more stunned. "This is above and beyond?"

"He sure thinks so."

She knew he felt the same way she did. They were on their own in this. Joule now regretted giving the officer the information they'd gathered. They'd told him about the tire tracks on Salvador Torres' old white chevy, they matched the images of the tracks next to Sarah's car.

At the time he'd seemed to make a note of it. But now, Joule was pretty certain he'd thrown all of it into the trash. In fact, when Joule mentioned that other tire patterns at the parking lot also matched tracks nearby, he hadn't even bothered to write down the two license plates she'd given him.

"Let's go."

Her brother's voice compelled her into motion. They headed across the hot parking lot. It wasn't made with black tar —as if they understood that would be a very bad idea—but it still reflected a day or more's worth of heat at her. She could see it shimmying upward around her when she caught the angle right.

Sliding into the driver's seat, Joule again wished she was the passenger. She liked being able to research things on her phone while she just rode along. Being a driver meant she had to pay attention, and that she was responsible. Not her favorite thing.

She turned the engine on before anything else, having already learned that getting the AC going as quickly as possible was more important than even her seat belt. Cage slid in beside her, the sound of his door closing sharp and harsh, letting her know that he felt as frustrated and angry as she did.

Somehow, he found a little more grace than she had. "Do you think that was awful because it's Sunday?"

She shook her head. "I think we waited an hour and a half to get those shit answers because it's Sunday. But I think the answers are going to be shit regardless. It's not like they were doing a lot of work through Friday."

The AC blew at her, the fan already cranked to the highest setting. Though the air wasn't quite cool yet, it was definitely colder than the parking lot.

She closed her eyes to relax, and she could hear her mother's voice telling her that being hot and then cold or cold and then wet, things like that, would make her sick. The evidence had come out since then, that it didn't work like that. But right now, Joule thought she might be sick, and it was easy enough to write it off as going from the too-cold air conditioning of the police station to the outside dry heat of the parking lot and into the quickly cooling interior of the car.

She put her hands on the steering wheel but didn't go

anywhere. "We have to pay to get the shoe sent out for DNA testing. Don't we?"

"Do we? Can we?" Cage asked. "They have it and as much as they are doing exactly jack shit with it, I don't imagine they'll hand it back to us. Or even let us do our own tests. We have to get the jacket and test that, I think."

Joule backed out of the parking lot. At least she and her brother almost always wound up on the same page. That was a comfort in the worst of times.

But Cage was still talking. "I'm really concerned that we found another piece of Sarah's clothing . . ."

"At least it's a jacket and not a shoe." She shrugged and aimed the car back toward the little house.

He frowned at her.

"It's not as essential," she countered.

"But it is," he said. "When the desert gets cold at night it may be even more so than the shoe."

Joule felt the shudder run down her spine. "We should get the jacket."

He only nodded and looked out the window.

They hadn't even seen it in person, only on the review of the drone footage. So maybe there was more evidence there.

"Should we go now?" she asked, ready to turn the car the other direction.

He put his hand out onto her arm. "There's something we need to do first."

24

Cage knocked on the apartment door, pleased when it opened that Brooklyn was ready to go. What he was surprised by was the duffel bag over her shoulder.

Then she announced, "I don't have everything, this is just what I could gather since we found that shoe."

What could she possibly be missing?

He caught a glance in his peripheral vision of Joule, looking the woman up and down. Probably wondering the same thing he was.

Brooklyn's blonde hair was pulled up in a ponytail and straightened to a near impossible point. She even had on makeup, but also sturdy hiking shoes and cutoff jeans shorts. She was wearing a lightweight but long sleeve shirt. Seeming to double-check herself before she left the unit, she paused then reached back around the counter, grabbing a completely white baseball cap and a pair of sunglasses.

With the cap in place and the sunglasses in hand she stepped out onto the walkway. For all that Brooklyn looked a little too-put-together to go into the desert, she was clearly better prepared than either him or his sister. Joule seemed to be realizing it, too.

Maybe his eyes had crossed because he'd been out yesterday without any sunglasses on. The desert here didn't offer any blinding whiteness. There were too many variations in the sand and the shrubs. All the brown broke up the view, but clearly, this was the better way to do things.

The three of them headed downstairs, the metal risers clanking under their feet. Then they were across the parking lot. With a glance back over his shoulder, Cage looked at apartment 104 but saw no movement behind the curtains. The white car stayed parked directly in front of the unit.

Nothing he could do now. *But he would later*, Cage thought.

He climbed in with Joule once again behind the wheel. Brooklyn immediately began talking.

"I don't have fingerprint powder or anything to lift a print with if we find it, but I don't expect to find anything out in the desert . . . I do have most of what we need to lift the jacket out and bring any evidence around it."

"Like the crime scene unit did when they collected the shoe?" Joule asked in the rearview mirror.

"Exactly. You want to capture the whole scene. If it's a body, it will leak fluids into the area. There may be associated evidence nearby, and we'll sift for it."

The bodily fluids were not anything Cage wanted to think about. So, he added, "It's a jacket, so I don't think we'll get any fingerprints."

"Right. But, if there are things in the pockets," Brooklyn added, "like keychains, or anything like that, we might be able to lift prints from that."

"But we can't lift prints, you said," Joule pointed out.

"I can't lift prints today. I've got a kit coming. I ordered it online, but we're out in the middle of nowhere. So, it'll be a few days before it gets here."

Nodding along, Joule asked, "What else do you have in that bag?"

"Gallon and sandwich sized plastic zip bags, paper bags. Digging tools and brushes to clear anything for a better view without disturbing it. I pretty much put together everything I could from the local store from what my sister told me."

Ah, she'd called her sister, the forensic scientist and put together a home version forensic kit. *Very smart.*

She was still going. "Brown paper bags are for anything biological. You can't put that in plastic. It'll degrade the DNA."

Turning around now, he watched as Brooklyn showed off the parts of her kit. A small folding shovel, large brown bags, which she'd apparently begged for at the dollar store. The kind with handles that groceries got packed in, as well as a set of lunch ones still wrapped in the plastic. She also had those thin plastic grocery store bags, certainly not professional, but he assumed it would do the job.

Reaching down into the bag again, she held up a small spray bottle. "I have Luminol. Actually, it's a different brand." She showed off the blue label.

"And a black light?" he asked.

She reached in again and pulled out an ordinary looking flashlight and smiled as she said, "Blue, but yes."

It must have been altered, not that he could tell. But given the hoard that she hauled into the car with her, he was going to trust her.

"Do you just do forensic science with your sister? That's why you know all this?"

"She's about six years older than me. So, I was in early college when she was finishing grad school. She helped keep me sane with my core classes. Helped me with essays for English and Humanities. And I posed as her assistant on a handful of cases."

That sounded incredibly cool to Cage.

"I certainly don't know exactly what I'm doing," Brooklyn said, shoving everything back down into the bag, zipping it up, and leaning back in the seat, "but I seem to be the best that we have."

He couldn't agree with her more.

"And I do have an on-call lifeline to a real forensic scientist. As long as we can get a signal. So, while she's not here, we'll bumble through with our best technique, and she can help talk us through probably."

Cage couldn't ask for more. It was clearly far better than what the police were offering.

The conversation lagged a little then. Aside from trying to find Sarah and working for Helio Systems Tech, the twins didn't know much about Brooklyn.

It was Joule who eventually asked over her shoulder as she turned off the main road, "Engineer or biologist?"

Brooklyn shook her head a little, not understanding the question.

Cage translated. "It feels to us like everyone at HST is mostly an engineer or a biologist." Then he pointed to himself and added, "herpetology specialty, Joule's an engineer in materials."

Brooklyn nodded even as she looked out the window, taking stock of the passing landscape. "Ecology."

They'd had some ecologists on site before, but he'd tended to lump them in with the biologists. Certainly not with the engineers. "Specialty?"

"I have a PhD in hydrospeleogeology."

"I'm sorry, what?" Joule asked. But she kept her eyes on the road . . . or the path. They'd moved from pavement to gravel and now to ruts in the sand. The noise of the town hadn't been very city-like, but even it had faded away as they got further and further out into the quiet. Only the occasional cry of an animal, zoom of a plane overhead, or the sounds of the car bouncing along followed them out here.

Brooklyn explained, "Hydro - speleo - geology."

Cage didn't doubt the PhD. Helio Systems Tech tended to hire highly educated people. "Given whatever that word was that you just spouted off, it sounds like quite the specialty."

Brooklyn laughed. He realized she was probably older than she looked. "I got into geology in undergrad and I grew up in the Mid South. My dad took us caving a lot as kids. It was something really cool that my sister and I could do together given the age gap."

He was putting it together. "Hydro for water. Speleo for caving. Geologist."

"You got it. I study how water moves in caves and how it forms them."

But he felt his eyes darting from side to side. "Are there even caves here? In *Texas*?"

"There's actually a bit of a system of caves in Texas. They're mostly slightly north of where we are setting up the job site. Concentrated in the Edwards Plateau. But there are a handful around here and they certainly will make a difference in how the system gets built."

"We haven't seen a hydro—speleogeologist—" he tripped over it a bit, "—on any of the previous jobs."

"Yeah, I'm not a permanent hire. I don't know if I will be. But I'll be honest, with a specialty like this, when I get a chance to do work like this, I'll take it."

"Alright," Joule announced as the car bounced more and more. "This is as close as I think I can get us."

She pointed to her phone on the dash mount where she had been tracking the system. "It looks like the brush gets denser out here. And it looked pretty solid ahead of where we are."

"Can I see the drone footage?" Brooklyn asked, leaning forward as the car came to a stop.

Joule put the car into park but left the engine on. They would take the AC as long as they could. Cage opened his laptop and handed it awkwardly into the backseat.

Brooklyn checked the screen, then scanned the landscape beyond the windows. "You know exactly which direction you're going?" her tone sounded like she had the same concerns they did.

"No, not at all," Joule said. "But the app on my phone does."

"And if the phone doesn't work?"

"Old school compass for back up." Cage patted his pocket.

Turning her lips in and pressing her mouth together, Brooklyn accepted that it was probably the best any of them could do. With the AC turned off, Brooklyn insisted on carrying the bag herself as they trekked out to where the jacket was.

"If it wasn't for the coordinates, we never would have found this," Joule offered as the three of them ringed the small bush the jacket was tangled in.

The wind picked up ever so slightly, and Cage was grateful. Even sweating wasn't that helpful if there wasn't moving air to lift the heat away from the body. Joule knew far more physics than he did, but he remembered that part.

Even thinking about that though had him motioning to his sister's bottle. "Drink."

"Good reminder," Brooklyn declared, setting down the bag that looked a bit heavy. "We hydrate and we get to work."

Sunglasses in place, she looked up at the sky. "I don't know how long this is going to take or how much more daylight we're going to have." But she pulled out the shovel and squatted down to get to work, issuing orders to the twins who followed along.

It took an hour. It was painstaking. She didn't want to budge the jacket at all. Cage had thought they'd simply lift it up, check the pockets for loose change, or even perhaps something solid and smooth that Brooklyn might be able to lift a fingerprint from.

Instead, Brooklyn seemed to want to take an entire box worth of sand out of the desert. She didn't want to touch the jacket.

"We can't move it at all?" Joule had asked as they were all sweating, working hard to not jostle it.

"Not until we get back and can see it with some light. I want to check for blood again." She'd already sprayed it with luminal, but it hadn't shown anything—much to Cage's relief.

From Joule's expression, he could tell she'd expected the worst, too.

It was Cage mostly who helped Brooklyn with the digging. Joule stayed upright, watching the landscape. "I'll make sure we don't get any snakes or scorpions."

But as they were caching the last little bit of sand that Brooklyn wanted to bring along, and Cage was eyeing the plastic lined cardboard box she'd put it into, he was thinking how he was likely the one to carry it all back.

Joule turned back to them, interrupting his silent concerns as she told them, "Look!"

She held the phone down where they could see it, the screen brightness turned up just to compete with the sun.

He didn't want to look, the heat was getting to him. He just wanted to carry the heavy box back. *Why hadn't he brought wheels?*

Next time, he told himself, he would.

"Look," she insisted again. As she and Brooklyn exchanged a glance.

Then Cage caught it, too.

"Oh hell," Brooklyn said.

25

She hated the heat, Joule thought.

In the past, she'd been glad it was a dry heat, just like everyone else. But she wasn't sure this would be worse with humidity. She wasn't sure it *could* be worse.

Maybe it was the news that bothered her more than the heat. She looked at her brother and Brooklyn, still crouching down. Brooklyn had considered taking the entire tiny shrub in the box with them. Cage had finally convinced her not to. Though Brooklyn had tried to call her sister to settle the argument, there hadn't been cell service out here.

Joule's phone had been hard pressed to hook up to anything either. In fact, they'd walked a while when they left the car with all three of them waving their phones around until she finally caught a signal. They'd realized then that they were heading in slightly the wrong direction before turning and aiming back for the jacket.

But once she caught a signal again and looked at where she was now, she recognized what she hadn't seen before. They'd only entered the coordinates to get here. She hadn't put them on the map when they were leaving the car.

Now she pointed at one dot on the phone screen. "This is the shoe."

Cage nodded, not liking the conclusion they were all seeing.

Still, Joule pointed to the next dot. "This is where Sarah's car was."

It made almost a disturbingly straight line to the jacket.

If they put the clues together logically, then Sarah had likely left her car and headed first to where the shoe was. She'd lost it somewhere in the vicinity of that spot, it couldn't have traveled far . . . at least Joule didn't think so. Then Sarah must have headed here to where the jacket was, losing it, too.

"This means," Cage pointed out into the open space as he stood up, "we need to be searching that way."

But he didn't quite point in one direction, he swept his hand across a swath of land.

"We don't even have the drones anymore." She wished she did, but it was growing late on Sunday. They couldn't just go get them back and borrow them anytime they wanted.

She was confident the whole thing had worked this weekend because they picked the drones up on a Friday evening. She and her brother knew from experience that, on Friday, people tended to leave the job site as soon as the last hour rolled around. But on a weekday, these people were far more apt to stay late to complete some kind of task. Maybe some experiment they were running that needed another hour or data that would just take a little more crunching to finish.

So, the likelihood of the twins running into someone if they tried to pick up the drones tonight was probably fine. But how would they return them? In the middle of the night? No one seemed to be on the roads late; they'd be obvious. If they tried to pick up or return the drones on a Monday or Tuesday, the odds were even worse. And they needed daylight to use them.

Joule had her sunglasses on, but still she held her hand over her forehead. As light as it still was now, the sun was starting to move down. There wasn't time to get the tech they needed anyway. "It will be the weekend before we can get the drones."

"*If* we can even get them again." Her brother nodded along, but they might have to risk it.

They were Sarah's only line of defense now. The police weren't doing more or couldn't. Even if the jacket was Sarah's . . .

Her brother seemed to have the same thought at the same time. "How sure are you that this is Sarah's jacket?"

The whole issue of the line pointing them in the right direction depended on both these pieces of clothing actually being Sarah's. "I'll know more if I can see what's in the pockets."

"If there's even anything there," Brooklyn added, still crouched down, taking care of the last of the evidence. She'd tried to make sure they didn't have any high expectations.

"If it's Sarah's—and I'm pretty sure it is—" Joule said, still scanning the bright horizon, "—There will be something in the pockets."

Brooklyn nodded along, catching up. The team hadn't been here at this job site that long and Sarah apparently hadn't been hanging around with her roommates much. They hadn't bonded—not the way they had when the roommates had been Sarah, Dev, Cage, and herself.

But Sarah was a woman who appreciated being useful. When there was a task, she always seemed to have something that would work right there in her pocket. A can opener, a Swiss Army Knife, a screwdriver, a quarter . . . something.

"Why don't you guys go do a preliminary search out there?" Brooklyn asked. "I'm going to stay here and take care of this. I want to be sure I have it all packed in as well as possible, because I'm not going to be able to call my sister until we get back into range."

"I don't think we should lose sight of each other." Cage looked between them.

Brooklyn agreed. "I didn't mean go out of sight but . . . it's flat." She motioned them to go, the irritation in her voice conveying something beyond what Joule recognized. But it didn't seem to be aimed at them, at least. "I think you can go a good distance without us losing sight of each other."

The twins headed out, Joule noting the position of the sun again. It was no longer high. Had it moved since she last checked it?

Cage pulled the compass from his pocket, wanting to be ready. It had already saved them once.

"So, the car was back there. Then shoe, then jacket," Joule pointed loosely.

"We go this direction," Cage started moving. It was the same place he pointed originally, but Joule thought it was just like her brother to double check.

They walked out, slowly moving apart from each other, knowing that they could cover more ground that way. Their footsteps traced a V in the sand behind them, but her eyes were glued to the ground in front of her. Lifting the sunglasses, she tried to focus more. At least they were headed away from the sun.

It was a strain, searching for the tiniest clue. Periodically she turned around, looking over her shoulder, checking to make sure she could still see Brooklyn who became smaller and smaller in the distance. She was about to say this was as far as they should go, when she heard a tiny sound.

"*What?*" she called over to her brother, who was suddenly farther away than she'd realized. He wasn't as far away as Brooklyn, but far enough that she had to call out.

"It was Brooklyn. She said she's done!" he called back.

Joule nodded and made a loop, not wanting to simply turn around and trace the same steps back. Once she was aimed back toward Brooklyn, she'd moved ten or fifteen feet to her left, but she only made it five feet before she saw the thing that the desert had almost consumed.

A lump.

Long and lean, it lay in an awkward position.

She almost didn't process it. It was desiccated, dried, and partially naked.

Then her brain turned on.

She sucked in a deep breath and yelled, *"Cage!"* quickly followed by *"Brooklyn!* There's a body out here!"

26

J oule stood over the body, still not quite processing what she saw. The parts of her brain that were working told her what to do. Her feet started to move.

She would walk a circle around it. See what she could see.

She found the head at one end. Curly hair, dark and dried, didn't even move in the wind. Traces of sand had piled up around the body, and small bushes grew at the back of the knees and the front of the chest.

Had someone lay down here to sleep? Had they wound themselves in between the small shrubs on purpose, perhaps to hide as best they could? And they simply hadn't woken up?

The bad thought had already wormed its way into her brain. She tried not to think *What if it was Sarah?*

Taking a wide berth around the head, Joule tried not to worry about the face. In the distance, she saw her brother running toward her. Not thinking, she turned and looked back. Brooklyn was headed her way, too. She wanted to yell out and tell them *don't run. Not in this heat.*

They couldn't afford to have anyone pass out. They couldn't carry anyone back.

Brooklyn had already carried the heavy kit this far. Someone would have to carry a box full of sand all the way back. And now there was a body.

Blinking heavily, Joule knew she was still too shocked to operate at full speed, but her next thought was *wouldn't the police at least come out for this?*

Then, *please, don't let it be Sarah.*

Though she and Cage had moved apart as they'd searched, he wasn't that far away.

"It's small," he commented as he got closer, finally slowing his pace.

"It's desiccated," Joule replied, not looking up. She wouldn't have described it as *mummified*. Nobody had wrapped it or preserved it in any way. "Don't they shrink when they dry out?"

Heavy breathing came from behind her. It was Brooklyn. "They don't shrink that much," the other woman added.

Joule turned, taking her gaze away from the hollows that had been eyes and the stretched gash that had once been a mouth. If it was Sarah, she wouldn't have recognized it. Which meant it still could be.

The body wore a T shirt and jeans shorts. But Brooklyn wasn't done.

"Desiccation can change the organs and the skin, but the bones won't shrink. This person was too small in stature to have been Sarah."

The confidence in Brooklyn's voice turned a key inside Joule's chest and she almost cried as the feeling let loose. In her own mind she sarcastically reminded herself this was the Texas desert, and she couldn't afford to cry and lose the liquid.

How much should she trust Brooklyn's evaluation? She wondered. But right now, the answer was *completely*. If someone who knew something—and Brooklyn did—was telling her that this wasn't Sarah, then Joule couldn't afford the emotional space to fight it.

"Who is it?" she asked.

"Could be anyone." Brooklyn moved around the body, once again squatting down and seeming comfortable at ground level. Then she looked away over one shoulder to her right, then back to her left. "People pass through here a lot."

"Cage saw people the other night out with Dr. Murasawa," Joule volunteered.

"That doesn't surprise me. They take different routes around here."

"It's not safe!" Joule burst out, maybe just glad that the conversation wasn't about how this body could be Sarah.

"It's not," Brooklyn agreed, looking up at Joule, her expression somber. "But you don't come through here unless this is safer than where you came from."

The water is safer than the land, Joule thought again. What might drive a person to make a journey like this, knowing that a certain percentage of them simply wouldn't make it?

"Do we call the police?" Cage asked.

Brooklyn looked down at the body. "Yes, when we get in range of a signal, we can pin the location."

Brooklyn stood up and they all held their phones high in the air again.

"I think we're going to have to go by distance and direction. This isn't working," Cage declared. "We know where the jacket is. We can lead somebody here."

"Will they even care?" Joule asked, angry that she felt she had to.

"It's a body. Legally, they have to do something and, legally, we are going to get in a lot of trouble if we touch it," Brooklyn warned.

Joule turned a circle again, her eyes scanning the area and this time she caught what she hadn't seen before. A flip-flop upside down about fifteen feet away. She'd seen the crushed water bottles and a gallon jug, all within eyeshot. Most had old labels, sunbleached and dirty. Bugs had likely made a home inside by now. There may have been fights for the last drops of water, Joule thought. She'd dismissed all of it as trash.

"Let's pace it off," Brooklyn declared, then asked Cage, "Do we have any kind of tracking system?"

Even as she asked that, she was moving around the body snapping pictures, hundreds of them. From what Joule observed, she took them high, low, and from every angle, flash on, flash off, all the options.

"Do you want to try the luminol?" Joule asked.

"Well, it's back in the bag and I didn't bring it on purpose. If I did anything like that here, I could be brought up for contaminating evidence. Truly all we can do right now is look."

It was Cage who pointed into the sky. "The sun's getting low. We need to head back."

Joule wasn't looking forward to carrying the box of sand. But she couldn't regret it either—anything that helped them find Sarah she would do the work for.

The other two turned and started back toward the car. Joule followed, hating the conclusions she was coming to.

Turning away from the body, she tried to sight a straight line to the jacket, then the shoe.

Which would mean Sarah was somewhere behind her now.

Alive or dead? None of them knew.

The flip-flop and water bottles, the bandana, and scraps of paper? They weren't trash. They were a trail.

27

They stood in a line, the seven of them, Cage at the end.

It felt good to be part of a block. He kept his arms crossed and his stance somewhat hostile.

"What's happening with the body?" Joule pressed.

They'd spent a good chunk of yesterday waiting, out in the desert, for the police to find them, then watching as the body was excavated. They'd all gotten hungry and thirsty and tired, being out long past when they'd expected. What they'd prepared for.

It was a smacking reminder of how harsh the desert was.

Even Brooklyn hadn't stayed to see the crime scene team do all the forensic collection. Though maybe that was because she rolled her eyes a few times. She'd whispered to him on more than one occasion that they were doing it wrong. "Even I know they should have taken samples much deeper and further out from the body."

Once Brooklyn had said that, Cage realized they were testing for bodily fluids leached into the sand as the body had decayed. They'd gotten only one sample. Maybe they'd gotten more later. But his faith hadn't been high yesterday evening when he was hungry and angry. And it was lower now.

They stood there, in their line, in the middle of the slightly too-cold Police Department. All of them waiting for the answer to Joule's question.

"It's been sent to San Antonio to the M.E.'s office. They'll take it from there."

"That's it? No investigation?" As much as Joule's tone kept an even keel and her hands stayed at her sides, Cage could tell she was holding back.

The officer narrowed his eyes and leaned forward. But his sister met the man, move for move, not backing down. Next to her, Aurora Walker glared and leaned forward as did Gisela.

Slowly, the whole line closed in, letting the officer know they didn't like the route this investigation was taking. Maybe that was why he changed tack.

"You guys need to stop going into the desert."

"*Really?*" Cage asked, the word bursting out before he could stop it. Now it was him about to let loose.

Next to him, he saw Amber's mouth fall open and her eyebrows rise, her slim fingers curling into tight fists.

But the officer wasn't having it. "There's too much going on out there that you don't know about."

"Like what?" Aurora Walker asked, her arms now crossing under her ample chest, her expression somehow becoming sterner.

"There's illegal immigration, for one thing."

"So?" the woman asked.

"So . . . it's mostly run by coyotes who won't hesitate to take you out if they run into you."

It wasn't the first time Cage had heard that.

"And . . . there's drugs. It's wide open space. All kinds of things are moved through there—weapons, drugs, people, stolen art worth millions." He paused. "Even the large animal trade."

Cage tried not to blink. That was news to him, and probably to his sister, too. Maybe to the Walkers but none of them let their expression show it.

"It's not a place for amateurs." The officer punctuated his comment by turning to walk away.

Cage felt himself boiling. *Was he even an amateur at this point with everything he'd faced?*

Could the coyotes actually be worse than the Night Hunters?

He was opening his mouth to demand an answer, but Aurora Walker beat him to it. "It sounds horrifying. So why are you leaving my daughter out there without even bothering to look?"

The officer turned back and blinked.

Score one for Aurora. He could see the admiration flit quickly across Joule's face before she hid it.

When the officer didn't answer, Cage pushed. Planting his feet like an anchor at the end of the line, he asked again, "So what are you going to do about it?"

"We're doing everything we can." The man reiterated, but it was a shitty answer. From the tightening muscles at the edge of his jaw, he knew it.

"It doesn't feel like much." Malcolm Walker's deep voice entered the conversation for the first time. "My daughter was last seen in that direction. There's evidence that she continued in that direction. You just told us how dangerous it is and yet you refuse to look for her . . . Your *everything you can—*" he made sarcastic air quotes with his fingers, "—looks a lot like sitting on your ass."

Damn. Cage fought to suppress the curl at the corners of his mouth. The Walkers came to smack down.

Malcolm had seemed steady and stable, but his anger was

flaring now. Maybe he wasn't as calm and collected as he always appeared. Yet somehow neither of the Walkers had lost their shit.

Though it looked like now the officer might.

His teeth visibly clenched. "If you go out there, you'll wind up disappearing, too."

He stopped and stared for a moment, trying to look each of them in the eyes, as if to intimidate. To make his point to unruly children who were playing basketball in a closed court or loitering outside the convenience store.

Cage was proud of his little group. None of them was having any of it.

"I see you're content to just let Sarah disappear into nothing." Joule took a full step forward, moving herself in front of the line. This time, her hands didn't hang idly at her sides. A gesture that Cage had always realized was more force than casual. Now they curled into fists, her arms moving out behind her as if she were ready to swing one of those punches that she trained for years for.

Both of the twins had second degree black belts in MMA. Though it had been a while since they had practiced, he had no doubt that as soon as his sister started to move, all the motor memory would come right back. And who knew what any of Sarah's roommates might throw? Cage could admit he'd underestimated them from the start.

"We're investigating the best that we can," the officer said, red starting to creep up his neck.

"Your best is serious shit." Joule called him out, and Cage wondered when she would cross the line and really provoke the officer.

"We have to go into the desert," Amber stepped up right beside Joule, "because *you* won't."

This time, in a surprising move, the red faded quickly down

the officer's neck. His expression softened, his arms crossed, and he smiled. He waited.

"You simply don't have the manpower to do the job you've been tasked with," Joule stated, her tone had evened out again.

"We don't have the manpower to chase *adults* who probably left *of their own free will*. And you just don't want to admit that your friend doesn't want to talk to you anymore."

It was harsh. Cage loved it.

He reached down to the side of his cargo pants, into the pocket he had left open, and pulled out his phone. He held it up to show that it was recording. "Thank you, officer."

Then he turned to leave, the entire line following him out into the parking lot.

It was Amber who pulled out her own phone, seeming to just check the time before she put it back into her pocket. She motioned to Gisela and Brooklyn. "We have to get back to work."

The three roommates had come out on their lunch hour.

"Are you going back out tonight?" Brooklyn asked the group at large.

Cage looked to Joule, then the twins looked to the Walkers. They all shrugged. But he understood what they all did: It wasn't an answer of *I don't know*. It was an answer of *what else can we do?*

Then the three roommates checked in with each other through a series of glances. Gisela stepped forward. "We have to keep showing up for work. But you'll have at least one or two of us each evening . . . or night. I'll go tonight."

"I will, too." Amber volunteered.

Aurora Walker stepped forward, hugging each of the girls, tears welling in her eyes. "I can't thank you enough." With her arm still slung around Amber's shoulders, she looked to the twins. "And both of you, too. I don't know where we would be without you."

What could they say? Cage thought. It was only what he hoped someone would do if it was him missing . . . or Joule.

They were compelled to be here. The world had taken too many people from them. There was no chance to go out and hunt down Dr. Brett and bring him back. They'd hunted for their father and knew what it was to give up. He wasn't sure he could handle that again.

If they could find Sarah . . .

Would it erase the sins of the past?

He didn't know. Instead, he cleared his tight throat. "All right. Tonight. Nine p.m.?"

Everyone but Brooklyn was attending. They all nodded.

"You all heard the officer the same as me," he said, "We need to be ready."

But for what, he really didn't know.

28

The desert air was almost cool, Joule thought. Though she had a lightweight jacket tied around her waist, she didn't yet put it on.

Her good walking shoes were laced tightly on her feet and bandaids were shoved in her pocket. They'd just bought the shoes the other day and hadn't had time to break them in yet.

Her brother was there in his ever-present cargo pants, with a lightweight long sleeve shirt already on. He didn't have the same kind of body heat that she did.

Next to her, Amber and Gisela showed up in bright colored cargo shorts, thick socks lining their hiking boots. Gisela had a tank top and a short sleeve jacket already on. Amber had a bright blue T shirt with a logo from a local cider brewery from some other state and likely some other job.

They'd all parked right near the tire tracks where Sarah's car had once been.

"What do we have?" Joule asked everyone, somehow stepping into the position of leader, but likely only for the moment.

"I've got Brooklyn's bag." Amber motioned over her

shoulder to the large backpack she carried. "I rearranged it, I don't like hauling a duffel."

The twins nodded at her. The Walkers didn't ask.

"I've got *this*," Malcolm reached to his side. His plasticky 1980s windbreaker having covered the gun to where Joule hadn't even noticed.

"Semi-automatic?" she asked.

He nodded. "Illegal eighteen round clip."

It was Cage who said, "I don't think it's illegal here so at least no worries on that." Then her brother moved his own jacket revealing the gun at his hip, too.

It was the one that their father had given them. But they'd bought another this afternoon for Joule to carry. Too new, too stiff, the holster clipped into the side of her pants was heavy. The weight and discomfort a reminder that she had deadly force on her now.

Both twins had the guns snapped in but had already discussed that as soon as they saw movement, they'd be undoing the snaps. She'd noticed that Malcolm didn't have his secured.

She was grateful now that her father had trained them carefully. The last thing she ever wanted was to kill the wrong thing. She had enough regrets in her life as it was.

It was Aurora who waved her hand up and down at Joule and asked, "A bow and arrow?"

"Arrows." Joule smiled and twisted to show off her quiver, stocked full. "Metal tips." She pulled the bow off her other shoulder where it had slung easily. "Compound, with a wide range."

"She's probably better with that than with a gun," Cage told them.

It had been a while since she used the bow. Luckily, the little rental house was out at the edge of town in the middle of nowhere. She'd called out to make sure no one was nearby then planted practice shots in nearby tree trunks. Then she'd made her brother come out to throw objects into the air and roll them along the ground for her to aim at.

Her skill returned quickly.

"Me, too," Amber said, pushing her hip out to one side, and pulling back the jacket wrapped around her waist. Her gun, like Joule's, was on the left side.

Interesting, another lefty. Everyone had a holster. No one had stupidly stuck their gun down the back of their pants. Even more impressively, Amber immediately added, "My mother is a US Marshal. I'm trained."

Which, ironically, left only Malcolm Walker as possibly the least handy of them with the weapon.

"We've got water, sports drinks, and snacks." Aurora changed the subject as she hefted a clearly heavy backpack and pointed at the one Malcolm carried as well. Shiny and new, but bright in color, they would not blend into the night.

That had been the point. They'd all discussed it. Malcolm's 1980s jacket was the same shade of blue as the sky. Aurora wore a white sweater. Joule's jacket was a pale pink. Cage had struggled to find something bright among his usual darker colors. He had on a bright blue national parks shirt, and Joule had managed to convince him to at least wear his lighter colored pants.

They wanted to stand out. They didn't want to sneak up on anyone. Because, if the officer was right, there were all kinds of things passing through here. All kinds of places that Sarah could have disappeared. Though Joule didn't like to think about it, all kinds of people that would have found it easier to kill Sarah than to let their secrets get out.

"So, how do we split up?" Malcolm asked.

"Before that," Cage told them, "Joule and I have some information to share."

"What's that?" Aurora asked, the tone in her voice latching

on, as if maybe they had just found Sarah and hadn't yet said so. Sadly, that was not the case.

"If you remember, we took pictures of the prints of the tire tracks out here the other night. The tires of the car that were parked next to Sarah," Cage pointed at the ground where the faint prints could still be seen if a person knew where to look, "matched Salvador Torres, who lives in apartment one-oh-four."

Joule held out her phone, having pulled up a picture of the man. She showed it around the group. Then added, "The prints from some of the other tracks out here match two of the other cars in the parking lot of the apartments."

Amber and Gisela looked at each other, worried now. Joule could read their concern. *Were they living in a building that was part of a criminal ring?* Could Helio Systems Tech have simply failed to check information like that?

It hadn't crossed Joule's mind before now. And she wasn't sure why it would have crossed anyone else's to find out more. It seemed more than possible now that was the case.

The Walkers nodded. Malcolm and Aurora's eyes turned to each other, sharing something the rest of them didn't know.

Joule could see something was coming. Sure enough, Malcolm stepped forward.

"We learned something yesterday, too."

29

Cage felt himself leaning forward as the cool night air wrapped around him. The shiver that ran down his spine had to be from the look on Malcolm's face and not the desert itself.

He'd not minded the open spaces during the day, and the low shrubs and jackrabbits were fine. But the snakes he'd seen, and the rumors of scorpions, still lingered at the back of his head. Now, after what the officer had said today, he realized there were other things in the desert far more deadly than a straight up poisonous bite. Cage only knew that he had to go forward because he really had no other options, so he could only hope that Malcolm's information was gold.

"Aurora and I went out yesterday asking around town. We just wanted to see if anyone had seen her."

"Someone had," Joule guessed immediately from the couples' expressions.

"They didn't admit it."

"So how did you know?" Cage asked.

"We asked around and no one said yes. But this woman visibly reacted when we showed her Sarah's picture. She looked at us, very worried. When we asked if she'd seen Sarah, she very clearly said *No, I've never seen her before in my life!* Then she slammed the door in our faces." Aurora glanced around the group, almost daring them to come to any other conclusion.

Cage agreed, that absolutely sounded like a liar. It also sounded like the Walkers had literally gone door to door showing their daughter's picture.

Joule seemed ready to open her mouth and ask a question, but Cage reached out, slightly wrapping his fingers around her wrist, telling her to wait.

It looked like the Walkers had more to tell.

Malcolm did. "We wrote down her address and stopped for a moment to memorize what she looked like. Then we kept asking down the street. But when we got back to our hotel, we put her address into our search or whatever Aurora did."

Aurora took over then, "The woman's name is Gretchen Mueller. She was relatively easy to find because apparently the police keep picking her up and arresting her. Nothing ever seems to stick or . . ." Aurora shrugged.

"Maybe she has a good lawyer," Amber suggested, though from the looks on everyone else's faces they were all still trying to figure it out.

"The shape of her house would not suggest that she has the money for a good lawyer."

Cage tried to absorb that.

"What is she getting arrested for?" Joule asked.

"Mostly confronting federal agents." Malcolm put his hands on his hips.

Cage felt his eyes fly wide.

"One time for assault," Aurora added. "Assault against a federal agent! But that's all we can find."

"Where was she arrested?" Cage asked. This was nuts. Why would someone like that, someone local, know Sarah? And why refuse to admit it?

"Looks like they were all near here. I mean, in this area of Texas, not specifically here." Aurora pointed at the ground under her feet.

Looking around the group, Cage saw no one else could quite process all of it into a cohesive story either.

Salvador Torres at apartment 104 knew Sarah but wasn't admitting it. It appeared his car had been parked next to Sarah's the night she went missing. Gretchen Mueller also appeared to know Sarah and adamantly denied it. She had a string of arrests for interacting poorly with Federal officers in the area. Sarah herself had gone missing, but articles of her clothing were showing up in what might very well be the beginning of a trail. *Maybe even breadcrumbs...*

Cage had puzzle pieces, but none of them clicked. A sweater with dangling ends to unravel, but when he pulled on them the sweater didn't seem to get any smaller. Nothing of value came undone.

The group as a whole seemed unable to reach any conclusions.

With a deep breath, Joule finally asked, "Does anyone else have any revelations?"

When she was met with more silence, she suggested, "Maybe we should get this search on the road then."

Cage pulled out his phone, the time letting him know it was just after midnight. As he and Aurora moved farther and farther away from the other two pairs, they kept their eyes on the ground, occasionally flicking up onto the horizon checking for movement.

Periodically, he would glance back over his shoulder, checking as the others became smaller and smaller in the distance. He couldn't help the sinking feeling that clenched his gut.

30

Cage clicked the buttons on the walkie talkie and then handed it over to Aurora. They'd been out for thirty minutes, and it was time to check in.

The walkie talkie hadn't buzzed at him, meaning the others hadn't contacted him, so he was reaching out.

The first buzz earned them a pickup.

"Hey, honey," Aurora said as Malcolm's voice came over the line. "We're doing the check in."

"We haven't seen anything," he answered. "You?"

"Just tracks. It's clear there's a lot of movement of all kinds of things through here, but we haven't seen anything in and of itself."

She was right. There were foot trails and Cage had seen other prints, maybe from bikes, even motorcycles. There were animal prints everywhere, some in groups. Aside from general classifications, he couldn't say exactly what was out here, and the two of them didn't see much of anything until they almost stepped directly onto it.

They had flashlights but weren't using them. All three groups had decided to let their eyes adjust to the dark, afraid that waving one around would draw attention to them, while blinding them to anything beyond the radius of the artificial light. And a flashlight might shine on something it shouldn't. When it did, it would alert everyone what they were looking at. So, they'd left them off. So far, it had worked for him and Aurora.

"Well," Malcolm sighed. "Consider Gisela and me checked in."

A moment later, Joule's voice came over the line.

"Same," she told him, "all kinds of tracks. We actually came across a jug full of water as if someone had just set it down and left it."

Strange that someone would abandon their water out here.

"Did you take it with you?" Aurora asked.

"Oh no!" Joule and Amber immediately replied in tandem.

"We have our own water and we're not touching anything. Not unless it's obviously Sarah's," Amber filled in.

For a moment, the distance hung between them, and it was clear nobody had seen anything that was Sarah's. Not tonight.

"Okay, then we're all checked in for the next half hour. We'll talk again at one." He didn't like the feeling of releasing the button to end the call. But he did feel better having heard everyone's voices. Mostly, it was talking to his sister and knowing that she didn't sound disturbed in any way that settled his feelings.

He kept moving in the same direction. Again, his eyes scanned the ground at his feet. A scared lizard, who'd managed to keep himself hidden until the last moment, scurried away before Cage squashed him. In the distance, a bush shuddered and a rabbit bounded away, a shadow hopping through the night.

At one point, they'd heard a rattle—the almost plasticky sounding shake of a snake tail. Aurora's hand shot out as if he was a child in the car seat next to her. As if her hand were enough to stop his forward momentum. It didn't matter, both of them froze.

They stood silently waiting, trying to pinpoint the sound without turning their heads. At last Cage managed to find it though the low light made all of it difficult.

"Over there," he whispered as softly as he could. He stayed as still as possible, moving only his eyes to direct Aurora where to look.

They stayed that way, in a standoff with the snake, for a good five minutes. Eventually it grew bored with them, turned and slithered away.

They shouldn't be out here like this. Him and Aurora. The snakes were home. He was the intruder. And the wildlife was hard enough to spot in the daytime.

They could have been bitten before they even knew it was near.

Aurora had a similar thought. "We're lucky this one decided to warn us first."

Did Amber even have any antivenin in that kit, and why would she? It was a forensic kit and an evidence kit so at best they could save things that were already not alive.

"Malcolm has a medical kit on him," Aurora assured Cage, but he didn't feel very assured.

Malcolm and Amber were the farthest away. Could they get to any of the others in an emergency? He didn't know.

When dividing up into pairs, they'd made sure to get a gun in each party. They'd made sure to split up their little already formed partnerships, too, hoping that they could share information and that a person coming from a different perspective on this would lead to better cooperation rather than echo chamber ideas.

He and Aurora crossed another set of trails and he felt like they'd covered no ground. They'd stopped and stood still for so long for the snake, that when the walkie talkie buzzed this time, it startled him.

He had forgotten to set the timer to make the call himself. What if the digital sounds of the walkie talkie had startled the snake?

Cage was beginning to think this was all a bad idea. Though he hated to admit it, maybe the police officer was right. Or maybe he just had a bad feeling about being out tonight.

All three groups checked in again, and Cage didn't want to say *we should turn around and go back this isn't working.*

Luckily, he didn't have to.

It was Gisela who huffed an irritated sigh and said, "Let's check in one more time and then we go back. I don't think we're finding anything of value out here tonight."

Looking at each other, Cage and Aurora nodded. Cage spoke their agreement into the handheld system.

"Joule and Amber agreed, too," Gisela told him and again they disconnected.

He set the timer on his cell phone, turning down the volume of the alarm and the volume on the walkie talkie as well. At least he was trying to think ahead.

They only had thirty more minutes to go forward. They didn't even have to go that far. Maybe because it was the last leg of the trip, or maybe because it was so late at night—he didn't know—he felt the twist of his stomach as he stepped.

Aurora at least had turned out to be a better companion than he'd expected. Her ample shape disguised the fact that she was fit. It was his mistake, he knew, for not recognizing that. But for all the walking and all the ways the desert night stole from the people who walked through it, she hadn't broken a sweat. She hadn't breathed heavily, and she had not once complained.

She was smart enough to wear good shoes. And Aurora was the one who'd suggested the bright colors, her own white sweater gleaming in the moonlight. Now, for whatever reason, maybe because it was the last leg of the trip, she started talking casually. Even if the topic wasn't casual at all . . .

"I felt that something bad had happened to Sarah when we didn't hear from her. I just knew it. But now I'm looking back at all the times I talked to her right before she went missing, all the times since she started the job here, and I'm trying to think *what did I miss?*"

"What *could* you have even missed?" Cage asked. "Unless she dropped big hints?"

"No, nothing like that. Sarah sounded happy here. She said she was volunteering at the Y and doing good work. And I had no reason not to believe her. Now I don't know if we'll ever know. But I'm starting to think that Sarah got herself into something and I hate to say it, but her disappearance may not have been entirely innocent."

Cage had wondered that, too. There were now two people in town who recognized Sarah and wouldn't admit it. At least two, maybe they just hadn't found the rest.

He was pondering that problem when he stubbed his toe on a rock. Frowning, he looked down, thinking it should have hurt more than it did, and realizing that the rock had moved. Too easily.

As he and Aurora looked at each other, questioning the oddity, they reached down in tandem. Even in the pale moonlight, up close it became clear: It wasn't even a rock. Just a plastic molding of one. The fake kind people used to hide pipes in the yard or small outdoor appliances.

Curling his fingers under the edge, he lifted it slightly. But before he could see anything, he heard shuffling noises and froze.

People. He heard people. Many of them. From all directions. Close.

He heard the snicks and clicks of guns being readied.

Across from him, he saw Aurora. Fear or shock or something was holding her unnaturally still.

Whatever was under the fake rock, someone was willing to kill to protect it.

All around him, people of different sizes held guns aimed at them. Some were handheld, semi-automatic. Some were assault rifles that would make it completely unnecessary for the handguns to even be here. One was a battered silver Colt revolver that glinted in the night.

His heart hammered in his chest.

The bad feeling hadn't been for Joule. It was for them.

But as he looked up, trying to make out the people at the ends of the barrels pointing at him, his mouth fell open as he recognized a face.

31

"All right, we're heading back now?" Joule asked.

Across the connection on the walkie talkie, she heard Malcolm and Gisela both agree. "We'll just turn right around and meet you back at our starting point. Cage, Aurora, check in?"

She released the button, waiting for her brother's voice. disconnecting them from the other line, grateful that Cage had had the idea earlier that if they were going to be out here in the middle of the night, with limited cell phone connection, that it was time they started having some kind of dependable communication on hand.

They'd spent the afternoon trying to find satellite phones but had settled on expensive but long range walkie talkies.

She buzzed her brother and Aurora and waited a moment but got no response. She buzzed again, then again. Nothing.

Joule and Amber looked at each other. Joule pushed the button one more time. This time, when no one answered, she became worried. Was Cage and Aurora's handset broken?

"Gisela, Malcolm?"

Malcolm answered right away. *"Yes?"* Of course, he sounded worried.

"I don't hear Cage and Aurora. Can you talk to them?"

"No." The word was drawn out with concern she knew she'd put there.

"Can you try them?" She wasn't going to worry, she told herself, not until she knew she had a reason to. But she hung up, motioning to Amber for the two of them to get started back to the original meeting point.

Malcolm and Gisela had gone northward. Amber and Joule had headed mostly east, while Cage and Aurora had headed more toward the south. They had all aimed east after the first check in, not wanting to get too far away. Heading back to the starting position was the correct direction. Joule also knew it was where Cage and Aurora would meet them if something had happened to their communication.

If need be, she and Amber could turn south and hopefully intersect the other two. She worked through all of it mentally, keeping her feet moving, until just a few moments later when, the walkie talkie sounded off again.

Malcolm's heavy tone came across, followed by a long pause and, "They're not answering for me either."

Fuck, she thought. *Fucking fuckballs!*

What was the protocol if none of them answered?

They had planned where to go, when to check in. But stupidly, they'd not made a decision for what to do if someone completely failed to answer.

"What do we do?" Gisela asked.

"We go back to our starting point." Joule was confident that was the right first step. And hopefully the only step.

Because as much as she had just thought that she and Amber could simply turn south and intersect the other two, that only worked if they knew exactly where Cage and Aurora were.

She'd been out here for several hours, stepping over trash, passing by small bushes, slightly altering her path to avoid things and at one point, staring down a pair of eyes that she was relatively certain belonged to a bobcat or a jaguar.

So the idea that she would just "see" Cage and Aurora and intersect them was not going to happen. Not tonight. Not with only the moonlight to guide them.

Beside her, Amber looked worried and Joule felt the need to maintain the calm.

"We head back." She told Malcolm and Gisela. "We'll meet you there."

If something had happened to the walkie talkie, she knew Cage would follow the same plan. If the batteries had died, if it had broken somehow . . . there were options, she knew. Options that weren't that bad.

She held tight to the faith of that.

Joule and Amber trekked back at high speed, not looking for anything other than immediate perils. She kept her eyes out for snakes, thinking she might trip over one if she wasn't paying attention. She buzzed Cage and Aurora three more times, but each time the silence greeted her back, her heart grew a little tighter.

She told herself there was nothing to worry about. Yet.

By the time it was their next check in, they were almost back to their starting point. Malcolm and Gisela picked up on the first try, nagging Joule again with the idea that the walkie talkies worked fine—that maybe there was a reason Cage and Aurora weren't answering. But she refused to be driven by worry.

Just a few minutes later, she and Amber were at the starting point, the first to arrive. But quickly, she spotted the two shadows in the darkness. They weren't that far away. It was creepy how close they could get and still be covered by the night, even when it felt like the moon lit up everything.

The looks on Gisela and Malcolm's faces told her they'd had no luck raising the other two either. Though of course they would have buzzed her and Amber if they had.

Her worry crept all the way in and finally took hold.

Cage and Aurora were not here. Despite the number of times she had told herself that they would show up and everything would be okay, it hadn't happened.

As the four who'd made it looked at each other, Amber asked, "What do we do now?"

It was Malcolm whose attention Joule caught. He, too, was missing his other half.

She pointed in the southeastern direction. "We trace their tracks until we run into them."

Her tone was decisive. She had to be.

They would run into Cage and Aurora.

Hopefully alive.

32

E verything was normal. And that was the problem.
Joule inspected the sand in front of her. It seemed at least as normal as she could imagine, from what little she knew.

Had that stupid fucking officer been right? Had they jumped in over their heads?

She huffed out a breath, hoping the others were watching for snakes and other dangerous animals because she was not. She was keeping her eyes on the clear set of two footprints leading away from her. They aimed in a southeast direction, away from the original start point. She regretted not memorizing everyone's shoe tread as a matter of course, but these could only belong to Cage and Aurora.

"Look." She pointed at tracks that came from the right and headed to the left. This belonged to a decently large group of people. Then again, she was no tracker. But it was definitely more than two. A few clean prints showed the direction the foot was aimed, indicating this group was heading north. The trail Cage and Aurora had left crossed over it.

But it didn't look like anything had happened. One trail was there moving south to north, and Cage and Aurora's footprints kept moving east. They stepped right through the first trail. Their footprints looked newer with cleaner edges. Joule concluded they had not run into any actual people.

Later, she found a set of paw prints—another cat, large enough to have her concerned. But again, these prints crossed Cage and Aurora's trail and appeared that they hadn't interacted at all.

"Wait." She motioned to the others as she leaned down.

Joule didn't want to get out her flashlight. It would be too bright. It would signal to someone else that they were here. And they were all saving their vision hoping to catch a glimpse of something on the horizon. Because surely if Cage and Aurora were out here somewhere, all they would need to do was put on the flashlight they had brought. It would be a beacon so they could be found.

In fact, the lights they carried had white, red, and flashing functions, so anyone stranded wouldn't even need to keep flicking the flashlight. They would simply need to have enough in them to push the button twice. So far, Joule had seen no such signal in the distance.

Now she pulled out her phone, turning the screen brightness up and aiming it at the ground at her feet.

"Shit."

"What?" Malcolm's voice was soft and strained.

"The cat print is *inside* the shoe prints."

The older man looked at her as if to ask *what importance is that?*

"The cat came by *after* they were here. If they were second, the shoe prints would have obliterated the cat print. Or at least messed it up."

Had they run into the large animal? The width of the tracks indicated it was sizeable. But she'd seen one and it seemed to want nothing to do with her. Maybe the one they found was rabid?

Using the phone, she traced the cat tracks to her left—where they came from—and then to her right—where they led. She wasn't quite willing to leave the trail she was on to track this other one.

"I don't know," she said. It seemed maybe insignificant other than the fact that the cat had crossed after they'd been here.

She filed it away for later. So many things filed away and no idea which ones would be useful.

"How far do you think they got by each check in?" Amber asked.

It was a good question. But Joule shrugged. It was one she didn't have the answer to. They were now moving really fast. "How long have we been following the trail?"

"About twenty-five minutes," Amber answered confidently. Thank God at least someone was paying attention.

Standing up straight, Joule once again took stock and followed Amber's reasoning. "We spent an hour and a half going out on our own paths. We checked in every thirty minutes, and they only missed the last one."

Amber nodded, picking up. "So, for an hour they moved outward away from our starting point. But we moved so much slower then."

She was right. They'd ambled and looked at everything before they turned around. "It took about half the time to get back. I would guess we're close to that pace now."

"Not quite."

Joule looked at Amber, wondering how she'd done the math wrong. If they were at that same path, and Cage and Aurora had moved the same way, then they were close to the one and a half hour mark . . . the point when the pair had stopped answering the walkie talkie.

Amber readily explained. "On the way out, we were watching the ground. We were being careful. The same was true with Malcolm and Gisela," she motioned. "You guys kept moving out, but you only arrived back at the start point five minutes after us. I would assume Cage and Aurora made about the same pace."

They had to assume that. It was the only good guess they had. There were several places where the footsteps had wandered off the line, clearly the two of them had checked something out, then continued on. So, the guess made sense.

Once again Joule was glad that she was in a group of smart people, and they'd been paying attention.

Amber continued. "I don't think we're moving quite that fast now though, because while we aren't scanning everything, we are following this trail. If we were moving as fast, we should have gotten as far as they got at the third check in, by about now."

That was the same conclusion Joule had arrived at, so what was wrong?

Amber looked at Joule, her expression somber. "We aren't at the end of the trail yet. The tracks are clearly still going that way." She pointed.

Gisela was catching on, but Joule and Malcolm still weren't. Was it because they were the partners of the missing people? She didn't like that possibility—that she wasn't seeing clearly because of her own bias.

Gisela continued, now filling in blanks animatedly with Amber. "We're past their first check in point. We have to be. Even though it's difficult to tell where exactly they stopped and checked in, we're probably past their second point, too."

Amber's voice lowered. "They lost contact between the second and third check in points."

So, it was possible that something had happened almost two hours ago.

Joule didn't like that math. Every second was a loss.

For a moment, darkness crowded the edges of her vision and stars sparkled at the periphery. Her throat tightened and her rib cage stopped moving. But she would not do this now.

Somehow, she turned it all off. She was Sherlock Holmes solving a mystery that was interesting but in no way a threat to her person. It was about someone else. Someone else's friend was missing. Someone else's wife. Someone else's brother.

Forcing a deep breath, she looked up at Amber and Gisela.

"We also haven't seen any evidence of them backtracking," Amber pointed out.

It was then Amber looked solemnly at each of the other three. None of them said it out loud.

Instead, she offered, "We must be almost near the end of their initial hour and a half of outward movement. And there is still no evidence of their footprints leading back this way. Wherever they are . . ." she pointed out into the wide darkness dotted only by moonlight glinting off unidentified objects in the distance. Amber sucked in a breath. "Wherever they went, they didn't come back."

33

Cage's eyes flitted from person to person. Each one held a gun aimed at either him or Aurora or at least in their general direction.

He was trying to casually make eye contact with Sarah, who stood almost calm at the other end of an assault rifle. She aimed at him not her mother. The subtle tightening of her lips, widening of her eyes, and nearly microscopic shake of her head told him it was best if he didn't let on that he recognized her.

Heart pounding and blood pulsing through his brain, Cage tried to take in every signal. Reaching out with his hand, he linked his fingers around Aurora's wrist. *What would she do if she recognized her daughter and threw herself at Sarah?*

He had to stop her from doing anything like that.

More importantly, what would these people do if Aurora burst out that they'd found Sarah?

Whatever had been under the fake rock had not been for them to see.

Cage tried to use that. He raised his hands, Aurora's wrist still in his grip as he turned slowly, hoping to find a leader. But he didn't see anyone who looked like they were in charge.

"We'll just leave," he told them. "We didn't see anything."

Laughter came from out of the darkness somewhere to his right.

Cage couldn't help it. His head turned to look. He half expected to see Salvador Torres walking out of the desert, laughing and clapping as if Cage had put on a good show.

But it wasn't Salvador Torres at all. It was someone he'd never seen before. He had long dark hair slicked back away from his face, a thin black mustache and bright blue eyes. He wore a clean tank top, black jeans, and cowboy boots. He would have looked ridiculous if something about him hadn't looked so threatening.

And evil.

Cage thought about the gun still at his side, and now he wished Aurora had one as well. She would be steadier with the gun than most of these fools whose hands shook, or they just held the gun out like on TV. In fact, she was probably doing better than he was right now.

He flicked his eyes to the side for a glance and found her completely expressionless. She had to have seen Sarah. Her daughter was alive and here. Cage held onto that hope. But then he wondered if Aurora had figured out what he did.

People surrounded them with their guns all aimed toward them, in the center of the circle. It was a supremely shitty scenario and one they were unlikely to pull the trigger on because, even if Cage and Aurora died, they would all shoot each other.

For a moment, his thoughts took flight, thinking how he would turn around and go back and tell everyone that he had seen Sarah. She was alive, not dead. Though he had no idea what she was doing here, he felt it had to be connected to the weird volunteering she said she did. But right now, he wasn't going anywhere.

As he moved his eyes slowly around the group, he tried to listen to what the man was saying.

"It doesn't matter if you saw anything. It's a risk we simply can't take."

Fuck.

He was going to walk the two of them out into the desert and execute them.

Would the others—who would look as soon as they decided Cage and Aurora had failed to check in—be able to hear the gunshots so far away? He knew his sister would trace his steps and find his body. His brain disconnected, unable to process his own imminent death.

Knowing how it would work, how he would feel if it went the other way. What if it was Joule? He decided he wouldn't let that happen to her. As if he had the final say on how this situation went.

Still his eyes walked around the group again. Many of them were holding their guns just flat out wrong. One young woman had the butt of her rifle jammed against her bicep. Another teenager—probably—struggled to keep the gun lifted at the end of his arm. Neither had fired like this before as both would likely hurt themselves and learn quickly.

If this were an alley, if there were cars, if there was *anything* he could duck behind for safety, Cage might have considered the option. As it was, all he would be able to do is run and give them a target in which they didn't have to shoot each other to take him down. Though he didn't trust that any of them could aim, it would only require one or two of them to get a good shot. That many guns and someone would get lucky.

Which would make him extremely *un*lucky.

Also, while Aurora was in excellent shape, he had not seen her run. Had no idea how fast she could go.

So, at this moment they were still alive, and Sarah was still alive, and he would take that as a small win.

Black Hair wandered into the group, blue eyes sparkling in the moonlight, making Cage wonder if he was high or just excited. Close up, Cage couldn't smell anything but sweat and maybe fear. There was no hint of liquor, no burn or tang that sometimes hinted at other drugs. Maybe the glint in his eyes was just evil.

"Hands down," he told them as he walked slowly in front of them, passing by the raised guns that stayed raised. The smile still played across his lips. It wasn't the smile of a kid on Christmas, it was the grin of a man who enjoyed torturing others.

This was not good. But Cage did as he was told and put his hands down behind his back. Surviving was step one. He'd learned that a long time ago.

Black Hair pulled out zip-tie handcuffs and as scary as the whole situation was, that move allowed Cage's rapid heart rate to settle *just a little bit.* Cuffing meant they were moving, maybe to somewhere separate to shoot them, but likely not. They were already in the middle of nowhere. There was no reason Cage could see not to kill them right here.

Black Hair motioned to one of the others, handing off a pair of cuffs and saying, "Get them tight."

Cage, lean and wiry, did his best to twist his hands and keep the cuffs from ratcheting down too far. But Black Hair had no such designs. He yanked to the point where, had Cage not been twisting his wrists, he would have lost his circulation. He could only hope that Aurora knew to do the same or that the timid soul cuffing her wasn't quite as ruthless.

As the zip-ties were tightened down, the guns around him lowered. Black Hair ordered all the others to load the guns into a duffel that he slung over his shoulder.

Once again, Cage's heart rate dropped just a tad, though it remained insanely high. Behind him, he felt a shove to his back that sent him stumbling forward a couple of jolting steps. He tried not to fall with his hands cuffed behind his back.

It was close, but Cage managed to stay upright. He tried to watch what was happening.

And he saw they were getting pushed further out into the desert and away from everything and everyone he knew.

34

Hours later—he didn't know how long it had been—
Cage was exhausted. His mouth was dry and dusty.
He'd been patted down and had his phone, walkie
talkie, wallet, and gun taken. The same for Aurora.

They'd been offered only sips of water by some of the
others walking with them. The others carried water bottles that
looked like they'd been used multiple times but catching something from one of the other people here was the least of his
concerns right now.

It had been long enough that he was coming to a reasonable conclusion that they weren't going to be executed. He
couldn't help but be relieved.

At last, a low building came into his view, and he tried not
to look excited by it. It was low enough that he probably could
have seen it for a while if he'd known what he was looking for.

Beside him, Aurora's footsteps had grown heavy, but so had
his own and so had the others in the group. They walked
without speaking, guns hanging heavy at their sides. Water
bottles packed in battered cloth bags or plastic bags from the

grocery. The bags often had holes. He wondered what was going on that they couldn't even get useful bags for their water.

The operation was clearly running catch-as-catch-can. Though he'd had plenty of time to wonder what was under that rock. And what in the hell Sarah was doing here.

He'd cooked up several scenarios, but there was no evidence for one of them over the other. Cage first thought that this could be the "volunteer work" that Sarah said she was doing. Though with what he could see so far, that didn't mesh with anything he knew of his friend. His second option was that this was a scenario that Sarah had gotten caught up in, maybe radicalized by, though he didn't even know what the cult was about yet. The last option was that Sarah was somehow a prisoner like him and her mother.

That didn't seem reasonable either. It had been over a week since Sarah had disappeared now. How had she not escaped? She was smart enough and stubborn enough to have tried and kept trying if she was being held against her will.

Cage glanced at her periodically, finding her in much the same state as the others: Dirty clothes, occasionally with holes. Her hair looked like it hadn't been properly cared for in a while. It was pulled back awkwardly into a poof of a ponytail without regard to symmetry or style.

But she'd walked for probably several hours and she wasn't talking, and neither was anyone else. The silence, cut only by the shuffling of footsteps and the scurry of an animal out of their way was unnerving. The occasional screech of an owl had more than just him jumping.

All Cage could do was keep moving forward. He hoped that the house would have food, at least water and a restroom. Not that his body was allowing him to know that he needed it. The desert was dry enough it was leaching liquid from him.

But there had to be something here. They surely wouldn't walk past the first bit of civilization—one it seemed they'd aimed for. As they got closer and closer, he discovered the building to be in much the same shape as the people: Standing, seeming to work, but not in good shape. Definitely not well cared for.

The back door opened as Black Hair called out, and the others filed in. Cage felt the air conditioning blow out of the door and wash over him and he tried not to show his relief. He knew instinctively that he couldn't afford to give anything away.

Black Hair waited at the back of the line, right behind Cage and Aurora, barking orders, though none needed to be issued. Everyone moved of their own accord, clearly having been here before.

Cage and Aurora were shoved through the door. He almost tripped again on the threshold, but he'd learned over the course of the walk how to keep himself upright. He breathed in the cool indoor air and watched as the others headed toward the left, down a short hall into two rooms. Others ducked into what must be bathrooms. They appeared to separate by male and female, but with the long unkempt hair and baggy clothes, it was difficult for Cage to tell for certain.

He wondered if he'd follow, but he didn't wonder long. He and Aurora were shoved forward into a larger living space. She'd stayed as silent as he had the whole time and now, she stood stoically, hands still cuffed behind her, next to Cage.

Though the building was horrifying, and even inside the paint was flaking off the walls and the carpet curled at the edges of the room, whoever lived here was doing their best to live it up. A large screen TV showed an old Arnold Schwarzenegger movie. Liquor bottles lined the bar top, three different mini fridges dotted the living room, with a freezer that could hold a dead body holding court in the far corner. There was a small kitchen, with a stovetop, refrigerator, and an oven.

Another man—clearly higher ranked than Black Hair—sat sprawled on the couch, legs wide, hands out, taking up as much space as he could with his skinny build. The humor in his eyes quickly turned to anger as he lashed out at Black Hair.

"Connor! What did you do?"

"I caught these two checking out a stash." The words came from behind Cage, false confidence filling the air.

"And you brought them *here?*"

"They can work." Black Hair—apparently Connor —countered.

"Look at them!" The man stood up, his fingertips barely holding onto the rim of what looked like a pretty good scotch— at least, according to the label on the bottle on the brass and glass coffee table.

He sidestepped around them. Taller than Connor, this man had shorter and better kept brown hair, brown skin, brown eyes. He was handsome enough to pass in the general public, but he wore a muscle T shirt and black jeans. He did not look like he had been in the desert for hours tonight. He glared at Connor, "They can work, but who's working to find them?"

He waved his hand up and down Cage and Aurora to make his point.

Then he punctuated his motion with more harsh words. "What were these two even doing out in the desert in the middle of the night in the first place?"

Lightning fast, his hand shot out and whacked Connor upside the head. "You're a fucking idiot. We can't keep them."

35

T hey'd been out here forever.

Joule knew she couldn't let herself get discouraged, though.

All four of them had stuck together this time, following the pair of footsteps until they'd arrived here. Suddenly, more footsteps came in. A lot of different sizes. Some old shoes, some flat soled, some sneakers leaving treads and what looked like a pair of cowboy boots.

The tracks messed up a large patch of ground around a large rock. Though Joule first gazed off into the distance, trying to see where the two tracks they wanted continued, all the tracks screwed up her brother's and Aurora's prints and she couldn't pick them out anymore.

When they got home, and she told herself they would, she would take up tracking skills. Animal or human, she would learn to hunt it.

"This time they interacted with someone," Gisela declared, clearly thinking the same thing as Joule.

"The footprints all overlap," Amber agreed. "Do we think they joined up with somebody?"

"It looks like a decent sized group," Malcolm added in.

Joule could only think how odd that was. All of it. Why would Cage and Aurora join some other group and stop checking in? Who were they? These were all questions she couldn't answer. She tried for one she could.

"Where do the tracks come from?"

They all understood and began tracing paths outside the cluster they could see. One by one, they whipped out their phones, activating the flashlight feature and aimed it at the ground.

Joule no longer cared if she attracted attention. Something had happened to her brother. The clues were here, she needed to see them. If someone spotted them, maybe right now that would be good. But she didn't find the tracks she wanted.

On the other side of the mess, Gisela called out. "Over here! I think I have incoming footsteps."

"Here," Amber replied, at almost the same moment, from the opposite side of the mess.

Joule stood up straight and looked between the two of them instead of at her own feet. "Don't mess them up with your own footprints."

She shouldn't have said it. Though Gisela humored her and nodded, Amber looked at her as if to say "duh." She should have known they would handle everything with care. It was good traveling with people who might be able to find her brother.

"Keep looking," Gisela told her. "They seem to come in from a bunch of directions."

So, Joule headed away from her new friend.

"Over here!" Malcolm called out from yet a different spot.

Fifteen minutes later, they had determined that all of the footsteps had originally come from south of the mess. But, at some point, they had moved out and around and come in from different sides. Joule refused to think of what kind of ambush that might mean.

"I have no training in any of this," Gisela offered her caveat, "but my best guess from the ways the toes are pointed, it looks like they came in from there." She lifted one finger toward the south. "It then seems they made a circle around this rock, then they left that way."

This time she pointed east.

"Agreed," Joule said.

Malcolm nodded.

Though Amber was still looking at the ground. "The rock looks wrong."

Joule hadn't paid much attention. She'd been so much more concerned with the footsteps—where they came from, where they were aimed, which direction her brother had likely been taken.

She had not let the thought pass that they might be looking for a pair of bodies. She was simply grateful they hadn't found any.

She watched as Amber jabbed at the rock with the toe of her sneaker. "It's fake!"

Her tone indicated she was almost angry at the discovery of exactly what she'd suspected. Reaching down, she curled her fingers under the edge of it and lifted it easily.

Was it paper mache? Joule thought even as Amber cried out, "It's foam!"

After she messed with it for a moment, she added, "It's anchored just enough to not blow away in the wind. *Holy shit!*"

The four of them moved quickly, and it occurred to Joule then that they'd all been looking at the ground, then looking at each other. And *not* looking off into the distance. Something wasn't right out here, and they needed to be watching out for surprises.

Amber held the fake rock up, tipped onto one edge. They

all looked under it, but no one aimed their flashlights into the space, as if something told them not to look too closely.

But it didn't matter. Her eyes had adjusted again, and she saw it.

Holy shit. What had they run into here?

36

They'd been pushed into another room. With a quick glance around—all he was afforded—Cage saw only two chairs and an old mattress on the floor.

Because none of it looked inviting anyway, Cage chose the mattress, thinking he might be able to work his hands down around behind him and under his feet and get out of the zip-cuffs.

"I saw Sarah out there," Aurora whispered to him with tears in her eyes as she stood motionless in the center of the room.

"Me, too." He smiled at her, stopping his movement for a moment. "She's alive."

She'd likely been here for the whole week-plus that she'd been gone. He hoped his likelihood of execution was low. But he wasn't sure, and he started trying to get out of the cuffs again.

Aurora saw him. "Not sure what good that's going to do."

"What do you mean?" He lowered his shoulders and wiggled, working his wrists over his hips, not without struggle. He was close. He could do it.

"So, you get out of the cuffs, then what?" Aurora sat heavily in one of the chairs and stared at him.

"Then we get out of here." He tipped his head, motioning to the window. It was covered with an old curtain that fit with the rest of the dingy room but looked like it might be blackout quality.

"What's beyond the window?" Aurora asked him as if he were being slow and he was starting to see her point.

There was open desert beyond the window—where they'd just walked for hours to get here. But . . . "There were houses the other direction."

"That's true, but which ones do we trust?"

"Which ones don't we?" he countered quickly, still not getting his wrists quite past his own hips. He waited a moment. He'd get it on the next try.

When she looked at him confused, Cage added, "What are the odds that any of them are worse than here?"

She seemed to think about that for a moment and Cage continued trying to get the handcuffs in front of him, then wondering if maybe he'd won the argument.

"Hey!" she said, quickly.

But he'd heard what she was warning him about. Footsteps tromped heavily in the hall. The jiggle of the loose doorknob came almost immediately. Cage barely wiggled back into place with his hands behind his back, sitting cross legged on the mattress before the door was flung wide.

Black Hair—Connor, he now knew—stood in the center of the space, legs planted wide, once again taking up space. Cage didn't like him any better for what he'd seen, but after watching the grown man get whacked upside the head like an abused toddler, he understood a little better.

Connor certainly acted like one of those men who knew nothing to do with himself, except to try to take up as much space as he could. As if that would make things any better for him.

He first looked at Aurora, then at Cage, then he grinned a grin that hit his eyes and announced, "I convinced him not to kill you."

"That's fantastic!" Cage issued in as sarcastic a tone as he could muster.

Truly, he was exhausted, and he had no idea if this was a game that Connor and Brown Eyes played with every newcomer. Was it an attempt to try to keep people like him and Aurora in line, or was there truly a question about his and Aurora's future existence?

Right now, the outcome was not execution, so Cage decided to be happy about it.

"However," Connor added, the darkness still wavering at the edges of his expression, as he tried to exert an air of authority over two people who almost couldn't care less. "You have to do the work. You have to blend in. You have to stay hidden."

He waited as if they would protest or have legitimate questions.

Cage and Aurora stayed quiet, both seeming to hold to the policy of giving as absolutely little as possible away.

Connor continued. "Your first run is tomorrow night. If it doesn't work out, you won't last long."

Cage guessed that Connor's continued existence, or maybe just his climbing of the ranks here, would also depend on their working out. Whatever that meant.

"Follow me." Connor turned and walked away, offering no help.

Aurora looked at Cage for a moment as if to ask, *did he need a hand?* Not that she really had one to give. He tipped his head as if to motion that he was good and managed to stand up smoothly, hands still tied behind his back.

Connor was already partway down the short hall. "You're here," he motioned Aurora to the left, "and you're here." Cage would go to the right.

Cage couldn't see inside yet, but guessed the rooms were divided by gender. Connor was at least gentler with Aurora as he nudged her into the room.

But she said only "Hey?" as she turned around and flicked her fingers behind her back at him.

Cage had forgotten to ask if she could feel her fingers. At least it seemed she'd managed okay.

With a sigh that he was being put upon to undo the shit he'd done, Connor reached into his back pocket and produced a wicked looking blade. Aurora didn't flinch as he slid the metal along her wrist and sliced open the zip ties.

"Turn around," he told Cage, still irritated.

It was only when the ties were released, that Cage realized he'd been in this position too long, long enough for his shoulders to be sore. But he didn't have time to worry. Aurora was gone into the room, Connor closing and locking it from the outside with a padlock that he had a key for in his pocket.

Cage paid attention.

Hopefully, Aurora was in the room with Sarah. As bad as this might be, she had reunited with her daughter. Sarah was alive and maybe Brown Eyes wasn't going to execute them. Not tonight. So maybe, just maybe, there was a way out of this.

Connor shoved Cage's back, sending him stumbling into the room where he was to stay. But he looked into the empty room and wondered what had happened to the others.

37

J oule fought against it with everything she had. Malcolm seemed to feel the same, but Amber and Gisela looked at each other.

Gisela tried to soften the blow. "We have to stop. We were only supposed to be out for a few hours."

"I have to call in sick to work. We can't stay out here." Amber looked at them as though pleading.

Joule was opening her mouth to say no, to say *then you go back*. Gisela laid a comforting hand on her arm as if that might make enough difference. It didn't, but her point did. "We're out of water and food. You're of no help whatsoever if you're not still upright." She looked Joule in the eyes. "And you and Malcolm both need to file police reports now."

Oh, the irony. Joule could only hope that Officer Dipshit wasn't there to play his *I told you so* card. What she really wanted to say was that the officers should have been out here. They should have been leading the searches, because maybe he was right. Maybe their little ragtag band wasn't good enough. They'd already lost a third of them.

Also, clearly Cage and Aurora had found *something*—something that the police probably should have taken care of a long time ago. But Joule knew she couldn't say that and she couldn't avoid filing the report. Even if nothing happened, or God forbid things got worse, they would need it to get professional help. That missing persons report and having it filed in a timely manner might be the only thing to save them.

Joule tried to rein in her thoughts from the thousand options she was sorting through. Go back out now with Malcolm. Go back out by herself. File the police report. Hire a PI. Hire an assassin, though that one she didn't know where to find.

None of these options were playing out. So, she sucked in a deep breath and nodded to Gisela. She had to agree. She had to, though it broke her heart to watch Amber and Gisela open the doors to their car and stash their gear.

Joule knew it was a signal to her. It was time to give up for now. Go separate ways. Gisela and Amber's words were encouraging and correct. She had to get some sleep.

But she also understood that while the two had lost a roommate and now two new friends, they had not lost the last member of their family.

As bad as Joule felt, she wondered how Malcolm was holding up. On the outside, he still appeared stoic and put together. But he'd lost his daughter a week ago. And, in the last six hours, his wife.

Amber and Gisela each turned and offered Joule a deep, heartfelt hug. It wasn't until she was squeezing her eyes shut, hugging them back, that she realized she was doing it. They hugged Malcolm too, but then they were backing out, driving off and leaving a pattern similar to the one that Joule and Cage had matched to Salvador Torres' tires.

Then Malcolm and Joule were each climbing into their own cars.

She was out of the sand and back onto the gravel road

before she could admit just how weird it felt. She so rarely drove without Cage. She was used to him telling her she needed to be the driver. That it was her turn. And suddenly now it was her turn because he was gone.

Though she occasionally ran errands or went to see a friend without her brother, the space now felt unerringly empty.

She'd pulled out quickly, trying not to cry, not to break apart. She stopped on the empty road and waited for Malcolm to catch up. Once she saw his lights behind her, she turned and followed Amber and Gisela.

Another vise clamped down on her heart. She could see Amber and Gisela pulling away up ahead, but she slowed down and waited for Malcolm, feeling a necessary kinship with the man now. She couldn't even fathom what she would do if he didn't show up tomorrow. Because there would be a tomorrow.

She made sure that the older man was tucked in close behind her, that he hadn't done something crazy like throw his car keys away and run out into the desert himself. Something that had crossed Joule's own thoughts.

Further into town, Amber and Gisela took a left back toward their little apartment building. Joule took a right. She was not looking forward to this.

In a few turns, she was pulling into the parking lot that she now knew better than she wanted to. She couldn't help just staring at the low concrete building with a slight overhang and squarish lettering that let everyone know it was the police department.

She waited until Malcolm pulled up beside her, only then putting her car in park. Still, she sat a moment with the air conditioner on. For just those last few seconds until his shiny new Buick was pulled up next to her old sedan, she pretended she was here for an entirely different reason. That Cage was simply running an errand with someone else, and this was a bad dream.

But Malcolm got out of the car, closed his door and turned to look at her over the hood of his car. It wasn't a bad dream. Something in his eyes let her know that he was already far too familiar with this process.

Joule headed in, holding open the door to the department, the cool air wafting out at her as she waved Malcolm in first— as if his going first might make her job a little easier. Nothing could make this easier.

After a few minutes of antsy waiting, they were led into the back to file the report. She was grateful that officer AssPants was not on duty right now and that they were assigned to a different officer—a young woman who seemed somehow completely indifferent to their plight.

She looked up, periodically asking questions and making notes as if this were some kind of doctor's office intake work. Joule answered every question, signed every form she was asked to, and tried not to show her worry that everything was getting filled out on photocopy forms rather than getting entered directly into some kind of database.

"So now what?" They seemed done, and Joule was waiting for any action.

But all she was told was, "The paperwork will be filed, and someone will get in touch."

"When?" She pushed. *Someone would get in touch???*

She tried to stay calm. She'd been willing to push and play the bad guy when it was just Sarah missing. But now, there was no good guy to play the other part.

"I don't know!" The officer said it with the up-and-down tones of a teenager being asked when they were going to clean their room. "As soon as we can get somebody to look at it."

Joule and Malcolm were being very clearly dismissed.

Malcolm leaned over the counter they were standing at, the only thing protecting the officer from their anger. "Is this because it hasn't been twenty-four hours yet?"

"That's not a rule." The officer shook her head as if he was being silly. "That's some bullshit from TV."

Joule was about to explode. "My friend went missing in a very similar place just over a week ago, and no one seems to be looking for her. We were told she wasn't gone long enough."

"Ohhhh," the officer said, taking an interest now. Something in her attitude looked like she chewed gum and twirled her hair when she wasn't being *a serious officer*. "This is different. You actually saw these two walk out into the desert. Nobody knows that for Sarah, right? For your friend."

"We found her car out there." While Joule understood that those were, in fact, differences between the two cases, were they really the kind of differences that meant one got investigated and the other didn't? Maybe, if she got very lucky, Cage and Aurora going missing would mean finding Sarah, too.

When they didn't move, the officer dismissed them again, "I told you, someone will be in touch."

Quietly seething, she and Malcolm walked out to the parking lot, heading their separate ways. She couldn't even speak to him, she might explode. She barely waved as she turned out of the lot and headed through town and across open desert on a paved state road until she arrived at another small enclave of homes. Letting herself into the tiny house all alone she headed into the bedroom and flopped down on the bed.

She was fighting the sleep that was desperately trying to overtake her out of necessity and wondering if she was the last surviving Mazur.

38

The phone rang, a harsh digital noise that made Joule sit up in bed disoriented.

It rang again. She should have put a better ring-tone on this new phone. It had been a while since she'd switched phones and numbers and she still hadn't put all the settings back.

She would have to ask Cage what that program was that he—

Cage was missing.

It all flooded back as once again the phone rang at her. She reached out to her side, tapping on the tiny table. Instead of just turning her head and looking, she pulled the phone closer to her face. An unknown number.

When everyone was accounted for, she would have ignored it, but now she tapped frantically at the button. "Hello? Hello?"

"I'm looking for Joule Mazur," the voice said. Masculine and deep, it offered mellow tones that she had not expected with the harsh wake up.

The light shone in through the curtains and she wondered what time it was. Holding the phone slightly away from her face and blinking, she said, "Yes, this is she," as she read that it was already 3pm.

How had she slept that long? Though she knew she needed it. She wondered what had happened to her brother in the hours that she had rested.

Had she rested?

Her head didn't feel like it, but the voice was talking.

"I'm Officer Jacob McQueeny. With Maverick County Sheriff's patrol."

Joule fought the urge to roll her eyes, even though he couldn't see her. The last time she'd encountered the sheriff's deputies, they'd been less than helpful.

"I'd love to come over and talk to you about your brother's case."

She blinked. *Was he being useful?* That remained to be seen, but she couldn't turn this down.

"Do you know where I am?" she asked. "Do I need to come to you?"

"It might be easier if I come to you. I'm also curious because your brother disappeared with Mrs. Aurora Walker as well."

Joule could tell by the way he said the name that he was reading it off the paper in front of him.

"I'm hoping to speak to Malcolm Walker also."

"Do you want us all together?" Joule asked, throwing her legs over the side of the bed and discovering she was still dressed from last night. She hadn't even gotten under the covers.

"I think that would be best."

"I'm in a rental home. We can meet here." Her eyes searched frantically around to see if she was ready for visitors before reminding herself, *Fuck it, her brother was missing*. She didn't need to get the house ready.

"Is thirty minutes good?" he asked.

"I'll get Malcolm." She didn't even entertain the option that Malcolm might not come. Of course, he would.

After getting a little more information from the officer, who seemed to have no need for any directions from her—then again, he'd almost definitely lived here longer than she had—she hung up and hit the button on her phone to call Malcolm.

But she immediately hung up again.

First, she called Cage. It rang and rang and rang and went to voicemail. She'd done this twice already on the sheer hope that he might answer and tell her where he was. He didn't. But it did feel good to hear his voice. Next, she called Aurora, wondering if Malcolm was doing the same thing. And again, it rang through until voicemail. Only this time, she was given the automated tones of the robotic AI, letting her know that the person whose number she had called was not available right now.

She didn't know how often she would call her brother's phone with hope in her heart. Then she messaged Dev and updated him. Just typing out the words broke her heart. But, tasks completed once again, she called Malcolm. He answered on the second ring. "Joule."

No *Good morning*. Not that he'd ever really given her one. She hadn't met the man until tragedy had already occurred.

"I just got a call from an officer Jacob McQueeny with the Maverick County Sheriff's Department."

"Interesting."

She understood Malcolm's lack of enthusiasm and she tried to muster some of her own. "He's on the case. He wants to meet with us."

"Hopefully he'll do better than whoever's trying to find Sarah." The disgust in Malcolm's voice bled through the line, and Joule felt that deep in her soul. She gave Malcolm all the information to the little rental house, as he actually needed directions again.

Then she brushed her teeth, showered off last night's desert dust, and pulled random clothing out of her closet without concern for how she looked. It felt good to be moving, to be doing something. She forced herself to eat a bowl of Cheerios, not questioning why it didn't taste like anything. Then she called her brother one more time, as if those few seconds would eat up enough space between now and when the officer arrived.

There was no TV she could bear watching, no house-cleaning chores, not anything to do to keep her hands busy. But then she saw the green and white cruiser pulling down her driveway, gold stripes reflecting in the bright sunlight. The door opened and the officer climbed out. Tall, with short cropped dark hair, his square face was partly covered by Oakley sunglasses. He was fit, his T shirt clinging tightly under the khaki he wore.

She could hear her heart saying she didn't need another uniform jockey but this was what she had. She opened the door, reading the nameplate with his title and "McQueeny" on it—double checking that he was who he was supposed to be—before she invited him inside.

Her life had taught her nothing, if not paranoia.

Even as he headed down the hallway, she heard the crunch of gravel and turned back to see the Buick coming down the drive.

"Malcolm Walker is here," she said, aiming back to greet the older man as he seemed to be out of the car almost before it was even in park. Luckily, there was no slope to much of anything around here and it wasn't going to roll away even if he'd left it running.

"Shall we sit?" It was Officer McQueeny who motioned to the table. Only then did she see he had a file tucked into the crook of his arm. It was far too thick to be for Cage or Aurora.

Maybe for Sarah—had anyone actually been working on her case, but Joule was relatively certain that wasn't it.

He looked at each of them before saying, "I'm here to help you find your missing loved ones but first I need to let you know I have an ulterior motive."

39

J oule blinked at Officer Jacob McQueeny. *Did she care if he had an ulterior motive?*

She looked to Malcolm who seemed to be thinking the same thing. But he was on his game enough to say, "Well, what is it?"

"My oldest sister is a professor of criminology and criminal psychology at UT San Antonio. The middle sister is DEA. I'm the youngest in the family, on my way to the FBI. That's my goal. Solving this case will catapult my application to the top of their list."

Family in the national narcotics unit? And in the Feds? What did that mean? Was it a warning? "Does that mean you don't care if my brother and Mrs. Walker and Sarah maybe get killed in the process, as long as you solve the case?"

"That's not winning!" He stumbled over the words. "I do care about finding them."

"And if you find them, and it doesn't get you into the FBI . . ." she prodded.

"Then we will have found two people—"

"*Three,*" Malcolm interrupted.

"Three people," Officer McQueeny agreed, though he looked as if he didn't quite understand why there was a third person being mentioned. "They'll be returned home. That's a win."

Joule looked to Malcolm as if to ask, *did he have a problem with this?* She wasn't even quite sure what the problem was, but McQueeny picked up on it.

"I didn't want you to find out later and think that I didn't care about the case, that I was ladder climbing or something."

"Gotcha," Joule said. He was ladder climbing, but if it found her brother . . . "I think I'm okay with your ulterior motive."

"I hope so. Because my mother is also a retired ATF agent." He tapped on his phone for a moment and held up a picture of what was clearly his family. All the women redheads.

Joule was getting more confused. Alcohol Tobacco and Firearms in the family too? None of these things really sounded like caveats and why did it matter? Why was he showing them a picture?

Jacob looked at them and grinned. "You'll be meeting at least some of them. I may be the person best able to solve this case, if only because of my family connections."

Ah, so he was going to access ATF mom and DEA sister and Criminology Professor sister to help find Cage, Aurora, and Sarah on his way to the FBI.

"I can live with that," Joule said. This time she didn't need to look at Malcolm. "We just need to find them."

Alive went unspoken.

McQueeny settled back in his seat, his legs widening, feet firmly planted beyond the legs of the chair, as if the chair itself weren't quite big enough for him. He tapped a couple of times at the thick accordion file he'd carried in and laid on the table. "I only have two names in the cases I've been assigned."

It was an interesting choice of words.

He continued, "But you two have said three. Who is Sarah?"

Joule and Malcolm explained, words tumbling out, stumbling over each other, trying to fill him in on all the information.

Malcolm got on his phone, then held the screen out to the officer, showing off the case number for Sarah's file. "You'll want to pull this, too."

Jacob was already thumbing through the old fashioned accordion folder. Joule realized it wasn't just papers inside, it was additional files.

He pulled out a slim manila folder and flipped it open. "This one?"

Malcolm looked through it. Most of the pages were new as if they'd been printed that morning.

A few of the pages did look like they'd been handled a little. Did that mean somebody was doing anything on Sarah's case?

"You have her file on you already," Joule pointed out, "But you didn't know Sarah was part of this case?"

Officer McQueeny looked between them. "I was assigned two cases: Cage Mazur." He pointed at Joule. "—and Aurora Walker." He pointed then at Malcolm, "—going missing together last night. Almost with eyewitnesses."

Another interesting turn of phrase, Joule thought. But he was kind of right. They hadn't actually *watched* what happened to Cage and Aurora, but it also wasn't the same as if they just hadn't come home the next morning.

"But this file," he tapped at the accordion again. "It's full of the people who've gone missing in similar ways, in the same major area, in the last three years."

He turned it around to show them the inside. Though it had about ten slots for folders, it was stuffed full of more slim files than Joule could count.

40

J oule watched as Jacob McQueeny grabbed a handy ballpoint from his pocket and a note pad from the accordion file and started taking down notes.

"Your daughter," he said as Malcolm let him take down info. Then he turned to Joule. "And your old roommate."

"We worked the same job on several sites."

He flipped to sparse pages in Sarah's report and said, "Helio Systems Tech?"

Joule quickly explained how the company worked—traveling from place to place, analyzing a site, setting up solar and hydropower for various communities, businesses, etc.

He nodded. "So, none of you actually live here in El Indio?"

"No."

"And how long has Sarah lived in that apartment?"

Joule found it interesting that she didn't quite know.

"Eight weeks," Malcolm said. Then he added, "She said the original end date was about now, but the project encountered a handful of setbacks." Joule turned to him.

She almost felt herself grin. *Didn't they always?* They were budgeted and planned for, and it almost never worked that way.

A battle plan never survived engagement with the enemy. The land surveys didn't come out quite the same as they had that first time. Or an employee had a different idea and the company tried to renegotiate.

"Alright, good to know. Aside from Cage and Aurora, Sarah was the most recent to go missing. But how did you lose three members of your unit in just over a week?"

Joule looked down at her folded hands, hating that this was a question that had to be asked, and that she felt responsible for the fact that it happened. She wouldn't make Malcolm be the one to admit it. "We were out looking for Sarah."

"Gotcha." McQueeny made a quick note in his tiny, neat handwriting. "You were out looking for Sarah, which is why you were in several pairs, and you had walkie talkies and check in times?"

"Yes." That was all in the report. *What had he thought they were doing?*

He looked at them and answered the question, though she hadn't asked it out loud. "I'm just double checking that all the information I have is correct. I don't trust all the intake officers or office assistants."

Joule didn't either. It made her trust him a little more.

Then he added, "You don't want to know what people are doing in the desert at night. But the fact is, I think you're about to learn. If you were out searching on your own, you may have learned some other things too, and I'm hoping you'll share with me."

Now, Joule practically grinned. They had not just learned other things. They'd been doing all kinds of work. She pulled out her laptop and tablet, tapping on one and handing it to him and then getting the other lined up for her next point.

"This is where Sarah's car was." She pointed to the red dot on the map.

He nodded though he must have had that in the file.

"Here are the tire tracks leading up to Sarah's car, and here's another set of car tracks next to Sarah's car." Joule flipped the laptop around this time, so the picture would be slightly larger. She pointed to what was almost an entirely uniform image of desert sand, low shrub, and the occasional rock. Then she flipped past it. "This is a close up on the tracks. We weren't able to plaster cast them—"

"You were going to plaster cast them?" he interrupted.

"One of the women, she's one of Sarah's roommates," Joule refused to use the past tense, "Brooklyn, has an older sister who is a forensic scientist. We also lifted fingerprints this time."

He turned back to his notepad and put down *get fingerprints*. "I want to see those."

"Of course." She couldn't help the way her heart beat in her chest, loud and bold for the first time in days. Someone actually wanted to help! Someone wanted to do something other than tell them they were stupid and that they should just let their friend die in the desert rather than look for her.

Still Joule tamped it down. There was more work to do to find them. Jacob McQueeny wanting to be in the FBI wasn't enough in itself.

On the tablet she pulled up another picture. "These tires on this car," she pointed, "match this track," she pointed to the picture from the desert. "They belong to Salvador Torres in apartment one-oh-four."

McQueeny nodded, moving the laptop in his left hand and holding the tablet up in his right so they were practically side by side. "You definitely have a match."

"There are three more matches in the parking lot for other tire tracks that were out in the desert nearby. We think Salvador Torres has something to do with Sarah's disappearance."

"Hold on." It was the first time McQueeny had put the brakes on her, and she didn't like it. "You've matched tires and you got a nice side picture of the car. But, if you look at the name on the sidewalls, you can see these are everyday tires. They're not even a Goodyear radial or such."

He paused, but when neither of them contradicted him, he kept going. "The car qualifies as an antique, but it's not getting kept up in mint condition, so the tires aren't either. Their commonness makes it difficult to say it's really a match."

Joule understood. But she had more. "We knocked on doors at the apartments and the woman in one-oh-three said she saw Sarah going by—to one-oh-four—several times a week. That she'd seen Sarah talking to Salvador."

"Okay, that's important." He noted it down. "It does make it more likely that they are his tires, but the prints alone aren't enough evidence."

Or were they?

Joule showed the picture again. "The tires aren't very new."

God bless Brooklyn for teaching her this. She leaned over the picture and enlarged it. "Look here, one—the treads are worn in the tire track image. Two—without actually getting a ruler out and measuring, I guess they are about the same amount of wear on the actual tires. See?"

He nodded. "But wear and tear on tires out here is common. People run them bald. It's not a rich community. It's still not enough evidence."

"Look." She ran her finger along the screen, pulling the picture aside and enlarging it even more. "Here. There's a piece of something stuck in the tire marring the tread."

He shook his head again. "It just means something was there in the desert. That mark could have easily been made after the tire was there."

"But that's not what happened." Joule frantically scrolled the screen again, trying to figure out amidst all the sandy white going by where exactly it was. But then she found it. "It repeats every time the tire makes a full rotation." She pointed to several spots on the picture.

He nodded. "Good work."

"It was Brooklyn," Joule said. "And look here."

She swiped three pictures over, showing off a squarish piece of gravel stuck in the treads of Salvador Torres's back tire.

41

J oule showed McQueeny all the information they'd gathered from the tire tracks.

"Here are the license plates of the two other cars that match tracks," she'd said, scrolling by the pictures, stopping just long enough for him to write them down. "I'd love to have them checked out."

The officer pulled out his own phone, a blocky, industrial black thing, and he started tapping something for a moment.

Joule and Malcolm stayed silent, the urge to fidget overwhelming. Her fingers interlaced with each other, and it made her think of Cage and the way he wore out the cuffs on his jackets, how he had a fidget toy in his hand or his pocket so often. She watched as Jacob McQueeny wrote down names and addresses, one of which was in a different unit number at the apartment building, and another of which appeared to be a visitor from somewhere on the other side of town.

He tapped at the paper and the neat, tiny addresses he'd written, sliding his notepad slightly closer to them. "I'm not allowed to share this information with you," he said, even as he tapped his finger and Joule nodded.

Malcolm got into the game then. "I think there's a bug on the wall behind you." He pointed over the man's shoulder.

McQueeny managed to sound interested. "Oh, is there?" He turned around and inspected the wall, lingering as he said, "I don't see it."

"Oh," Joule grinned as she snapped a picture of the second address, "I think it's gone now."

Malcolm smiled sideways at Joule as Officer McQueeny turned back around. "Oh, well. I'm sure it's not important."

The officer nodded and moved back to his paperwork. Joule was going to like officer McQueeny.

She did have to say, "We didn't find any gravel or specific identifying marks on the other tires, unfortunately."

They worked piece by piece through the evidence. Until they got to the body they'd found in the desert.

"It hasn't been ID'd yet?" Joule was stunned.

"No. Not only does the preliminary information not match any missing persons that have been filed, the body was also older and desiccated. Therefore, it's a very low priority for the San Antonio Medical Examiner's Office."

Joule hated hearing that. She was certain that finding a body so close to where Sarah was last seen had to mean something. But it couldn't tell them more if no one examined it.

While she tried not to sulk—there was no time for it—Malcolm talked to the Officer about the things he and Aurora had remembered from Sarah talking to them before she disappeared.

Officer McQueeny then looked to Joule. "When you talked to her, did she say anything unusual?"

"I didn't talk to her recently," Joule had to confess. "We hadn't actually talked in a handful of weeks, though we did chat on social media or via email. We were roommates on a previous job. My brother and I, we lost a good friend recently —" It was still hard to say even that. "So, we took a leave of absence. We aren't part of this job. We weren't here until after Sarah disappeared."

Would they have been assigned to this job if they had stayed on with HST? It was plausible.

McQueeny turned his attention to Malcolm then, "And you, when did you last speak to your daughter?"

"We spoke to her every several nights. Family check-in, that kind of thing."

"Wonderful." McQueeny didn't look up from the notes he was taking. "And what, if anything, unusual might she have said?"

Malcolm went through all of it, recapping his and Aurora's recent conversations with Sarah. But Malcolm didn't change his tone at all, didn't give any hints about what he thought of the things Sarah had said. Things he'd already told Joule and Cage. He was probably hoping for McQueeny to sort the information for himself.

McQueeny stopped him when he talked about Sarah volunteering. "At the Y?"

"Yeah," Malcolm nodded.

"There's no Y here. She would have had to go into San Antonio on a regular basis."

"She didn't mention that. And after she went missing—" his voice cracked but he kept going, "—we got her phone records from our cell provider." Malcolm had brought a bag with him. He and Aurora had become quite the sleuths in their search for their daughter. He pulled out a stack of printed papers and laid them on the table for the officer. "Phone records from Sarah for the last month. I can get further back."

There was a pause then Malcolm filled in information that was new to Joule, too.

"She wasn't going to San Antonio often enough for her to be regularly volunteering two nights a week at the Y. Look where the cell towers ping." He pointed to several names on the list of each tower Sarah's cell had linked to and when. "She *is* going into the desert on those nights, it would appear."

McQueeny had shuffled through the pages, pulling out the call and text lists. He seemed to have noticed calls to a couple of numbers. "Hold on a second."

He punched them into his tiny industrial phone. Then he said, "Your tires *are* a match. Because this phone number that she contacted repeatedly, and it contacted her, is registered to Pablo Torres."

"They've got to be related. That's the name that holds the lease on one-oh-four."

"How did you find that out?" McQueeny eyed her, but Joule just pressed her lips together.

She nodded her head and left it at that.

Things finally felt like they were clicking. She didn't know yet what the puzzle picture was, but at least a piece of it was coming together. "Sarah had been calling Torres and Torres had been calling her on a reasonably regular basis?"

McQueeny turned the phone log around to face them. She could see the number came up often. One of them should highlight it.

Malcolm then told McQueeny about when he and Aurora had been knocking on doors. He held up his phone once again. No picture. Just information.

"Hold on." This time it was McQueeny who held up the phone to Joule and Malcolm. "Is this her?"

It was not a flattering shot, and Joule didn't know if that was the same woman. She hadn't been there. But Malcolm did.

"Yes, that's her. She looked a lot better at her door though."

"Well, this is a mug shot."

"Ah yes. We found out she's been arrested multiple times for run ins with Federal Agents."

Again, McQueeny looked at them as if to ask how they'd

gotten that information. Again, both Joule and Malcolm ignored the implied question.

But the officer wasn't done. "I think I found something that might help."

Joule's heart, pounding heavy and full of hope, came to an abrupt stop. She leaned forward, hand splayed out on the table as the officer spoke.

"One of the arresting officers here," he showed the picture again, "is my mother."

The ATF one, Joule remembered as she read the name Maeve McQueeny.

But the officer was still going. "I think I know what Sarah was volunteering for."

42

Joule's phone rang. It was sitting in front of her, face up on the table, and she reached out to answer it. But a quick flat handed gestured stayed her.

"Who is it?" Officer Jacob McQueeny asked.

"It's Dr. Chithra Murasawa. Sarah's boss, from Helio Systems Tech. She's mine and Cage's old boss, too."

"Okay. Answer."

Interesting, Joule thought. McQueeny was monitoring her calls now, but maybe that was important. *What if Cage or Aurora called?*

Even as she hit the button, Joule glanced toward Malcolm, who seemed to be processing the same idea. She almost didn't get the whole name out. "Dr. Murasawa—"

"Joule! I just heard. I'm so sorry. I know you were all out last night just trying to find Sarah."

And then this. It was what it was, and she couldn't let it be anything more. She couldn't afford to think about what her life might be like if her brother didn't ever come back.

But Dr. Murasawa was still going a hundred miles a minute. "You have all of us. Right now, if you want. It was finally enough paperwork and not cases where someone might have wandered off. The bosses finally pulled the plug. We're stopping all work and helping."

Joule was feeling the warmth as the offer infused through her system, though McQueeny was looking surprised. Apparently, he then decided to jump into the conversation himself, rather than letting Joule be a go between through the unwitting third party of her boss and him.

"Hello, Dr. Murasawa? This is Officer Jacob McQueeny with the Maverick County Sheriff's Unit."

"Officer?" Murasawa sounded as relieved as Joule had felt. "Are you on this case?"

"Yes, ma'am. And on Sarah's, too." He almost let a wry sound escape. "Well, I am as of a few minutes ago when I was informed how the cases are related."

Joule almost opened her mouth as if ready to say *and on three hundred others apparently,* but she held her tongue. If McQueeny was helping them, she needed to let him make the best decisions he could. She didn't know enough in this area to override him.

"What does that mean?" he asked Murasawa now. "When you told Joule 'you've got all of us'?"

"I have a unit of almost thirty engineers, computer whizzes, and bioscientists ready to help in any way we can. Our job is to install a solar panel array and a small hydroelectric dam. But we have finally halted the work in order to find our missing people."

She paused. "So, we can give you about thirty, smart—but probably untrained—hands on deck to help search, research, whatever you need. Full-time."

"That is a wonderful offer, ma'am. And I am going to take you up on it, just not right now."

"Understood. What should we be doing in the meantime?" Dr. Murasawa was the best.

Joule knew her old boss had previously risked getting at least written up and possibly losing her job. And she wouldn't make the employees under her risk that. Chithra Murasawa would make it clear that it was entirely her decision. But she'd finally made it work. Until somebody overrode her, the team had everyone they needed for the search.

"Have everyone who interacted with Sarah put together everything they can remember about her activities from when she arrived in Texas until she disappeared. Use cell phones, emails, everything. Hopefully, I'll get back to you in a few hours with more of what we need."

"Do I need to send my employees home to rest after that. So they can be available this evening?"

McQueeny had been holding his pen between his two hands, and now, surprised, he dropped it and leaned back in the seat. "I don't know about that yet. We're still formulating our plan. There's a lot more going on here than we initially thought."

A pause from Dr. Murasawa let Joule's brain wander.

Cage and Aurora had only gone missing just after 1am last night. It was a good reminder that they hadn't been missing for very long—despite the fact that it felt like forever.

In a moment, her boss's pause became clear. It sounded as if she were talking to someone else in the room with her. The sound faint, but the words detectable.

"Are there satellites overhead? Over the desert last night?" she asked someone.

"There are always satellites overhead," a male voice responded. It was far enough away that Joule couldn't identify it. She even had trouble picking out the words, but she managed.

"Anything like Earth imaging?" Dr. Murasawa asked him.

"Hold on."

During the brief pause, McQueeny turned to look at Joule

and Malcolm as if to ask if this was good help, help they wanted. It was Joule who nodded at him. *Yes.* She knew Dr. Murasawa could and would take over if she had the means to do so. She wasn't bad at it when she did.

She was still talking to whoever was with her. "With something like that could you be able to pinpoint two people?"

"Pinpoint their location? And time?" the voice in the background answered. "Some satellites can. The problem is getting access to them."

"Wait!" Joule broke in. "What?"

She could almost hear Dr. Murasawa turning her face back toward the phone. "I've got David here on the system."

"Hi, David!" Joule's heart swelled. He'd been the data analyst in Alabama. He was good. Overwhelming relief flooded her at the sound of his voice.

"I owe you and Cage one," he called out across the room. "More than one."

"You don't owe us anything," She almost yelled it back, though she was plenty close to the phone. It was so good to hear from a friend.

"I do. And I've got you."

She would take it, but then she added, "It was more than two people."

"I thought it was Cage and Aurora?" That was Dr. Murasawa.

"It *was* Cage and Aurora," Joule said, "until sometime between one and two-thirty in the morning. That's when we discovered the tracks. We think the tracks relate to whatever kept them from checking in, which means probably closer to one a.m."

"Go on." She could hear the tension in the doctor's voice and Joule watched as the officer leaned forward, pen ready for more tight notes.

"There were a lot of footprints," she told them.

"Human?" the officer asked.

"Yes. Human tracks that crossed their path. It looked like the new tracks surrounded Cage and Aurora's footprints, and then they all went off together."

"How many?" This from David.

"I don't know."

"At a minimum?" Murasawa pressed.

"Ten. It could have been twenty though. Everything was jumbled." But even as Joule was talking McQueeny was picking up his own phone and dialing up someone.

She heard the faint ring though her concentration stayed on Dr. Murasawa as the woman once again sounded like she was talking over her shoulder. But this time with McQueeny talking to whoever he was talking to, Joule couldn't hear the answer.

43

J oule stood once again in the open desert. Though her car was nearby, and she was experiencing the urge to simply flee, she couldn't. So, she stayed in the last place she wished to be.

She'd half expected to be here with the entire crew from HST, but surprisingly, that wasn't who was beside her. Gisela, Amber, and Brooklyn had turned up, having done their part to put together Sarah's timeline already, they'd headed straight here.

In fact, they'd called Joule almost the second Dr. Murasawa had hung up. They'd all decided that—given the women's specialties—they were far more useful out here than at the job site. Those still with the boss were reconstructing a timeline, overtaking the computers, and attempting to crack some satellites.

McQueeny had told Dr. Murasawa outright, "I can't authorize this." To which the professor had said, "You aren't authorizing it. I am. But if I give you the information, you can use it?"

"I don't know." At least he'd been honest, but Joule had felt her heart sink, until Jacob added, "But if you give it to Joule or to Malcolm . . ."

"On it!" Dr. Murasawa had said.

Now Joule was waiting to hear if they'd found anything, though at this point it had barely been an hour.

McQueeny had told them to eat and then gathered this little ragtag band out in the desert.

As she stood there waiting for instructions, Joule watched another car pull up. The driver, the older redhead from the pictures, had with her a woman who looked remarkably like her. These could only be McQueeny's mother and sister, called in to help officer Jacob on his way to the FBI.

As long as her brother and Aurora and Sarah were found in the process, Joule found she didn't much care.

As the women got out and Joule got a better look, she realized they were exactly who she thought. Jacob stepped forward, offering a "hey mom" and a quick hug, but as he turned to introduce them the younger one stepped forward.

"Kathryn McQueeny," she held out her hand, shaking Joule's hand first, and then Malcolm's as if she already understood that these two were the major players in this horrific little game. Waiting politely behind her for an opening, the mother did much the same, though slightly less forcefully.

"Maeve McQueeny, former ATF."

"She says *former*," Jacob told them, "but she retired only two years ago and she still works full time for them. They keep calling her in to freelance on cases. So, she is as current with cases in the area as she can be."

Malcolm's brows were pulling together, his mouth tightening at the edges, "Why do we need ATF?"

He was right. All the help was great, Joule thought. But she could understand Malcolm wondering about the ATF and DEA. Then again, he hadn't seen what was under the rock.

Whatever it was had been wrapped in plastic and Joule knew that couldn't be good.

"One," Jacob told them, addressing the entire group like a teacher or a scout leader. His hands were up, gesturing as he spoke. "She's worked a lot of cases out here in the desert. She's an excellent tracker. So is Kathryn. Two—before we got the calls and everything started moving, *which is great by the way,* I told Joule and Malcolm that I think I know what Sarah was volunteering for."

"She sure wasn't with the Y," Malcolm huffed, for once, seeming irritated at his daughter for her lies.

Jacob nodded at him. "Given that Gretchen Mueller recognized her—."

"Gretchen Mueller?" Maeve McQueeny interrupted.

Jacob turned to his mother. "Yes."

"I arrested Gretchen Mueller on more than one occasion."

"Did she serve time?" Joule asked.

"No. We always found a way to let her off."

What? They *found a way to let her off?* Joule couldn't quite process that. Her face must have showed how confused she was, because Maeve answered.

"She was with an illegal organization trying to cover the area here." She waved her hand out into the desert where three people had recently disappeared and broken Joule's heart. "—to leave water and provide safety for immigrants illegally crossing the border."

Was Sarah doing that?

But Maeve was still going. "The group, loosely an organization—just enough of one to collect donations of clothing and food and money—they provide clothes, occasionally safe houses, and water and supplies."

Holy shit. Joule thought. "You think that's what Sarah was doing?"

"I'd guess so. It matches where her cell phone pings." Jacob must have sent his mother the records. "I don't know how she got involved with it, but yes."

"Salvador Torres!" Malcolm muttered and he was right. That would be the obvious choice. The man lived in the same apartment building and one of them had befriended the other somewhere along the way.

Joule wondered if the migrants had somehow taken Sarah, then her brother and Mrs. Walker. She clung to it, thinking she could still find them all then, that the three might be alive and okay, even though that line of reasoning made no sense. Why would someone just trying to get to a better life do something like that? So, she asked her next reasonable question.

"You said that you found ways to let Gretchen Mueller go each time she was arrested?"

It was Kathryn who stepped in then. "There's a hard line between the morality and the law. A lot of people completely disagree with the illegal immigration that happens through here."

That was really difficult to distinguish, Joule thought. She struggled to tell what Kathryn's opinion was given the expression on her face. She was excellent at just stating facts. Then again, her brother had already told them that she was a professor at the university.

"But regardless of their stance on the act of crossing, many people still cannot handle the immorality of leaving people in the desert to die, bad choices or not." She paused and her expression turned grim. "The problem is the migrants are only a small fraction of what's out there."

Gisela spoke up, maybe a little worried for herself for the first time. "I don't understand. What kinds of things are out here besides people?"

"Well," Kathryn said, "I think the easiest way to put it is that my mother is with the ATF. And she's intimately familiar with what travels here."

44

C age had a bruise on the side of his face. It hadn't yet bloomed full purple yet, but he could feel that it was going to. It pulled every time he spoke, but he worked not to let any of it show.

He'd known from the moment he'd been hauled in here that it was going to be a mess like this.

Wishing he had his gun with him was a strong desire, but also a recipe for disaster. If he had one, then everybody could have one. And these half-starved, angry, crazed fools would have killed everyone in seconds.

Just in case things couldn't get any more bizarre, he was now standing in the large central room of a cave.

There was only one person here who seemed older than Cage. That was concerning in and of itself. Cage also understood that, given his tall, lanky build, he was often mistaken for younger than he was. It was entirely possible he was getting underestimated. He wanted to let that stand—and pray that it was right—as long as he could.

The one man who was older sat quietly on a mattress in the corner, near him, a floor lamp glowed bright—one of several scattered around the space. His shoulders hunched in as though he might make himself small enough to disappear from the situation ... and the violence that permeated the space.

One of the teenagers was running the show, and his initial greeting to Cage had been a cuff upside the head as soon as Connor had shoved him in and turned around. Cage had taken the expected move with as much grace as possible.

He'd wanted to get a better lay of the land, see how the group was working. It was clear from the moment he walked in that they'd set some sort of hierarchy. It was also clear that the hierarchy only came out when it was just them. Connor with his gun down the back of his pants clearly ruled over whatever hierarchy existed here.

But Connor had left hours ago.

Cage had been trying to sleep but had to do it with half an eye open. He had no allies here and he knew it.

Now, he was beyond hungry. He sat in the corner, his back against the rough stone wall, another old worn mattress on the floor his only furniture. There were no chairs in here. Probably these boys—because they weren't men—couldn't be trusted with anything they could pick up and fling around like a weapon.

Cage had made it hard to get behind him and he'd done that on purpose. He needed to see all comers and get as much sleep as possible. Aside from his rough entry, the place had stayed mostly quiet during the day.

The big teenager in charge, his long lanky hair greasy from lack of care, sat with his knees up, forearms resting across the tops, hands dangling as if to say he could afford to not be ready. Cage knew the stance. The kid would glare around the room as the others slept off and on.

As far as Cage could tell, Teen Woof there didn't sleep.

He himself had been up for over twenty-four hours. Still, he'd managed to drift off a few times. More than once he hadn't realized he'd done it until a fist caught him upside the head, right in the forming bruise.

When it happened again, he realized he'd been out cold. Not surprising, but he jolted awake. He managed not to yelp and looked up.

"Food's here," Teen Woof announced. "You don't get any."

Cage stood then, his one apparent advantage his height. Looking down at the weasel, Cage wondered, *was he the only one in here tall enough to do so?*

No, the man sitting in the corner trying to disappear into the peeling paint would be taller. But he probably never stood to his full height.

"I eat," Cage announced to Teen Woof in his most simple tone.

The kid's retaliation was clear in the crunch of his expression into immediate rage at being countered. In the time it took for his hand to come swinging up, he telegraphed enough to tell Cage what was coming from a mile away.

With a sharp move upward with his left hand, Cage blocked the coming punch. A simple swing had him wrapping Teen Woof's arm and controlling it now. His right hand snapped out, grabbing the throat of the young man who thought to attack him and control the food.

Cage pushed backwards while pulling on the arm, applying pressure to the throat but not enough to cause real damage. Just enough to hurt. He said only, "I eat. Everyone eats."

Around him, dark eyes popped open wide, reflecting the dim light of the room. The tray of food had remained untouched, though clearly everyone was quite hungry.

As best Cage could tell, he and Aurora had arrived early in the morning. It was now late afternoon, judging by the slant of the one thin beam of light that came from some opening far above them. He hadn't seen other food come in here unless he'd slept through it, or the group had been given breakfast before he arrived. If they had, it wasn't going to be a Continental hotel thing, he knew.

It was possible none of them had eaten since this time yesterday.

But Teen Woof wasn't taking Cage's simple statements well.

Sure enough, a foot quickly came out. Cage was quicker.

He was playing some of his most valuable cards early, letting them all know that he could do this. For a brief moment, he sent up a prayer of thanks for all the times that he'd had to run five miles and his knees had hurt and his parents had told him, "You can quit. But if you quit, you don't get the black belt and you only have two more miles to go."

He'd understood then that where he was was zero. Except it was so close to the goal. In the end, he and Joule had each gotten a second degree belt in MMA. By the time he'd made it out of his early belt classes and into the upper levels, the school had been teaching the kids how to fight dirty if they had to.

So now he did.

45

The hierarchy in the room had shifted. Cage could feel it.

But for how long? Were there any other comers waiting in the corners?

His position was precarious and dangerous.

He knew it would be easier to sit back. He did not want to take another cuff upside the head—though he could physically take it and grit his teeth again, he couldn't hold the room if he did.

He hadn't slept enough to afford not to eat, and he couldn't handle the way some of these kids hung back. Some of them were just *kids*. Cage knew he couldn't let it show how much that broke his heart. There was no room here to care, only to rule or find his position in the order.

Trying not to huff out a breath into the cool air that smelled of wet stone, he stared at his opponent quietly. He would have gladly occupied the bottom rung if it hadn't come with abuse. And he might even have put up with it for himself, not rock the boat, but not for kids. So here he was, locked in a death glare with Teen Woof, whom he'd since learned was Terrence.

The asshole still fancied himself in charge and was using food to maintain his control. How long had Terrence held the room? Because some of them had still looked to Terrence before they ate.

It would be a while before Cage could convince anyone he should hold his new position.

He knew he didn't want to be here long enough to do that. He didn't want to be king of the rat cage.

But what could he even do? He ate food that was mostly pointless. Aside from the fact that he could tell himself it was calories, and it would keep him alive until he got out of here, it tasted like nothing, and it was tempting to toss it aside or give it away. But he methodically chewed and swallowed as he tried to figure out what could be done.

Could they form a union and go on strike? That seemed highly unlikely. He didn't yet know what they were being kept for, but he had his fears. He was also quite confident that any attempt at refusal to do as told would be met with bullets. There had been that discussion of killing him and Aurora simply because of who they were.

That had made Cage realize something.

He ate the food quickly and leaned back against the wall before giving everyone the stink eye and closing his eyes. They would have to gang up on him to hold him down. He knew that they could. His only hope was—though it had not been a strategic move on his part—that he was the one who fed everyone.

He didn't actually sleep. He couldn't afford to, so he only dozed lightly.

No one came at him. He could see Terrence sitting in the corner, bruises blooming around his throat to match the ones on Cage's own face. Cage didn't think the new bruises would be that noticeable to anyone else. Everyone here looked more than a little battered.

Cage didn't know how long that quiet stand off lasted, maybe an hour before the door opened.

When Connor came in Terrence still stood up, as if to lead the way. He offered only a quick side eye toward Cage as if to ask if he would challenge the move again.

Cage wouldn't. It served him well for anybody coming into the room to think that the pecking order had not changed. So, he hung back, positioning himself as the last one out, and taking a cuff on the shoulder for doing so.

They were trekked back to the house, maybe thirty minutes of walking and stopping. They waited for something—Cage couldn't tell what—then were shuffled in through the back door. In the living room, they were lined up behind the women. He spotted Sarah and Aurora and fought the smile that wanted to show at just seeing them.

Aurora looked upright. That was good. Cage could only hope the women had a far more civil society than his own.

At the front, all eyes duly focused on him, Brown Eyes sprawled on the couch. His legs were spread wide again, another glass of amber liquid dangled from his fingertips. If he were smart, Cage thought, that wouldn't be whiskey or bourbon, but simply tea. He could let everyone think that he was drinking all the time and maybe not on his A game.

But then Cage caught a whiff. The whole room had the slice in the air of alcohol. It *was* actually bourbon.

Brown Eyes took a too-casual sip and issued his orders with the calm certainty of a functional alcoholic. As he told them what the plan was for the night, what they would be doing, Cage felt his brain expand in his horror.

This was no casual operation, and it wasn't just this one group. Brown Eyes, like Connor before him, wasn't in charge of this thing. He was merely a cog in a much, much larger machine.

No wonder Sarah had been here for a week without escape.

Cage began to wonder if they would ever get out.

—————

46

"No, not you," Kathryn told her, making Joule step back for a moment, a little surprised.

"We're following footprints," Joule reiterated, clutching her little cluster of blue flags that Maeve had brought with her.

Kathryn and Maeve had assigned them to each choose one footprint and try to follow it. They'd handed out little tiny colored flags and explained how to put the flag near the footprint but not in it.

Brooklyn was once again irritated. "My plaster cast kits don't arrive until tomorrow. The mailing was a bitch. I bought a bunch of them."

In that moment, Joule maybe loved her a little bit. They'd all been hunting for Sarah, but the fact that the coworkers were willing to put this kind of effort in gave her hope that all three of the missing could be found.

"I was just going to follow the footprints, like we were told to," Joule realized she was defending herself.

Kathryn reiterated, "No, not you or Malcolm."

This time Malcolm, who's hand was already out to accept flags from Maeve, flinched as Maeve pulled them back away.

"Why not us?" he asked, his voice deep and concerned.

"You're biased."

Of course, she was, Joule thought, *they all were.*

But Kathryn understood that too. "You two are the *most* biased. So, you're going to come with me."

Lovely, Joule thought. She had been happy to try and find her brother's footprints and follow them. Her bias wasn't in doubt. But what was she going to do now?

Kathryn motioned for her and Malcolm to step around the fake rock without stepping into any of the footprints there.

They'd already set up a chart whereby each of them pushed their foot into the sand and Maeve began by marking who's print it was so they could rule out impressions and avoid going in circles tracking each other.

Now, Joule and Malcolm stood in the middle of the mess and were told, "Get a good look at the fake rock. We can't lift this one yet, but we're going to go look for more. If there's one here—"

"—There will be others," Joule filled in.

"Exactly."

It seemed like a ridiculous system, and Joule was certain the fake rocks would be easy to find. If someone was storing something under them, then surely all her little team would have to do was lift the fake rock and find it.

She could only assume that they would call Maeve over to catalog it. Since Maeve was ATF, Joule assumed they would find ATF related findings under the rocks.

It turned out to be a harder task than Joule expected. She quickly located another reasonable sized rock. But when she happily reached down to curl her nails underneath it and lift it, she met only with the scratch of a rough surface against her nails and the weight of a real rock.

How had she made that mistake?

Using her foot she pushed against it, but the weight held up. This one was actually a rock.

They'd moved far enough away from the group that maybe the others didn't see that she was being a dumbass.

Kathryn let her off the hook though. "The fake rocks only look fake once you figure out that they're fake. It's actually not a bad system. Look," she waved her hand outward, indicating the wide open space. "There are so many rocks out here to check."

While Joule had considered the desert simply a sea of sand and shrubs before, she remembered bumping her toes in the dark on rocks. Even the little ones were heavy enough to hurt and big ones were enough to trip over and cause real problems.

It was a good half bottle of water and thirty minutes later that Malcolm called out, "I think I've got one."

"Don't touch it!" Kathryn warned even as he was reaching down.

She hadn't stopped Joule from trying earlier. It must have been that she realized Joule's rock was real. As she walked over to where Malcolm waited impatiently for them, Joule tried again to categorize what made the fake rocks look fake. And again, found that it was harder to tell than she'd thought. Maybe just nudging them with her toe was the better test. "Why can't we touch them? Fingerprints?"

"Maybe prints, definitely DNA . . ."

"Someone would test the rock for DNA and come after me?" Joule was stunned.

"Someone at the ATF could test the rock for DNA and yours might contaminate a sample that could otherwise be used to help convict someone."

Well, hell.

Then it got worse. "We don't know what capabilities the operations out here have. We suspect it's very lowbrow at the bottom of the chain, but high tech at the top. So, no, you don't want to leave any way for them to know you were messing with their stash."

Stash.

Kathryn paused, "If they think you've interrupted their operation, they will take you out. What passes through here is more valuable than any human life. The fact that you're all out here searching around their stuff is problematic in the first place. It's why you lost two people last night."

Fucking fuckballs.

The words of Officer Asshat came back to Joule: they shouldn't be out here. They didn't know what they were doing.

But the fact was, no one but them was out here looking for Sarah. Everyone else had seemed perfectly willing to let her disappear into the sand and never be heard from again. Joule's fervent hope right now was that the loss of Cage and Aurora had sparked enough interest and enough talent from the McQueeny family to get something done.

"Here," Kathryn dismissed that harsh warning as though she were telling them not to get stung and shuffled around a little.

Reaching into her pocket, she pulled out an extendable pointer and tried to shove it under the edge of the rock to lift it. Quickly, she realized it wasn't quite sturdy enough to do the job.

So once again, Joule found herself traipsing around and looking for bushes with branches sturdy enough to work and weak enough to snap off. She came back a moment later.

"Excellent," Kathryn grinned, and Joule felt proud she'd at least done this right.

She was happy for the professional help. Apparently, they'd been doing it all wrong. As she shoved the knob of the branch under and they lifted the rock together, Malcolm leaned down and looked under.

"It's empty," he declared.

"It is but it's not," Kathryn offered with a half-smile. "Look at the impressions."

That task, Joule found, was a little harder. Katherine McQueeny pulled out her phone, flipped on the flashlight, and held it at a low angle creating a few shadows.

"They were wrapped. No one would put one directly into the sand because it would cause problems. But look. Can you make out the shape?"

It was guns, Joule saw, and not small handguns. Not the kind you could pass at a gun show. No.

"A couple of decades ago," Kathryn started after she snapped a few pictures and carefully lowered the rock back down into the exact same groove. It seemed she didn't want anyone to know she'd been here either. "The Hells Angels organization was brought up on racketeering and weapons charges. They were running guns and drugs from Mexico to Canada . . . in addition to all their charitable efforts. They had connections directly into the IRA—"

"*The Irish Republican Army?*" Malcolm seemed surprised, but Kathryn only nodded as if it should be clear.

"That crack down shut down a lot of the pipeline of illegal weapons in and through America." She stood upright then, done with this particular, empty, fake rock. She waved one hand around, gesturing like a hostess to the open desert. In the distance, Joule could see her friends carefully planting little colored flags.

"Want to guess where the traffic moved?" Kathryn McQueeny asked.

Joule didn't have to guess.

In the distance she could hear the group start to talk excitedly, their noise level rising. It was Jacob and Maeve who called back to Kathryn, "Come over. We've got something!"

47

They walked the desert on a long trek through the waning day. Cage was grateful that he'd had decent shoes on when he'd been taken. The weight of the backpack that he had over one shoulder bothered him. It hit his hip with each step.

He'd initially put both straps on, but a wide eyed, very subtle head shake from one of the younger boys—one that Terrence called "Rana" for "frog"—had made Cage slide his arm out of the strap.

This hadn't been the kind of kidnapping he'd always imagined. No hand over his mouth from behind. No chloroform. No being stuffed in a trunk.

He couldn't say he'd gone along willingly, but he'd walked the distance himself. The guns aimed at him had certainly been coercive. And now, nobody was holding a gun on him, but he was unshakable in the belief that if he tried to flee, a bullet would be in his back before he could get fifteen paces away.

From behind him Aurora moved forward, shuffling along, as if trying to get ahead of him in the group. He turned to see if she had something to say—not that anyone has spoken since they left the house—but she didn't even look at him. She just stared straight ahead. He let it go, hoping he would figure out what she was doing.

He'd seen Sarah again. His friend didn't look great, but she looked healthy enough. She had fading bruises, indicating it had been a while since someone had laid a hand to her. He didn't get a chance to ask, and she stayed toward the back of the group as well.

Aurora had been back there with her. Why were they splitting up? Wouldn't mother and daughter stick together? Safety in numbers, happy to see each other, and all of that.

But, as Aurora passed him, she bumped into him, her thick fingers pressing into his palm. He felt it then. On any other day, he would have thought it was a dollar bill. Now he knew it was paper, and both he and Aurora knew he was smart enough to surreptitiously slide it into his pocket and not read it until much, much later.

The group continued forward at a reasonable clip. Cage had to assume they were counting on the creeping darkness to keep them covered and that no one would find them unless they stumbled directly on the group—much the way he and Aurora had.

Connor led at the front with his greasy hair and black jeans and his ridiculous Colt in his hand. He walked by himself a decent distance ahead. There had been no instructions specifically to do this, but Cage had followed the group and they were keeping pace.

For a while he conjured the kinds of psychological experiments that tested his ability to learn and modulate just based on the actions of others around him. He wished he'd had more psych classes.

They'd already walked over an hour, as best Cage could tell, and while Connor seemed confident of their direction, Cage couldn't be. He wished he'd learned to navigate by the sky better. The last of the light shifted around him, indicating they took a circuitous route, he thought overall, they had mostly gone in a straight line. The question was, *where?*

Though it had been daylight when they started out, the evening had begun to set in. Cage had a feeling that they would be walking until it was actually dark. As they moved, he shifted the backpack to the other shoulder and looked out across the horizon. His sister would be searching. Malcolm would be with her. Probably Amber, Gisela, and Brooklyn as well.

Five people looking for him.

The group he was in was relatively large. Surely, they could be spotted . . . if someone got close enough.

The others would almost definitely be out tonight. Could he be seen? He wanted to shield his eyes from the setting sun and search for them, but the last thing he could do was give himself away.

Cage considered if there was a way to get a light or even something reflective on him so he could be spotted easier. But before they'd left, he had been inspected. His bright t-shirt stripped away and traded for an older black one. He saw now that Aurora's pale sweater was the only thing that had survived. Her brighter clothing had been swapped out for more muted pieces. They were meant to blend in.

Though he didn't know what was in the backpack, as they moved it felt heavier and heavier. He noticed up ahead, some of the smaller ones in front of him seemed to be feeling the same. He wanted to step up and offer to carry someone else's. He watched Aurora and she, at least, did okay. But he didn't do it, because he knew the offer to help could get them both in trouble more than it was worth.

He was beginning to understand why people didn't break out of this. He hadn't even been here a full day yet, so maybe his attitude would change over time. But right now, he was determined to cling to his *live free or die trying* attitude.

Right now, that meant surviving. While he was at that, he would gather as much evidence as he could. So, he walked, and he stayed silent. He kept his mouth closed aside from a few sips of the water he carried with him.

He now looked a lot more like the people that he and Dr. Murasawa had seen the first night, though he still thought those people were immigrants. And these people he was with were something wholly different, at least they were now.

Subtle motions came from Connor at the front of the pack. Cage would have missed them if he hadn't happened to be looking that way. The darkness had fallen enough that it was getting harder to see, even though his eyes had adjusted.

Connor had already made it clear that they should trail him by a reasonable distance, but he now motioned for them to stay even further back.

What was happening? Cage didn't know. He was about to find out.

But nothing happened quickly. He kept walking and his brain wandered. He knew a kilo of cocaine was actually a weight of measure, but he didn't have a good enough sense of it to know if he carried a certain number in the backpack. He didn't even know if he had cocaine or what it might be. His backpack seemed relatively stable—packed tight—but ahead of him he could see Aurora with a long, awkward duffel bag. Hers seemed to rattle.

They weren't carrying the same thing.

An interesting operation, he thought, not focused on one product. Was the economics better if they diversified? When was the last time he'd had a class in economics? And had any of the people running this show had one? Probably not.

Once again, he slid his hand into his pocket, feeling the tiny slip of paper. His curiosity tried to get the better of him, but his sanity held back. It would simply have to be read later.

As he trudged along, Cage tried to keep his eyes on what

was happening. He was paying attention when Connor casually disappeared from the front of the group. They all walked a bit further before Terrence stepped forward, as did one of the women.

"We know where we're going," he said.

Though Cage didn't like it, he didn't get a say. So, he only watched as the women headed one way, and the men—boys, really—went a different direction led by Terrence.

Huh. Despite Cage's tentative control of the room back at the house, Terrence was still in charge out here. There was something here that the rest of them knew that Cage didn't.

48

Terrence had binoculars. Cage wished he had a pair, too.

In fact, Terrence had a second set of binoculars, and he'd handed them off to one of the youngest boys, charging two of them with moving a good distance south of their current location to watch from there. Obviously, Terrence wasn't going to hand one of the prize pieces to Cage—who was assumably now his mortal enemy.

Not a good position, Cage thought, none of it. Not his position in the pecking order inside the cave or out here. Not what they were clearly doing out in the desert, and not his chances of getting through this unscathed . . . or at least not any more than he already was.

Terrence had instructed them to leave the things in their packs in several locations, the teen puffed up with his assigned duties. One set of bags had been emptied under a fake rock. In another spot, he'd had them dig. Of course, Cage had been on that team. He was pretty confident they weren't being fed well enough to do the kind of manual labor that was required of them. But he'd done it anyway.

Curiouser, curiouser. Now they'd stepped back, bags empty, and they all watched the locations, though what they were watching for, Cage could only guess.

The women were completely out of sight, and they themselves were a good distance from the items they placed. The situation was becoming clear, whatever they were running— and he was pretty certain that what they had handled tonight was guns on the women and drugs on the men—was getting left out here in the desert and observed for pickup.

He wondered if there'd be cash in exchange, but who even ran a cash society these days? He thought it would have been funny if he wasn't out here concerned about his ability to survive dangers both desert and human based. He watched quietly, thinking about the things he buried in the sand: dense, plastic wrapped bundles that he couldn't identify.

The wrap was clear with a faint blue tint. There were too many layers of it to see what was inside. It could have been bricks of cocaine or boxes of pills. Though, as soon as he had that thought, he talked himself out of it. The bricks were too heavy to have as much air as a box like that would have.

He'd contemplated escape more than once already. But it wouldn't be tonight. If he was ever being heavily watched, it would be in these early days. He couldn't make an attempt with a real chance at making it until he established himself as a complacent player. And, if he did just make a run for it, what would happen to Sarah and Aurora?

Nothing moved in the desert, so his thoughts followed that line of reasoning. Was that why Sarah had stayed where she was? Had she grown concerned about the others? Or had there simply been no avenue of escape?

He tried to keep his focus on following the operations, but it was boring, and his brain wanted to wander in a way he couldn't let it. He told himself that watching meant he could gather as much evidence as possible while he was out here.

That way he could help whatever organization might rescue them from their kidnappers when the time came.

A light slashed across the sky and one of the kids uttered, "Estrella fugaz!"

Cage knew that one and he replied without thinking. "It's more likely a satellite."

"Shut the fuck up," Terrence growled and Cage rolled his eyes before turning back to his musings.

He tried to figure out where he was. His phone had been taken and his personal geolocation skills were pretty close to crap. What was out here? What landmarks could he pace off from? He needed something that could get him back to this position later. If he could get an investigative team close enough, perhaps a drug sniffing dog could figure out exactly where the drugs had gone.

Aside from being plastic wrapped, they didn't look to be that well concealed. When he'd finally opened the backpack he'd been given, Cage had almost expected to find little packets of heroin hidden inside hollow dolls. He'd seen TV shows where the rubber dog toys dissolved in acetone becoming the drugs themselves.

But this wasn't that. This was far more bold, far less concealed.

Sure enough, more time passed as he sat there bored, looking for landmarks and checking for future avenues of escape. He watched his own merry little band of drug runners like a hawk. The group in turn watched their stash like a hawk.

Cage could only conclude that Terrence was doing Connor's bidding. Whatever they were watching, it was important.

"Over there!" One of the younger boys was pointing excitedly into the distance.

Terrence lowered the binoculars for just a moment to get a

reference and then swept them back up. The kid had seen it with his bare eyes.

Cage and his sister had both inherited very good vision from their parents. As he turned and looked, he wasn't surprised to spot the small bit of movement on the horizon. Very quickly it became four distinct figures.

Interesting. There were twelve boys and young men who carried the supplies out, but only four had come to pick them up.

As the four got closer, their silhouettes became clearer against the starry backdrop of the sky. They walked with the confidence of people who gave no shits about the fact that they were in open desert. Unlike the group, they moved with purpose. And, sure enough, as they got closer, Cage could see the arsenal each one wore strapped to himself.

These men made him concerned. If Terrence had a weapon on him, Cage didn't know, but if he did, he had to be the only one. Cage had been offered no protection for himself and he didn't see any obvious guns or even knives on the younger kids, a fact for which he'd previously been grateful.

Now he realized the people they were dealing with were not people like the ones with him. Not people using kids as couriers. That meant if anything went wrong on this pickup, both sides thought his entire group was expendable.

49

Joule turned suddenly at the sound of the other group getting excited. She was surprised that she could hear them even from over here, letting her know that *something* had happened.

She looked to Kathryn. "Can I go join them?"

She was barely able to make out the group if not for their excited twitters given the way the sky had darkened. Maybe it was a desert thing, but it had happened fast.

To a certain extent she would have liked to have made the decision to join the others or hang back herself. But, on this very first night—hopefully the only night they would have to look—she wanted to trust the experts.

These people had come out of their own free will to find her brother, to find Aurora and, hopefully, Sarah, too. God help her if they weren't all three in the same place.

"Yes, let's go," Kathryn said even as she stayed crouched down, snapping a few last pictures of the fake rock itself.

Malcolm and Joule were already cutting across the desert, heading back toward the others. They cut as straight a path as they could, veering only around rocks and small shrubs. Gisela and Amber were waving them over excitedly. Despite their cheer, Joule felt a shiver and reached down to pull her jacket from around her waist and slide her arms in.

"Look!" Amber called out, even before they were really close enough to look. She pointed out through the desert. "The tracks head this way. We checked everything."

Joule turned to look behind her at Kathryn who was bringing up the back.

Brooklyn turned their way and chimed in. "Maeve had us check footprints, and there aren't enough of us to follow all of them. So that's interesting."

Maeve stayed back, arms folded, letting the young protege take over the discourse.

"Maeve talked us through," Gisela added, just as excited. "So, it looks like this group of people came up from that direction." She pointed from the south, much the same direction as Joule and Malcolm had just now come from.

It was what they had suspected last night—or early this morning—when they'd first seen the tracks. But Gisela kept going.

"They came most of the way as a group, walking all together, although not in any noticeable formation."

Amber butted in, waving her hand to demonstrate as Joule got close enough to really see what they were talking about. "They spread out as if specifically to encircle your brother and Aurora."

She looked first at Joule, then at Malcolm.

It was Malcolm who said the words. "We're confident now that they were kidnapped."

Behind Amber, the other searchers and Maeve nodded. The agent added, "It wouldn't be the first time."

"*What?*" Malcolm asked, surprised, putting voice to Joule's sudden morbid curiosity. *Who was kidnapping people out in the desert?*

For a moment the expression on Maeve's face told her *you don't want to know.*

But that was a luxury that Joule no longer had. Maeve seemed to quickly understand that.

"Illegal factions, as Kathryn mentioned. The drug, gun, illegal animal trade . . . it all runs through here."

Joule had hoped that wasn't the case with her missing family and friends. Honestly, she'd hoped her brother had just wandered off and they would find him and Aurora lost in the desert somewhere. They would need water and help getting home, maybe an IV at the hospital, but that would be the worst of it.

It was very sad in her mind that near starvation and being lost in the desert had been her best case scenario. She nodded to Kathryn, accepting what was likely true. She hung back at the edge of the group, her heart on pause as she waited for someone to tell her that they wouldn't be able to get Cage and the others back, that they were lost to a system too big to fight.

But no one said it, and for that Joule was grateful.

Brooklyn missed the underlying horror of the conversation, and she filled in the gaps, at least with a little less enthusiasm. "So, the group surrounded your brother and Aurora."

There was a moment as they all had to stop for a moment and think about what the larger implications might be.

"Then Cage and Aurora head off that direction with the group. There are enough of them that following this set of tracks should be easy enough," Amber added in.

Joule felt a lift in her chest. They had done the initial work, the necessary set up. Now she could follow the tracks and trace her brother. Right?

Hope burrowed its way into her soul, though she tried to stop it with her own information. "We found evidence of guns under the other rock over there."

"I'm sure there's plenty more around here," Maeve added.

"That's enough for ATF, isn't it?" Kathryn moved to stand beside Joule and Joule was watching the conversation as if it were a tennis match. Where was this going?

"Do you want to call it in?" she asked her mother.

"I don't think so," Maeve said.

Joule almost blurted out *"why not!"* but managed to hold her tongue. The two women had clearly done this before. The conversation had an undertone that she couldn't read, but she hoped if she waited it out, they would help her understand.

It was Kathryn who looked to Jacob. He wore an expression indicating that he wasn't so fond of the idea of handing the case over to his mother. Joule caught on then: This was his ticket into the FBI. If they handed it to his mother, he'd have to find another ticket.

She had to ask, "Shouldn't it go to the agency best suited to bring the *missing people home*?"

She emphasized the last three words. As much as she was more than willing to help Jacob achieve his dreams, she was not going to sacrifice Cage, Aurora, and Sarah for an FBI badge he could get later. She wouldn't sacrifice even one of them.

"Actually," Maeve said, standing back even as she pulled out a satellite phone that made Joule jealous, "ATF isn't the best place for finding missing people. It's not in our jurisdiction. Though it is something that happens as a side effect of our work far more often than you might expect, it's not what we're trained for."

Joule nodded along, but she wondered how much of that was true and how much of that was about keeping the case with her son.

Maeve turned to Kathryn, surprising Joule. From the looks of it she even surprised Malcolm.

"I think you should take it."

"What?" Joule asked again, though Kathryn was already nodding.

Maeve explained. "If I call it in, it's a case. The ATF takes over from here. If Kathryn takes it, it's a research paper. We can all be involved, and we don't have to worry about any agency sending in new investigators and we don't have to hand things over if jurisdictional lines get crossed."

Interesting, but was that the right thing to do? Was the best-case scenario for finding her brother having the work of his rescue be part of a university research paper?

Still, as she watched, the three McQueenys looked at each other, seeming once again to have a conversation underneath the conversation—one Joule could not yet read.

Whatever it was that they didn't say, they all understood. They looked to each other and nodded in agreement. Joule shivered, though whether that was from the rapidly dropping desert temperature or something she didn't realize she was picking up on, she didn't know.

Whatever Cage's fate was, Joule thought, it had been decided without her.

50

S he wanted to fight and claw like a wild cat. She wanted to stay out by herself. But Joule reluctantly agreed to wisdom and headed back in with the group.

"It's past dark. You don't want to be out here alone now." Maeve offered the solemn advice, letting Joule know that they wouldn't be staying with her.

It was Gisela who looked at her solemnly and said, "We're not going to lose you, too."

But Joule wasn't confident she cared enough to "not get lost." Would she care if she wound up with her brother?

It was Jacob who seemed to pick up on that. He leaned down and he didn't whisper but his voice was soft as he said, "There's no guarantee you would wind up with him. There's more than one faction out here."

"They have territories?" *It was all too much.*

"They do," Maeve answered, but she was already picking up her flags and aiming the group back toward the cars. It was still a distance back. "Even though we've been able to find some boundaries sometimes, they shift constantly. In this section of the desert, there's an entirely different world. It's overlaid on the one you occupy. You should never have crossed paths with it."

"Sarah did," Joule said as if that were some kind of excuse.

"It's true, but Sarah purposefully did it." Kathryn's words hit like a brick and for the first time Joule felt a shot of anger at her friend. Though Kathryn added, "She was helping people, just like you and your brother and Aurora. I don't fault her the choice," the words were a harsh dig, because Joule was starting to do exactly that.

Aurora and Cage were missing because of looking for Sarah. And Sarah had been out here of her own accord. She'd known the risks and she'd still come out.

But the others weren't going to let her stew in it.

Jacob simply said, "You need to go home. You need to get some sleep. I know you didn't sleep last night."

How did he know? Or was that just something you could say to every person who had a recently missing family member?

No. Joule refused to think in terms of 'recently.' That would mean there might be a time when Cage was missing 'not recently.' Unfortunately, she already knew the answer to that.

Cage had been her rock when their mother died. And she had been his—the stoic one, understanding that with everything going on in the world, there hadn't been time to mourn. Cage had been her link to the grief that she should have been feeling but couldn't.

When their father disappeared, it was one of the few things that the twins had ever argued so vehemently about.

Now who was left? She had friends. She even had Ivy and Kayla. But no one was or could ever be as close as her twin.

She had to get Cage back. Though her feet were walking the opposite direction from where he had gone, she would not give up until she found him. The sharp pang of guilt dug into her guts and twisted. Had they given up on their dad too easily?

She had been the one who insisted that Nate was dead. Had she been wrong?

There wasn't time to answer her own grueling self-inquiries as one of their phones started pinging. They'd finally walked close enough to a cell tower to connect back up.

Luckily, they'd been able to note the points where the group had surrounded Cage and Aurora and where the rock stashes were. Kathryn and Maeve had both pulled out their sat phones, though Maeve had only waved hers around without using it.

Uplinking with it would have put the case on the ATF radar. Kathryn had been the one to use the data to pinpoint the spots. Joule, once again, was struggling with handing over the search for her brother to someone much better educated and more knowledgeable about what they should do, but who would never have the drive to find him that she did.

Her own phone began pinging and Joule was unable to even check any of the messages they were coming in so fast. She couldn't click on a single one to capture it. Still, she stared at the phone hoping that one of them would say "Cage."

She'd had no contact from him since that last check in on the walkie talkie.

All around her, phones pinged in unison and discord. She gave up trying to see what was coming in and just waited for the phone to process it. Joule looked around, hoping someone would say something interesting.

A handful of her pings were from Dr. Murasawa, and several were directly from David.

The ATF was out here tonight. So was the Maverick County Sheriff's Department, and a San Antonio criminology professor. They might be here to help but Joule had her own network, and they were chiming in.

Amber—whose phone had begun going off first—maybe she was on a different cell plan than Joule and Cage?—said, "Holy shit, this is amazing."

Immediately she and Gisela began saying, "Crap, crap, crap!"

As Joule's notifications finally began to slow down and she tried to open them, nothing wanted to load. Amber confirmed she was having the same problem.

"I managed to read the message, but I can't open any of the pictures."

"We have to get back into better cell reception territory," Jacob announced. "Let's all get back in our cars. Go somewhere central in town and work there."

"I need food," Gisela announced.

For the first time, Joule felt her guts twist. *What had she even eaten today?*

Tall and thin, she didn't weigh enough to afford to skip meals. Yet she knew she did. Still, usually she kept better track than this. While everything going on was an ample excuse to screw up, there was no excuse for not being able to find her brother simply because she hadn't fed herself well enough.

"There's a diner in the middle of town with a patio," Amber said, "I think they are open until midnight."

Everyone was quick to agree, even Malcolm.

Joule found herself back in her car. Having driven here alone, she was granted a few blessed minutes of silence, but she couldn't handle it. She hit the radio, waiting for the car to pick up San Antonio Public Radio. She needed to listen to someone else's problems for a while.

Unrest in China. Disputed borders near Russia. Those things she could handle. They were worse than her own problems, she could tell herself. Her brother was one person, these were whole nations at risk. They were easier than her own problems, too. So far away she couldn't have any responsibility for them.

Right now, she had felt the sole responsibility to find Sarah rested on her, even though she knew that wasn't true. Still, she understood that while others were searching and doing the work, she would be the one to carry the mantle when they gave up and tapped out. When they could no longer afford to leave their days behind to find her brother, she would still be here. When they couldn't sustain the effort, she would have to.

Jacob wanted to get into the FBI. He had a burning drive to solve this case. But if he didn't solve it, his family wouldn't be blown apart. Only hers and Malcolm's would. But she still had to wait to tell if he would be capable of carrying that weight for a long time if necessary.

Joule knew that she could, but she had to make sure that it didn't go that far—because she alone would carry that responsibility. And it might be too much.

Before she knew it, she was sitting at a cluster of tables that had been pushed together, chairs in an awkward shape around it. Some of the group had been passengers in cars and had been able to pull up information while the other drove. Amber now shared pictures that David had sent from satellites he had hacked.

"This doesn't look like legal information," Jacob said.

Joule shrugged. "So, you can't use it against the cartel when we find them."

Had she really just said *cartel*? No one had spoken the word out loud before. If it was the truth, she would speak it. "But we can use it to find our missing people, right?"

"Absolutely."

She was grateful for the conviction of his answer.

"Has anyone opened Dr. Murasawa's email?" Brooklyn asked.

Joule shook her head no. She was still scanning through everything, desperately hoping for contact from her brother and realizing it was her turn to contact the phone company. Trace all the info the details could give up.

Still, she and her brother had given each other access to

their phones. She'd tried last night before going to bed, but nothing had loaded from after him going out with Aurora, and they'd had some walkie talkie contact after that, so it seemed useless.

Wanting to leave no stone unturned, she pulled up the app again now. This time it loaded.

Her heart beat faster, pounding in her veins until she couldn't hear the conversation around her.

"What's wrong?" Amber's voice sounded like it came through water.

What was she seeing?

"Look." Joule held the phone out, showing everyone.

The tracking app had pinpointed Cage's phone much further out into the desert than they'd been able to follow.

51

———

Dr. Murasawa's team had not been asleep at the wheel. Though they hadn't been at the search, they'd been working just as hard at finding the missing.

David had sent reams of satellite pictures. Joule was grateful there were as many of them around the table as there were. It would take everyone just to sort the data.

They ordered burgers and a few got salads. She got a sugar laden soda, fries with cheese, and a double cheeseburger. She needed every calorie to counter all the shit she was burning.

Pulling out her laptop, she connected to the hotspot Kathryn McQueeny offered up.

Though Jacob had started to connect in, Kathryn held her hand out and stopped him. The McQueenys once again stayed any contact that would link this work to a specific investigative unit.

Kathryn reminded him, "Anything that runs through you might get filed with the Department."

Soon, they were up and running.

Joule had the large screen to look at the pictures. David had hand drawn a line through the pictures following the tracks he'd been able to hone in on. The fact that satellites were able to distinguish footprints—which were simply varying shades of shadow in the desert—was simply mind-boggling.

David had even commented in his email that because they'd been able to tell him where to start, he had been able to follow the tracks himself and had still gone cross eyed trying to trace it.

Joule could not have been more grateful for his work, but as she held the picture from the tracking app on Cage's phone up next to it, everyone crowded around.

She didn't have to say it. The others did.

"They're identical."

"Looks like he had his phone on him for quite some time after they got caught up."

"Look where it ends."

"Jesus Christ. How far did they walk?" Gisela exclaimed.

"I don't know how far that is," Joule said. There were no landmarks really to judge by and the path had direction, but it meandered.

"Look when the phone was turned off. It's almost four hours after the last time we checked in."

"What is that app running on?" Jacob asked. "Did you not check it before now?"

Joule explained that she'd tried it before, "So I don't know why it loaded now."

It was Maeve who told them, "It means he pinged another cell tower before the phone got turned off and the data finally registered."

"Did the phone get turned off or did it get destroyed?" Jacob asked.

Joule hated not knowing. "It's hard to say. The app doesn't track that kind of information. At least not that I know."

She could see that her brother had 32% battery when the

signal stopped and that he'd gotten two of her text messages, asking where he was. But there was no reply typed out to her.

Jacob was leaning over her, looking back and forth between the multiple screens. The others all crowded in but let him have the prime territory.

"Send me that picture?" Kathryn asked.

"Of course." Joule then asked the woman if she wanted the login to Cage's tracking app.

Kathryn McQueeny readily agreed. Her brother would have no secrets, but right now, Joule couldn't care less.

She would want them to do the same if she ever disappeared. She had to make the same call for her brother.

It was Brooklyn who turned to Malcolm, "Do you have anything like this on Aurora's phone?"

"Possibly, but I'm not the tech guy. It's more likely Aurora was tracking me than that I'm tracking her."

If and when they found Aurora, he would be learning all of the things that Aurora knew. He would never again be stuck like this. Joule could read it in his face.

She hated the *if* part of the *if and when*. She told herself, *when* they found the missing ones.

Dr. Murasawa had sent information as well. Hers was radically different. She'd started with the drones at the job site, which wasn't that far away from where they were out in the desert.

The solar array was getting installed beyond the town of El Indio. While it was south of where Sarah had initially disappeared and where Cage and Aurora had disappeared last night, the drones could cover some space.

Unlike when Cage and Joule had gone out with them, and had stayed close, keeping the drones in sight for fear of losing them, Dr. Murasawa seemed to have put together a little team that had no such concerns. Even her notes said, "I flew them as far as I could, until I was no longer certain I could get them back with the power that I had remaining."

They zigzagged, sending drones out in multiple directions, grabbing high quality images of the ground beneath them. Again, Joule saw nothing but sand and shadow, brush and rock. However, the images caught a group of five people heading north.

Through the video, Joule watched them trudge slowly through the desert. She put her finger on her own screen, motioning to Maeve and Kathryn. "Are they important?"

"I don't think that they're in the same situation that your brother Aurora and Sarah are," Maeve dismissed the group.

Joule understood. These weren't people with one of the local cartels.

"These are just migrants," Maeve said with such conviction that Joule had asked, "How can you tell?"

The woman pointed out the clothing and the lack of organization, though none of it seemed any different to Joule. But what did she know? Maybe her brother was out in the desert tonight in full tactical gear.

Kathryn had been busy on her own phone. Though Joule had assumed she was cataloguing pictures, it appeared she'd been in Cage's tracking app.

"He got two text messages from you before the phone turned off."

"Yes," Joule agreed. She'd already seen that. It wasn't like he'd answered.

He would have had he been able to, she knew. So, the phone had been taken away from him or something.

The look in Kathryn McQueeny's eyes as she held the phone up was more severe. "If they destroyed the phone, then they lost this information. That would be good."

Joule didn't understand. But Kathryn wasn't done.

"If they kept the phone . . ."

Something about the tone told Joule what McQueeny suspected. Her breath sucked in, and her eyes closed as Kathryn asked.

"He has the same tracking app on his phone for you?"

Joule nodded and her heart almost stopped beating.

"Yes." The word slid out slow and low as the implications of that sunk in.

52

Cage jolted awake, not entirely able to discern what had woken him.

For three nights now he'd barely slept. They'd been in the cave, then, last night, they'd been shoved here, into the back room of the little house. Every time he did start to rest, he came alert at the slightest shuffle or noise. The cave echoed sound and the room was full of others also shifting in their sleep. This was almost too quiet.

It appeared none of them slept deeply and Cage was no exception.

He opened his eyes into the pitch black of the night—nothing seeped through the blackout curtains. Maybe it was the early morning hours, but still he was grateful that no one could see him. With effort against the pressure of his pulse, he tried to keep his breathing low and slow. Whatever had alerted him needed to not know it had done so.

He'd watched Terrence the past few nights as they were all shuffled out into the desert for long treks. It was the same story both times. Something was carried out in backpacks and duffel bags and left for a small, heavily armed contingent to gather it.

Connor, it appeared, never touched the stuff. Terrence handled everything, Connor only pointed, sometimes with just the barrel of the silver Colt he liked to wave around. If he had to handle anything, he only did it when he was wearing leather gloves.

Cage was beginning to wonder if Brown Eyes even touched it at all. Maybe even they didn't know what it was and were merely content to be the distribution center using teenagers and young adults as their mules.

A soft shuffle from across the floor now told him something moved. Cage didn't.

Near him, one of the teenage boys rolled over on one of the mattresses that had been thrown on the floor, a soft mutter coming from his throat. What Cage now recognized was that the footsteps didn't stop with that noise.

Time for a test.

Cage breathed in deeply, a heavy sigh that hopefully signaled deep sleep, then he shifted just slightly onto his right. This time he closed his eyes. Though he hadn't adjusted yet to the dark, there had to be a small amount of light leeching in. He wouldn't want someone to have the advantage of dark adaptation and see his eyes open. Cage would have to go by what he could hear.

As he rolled over, the footsteps paused.

Shit. Whoever it was was paying attention to *him.*

He couldn't help but tense every muscle in his body, though he worked hard to make it seem on the outside as though he were still asleep, still relaxed, still oblivious to the world.

It was an indeterminable amount of time before he heard the shuffling softly begin again.

The steps seemed closer. Had he missed a few? Had he possibly dozed off for just a moment?

Cage knew he was tired enough that anything was possible.

What he was certain of though, was that it was Terrence and that it wasn't anything good.

Another step, another shuffle. He was close now, almost in striking range.

One deep breath.

Cage heard the footstep right near him. He considered rolling away but instead he rolled toward the feet. Just as he heard the fabric of the mattress rip behind him from something sharp aimed at where he'd been lying.

If he hadn't rolled when he did . . .

It might not have killed him, but it would have done serious damage. Lord knew, in here, infection was a high possibility. No more. He wasn't going out like this.

Cage used his momentum and kept rolling, crashing into the legs of his assailant. He wrapped his arms around the other's calves as he moved his own legs and tried to get to his feet.

Sure enough, there was a heavy thud and a startled *ooof!* as the kid hit the floor on his back.

The sound alone was enough to tell him it wasn't Terrence.

Son of a bitch.

Cage was on his feet, rolled upward on his toes, his knees bent, his hands out at his side, finally able to make out a little light coming in from the gap at the top of the room that he could match to the sounds he heard.

The kid scrambled to his feet quickly, backing away.

As he swept his gaze, Cage was glad to see the room became clear. Cage had been in the dark for some time now, and he was adjusting. To top it off, the metal of the blade was dull, but it was still enough to reflect a bit of light so that Cage could see where it was.

And that he was too late.

The blade had been palmed and was already swinging at

him again. The unpracticed hand was thinking to slash rather than stab and twist.

It should be easy enough to block—two fists up and swinging to the left. Cage knocked both his fists down across the striking arm and heard the noise in response. He would have liked to take control of the kid's arm to grab the knife and gain charge of it. But it wasn't that easy.

The kid wasn't that good. He jumped out at the contact. That kind of strike didn't feel good, Cage knew that much.

It had been too hard, too painful for some kid whose heart wasn't in it. His fist opened almost involuntarily, dropping the knife to the ground.

But Cage couldn't tolerate attacks. Grabbing the boy, Cage used his forward momentum against him and slung the kid back onto the mattress. Of course, that didn't go as planned either.

The boy tripped on the edge of the thick piece and went sprawling, his head hitting the wall with a slightly sick thud. It was a worse sound than when he'd hit the ground.

Fuck, Cage thought.

He turned for a moment to check on the boy, but the kid stayed down, slumped against the mattress. His assailant ended up with his hand to his head, not knocked out, but willing to be down for the count.

Another noise popped from behind him. Whirling around, Cage found what he thought at first now turned out to be true.

Even though the kid attacking him hadn't been Terrence, it had clearly been Terrence's plan. Terrence was on his feet now.

Cage had had enough.

He stared at Terrence in the dark. Just enough light came in to let him know he was looking the young man in the eyes. "Not man enough to do your own job?"

Confident that would enrage him, Cage was happy when it

elicited a snarl. Still, he couldn't afford to outwardly react. It worked almost too easily.

"I run the show," Terrence growled out.

Cage couldn't help it. The laugh bubbled up out of him. "The show you're running is a shit show, Terrence, and the way you're running it you're not going to be king for long."

Cage gestured with his hands out to his sides, showing off Terence's "kingdom."

He'd been cocky, trying to bait the asshole. Cage wasn't prepared for the hands that grabbed him, locking onto his forearms, fingers tightening down hard enough to bruise.

They held him tightly while Terence picked up the abandoned knife.

53

"We didn't find anything useful," Jacob told her over the phone, and Joule hated the answer. She needed these calls to yield more, to move more information or tell her they'd found her brother and Cage was coming home.

She'd wanted to go with them but understood why the Maverick County Sheriff's Department was not going to let her help them serve a warrant in the middle of the night.

The footprints in the desert that David and Dr. Murasawa had followed via satellite led to a small town—maybe just a cluster of homes. Though the footprints didn't do them the favor of leading directly into one home, there was a house right near there that had a history of criminal activity.

The sheriff's deputies had served the warrant and searched the place.

"What *did* they find?" Joule asked. She had to at least know the pertinent follow-up information. She wouldn't lose her brother because she didn't dot her I's or cross her T's.

"Only the Lopez family. Father, mother, high school aged daughter, junior high age son."

"There's a school out there?" Joule asked.

"No. They bus to one of the schools at the edge of San Antonio."

"Damn." The word slipped out, but Jacob McQueeny murmured along, agreeing with her.

That wasn't the issue, Joule knew. The Sheriff's Department was only allowed to look for what was listed on the warrant; they were constrained by what they could convince a judge they might find. She wasn't.

Joule tucked away the name Lopez for future reference. She'd found the address herself when Jacob refused to give it to her. He must know that, with all the technology available today, she would do exactly that. If necessary, she would go visit the Lopez family herself.

"Other footprints?" she pushed.

"There was nothing there. Nothing out of the ordinary. We had the warrant, and the warrant is limited," he reminded her, "But even beyond the warrant, we didn't see anything."

"There are other houses in the area," Joule added.

"But we can't just get a warrant to search them. And it doesn't help that we served a warrant and didn't find anything."

Her heart sank. It was 3am and she'd been hoping for good news.

No, she'd been hoping they'd tell her they had her brother, and she was to come collect him. But she'd have settled for good news.

This was her fault. She'd told Jacob to call her when it was over. She'd known they were waiting until the middle of the night to serve it.

"We woke the Lopez family and bothered them for nothing." There was a shrug in his voice.

Assuming the Lopez family weren't involved in this, she thought. Maybe they were just better at hiding it than the Sheriff's Department was able to find. Right now, to Joule, everyone looked like a suspect. Everyone would be treated like a suspect until she found her brother.

With so little information to be had, Joule found she didn't even have more questions. She thanked McQueeny and hung up, angry at yet another failed avenue.

The phone had woken her from a deep sleep—the first in several days. The little search team had been out again last night following footsteps again.

The tracks were fainter now, much fainter. It was just enough to find reminders that they were on the right path when they followed the images and locations from David's satellite hack. Joule tried not to draw conclusions between the fading footprints and the likelihood of ever seeing her brother again.

They were simply trying to see if they could find any information along the way—anything they could take to the sheriff or the DEA or . . . anyone. But they'd not gone the whole distance. It was too far, and Jacob, Kathryn, and Maeve all suggested that they not give indications of where they were headed. They shouldn't trek up as a group and give the houses at the other end of the footsteps any warning that they were coming.

It wasn't like the HST workers could do much of anything if they found it. Though Joule was more than content to think she and Malcolm would just be angry enough to break laws and break their family out, the others wouldn't be so rash. But who knew what was there?

Joule sighed into the dark. She was awake now and her brain was churning even though she should be going back to sleep.

She'd spent part of her day following along as they brought Gretchen Mueller in for questioning. But the woman had given up nothing. The Sheriffs had let Joule watch through the window into the interrogation room, though she'd not been allowed to say or do anything other than observe.

She'd been impressed with Jacob. He pushed. He'd said, "We know that you know Sarah," and he'd slid Sarah's picture across the table.

Gretchen calmly shook her head. "I don't know her. I've not seen her before."

For a moment Joule had wondered if Jacob might have been able to catch the woman. If he'd said, "We know that you know Tara," and let Gretchen correct him. But he hadn't done that, and the opportunity was gone. So, all Joule had to go on was the flicker in the woman's eyes as she looked at the picture. She looked sad, as if she regretted what had happened to Sarah. Joule wondered if she might have been able to bank on that sadness in a way that Jacob McQueeny had not.

Had she been able to go to the woman herself, slap her hands on the table and say, "my brother is missing now too!" and beg for help finding him, it might have worked. Joule was not above begging at this point. Cage had been gone too long. They passed out of the "Golden Window," and they'd passed Sarah's golden window a long time ago. So Joule was more than willing to leverage her fear and her need to reunite what family she had left to make Gretchen Mueller talk. But she hadn't been allowed and the moment had slipped away.

Jacob said he'd consulted with his DEA sister Lindy. Though he'd not handed the case over to the agency, Joule was glad that at least the DEA was involved. Any advice they had might be put to good use. Joule began to wonder if letting the sheriff's department handle the case was truly the best track. In fact, she decided it wasn't. It couldn't possibly be. But it was 3am and there was nothing she could do about it right now.

She punched the pillow, partly because it was flat, and partly because she was. She needed to hit something, to feel the smallest pushback from something real. She wanted to believe that she would know if Cage had left this world. He was after all, her twin. She should know if something had happened to him.

She'd had a bad feeling the night her mother had died. But it was no evidence of any psychic ability. The family had been hiding from the Night Hunters, the twins down behind the washing machine. When her mother had said, "I've got this." How could she *not* have had a bad feeling?

The answer was that Kaya *had* gotten it. She'd saved them all. But not herself.

Then, even when their father had gone missing, he'd gone off to protect his children. He'd been absolutely crazy, his grief utterly obliterating his decision-making process. His choices had come from a twisted combination of revenge for his wife and love for his children.

But with Cage being missing, there was no purpose to it. There was no greater good that anyone was trying to serve.

Her brother was simply gone.

Joule had already given Jacob McQueeny forty-eight hours. Looking over at the clock, she saw it now had a four on the front of the number.

Excellent. McQueeny had two more hours, and then she was taking matters into her own hands.

54

His arms were held out, his torso exposed, and Terrence now held the knife.

Cage pulled his arms inward, testing the strength of those who held him. They were firm. Firm enough? He didn't know.

This could go poorly, very poorly, for him. Even if he won this fight, what did he win? But if he lost? Cage had some very good guesses how badly that would go. There was no conceding here. So, he had to fight and he had to win.

"I've had enough of your bullshit," Terence said.

Cage fought the smile for a heartbeat, before deciding to let it bloom.

"What's so funny?" Terrence demanded, his knuckles white where he gripped the worn handle.

"You swear like a child, you absolute fuck knuckle." Joule would be proud of him.

More importantly, it had the desired effect, making Terrence lunge.

Placing all of his weight on the two holding him, Cage

jumped. They'd left his feet unattended, and he would have thought that they would have learned.

Besting Terrence would not be easy this time, not with three of them. So, Cage went for it. He kicked Terrence in the chest, using him for force and the hold on his arms as anchors as he flipped up and over.

It was a move he'd never tried before, and it really didn't work.

The two on either side of him were not prepared either for his weight or for the twist in their hands, and they let go far too early. Cage managed to get his hands down and barely stopped the hardwood floor from cracking his head as his rotation carried him around just enough to jam his toes into the ground. At least it wasn't his knees, or his face.

He scrambled to his feet, the knife on the ground between him and where Terrence had dropped it from the sudden kick. Dude was trying to get up off his back. Unfortunately, the fucker had fallen onto a mattress, having gotten a much softer landing than Cage did. The only good thing it did was make it a little harder for him to get up.

Taking advantage of the half moment that he was granted, Cage let the anger of the situation diffuse through him. The two who held him were ones that he had fed.

Turning, he glared at them. "Are we done?"

Neither answered. Their eyes moved toward Terrence as if to ask him what they should do.

"Grab him!" Terence commanded, though as they started to move to do his bidding, they were more tentative this time.

Cage balled his hands into fists, only making threatening gestures at this point. He wasn't ready to throw anything. But he stared at Terrence, who was once again standing on his own two feet and staring Cage down.

Cage opened his mouth, hoping his words carried to the ones who had held him. But, as he began, he realized the whole room should take it as an address. "If you side with Terrence, you get what Terrence gets."

Terrence's eyes narrowed but, for half of a heartbeat, there was a flicker of fear.

Good, Cage thought.

On either side of him, the two still remained uncertain if they should reach out and hold him or not.

That was okay. Maybe he would get a fair fight.

Between him and Terrence, the knife still lay on the floor. Cage thought of the old adage about not starting a fight, but ending it. His original intent was to meet aggression with aggression. But if he did, then Terrence would always step up.

Instead, he would have to go for intimidation. Stepping forward, he moved himself closer to the knife than Terrence was.

"Try me," he said, and kicked the knife to his opponent.

Startled at the gesture, Terrence reached down and snatched it up. A snarl curled his lips, as though Cage had made a mistake, as though he didn't realize he'd been set up.

Cage could only hope it worked, but he didn't let any of that show on his face. He could only hope the two beside him didn't interfere. If they thought the tide was turning, and Terrence might get ahead in this fight, they might try to hold him down again. And that could be the end of him.

It was possibly the worst decision he'd ever made. But as Cage watched, the two beside him slowly backed up, surely afraid of a man willing to kick the only knife to his opponent.

Terrence was not as unskilled as the first attacker. And Cage didn't have enough eyes or arms to worry about what was behind him. He could only hope they were intimidated enough to stay put.

Terrence lunged, stabbing with the knife. But Cage saw it coming and deftly slid to the side. He would have liked to reach up and block him—jabbed or grabbed something—but

Terrence was quick. Maybe quicker than he'd been the first time.

Maybe he'd learned. But Cage had learned, too. This time when Terrence stabbed at him Cage was ready. He didn't even go for the knife. He stepped aside and then forward, moving into Terence's personal space, putting the knife beyond him. He now had to control the arm before Terrence could try to turn the knife and stab him in the back.

Cage once again wrapped Terrence's forearm, controlling it. He shouldn't be able to use the same move twice, but he did. And it told him a lot about Terrence.

He took advantage of the surprise. Bringing up the heel of his hand under Terence's chin at a high speed, Cage heard teeth clack and maybe crack as his opponent's head whipped back with the startling hit.

The kid howled and Cage felt a momentary pang of pity. The kid was surely just a product of his environment. Too bad. Cage didn't start this fight. He'd ended one before and it hadn't been enough. He had to do more this time.

He had to make a move now, one that was solid enough and strong enough to quell any future attacks, too. Though he hated it, he used the arm he held and swung around so he could face the rest of the room.

Cage repeated his earlier warning. "Anyone who sides with Teen Woof here gets what Teen Woof gets."

He still controlled Terrence's arm, and he had to be quick before the kid recovered and made another move. So he brought his free elbow down across Terence's forearm and heard the sickening crack of bone.

55

The car was still here.

Good, Joule thought as she put her own car into park.

She sat for a while, just beyond Gretchen Mueller's driveway. Though nothing else had happened, at least she was doing something. She contemplated going into San Antonio to get a rental car. Was she too late for that though? She was already sitting here in her own car, and maybe alerting Gretchen that things weren't as they should be.

Also, a rental car would be shiny and bright, it might stand out and be just as recognizable as her own car. Joule held onto a brief thought of driving out into the desert in the rental and throwing fistfuls of sand at it to make it dirty. But she'd have to use a hose to make the sand stick. *Maybe,* she thought, maybe if she needed to do it. Maybe if Gretchen Mueller recognized her car.

It was an hour before anything happened. And what happened surprised Joule.

The door open and Gretchen Mueller came out with a baking dish in her hands. She walked her very short flagstone front path to the edge of the road where there was no sidewalk. It didn't matter though. Joule had already seen that there wasn't enough traffic in El Indio, and probably not enough taxes either, to warrant the building of sidewalks.

Gretchen Mueller walked slowly, balancing the pan. Given the towel she carried it with, it must be hot. Had she been baking this early in the morning? It would appear so. She made a sharp 90 degree turn into another yard that didn't even have flagstones, just a worn path through the gravel. Balancing the pan against one hip, Gretchen knocked on the door, then knocked again waiting until the resident opened.

When it finally happened, it was a small, frail woman, much shorter than Gretchen. The woman, who was old enough to be Gretchen's grandmother seemed incredibly grateful and held out her hands for the pan. But Gretchen refused and seemed to insist on carrying it inside herself.

A secret rendezvous? Joule thought. Using a frittata for cover? But no, Gretchen reappeared a few moments later, seeming to have simply done a good deed for her neighbor.

Not what Joule wanted, although honestly, maybe what she should have expected for a woman who had been arrested multiple times for helping migrants. Maybe this wasn't the place to be. She thought they'd already interrogated Gretchen. Gretchen was lying low, making casseroles for the neighbors.

The person they'd missed was Salvador Torres. Though Jacob had told her several times that he'd tried to get a warrant for the matching tire prints, even with the gravel stuck in the tread it wasn't enough.

Not enough for the Maverick County Sheriff's Department. But it was more than enough for her. Putting the car in gear, she drove past Gretchen Mueller as the woman walked back toward her own home.

There was no hint of recognition on the woman's face, perhaps only curiosity that a car she didn't recognize was driving down her street. El Indio was small so she should have been suspicious of a car she didn't recognize. But it was possible that the addition of the HST workers had made the town more lax about that.

Joule was done with this. Luckily, heading to the other side of town was just a short jaunt. She stopped herself along the way, driving through the one little place that served breakfast lunch and dinner. The heat seeped in through the car window when she rolled it down to pay, and though it was morning, there was only so much the air conditioner could do.

How many of these stupid breakfast biscuits had she had? It would have been more if she hadn't skipped breakfast so many mornings. She took the bag, smelling the desert on the air more than the food.

This was more like home cooking than what she usually got at a drive through, but nothing she could synthesize right now. Still, she chewed and swallowed. She needed the energy.

There was no excuse not to be in the best shape. But because she was eating methodically, she ate fast. Wadding the wrapper, she threw it into the passenger seat. She'd get it later.

Then she was there at the apartment building. Her car had been here enough times before so, unlike at Gretchen Mueller's house, she shouldn't look out of place. But this time she was done watching and waiting. The white car was here. Same plate. Joule was confident the gravel was still there, wedged into the treads of his tire.

Cranking the key and turning the car off, she opened the door and tumbled down into the heat. It wrapped around her, and she took whatever strength she could from it. Even if she didn't like it, at least she didn't sweat. She didn't even have the energy for that.

Joule channeled all of it instead and, had anyone been watching, they would have seen her marching angrily across the parking lot. She picked her way right through the small hedge of scraggly bushes directly to apartment 104 where she banged on the door.

Nothing happened. She banged again. And again.

The elderly woman in the next apartment opened her own door and frowned. "Honey. What are you doing?"

Joule didn't even answer. As if it weren't obvious. She banged on the door again.

When nothing happened. She impulsively grabbed at the knob and turned it, surprised when it twisted beneath her hand.

It had to be a sign.

Whether it was from the gods or whatever demons had her brother, she didn't know.

But she was done messing around. Joule swung the door wide and looked inside Salvador Torres' apartment, surprised by what she found.

————————

56

"I don't know about your friend," Salvador Torres insisted. He stepped forward, filling the now open doorway and blocking her view inside.

His voice was firm, but he wasn't impolite about it. Which was surprising—and telling—given that she'd just opened the door and almost walked in after he'd blatantly refused to answer her knock.

Joule was done with bullshit. She shouldn't have been so bold, but she had nothing left if not boldness. "Yes, you do. You know something."

He looked at her a little askance. "I heard you were out in the desert looking for her."

"You heard about me? Being out in the desert looking for Sarah?" Joule crossed her arms and cocked one hip out, her eyebrows following suit, as she questioned why he knew anything about her at all.

He pressed his lips together, giving nothing more.

She didn't have time to waste on his self-preserving silences. "So, you, or someone you know, was headed out toward the desert and saw my car?"

He only blinked. She read it as a yes.

"Were you following us?"

"No." This time his answer was clear and crisp. The other one had been a yes.

"If you weren't following me, then you were headed out to the desert anyway on your own," she pushed, testing him. His lips pressed together. "You were going to the same spot, but we happened to already be there."

When he didn't say anything, she tried to hold back, but it boiled out of her. He was leaning on the doorjamb and blocking her way inside but looking so casual. She hated him for it. Her emotions were running wild, and she was losing the tether.

"Your interference got Sarah kidnapped or killed! And trying to find Sarah got my brother and Sarah's mother also taken!"

"*What?*" Salvador asked. He stood up straight at the idea of it.

Almost before she could react, he reached out, grabbed her wrist and yanked her inside, slamming the door shut behind her.

Joule should have been faster. This wasn't a good position to be in. She was on his territory, and he hadn't proved himself useful yet. He was likely even dangerous. But she was in, and unless she wanted to scrap the whole thing and turn and at least try to flee, she should see it through.

It would have been better had she told anyone where she was going.

She hadn't turned off her tracking app though. Maybe that would save her. Maybe it would get her killed. She didn't know.

Deciding to stay and look as confident about the decision as she could muster, Joule looked around the apartment. The easy conclusion was that it had been decorated by Salvador's grandfather, or maybe his grandmother. What looked like hand-tatted doilies sat in a neat row, one on each of the back headrests of the couch. Another was draped over each of the arms.

A recliner sat at the edge of the room, just under the front window, a throw blanket disguising what she could see from a few edges was worn and tattered fabric.

"You're missing two more?" He seemed genuinely surprised and concerned.

Joule felt the last of her worry disappear. It was probably a shitty decision, but she didn't feel afraid of him. She was likely playing this poorly, but she suddenly felt that—whatever he was—he wasn't the problem.

"What do you mean my interference got Sarah killed?" He was pushing her this time. And this time she held her tongue until he talked again. "You're right. We saw your cars. We were headed out Monday night. But when we saw you, we didn't even get out of the cars, just turned around and called it off."

She still didn't say anything, hoping for more.

He gave only a little. "Because of you, we didn't get water into the desert."

"You and Gretchen Mueller?"

He tried to hide it, but his head snapped back just a little at the mention of the other name.

Click, Click, Click. Little puzzle pieces snapping together.

"You know," she tried to play casual like he had, "Mueller's on the DEA's radar."

"Of course she is, they've arrested her several times."

"But not you . . ."

He crossed his arms again, huffed out an irritated breath, and looked off to the side. The white tank top, maybe even the same one he'd been wearing the other day, straight black jeans and bare feet telling her he hadn't intended to go anywhere. At least not right away. "Gretchen takes the fall. She's in her fifties. She's white. She's blond, blue eyes. German ancestry. She figured she'd be the last one of us who would actually get blamed."

"What else do you do?" Joule asked, curious if it lined up to what she'd been told.

"Food, water, clothing, occasionally directions . . . medicine." He shrugged. "We try to interact as little as possible. Just get them somewhere safely and alive. It's a hard road."

Joule felt her eyes narrow, there was something in the way he said the last part. "You know the road?"

He caught on. Meaning she wanted to know if he had traveled it himself.

"My parents and my older brother did. I was born just after my family got here."

Something in his eyes told Joule to wait him out.

"My brother didn't make it. He was six. He got all the way into the U.S., partway through the desert." Salvador waved his hand toward the back of the apartment, as if motioning into open land behind him. "He got a fever—something he caught along the way. My parents carried him and tried to help, but they had no real medication, nothing like that."

This time the lull in the conversation had him turning and looking at Joule, really looking at her to see if she understood. His arms uncrossed, straightening down his sides, fingers curling almost into fists. Not quite in anger, if she was reading it correctly.

"You can't tell anyone what I just told you."

"I don't want to tell anyone anything," Joule admitted. "I just want my brother back. I need Sarah and Aurora Walker back, too."

"What happened to your brother and Sarah's mom?" Salvador asked. This time he seemed to really want to know. He motioned her into a seat on the blanketed recliner. And she took it.

Joule needed to ask more about what they were doing out

there and when and what they might have seen. He had to know or at least have an idea what was happening beyond the migrants.

So, she told him what had happened to Cage and Aurora. About the trail the group followed trying to find them.

Salvador nodded slowly. This wasn't news to him. Which was news to her.

He swallowed and said, "Yeah, about that . . ."

57

Cage held the binoculars loosely in one hand. They were good sturdy army issue, heavy and loaded with bells and whistles. Connor handed him another pair and Cage used the strap to hang them around his neck.

He was the only one who'd been pulled out here into the living room, and he tried to listen while at the same time figuring it all out. He didn't recall Terrence having been pulled aside, but Cage might have slept through it? Or Terrence might not have visited the living room like this. Maybe this was simply first stage training.

Last night when he'd broken Terrence's arm, the young man had howled and the whole room had looked up in shock. Immediately, they all scattered back against the walls. Cage hadn't understood until the door had swung wide, slamming into the wall. The doorknob would have punched a hole had the hole not already been there.

He was still ratcheting Terrence's arm in close to his body, the broken bones mushy beneath his touch. Cage fought letting his own revulsion at that show.

Connor stepped in, gun swinging wildly as he aimed at everything and nothing.

Cage filed that away, too. It was a huge Colt revolver, but Connor didn't wield it well.

"What's going on." It wasn't a question but a demand for answers.

Terrence was whimpering. And Cage tried not to apply any more pressure than he had to. This was it.

Cage turned and looked Connor square in the eyes and said, "I'm Terrence now."

Connor had looked briefly to Terrence who had stared stoically, jaw clenched, until Cage squeezed his arm softly. It put enough pressure on the break to convince him. This time, Terrence didn't yelp but only nodded at Connor.

"All right. You're Terrence," Connor acknowledged. He slid the hammer back into place and then slid the gun down the back of his jeans.

"His arm is broken," Cage said, "he'll need care."

"Good luck with that," Connor offered with no concern at all before reaching all the way to the side where the door still swung wide. He grabbed the knob and pulled it awkwardly through its full semicircle arc to close it.

Even as the door had clicked shut, Terrence growled. The knife had flopped from his fingers onto the floor. Finally letting go, Cage leaned over and casually picked it up, folded it back together and stuffed it neatly into his pocket.

He looked around the room exerting every level of authority he could muster. "Does anyone here know how to set an arm?"

No one answered.

"Well, I think I can do it," Cage told Terence, staring him down. "So, you can accept my help, or you can live with that." He pointed slowly.

Terrence was trying to work only his shoulder, pulling his

injured arm across his body and holding it with his other hand. Still whimpering, he looked about to vomit. Cage understood. Intense pain could cause that, but the last thing he wanted in this room was vomit.

Still, he couldn't afford to give an inch. Turning in a small circle, he made eye contact with each of them in the dark and repeated his earlier comment. "Anyone siding with Terrence gets what Terrence got."

He waited until one by one they nodded.

The room had settled into an uneasy truce then, and no one had slept. He'd not been able to set Terrence's arm. Nothing had existed in the room to do the job. So now he stood here in the living room, being told to go and pick up bags from the corner. He took a half second to look around for the material he needed.

Cage also tried to pay attention to the protocol. He'd said he was the new Terrence. He didn't know what would happen to him if he was incompetent at it.

He would move all the backpacks and bags, line them up in the hall to be carried. He got to decide who carried what—at least for the men. The bags were different sizes—and so were his workers.

Once again, he did not think there were guns in these bags. He was growing convinced that someone would come out from the women's room and pick those up and distribute them to the other team.

"You're dismissed . . . *Terrence,*" Brown Eyes said, finding himself amusing.

Still, it was better than when they called him Faraday. They'd pulled it off his driver's license, and while he didn't want them to call him "Cage" either, having them sneer at the name his mother had given him had felt worse than being called Terrence.

"Can I take some of these magazines?" Cage pointed at the

coffee table. Old issues of Guns and Ammo, Psychology Today, and even People littered the glass surface.

"Whatever," Brown Eyes dismissed him. "I mean, if you need that kind of reading material."

Cage didn't contradict, just rifled quickly through, looking for the sturdiest ones. He realized they were addressed to someone who clearly was not here. What had happened to the owner of this house? Or were the magazines just arriving long after they'd sold it? He didn't want answers.

"Can I take one of the T shirts from the pile?" Old clothing was thrown in the corner of the room.

"They're hardly worth your time."

"That's the point," Cage said and immediately wondered if he'd given too much away.

Brown Eyes looked him up and down, finally realizing Cage wasn't just looking for reading material, but still not quite sure what was going on. "Sure. Take two."

He gestured toward the discards before he took another sip of his bourbon, not once moving from his too-casual seat on the old couch.

Cage took his finds and headed down the hallway. As he set the bags down one by one, he tried to line them up according to a plan and remember which ones were heavier weight, so he could give the lighter weight ones to the younger teenagers.

No one was watching him. He could hear the tv in the living room so he quickly unzipped the end of one bag and peeked inside. Plastic wrapped packs again. Only this time, he touched. Reaching in, he squeezed at them. It felt like stacks of paper, but he didn't have time to go further.

Cage began wondering if there was a way to get just one piece, a small sample that he could take for evidence. Not enough to throw off the weight for anyone claiming their stash. But that attempt was for another day.

The note he'd gotten from Aurora had only said that she

and Sarah were okay. It was good news, but not a lot of help. He'd had to wait so long to read it, needing to know he was alone and that he successfully hid that he was getting messages from the women's room. But now he needed to write back. He needed a pen.

With the bags all lined up, he let himself back into the men's room and noted that it hadn't been locked again. He held up the magazines and the old T shirts and turned once again to address the whole room. "I need a pen."

Silence.

"Who has a pen?" He was more forceful this time and one of the younger boys leaned over reaching his hand down between the mattress and the baseboards. That was a move Cage wouldn't have done, not knowing what might be down there. He didn't quite trust the place and he shouldn't. But the kid did manage to produce an old ballpoint pen.

"Excellent." Cage walked over, held out his hand for it, and pocketed it. Better if no one knew what he was doing. Then he turned to Terrence. "Do you want your arm set?"

It had been hours already, beyond ideal. But there had been nothing to set it with before. When Terrence didn't respond, Cage told him, "It's your choice."

Another blank reply had him turning and walking away. He sat down on the edge of the one empty mattress. Had they saved it for him? There was still so much to learn.

Thumbing through the magazine, he found a page that had enough blank space to write a return note to Aurora. He ripped the sheet out and folded it neatly stuffing it in his pocket. He wouldn't write on it yet. He wouldn't do everything all at once in front of these boys. Let them think him odd, he didn't want to play his hand.

Then he went about reading People. These were clearly at least three months old. Not that he usually read it though, so it was new to him, almost a respite from the dreary surroundings.

But it wasn't long until Terrence stood up and walked over, his elbow cradled in his opposite hand, his forearm laying across the other. He said only, "Splint it?"

"Okay." Cage acted as if it were no big deal.

Then, later that night, when they were out in the desert, Terrence with his magazine wrapped arm further back in the line this time, Cage brushed by Aurora and handed off his note.

58

Joule sat across from Jacob McQueeny. She had managed to sleep in this morning having been up most of the night. This time, she had information for him.

"Salvador Torres and Sarah and Gretchen Mueller are part of a group with close to fifty people. They help the migrants cross the desert." She laid out a little more info that Salvador had given her.

"Not surprising," Jacob said. "The only surprising part is the number. That's a reasonable portion of the town."

"They're not all from El Indio," Joule told him before she thought about the wisdom of it. She'd already decided she would tell him only some of it. Salvador Torres had given her no other names than the ones she brought to the table. So, she didn't have that information to share, but had the numbers and their locations maybe been too much? She did not want to get these people in trouble. Certainly not before her missing were found.

Honestly, she didn't want to get them in trouble afterwards either. She appreciated the work. They took a huge risk each night they did it.

"They leave out food, water, medication, birth control, clothing." She wondered if Jacob McQueeny was surprised by any of it. He didn't seem to be, though Joule had been.

What Salvador had explained to her about the coyotes and their willingness to take money and sell people in exchange was concerning. The goal of his group was to get as many migrants through on foot by their own hand as possible.

"They don't interfere," Joule told Jacob now. "They avoid interacting with the coyotes at all costs. They aren't prepared for a fight."

They just tried to give the people the means to get themselves away. Or at least that's what Salvador told her. For the first time she realized she'd eaten it up with a spoon. Now, only Jacob's healthy skepticism reminded her that she should dole up some of her own.

"Do they think their people get through?"

"They don't have people. They don't follow anyone. Just have points where they leave out what they collected. Some do and some don't." She paused. "The drop points have to keep changing. So word seems to get around among the migrants that they should look for the things, but to avoid the cartels, they have to find new places and not interfere with the drug drops. They've had trouble in the past with some of their groups getting surrounded and going missing."

That had perked Jacob up and he began asking questions.

Joule was glad she could answer this. She felt she had been smart, taking out her phone and tapping out notes getting dates for at least proximities whenever Salvador Torres could offer them. Now she used those notes to help Jacob who pulled out his own device and compared his own notes to the information.

"This one is actually really close to this missing file." He held up the phone and she tried to read a very tiny copy of an official document. All she could make out was that it was a missing persons' report. "Two young women from San Antonio went missing together. Street workers out beyond the edge of town."

He pointed to another couple of the approximate dates she'd given him. "These don't seem to match anything. But this one—" He pointed at another. "The family reported a young couple missing."

"They were illegal immigrants and they were reported missing?" Joule had always thought that wouldn't happen. Staying hidden was key, wasn't it?

Jacob held the file up toward her. "It's very uncommon. But they felt that what had happened had been so severe that it might be useful to help others. Or for filing for political asylum and mostly for getting them found."

"They went missing from one of the groups that Torres and Mueller were helping." They'd seen them twice, Salvador said. Then there were fewer of them the third time they'd seen them. For some reason, this group had hung out in the desert in the same place for a while rather than moving north or east and out of harm's way.

They had been searching for their missing, Joule realized now, and she felt a deep pang of painful kinship.

She looked to Jacob. "What's next?"

"We go out again. This time, let's see if we can take the drones that your company has?"

Joule didn't doubt that Dr. Murasawa would find a way. She just had to be sure her old boss wasn't shut down before this was over.

"On it," she told him.

"We'll meet out there tonight and follow whatever footprints we can find." He looked at something that came in on his phone then turned his attention back to her. "Clearly this has been happening for a while. Definitely a trafficking situation."

Joule's heart clenched. All along she had wondered about human trafficking. "They sell them?"

Jacob looked away for a moment as if knowing she wouldn't want to hear it. "I think they have to."

"What do you mean?" Her heart was pounding. She needed these answers, and she so badly didn't want them.

"Look how many go missing." He pulled up information from some of his sister's earlier research. It showed tracked footprints and how the research team had tried to follow them through, find out where they were going, how many disappeared. "Even with conservative estimates, there's far more going missing than the people working for them."

"Do you think they position them at different places around the country? Or along the border?" She reached for something better than being sold into some kind of awful situation. For her brother, and for Sarah and Aurora. Not that working for the cartels was easy or even safe.

"They might. But it's still human trafficking."

True, Joule thought. And it would make it that much harder to find Cage, Aurora and Sarah.

59

Cage stood in the hallway, pointing to each bag as the young men came out of the room. One by one they picked them up. At the back of the line was a man who appeared to be notably older than the rest of them, one whom Cage called Dodger to himself now. His age alone made Cage wonder about his fate.

He was meek and compliant, and Cage hadn't heard his name at all. In fact, he was relatively certain he'd never even heard the man speak. He gave him one of the mid weight bags. Then Cage handed Terrence one of the heavier ones, listening to the kid grunt as he threw it over his good shoulder using only the one. Cage meant it as a level of respect, though he had no idea how it would be taken.

Then they were outside, standing around and waiting until the women came out, their own bags slung over their shoulders. Though they didn't say anything, and managed to hide it fairly well, Cage saw both Aurora and Sarah's eyes go a little wide as they saw him standing at the front of the pack. He had the binoculars in hand and was clearly leading the group. It wasn't lost on him that he was now running drugs.

In reality, he'd really only stepped up a level inside the cartel. He wondered if he were caught and arrested by one of the agencies, if he would be able to explain it away. Then he reminded himself that Joule would get him the best lawyer.

Then Connor appeared, wearing the same thing he always did. Did he just not own anything different or were these the exact same clothes Cage had always seen on him? Was he in the same position as Cage and the others? Stuck between the house and the caves, being fed oatmeal and tossed the occasional old apple?

It made Cage assess his own situation. He was going to need to wash his clothes and himself soon, and he wasn't certain how that was going to work. But it was beginning to appear that Connor was no more free than any of the rest of them. He was just the asshole at the front of the line. And Cage was now second asshole.

They were all walking out into the desert in seemingly no real direction. This time he was paying as much attention as possible, adding what he learned to what he'd already gathered. They headed an entirely different direction than any other time. *Not helpful*, he thought.

Joule and the others would be trying to find him. This— along with the sheer distance from where they'd started— would definitely make it harder for them to pinpoint where he was.

Despite his newfound nervousness of being the one with the binoculars for his "team," he followed along. The men and the women stayed mostly separate. It took a little while, but he and Aurora managed to bump up against each other again. This time he passed his paper to her, a little surprised when another note came back to him. He held it palmed where no one could see it, not even willing to risk sliding his hand into his pocket yet.

They would start checking pockets soon. They had to. And

a note from Aurora could be problematic. He hadn't even thought of that the first time. He hadn't had his pockets checked since the first night. Maybe they just assumed there was nothing the lowest members of the group could pick up and save. But as he looked around, Cage thought even a rock would be useful.

His brain churned. If he got close enough to Connor, could he get the gun? But Connor didn't get close enough to them. Though Cage hadn't noticed the first night, as he remembered it now, even then Connor had walked a good distance in front of the group. Cage had thought of it as a leadership position at first, but now he was more than certain it was to keep Connor from getting scooped up if anything happened to the rest of them. If there was a raid, if whoever was picking up the drugs and guns decided to open fire, whatever happened . . . Connor wouldn't be in the crossfire.

At last, Cage tucked the paper into his pocket. They were closer now to the drop point—at least according to Connor's motions for the two groups to separate. Then Cage walked and walked until he could barely even see the women. At least he could still see Connor clearly and Connor was mostly headed in that same direction. Chances were that Connor stayed in between the two groups, keeping an eye on all that happened.

Though it had been dusk when they started out, it was beyond full dark now. Cage was beginning to consider himself a bat. His eyes had fully dark adapted to the night. He didn't even think about it on these walks. But he was staying in the cave or that room that had blackout curtains. These people did not want the group found. He saw the sun only for a little bit at sunset. Jesus, he needed some vitamin D.

He thought again about running, but there was nowhere to run. Even right now, if he ran, Connor would shoot. And Connor didn't have to be very good with the gun, he just needed enough bullets. Though Cage didn't know what caliber the Colt was shooting, they weren't .22s. The bullets would be large enough to stop him. They didn't even have to kill him, they just had to make it so he couldn't keep running. Which honestly, as far out from civilization as he was now, any bullet would do the job, given enough time and enough blood loss.

If he got far enough away to hide, that wouldn't work either. Connor and Connor's gun were enough to make the others do his bidding. They would search for him for hours. While Cage may have taken over the room from Terrence, they would all still take orders from Connor. If Connor told them to split up and find Cage and turn him in, no one would walk past him. They were all too afraid of the rangy, lean man whose eyes held nothing behind them but emptiness.

They would turn Cage in to be killed to save themselves in a heartbeat. He knew that.

None of that accounted for what would happen to the others if he did get away. They might be punished or executed. Especially Aurora, since she came in with him. At the very least they'd be moved far enough to never be seen again.

So, he stayed with the group, held onto the heavy binoculars, and made his way out to the drop point. Though Connor stayed at a distance, he motioned them to leave their bags buried in the sand and under a few key rocks.

As Cage dug, he tried to figure out how to do some careful recon. He put the bag into the hole and began covering it. Could he open a zipper? Pull out a piece?

What if they searched his pockets? What about the next day when the others—the ones who picked it up saw that their stash had been tampered with? If he stole something, he'd have to get away within twenty-four hours. It might be even less time. That was the only way. The alternative might not be survivable.

Cage had kept alert, though he didn't talk much at all. Just motioned the spare binoculars to one kid he almost trusted who did the work. He did see that the women's group, though they were still far away, didn't seem to get the same kind of instruction from Connor.

Interesting. Cage's own lack of knowledge gave Connor more work, and Connor didn't seem pleased by it. Also, Cage noticed they hadn't gone to the same place twice yet. It had only been a few nights, so who was to say what the pattern was? But it made him wonder how long Terrence had been, in effect, the king of the room. How long until Cage had Terrence's knowledge?

There were too many questions.

The bags were set. With Connor off in the distance, he hunkered down with the binoculars to watch their stash. Motioning for the kid to hand the spare pair back, he next handed them off to Dodger, wondering if it would get him in with the man and what that would mean.

Someone here had to know a lot more than he did. For whatever reason, there was something about the quiet older man that made Cage want to bet on him.

They waited an interminable amount of time until another group showed up. These six were dressed in nicer, cleaner clothes than the first batch. Again, they were strung with weapons, making it clear that if they didn't like what they saw, they could easily mow down Cage's entire group.

It hit him then: it was now *his group*. The responsibility of that weighed heavy, shocking him at the pressure of it.

On the way back, he made a point to hang back, trailing along behind the rest. Pulling up the slip of paper Aurora had handed him, he wondered if it was bright enough to read and if he could do it without anybody seeing.

He paused, waiting for the right moment, for the clouds to pass by and the moon to shine brighter. And when he read it, he took a deep breath.

He had his work cut out for him.

60

They'd come back in the early morning hours, directed this time to a new cave again with a large enough cavern filled with old mattresses. Cage saw food in a bag left on one of the beds. It wasn't enough, but it was better than nothing.

One of the kids started to reach for it, but Cage put a hand on his shoulder, using a firm enough squeeze to make him stop. If he ruled the room, he had to rule the room. He opened the bag with a hard look around and no audible protests.

He found an assortment of fruit. *His captors weren't as dumb as he thought.* Or the possibility that one of them was psychic crossed Cage's mind, giving him pause. That would make escaping very hard. Luckily, he didn't give it much credence.

More likely they needed to keep the people in enough health that it didn't cause problems. Every body in the desert could bring another pair of official eyes aimed at them. That would be the last thing they would want. Fruit was cheaper.

Opening the bag, Cage rummaged through. He found apples, a few pears—two of them dented—some not great bananas and a few oranges. But not enough for everyone.

There was nowhere safe or clean to set it out and sort it. Nothing to do but hand it out in some honest reasonable fashion. He hadn't been here when Terrence had been handed anything good, but Cage couldn't imagine it had gone fairly. Now, he was in charge. Time to get to business. His people were hungry.

He peeled the bananas, breaking them in half and handing a half to each person. He didn't want to handle all the food, but he didn't want to get into any shit in which he gave bruised fruit out and it was interpreted as more. Or, that it was unfair.

The halves made it around the room, and after a quick count he broke the remaining bananas into smaller pieces and handed those out, too.

"Hey, why is mine smaller?" one of the youngest protested quickly. Of course, he'd seen the difference.

"Because you're smaller and I gave you a lighter bag. If you'd like to bump up and carry one of the heavier bags next time, I'll give you one of the bigger pieces," Cage told the kid with a confidence that he didn't really feel.

The boy quickly popped the smaller chunk of banana into his mouth and didn't say anything else. The heavier bags were heavy. It was a burden to carry them through the desert.

Cage went after the oranges next, using the knife he'd taken from the fight with Terrence—confident it wasn't clean, but it would have to do. He managed to hand a quarter to each person. He divvied the apples and pears giving more to the bigger guys again. He checked for dead spots and knew that had he not been in charge no one else would have done this for them. Cage tried not to let that get to him.

He was handing out the wide slices when he noticed two of the younger boys lingered in the corner looking awkwardly at the food that they held. He didn't know how he figured it out, but he caught on quickly. He offered a pointed nod to them.

The look alone seemed to work, and the two boys moved

around quietly asking until they found someone willing to trade. One of them had given away his banana and the other his oranges. It wasn't great for nutrition, but there was nothing great here. Cage wasn't going to force them to eat food they didn't want.

He made himself the last one in each round of food delivery. When he turned up one apple slice short, he went without. One of the kids came closer and silently tried to hand his own apple piece off. Cage refused at first, but then the kid pointed out that he didn't like apples anyway. Cage traded one of his remaining pear slices and hopefully made a friend.

He needed loyalty. First, he had to figure out how to do it.

Cage thought about Sarah's note that Aurora had passed him. She was full of good information—on how the room ran, who was in charge, when the bosses slept.

Between the three of them, Cage had no doubt that they could get out. But he was curious how long it would take and what shape they would be in when it happened. Also, he knew some of them here would likely die in the process.

It wasn't a decision he was willing to make. He reminded himself that he wasn't making it. If they didn't get out, some of them would die here. There wasn't enough food. Hell, he had been the one to provide Terrence's medical care, even if he'd been the cause for needing it.

There was more than enough alcohol and guns in the living room that, if nothing else, someone would get shot.

Connor didn't have a conscience, so his threats would likely come to fruition sooner rather than later. Faster if Cage couldn't keep them all together.

He sat on the mattress and watched as they each moved to a separate spot in the room. They curled into a mattress or tucked themselves against a dry wall that formed a corner, getting ready to sleep.

"No," he said. "No sleep yet."

Several looked at him oddly, a few who hadn't spoken to him. But he spoke to them.

He asked, "Have any of you heard of Night Hunters?"

61

J oule was drowning. It had been three more days.

She'd yelled at Jacob McQueeny. *"How do you not know anything more yet?"*

How had they not had any more clues than the ones she'd provided herself? *She* had tracked down and interviewed Salvador Torres. *She* had followed Gretchen Mueller. *She* had talked with David and gotten links to his steady stream of satellite information.

"We can't do any of the things you've done. They aren't legal for us, and they're barely legal for you," he'd countered calmly as though dealing with irate family members was just part of the job.

She couldn't be "just the job." *Cage* couldn't be.

Even though she'd agreed to exactly that several days ago.

"What new information do you have?"

"We don't have any," Jacob said, shaking his head. When she seemed ready to press him again, he added, "Look at the data on the files I gave you. Some of them are several years old."

Jesus, Joule thought, mentally tabbing back through what he'd given her. He was right. Many of the missing person's reports were several years old. As many as there were, the disappearances occurred only once every handful of months—or at least the reported ones did.

There were probably more unreported in between. But McQueeny didn't have access to that and neither did she. What was she going to do? Knock on doors, ask who they were missing and when? No one who would tell her that would have forgone filing a report.

Shit.

But what could they even do if they didn't have anything new to work with? Was she going to wait two and a half more months before they got the piece that they needed? Did someone else have to die or disappear first?

She wasn't going to survive this. "What about Gretchen Mueller? Salvador Torres? What about their group?"

She had given him so much information, or at least she thought she had.

"What they're doing is only borderline illegal."

"Borderline?" Joule asked. "It either is or isn't."

He didn't address that. "What we know that they do isn't. The best we can get them for is littering. And no one's going to shut them down on littering charges."

At least the Maverick County Sheriff's Department wasn't trying to nab the people helping. Though he promised he'd stay in touch, he didn't have any more to give and she'd run out of questions.

Joule was worn out from her own high-strung nerves.

Dr. Murasawa and David and the HST crew were also exhausted. They'd gone back to working their day jobs to at least some extent—trying to keep Murasawa's decision to make the search a priority from being too painfully obvious up the ladder. And they needed to deliver a system to the client; it was already behind schedule before Sarah disappeared. They'd needed the break last night.

Jacob McQueeny, as well as Maeve and Kathryn had warned them to take the night off and lay low. Some message had come in from Lindy, some concern about a DEA bust in the area, and they didn't want anybody out who wasn't supposed to be.

Joule had hardly listened.

She didn't have a job to keep going to for her paycheck, though she was slowly draining their savings account. Lord knew they'd been doing that since they'd left their jobs in the middle of the mosquito incident.

How long ago was that? She thought it was more than a month now maybe. She could no longer count the days. She could see the weight loss in her cheekbones, and the lack of sleep in the hollows under her eyes.

It hadn't occurred to her until now how many of her conversations had happened with her brother until he wasn't there to have them. She hadn't noticed until now that so many of those conversations were the good kind—the ones where they would question the world. They wondered how to fix the government. The ones where they said, "Let's do something for Kayla and Ivy. They've been so good to us."

Now, she thought about her friends again, but this time in a selfish way. Joule picked up the phone and dialed Ivy's number.

Her friend answered on an anticipatory breath. "Hey Joule, is it good news?"

"It's no news," Joule said. The phrase popped into her head that that must be good news. But it wasn't. It wasn't now, when every moment led them further from Cage's disappearance. But it had always been Ivy's first question these days. Her second question followed like clockwork.

"Do you want us to come out there?"

Joule had been saying no. Saying, *I don't know what you could do*.

This time, Ivy pre-empted her. "I don't know what we could

do either, but we are extra sets of hands and eyes. And we're familiar faces and warm hugs."

Jesus, Joule thought as she felt her body almost break apart. In that moment, she let go. She had to. She was holding herself together with hope and work.

It was the right thing to do. In fact, she was late to the game. She said, "Yes. Yes, please come out. I have a house . . ."

Dear God, was she going to put them in Cage's room? Was that an admission that he was gone? In another way, she understood she was just grasping at the most vital things that she needed.

It was already late in the day, but Ivy told her, "We're almost packed already. We'll leave soon and make the first few hours tonight. Then we'll be there at some point late in the day tomorrow."

It sat on the edge of Joule's tongue to tell her friend—and almost surrogate parent—that it was okay, they didn't have to come. That she'd overreacted. They shouldn't worry.

But she didn't say it, she couldn't.

It was a lie anyway. She wasn't okay. They *should* worry. She needed them.

Jacob McQueeny had promised he was working on it. She'd let it ride. Now, with Kayla and Ivy on the way and the sun going down, she was somehow lonely, lonelier than she'd been. And bored!

How could she be so bored when she was strung so tight, all the feelings completely at odds? Yet, there they were, winding her up as tight as could be.

She hopped in the car, grabbed herself a drive thru burger and promised herself once again that she would begin eating better. She would buy food at the grocery store and maybe cook some of it for herself.

She promised she would start tomorrow, when Kayla and Ivy arrived. Tonight, she was heading out.

The car took the turns as if it knew where to go. It was a Monday. She knew what should be happening if the schedule was still the same. She tried to stay a good distance back. Not sure if she'd accomplished it. She sat on the side road watching for over an hour before she was able to put the car in drive and follow along, and then she tried to stay unnoticed, not sure if she was accomplishing that either.

Eventually she turned off the road to wait. Maybe she was too confident, but Joule believed she knew where everyone was going. She sat for ten minutes, hoping that that was long enough. Then talked herself into another ten minutes of waiting before she started the car again and headed out into the desert.

She was following Gretchen Mueller's tracks, hoping she could find where they parked the cars.

62

They looked at her oddly as she put the car in park. Climbing out boldly where she hadn't been invited, Joule closed the door behind her as if to punctuate that she wasn't afraid.

Trying to look casual, she scanned all the faces in front of her, not seeing Salvador Torres at all. The one she paid attention to was Gretchen Mueller. And there wasn't a flicker of recognition from the woman.

Wonderful.

"My friend told me to come here if I wanted to help?" Joule lifted the tone at the end, making it into a question as she held her hands up. "I didn't bring anything with me. But I can next time."

"Don't worry about it." One of the young women said and then looked her up and down. "You're at least dressed pretty well for it."

"Am I?"

The woman nodded. "You blend in."

Interesting Joule thought. When they went out searching

before, she had wanted to stand out. Be different from the sand and brush. Make sure anything that was out here could see them and see that they were no trouble. She'd chosen this clothing tonight simply because it was lightweight. The lighter color was to reflect the heat of the day, and the length was enough to cover her for the cool of the night.

Most of the workers—or maybe volunteers—hung back, seeming to go about their own business. They searched in the trunks of the cars and opened huge coolers, pulling items out and sorting things from one bag to another. Most of the bags they filled were just pale-colored, used grocery store plastic. The people sorted items into them and tied the tops into knots before setting them aside.

One guy had brought a reasonably thick dowel rod, and he strung his bags along it to make for easier carrying.

Smart, Joule thought. But her watching and cataloging what was actually happening at one of these gatherings was interrupted by one of the women who had been standing with Gretchen Mueller.

"Who told you about us?" There was a tone underneath that let Joule know that the woman was worried.

"Oh." She smiled and tried to sound casual again. "My friend told me about this a couple of weeks ago. She said she came out with you guys a bit. Youngish—my age—woman. African American. Wears her hair in a ponytail pulled back. Tara."

"*Sarah,*" Gretchen Mueller corrected immediately.

Joule couldn't help the way her eyes flicked to the woman's face.

Small crow's feet at the edge of blue eyes widened as she realized what she'd done. She did know Sarah. Joule had baited her for exactly that. She waited until Gretchen spoke again.

"You're looking for Sarah." It wasn't a question or an accusation. It just hung there, somewhere between them until the light desert wind blew it away.

Joule couldn't fight it anymore. She swallowed hard and nodded. "She's my friend and she's been missing for two weeks now."

The two women both nodded and Joule realized they'd caught the attention of the other people in the group. The young man that had been stringing his bags on the dowel stepped forward. "Do you have any idea where she is?"

"Not really," Joule said. "A bunch of us have been out looking for her though. About a week ago my brother and Sarah's mother were taken, too."

"Fuck!" the woman next to Gretchen said, turning around as her hand flew up to her mouth. Gretchen reached out putting a soft hand on the woman's arm. As if there were any comfort for this kind of thing. Joule didn't offer any since it would be false. "That's what we were afraid of."

"Does it happen often?" Joule asked.

The women shook their heads, but one of the younger men stepped forward. "We have to define *often*."

His friend, a caramel haired young woman who could have been a high school student told Joule, "Three years ago, one of the other group members went missing. And more than one of the sets of people we've run into have said that they had people stolen."

The man nodded, picking up the thread. "They get surrounded and, if they're lucky, *some* of them get away."

That sounded about right, Joule thought. "We looked at the footprints and that seems to be what happened to my brother and Mrs. Walker."

After that, the dark night air went deathly silent, only the moon lighting the space between them. No one had anything else to offer her.

"But I am here to help tonight." Joule then added her other

hopefully bonus information. "I spoke with Salvador Torres, and he told me a little bit about it."

"He's not on tonight," Gretchen said. Joule only nodded, having figured that out for herself already.

"We go out most every night," Joule volunteered, then wondered immediately why she'd said it. She could only hope it worked for the best.

The dark-haired woman standing next to Gretchen opened her mouth to answer but Gretchen's hand came out as if to hold the words back.

"Who's we?"

Joule took a deep breath. "We've been working with Jacob McQueeny from the Maverick County Sheriff's Department." She did not add in his sister was DEA, that his mother was ATF, and another sister was a criminology professor who was also working the case . . . If the slow grind they had halted to could be called *working*. But maybe Gretchen would recognize the last name?

If she did, she didn't say it. She just grumbled, "The DEA doesn't like us."

"I got the impression that it's otherwise," Joule countered, once again, opening her mouth before even thinking about it. She had to remember these people might not be her friends.

"I've been arrested four times," Gretchen pointed out.

Joule immediately added, "And you've been released four times. With no charges."

The others nodded along. It was Gretchen who stepped forward.

"How do you know that?"

Joule took a deep breath as she looked at Gretchen Mueller. What would this woman do to her? What bad decisions had Joule made on not enough sleep and not enough food? She should never have played that card.

But it was too late now.

She should have told Ivy and Kayla at least where she was going. They were on the road. They wouldn't have been able to stop her. But at least someone would have known where to start looking for her . . .

63

Reminding herself that these were not the people she should worry about, Joule tried to fix her massive gaff. "Jacob McQueeny knows who you are."

"You're why they called me in for questioning!" Gretchen accused once again taking a step forward. Only this time it was her friend and one of the other younger men who put their hands out as if to hold her back.

She stopped and Joule was grateful that no greater restraint was needed. Not the best way to fix things. *Shit.* "I'm sorry about that. I truly am. I'm trying to find my missing twin brother. And they knew you were out here in the desert. Again."

The conversation paused and this time Joule decided that maybe she should play all of her cards. "So that you know, he told me the DEA doesn't *want* to hold you. The best that they can get you on is littering and no one will charge with that. As long as you don't do anything illegal in their faces, they don't want to take you down. You're not who they're after. I think they're more concerned that you'll get in their way or that you'll wind up missing."

She choked on the last word. Cage had been gone for far too long. Pressure dominated the back of her eyes and suddenly the desert was as gritty as the beach.

She couldn't cry now. Not in front of these people. Not when she stood in the desert alone, surrounded by people that she didn't know if they were enemies or friends. She reminded herself that if anyone could survive this long it was her brother.

"The Maverick County Sheriff's Department knows that because..." Gretchen Mueller pushed.

Joule remembered, these people didn't have a connection to the DEA or the ATF. At least not that she knew. She answered as generically as she could. "They brought you in. They check your records first."

Okay, she maybe wasn't quite playing all *her cards.*

The others looked at Gretchen as if to say, *maybe that's not such a bad deal.*

"Can I help tonight?" Joule tried again, fully expecting them to send her away. Though Gretchen still looked like she might, one of the younger men stepped forward taking over.

"We can always use an extra pair of hands."

Joule held hers out. "Thank you, and I promise I'm not going to give anyone your secrets."

Within a few minutes she was trained on what to put in each of the bags, a blister pack of Tylenol, 2 peanut butter sandwiches, apples and a guava.

No bananas. Joule was thinking that they came in their own peel. They should be—

"Bananas go bad too quickly."

She must have said it out loud. She needed sleep and food and none of that mattered. She couldn't stop until she found Cage.

She later realized she'd never introduced herself. With her hand out, she said, "I'm Joule Mazur. My brother who went missing is Faraday. He goes by Cage."

The kid working next to her grinned and laughed. "That's a fantastic nickname."

Joule couldn't help her return smile. It was the first time she truly smiled about her brother since the night she'd lost track of him.

"I'm Eric." He held up one of the guavas. "They're heat resistant, but buying a lot of guavas generally tips people off that this is what we're doing."

He put it into the bag along with a pair of cheap, light-weight sweatpants. Then the young woman ripped open a massive multipack of white T shirts, sorting a few of those into packs. They rationed two gallons of water for each bag.

One of the women had brought a small wagon to tug along. It had been retrofitted with all terrain wheels and looked like it belonged to a toddler trying out for the X-Games.

In a few moments she was paired with Eric and Lily, each of them loaded up with heavy bags and jugs of water. Eric hadn't given a last name but appeared to be of Hispanic origin. They headed off in a direction the two already knew and Joule followed along. Her eyes scanned the horizon as if she might magically just see her brother tonight.

Eric quickly turned his head back and asked her, "Do you speak Spanish or Portuguese?"

Joule shook her head at both. "I had Latin in high school, so I understand some of it, but I probably can't generate enough."

He nodded. "I do. So, I've got us covered if we run into anyone who doesn't speak English."

"Does that happen a lot?" she asked.

"Enough," Lily filled in.

The trio was quiet for a while, heading off in one direction as she watched other pairs go another way. After a bit, the question she'd asked before but not gotten an answer to pressed at her and she asked it again.

"Why do they do it?"

"Why do we leave out food and clothes?" Lily asked.

Joule almost laughed. "That part makes perfect sense to me. Not what you do, what they do." She waved her hand to the open, empty desert without a glimpse of her brother. "I mean, why do they cross? The journey is often fatal."

She thought of Salvador's older brother, who hadn't seen seven.

Lily was ready with an answer though. "Where they come from, it's worse."

That was hard for Joule to imagine, despite having lived on a street with the Night Hunters, and having lived with the mosquitoes. She'd thought that her home was bad, unsafe. She'd tried to figure out where she could move that would be better. But it was nothing like this.

"How is this better?" she asked.

"It's not that *this* is better," Lily told her. "The journey is rough, and it might be just as bad—just as likely to hurt and kill them as where they came from. But if they can get through to the other side, that's better."

"How bad is it where they're from?"

"No jobs," Eric answered. "No security nets. There's no government provided food, no housing. Not even the kind of charity that exists here in the US. People don't have it to spare. Aid organizations can't reach all the small communities, so they lose their homes. They starve. Families are often out on the street. So why not be on the street moving towards something better, rather than staying where things haven't been decent for a decade?"

"It's getting worse, too." Lily added in and Eric nodded his agreement. "It's very hard to drive the cartels out of the city. So, more and more cities are getting taken over. Border towns are prime property for activity because it's not just people moving across these borders."

That one Joule had heard before. This time she was

nodding along as she walked behind them, still scanning the desert. Still held upright by hope.

"The Rio Grande dried up last year for the first time."

"What?"

"The first time in any of our lifetimes. Even in my grandmother's," Lily told her.

"Yeah, there are portions of it you can walk right across." Eric told them. Still holding his dowel on either end, helping him carry a heavier load than either Lily or herself, Joule noticed. "In the past, when it got very dry it was still muddy, but it's nothing now. Just dusty riverbed."

"So, climate change is forcing people out of their homes?" Joule said as if to solidify it.

"Exactly. If you live in a rural area and have no steady income, you need chickens and farm animals and a garden. How do you do that when the river is dry? It's that and horrifying government policies that create untenable situations, dangerous ones."

Joule carried the bags on her arms, the plastic cutting into her skin. This was turning into the longest grocery run she'd ever made. Each time she set down a bag, she was relieved. But she couldn't drop them, only place them where the other two showed her. The three of them made what appeared to be a well-known loop for Eric and Lily.

Though her load was heavy, it probably wasn't as heavy as what those coming through carried. She told herself that and appreciated each piece she got to set down. Her back thanked her, too.

She'd been scanning the horizon and the ground all night —hell, she'd already found a body out here. At last, she spotted something and veered over to check it out.

It took longer to reach it than she expected. Enough time for Eric and Lily to really question her. But it grew clearer as she got closer: a duffel bag. It sat in the dirt in the open as if someone had dropped it and decided it wasn't worth it to pick it back up.

"We should take this," she said.

Immediately both Eric and Lily ushered a stern unison, "No!"

Eric held his hand out, grabbing her forearm as if his grip could stop her. "We shouldn't touch anything."

That made sense, but Joule didn't need sense. She needed to find her brother. Looking around, she saw no one in the vicinity. She stepped forward.

"Don't touch it!" Lily's voice was sharp. "We really need to get away."

"I need to see what's inside." Joule countered. She might not have cell service out here, but she still had a camera on her phone. So she began to take pictures. Once again, she lamented not ordering the satellite phone. It would have arrived by now. But their hopeful stance had been to save the money because surely they would have found Sarah before it arrived.

Oh, the irony of that thought.

She would have been able to pinpoint her location, even out here. More than that, she should have told someone— anyone—where she was tonight. But she was almost a pro at taking evidence pictures now.

Snapping a small, crooked twig off one of the nearby brushes, she hooked the spike into the tab of the zipper, pulling it back. She was not prepared for what she saw in the bag.

64

"The body was identified as Gregory Winters," Jacob told her. Once again, he was sitting at her small table, the two of them having their little update.

Joule shook her head. The name didn't mean anything to her. Her phone buzzed with another update from Kayla and Ivy. They should be here in the next several hours.

But she put her focus back on Jacob who was saying, "Also known as Marry Me Maribel."

"Oh." Joule felt her mouth go round. *That* name she recognized. There had been pictures in the missing persons report. "He was one of the two who went missing last winter. The two sex workers?"

"The family said she preferred 'she.' The cause of death was a bullet wound."

Joule hadn't seen one. But it hadn't been daylight and honestly she hadn't even recognized that it was a body when she first approached it. The sand had blown up against it. The clothing had draped over oddly from the wind. She hadn't been expecting a body.

"That's not good news," she said, and Jacob didn't counter

her. "If the people reported missing are turning up dead . . ." she didn't want to finish the thought.

"It's a shitty thing," Jacob added, tapping at the folder. "But I suspect she didn't fit neatly into what they needed. So, they disposed of her."

She sounded like a napkin, Joule thought, *or a used bag instead of a person.* That made her heart break. All of it was wrong. So wrong.

"Maribel was vulnerable in the first place because of the work she did." Her words came out with force behind them, anger at the general unfairness of the world.

Jacob nodded.

"And Misty Avington, who went missing with her?"

"She still hasn't been found." He sighed, and it occurred to Joule that this was her life, but it was his work. Hopefully her ordeal would be over soon, but he would inherit another one. "We put extra patrols in the areas where they work."

"Have more gone missing?"

He pointed once again to the files he seemed to always carry with him now. "Obviously, but none from that group."

Small comfort, Joule thought.

She looked over the autopsy paperwork, reading that a large caliber bullet was lodged near her spine. She didn't even think to question whether she should be allowed to read these reports, just went through them. The clothing appeared to be Maribel's own. She wore no shoes, though when she'd gone missing, she'd been in platform heels. She was one of the more recent disappearances. "She . . . mummified that quickly?"

He nodded. "The desert is harsh. Hot and dry."

Joule flipped through and began to put more pieces together. "How often do the cartels trade territories?"

"It can happen at any time." But Jacob seemed to understand where she was going. "But, given the timeframe, this was probably the same one that's still there now."

He didn't say "the same one that still has your brother, and Sarah, and Aurora."

Joule could only hope that they still had them, that they weren't dead and left to rot in the desert. *Like Maribel.* That they hadn't been traded or sold to some other place where they would be that much harder to find.

For a moment, she could imagine herself beating the information out of someone in an interrogation room. It was a thoroughly fantastical thought. It would never happen. She'd never be allowed into the interrogation room with her rage.

It was time to come clean to Jacob. What was done was done, and he couldn't stop where she'd already been. "I went out last night with Gretchen Mueller."

Though she'd learned a handful of names of the others, she gave none of them. Gretchen was already a known quantity. Using her name did nothing.

"Did you now?" He closed the file, placed his fingers on top of it, as if he were trying to hold himself back from saying more.

"We put out water and food." She didn't offer anything else, didn't mention how shocked she'd been at the birth control. That she'd learned up to ninety percent of the women expected to be raped at some point along the path.

She sat with that today, because *they still went.*

"We found a duffel bag," she finally told him.

"You didn't touch it." Not a question. A statement that he clearly didn't quite believe.

"Not with my fingers, no."

From the way his brows pulled together and his jaw ticked, that was not the answer he was looking for.

"Do you want to know what was in it?" she asked.

"Did you *take* it?" This time he sounded incredulous.

"No. I left it where it was. I never budged it. I used a twig to pull back the zipper. I looked inside, did not touch it with my fingers. Then used the twig to pull the zipper back into place."

"I hope no one saw you," he said, but he sounded as though he didn't quite believe that either. His tone was stern and dire.

"Me, too." It was the only answer she could give. "Do you want to know what was in it?"

He sighed. His head dropping into one open palm. "Of course, I do."

"It was animal body parts." She dropped it on him the way it had hit her. With no warning, nothing to stop the churn in her gut at even just the thought of it. Just mentioning it had her feeling the revulsion again.

"What?" But he didn't need her to repeat it, he was just processing the incredulity of what she'd said. Then he took a deep breath. "Oh, fuck."

65

Cage hadn't been prepared for them to say *yes*.

When he'd sat down to tell the story, he thought he would tell a story showing how he was brave. At least the way he told it, it would make him seem that way. It was necessary for his leadership in the group.

He told them a story that would make it clear that they were all better off if they stuck together. They would need that if they were going to get out of here. And he told them a story that he hoped would show them that he'd been in worse situations than this and survived it. Or at least, he made sure it sounded that way.

But when he'd asked if they'd ever seen a Night Hunter, he'd been surprised when one young boy had held up his hand.

"Like big dogs?" the kid asked, his English broken and stuttered. He made motions on his shoulders and indicated the size of the haunches of the Night Hunters. He pulled his fingers out in front of his face, indicating the long snout. Then held his hands up like claws to indicate the faces.

"Teeth?" Cage had asked, but the kid hadn't understood.

Not until another had turned and translated into Spanish.

Cage caught the word and, given his years of Latin in high school, he felt he should have been able to come up with it. Of course, he couldn't.

The first boy now nodded and quickly spoke back in Spanish. The second kid translated his answer as, "Too many teeth."

Cage didn't know if that meant that it just appeared that way when they growled or bit. Because that certainly was a scary thing to see, and it did seem in the moment of terror as if they were all slashing teeth. Or maybe the kid understood that the Night Hunters did not have the same teeth as dogs.

It had been Dr. Brett who'd explained to Joule and Cage what they had found. They'd noticed that the teeth in the Night Hunter they'd autopsied hadn't matched the veterinary book they'd bought. But it was Dr. Brett who told them that any change in the teeth—any change in dentition—was a speciation event. The Night Hunters were not dogs, but some entirely new species.

It had taken a little while, but using the second kid to translate, they'd cleared up that the boy had seen the same thing as Cage.

Cage had then returned to his story, telling the whole thing. Normally, it wasn't a bedtime tale. It was far too concerning. He watched as they curled into their corners and tucked themselves along the mattresses, each of them leaving space between them and the next one.

But how could the story of the Night Hunters be any worse than what they were already facing? He told it to his captive audience, trying to make a point.

He was surprised then as, at the last moment, Dodger moved. As the others dropped off to sleep, he stepped up close to Cage and pointed to his own chest. Then to his eye.

Cage didn't quite follow.

Dodger pointed to his mouth and made a claw hand.

Cage was still trying to put the information together. He

was more than grateful that Dodger was finally trying to communicate with him. And he was even more relieved when the boy who had translated earlier spoke up, even though he didn't move from his spot on the mattress. "He's seen them, too."

Cage felt his head snap back again. "Where?"

This time, Dodger actually spoke. The rapid-fire Spanish, far too fast for Cage to grasp even a word or two.

The first boy had been from Honduras, and it was a surprise to Cage that he'd seen the Night Hunters there. But now, Dodger said, through his translator, "In the mountains outside of Lima."

"*Peru?*" Cage hadn't been able to hide his surprise.

Dodger nodded.

Holy shit.

Cage had thought the Night Hunters were something that evolved locally in his own neighborhood. Honduras was far enough away to be concerning, but Peru was an entirely different continent.

Now, as he sat out in the desert—with yet another set of bags planted, binoculars to his eyes, watching for the staff—he started to spot the ones coming to pick up the goods. He thought again about the Night Hunters.

Cage scanned the land, he had to stay alert. But he also wondered if he hadn't seen any big cats because they'd maybe already been picked off.

He'd gotten a return note from Aurora.

She and Sarah had found a pencil and an old chopstick. Though it wasn't as fast as her usual skills, it was good enough. She was making work of redoing the front of the sweater. Aurora was the knitter, Sarah was feeding her what to knit into it. She had started a few days ago and managed to stay awake enough that she was nearly finished.

The note in his pocket now simply read, "ready by tomorrow night."

It wouldn't be enough. Not enough for him to open one of the bags and steal evidence. It wouldn't be enough for them to make a run for it. But hopefully it would get a message out. If only someone could find it—someone who knew what it was.

Still, right now, it was the best they had. They wouldn't set it aside until there was something better. But as soon as the opportunity presented itself, Cage would make his move.

His main problem was that Conor didn't like to present himself.

Cage discarded the idea of opening one of the bags and stealing evidence. As soon as the collectors carried it back and opened it, it would be discovered that someone had cut into it. He could imagine they didn't count every single piece, that a half ounce could go missing. But he had only the knife with which to open it and no way to put it back and even come close to looking like it was untouched.

Any decent accounting would see that something was missing.

Still, he'd reached in and risked leaving fingerprints and DNA and squeezed one of the bags. He didn't have gloves, so he made a calculated risk.

The contents slid around a little bit. He'd tested them again and come to believe he was transporting patches—the kind that would be used for nicotine addiction. Or maybe, as he'd heard, for easy fentanyl delivery. Because surely, they weren't smuggling anti-smoking patches.

He watched as five approached this time. Clad in their dark clothing like usual, they looked like total badasses out in the desert, armed to the hilt. He'd not yet seen them use one of the weapons, but he couldn't afford to assume they wouldn't.

Maybe they were merely intended to be a deterrence. But he couldn't bet on that. Still, Cage had begun to be less and less afraid of them, less and less concerned that they would simply open fire, and more and more curious if they even could.

Did they even carry ammo? He didn't know. Not anything he could see through the binoculars anyway. That didn't mean the weapons weren't loaded. He tried not to let his apathy make him stupid.

Hanging toward the end of the group on the walk back to the cave, he decided he was in the wrong place. So he pushed his way forward, hoping for a chance at Connor.

66

She'd tried to take a nap. It was clear she wasn't getting enough sleep. But it didn't work.

Joule tried to watch TV, but the idea that she might not hear a car approaching was too much. So, she sat with a cup of herbal tea, full of caffeine and loaded with extra spoonfuls of sugar, and waited on the couch.

Kayla and Ivy were close, she told herself, any minute now. She'd heard a car approaching a while earlier, but it had gone right past the house. She'd given good instructions and Kayla's nose for detail should have made it impossible for her and Ivy to go by without stopping. So, it wasn't them.

Not much traffic out here. Thinking of the time she'd sat in front of Gretchen Mueller's place, she must have stuck out like a sore thumb. How had they not caught her? Or had they, and Gretchen had just acted like she didn't know Joule when she'd turned up last night?

There were no answers. Not yet, and maybe never.

The one thing she did know was that she could no longer do that since she'd introduced herself to the woman.

A faint whir revealed itself and slowly it became the crunch of tires on old road. Unable to sit still, she set down the tea, headed toward the window, and looked out anxiously. Her heart soared at the car she recognized. She expected to feel numb, instead she was whipped wildly from one extreme emotion to another, even if the situation didn't warrant it.

Joule had already moved Cage's things off the bed and changed the sheets, though she'd left the old ones in a pile in her room. Would they become one of the last things he had ever touched? She told herself she would wash them when he came home. Not *if*.

The car parked behind hers, the doors opening as Ivy tumbled quickly out of the passenger side. Joule was out the front door and enveloped in a sturdy hug that lasted longer than she expected and maybe not quite as long as she needed.

Then even Kayla was stepping forward for a rote wrapping of the arms and a quick squeeze.

"You don't look okay," Kayla said.

Joule could only grin, "I'm not. How could I be?"

"Exactly," Ivy told her, draping her arm around Joule's shoulders and using it to pull her close and steer her back toward the house as if even walking on her own would be too much.

Joule felt her bones weaken, as if her joints were disintegrating, as if her own resolve was the only thing keeping her upright for these past weeks. Now that Kayla and Ivy were here, something in her decided to let go—just a little bit. She was sobbing before she knew it.

"I can't," she barked out her broken sentences through gulped air. "What if he . . .? What if . . .?"

Ivy shook her head, "I know. It's a worry. And it's okay to ask. But we're not going to believe it."

Joule looked at her as if to say, *how would they not believe?* Where should she find that faith?

"You have a dream team here." Ivy looked her deep in the eyes before pushing the front door open.

Joule took a deep breath. That she did.

She had a sheriff's deputy with big ambitions. She had an ATF agent, a criminology professor who knew the area, and DEA agents that she could get to if she had to. She had her Helio Systems Tech team, too. They were not only brilliant but driven to find two of their own who were missing. And now, Kayla. Also, Ivy was an art historian. But during the time she dealt in art and the work she'd done restoring historical homes, she'd learned to read people. She saw connections between things that Joule and Kayla didn't.

Kayla was a technical whiz. She made systems and organized things, and they could definitely put that to use now.

"First thing," Kayla said, "Ivy told me we need to feed you." Joule laughed. Kayla would say it and Ivy would be the one to dictate it. "Where is your kitchen?"

Joule led them inside, pointing to the bedroom to put their things down, which they did, with a solemn reverence knowing that they were getting Cage's room. Then Ivy apologized.

"We took a little longer on the way here. We stopped to look for a grocery store. There's fresh bread now, though, and blocks of cheese."

Kayla searched the kitchen cabinets and pulled a pan out and proceeded to make perfectly crispy grilled cheese sandwiches. As Joule sat by, just waiting—as it was all she could muster—Ivy chopped vegetables, made a salad, and pulled out a bottle of dressing. Both foods were shoved in front of Joule with no questions. She was simply expected to eat.

Next, the two women sat down at the table and joined her as if they needed to demonstrate how to do it.

Maybe they did.

Kayla had mastered the grilled cheese and where she'd sliced it, the cheese melted and pulled apart into perfect strings. Joule told herself she would be okay once the food was consumed. But then they began moving around. They cleaned the dishes, rinsing them and putting them in the tiny dishwasher.

"The dishwasher smells," Kayla said.

Joule shrugged. "I don't make enough dishes to wash it often."

"You've got to do it every three days anyway." Kayla said, noting it was still barely half full. Despite that, Kayla put the soap in and ran it, no further censure of Joule's poor house-keeping skills.

It was Ivy who shoved her back to the bedroom. "You need to rest. Kayla and I are getting to work. You can take some time off and then you can take over when it's time for us to go to bed."

"But you drove all day," Joule pointed out.

"We took turns napping in the car. We're ready and you need sleep."

Then she was gently shoved into the bedroom, the door pulled shut behind her. She wanted to tell them what they needed to know to get settled, what the passwords were, how to operate the tv, where to find things. Then again, they would ask if they needed it. And Kayla would either figure out the systems or reset them to make them work for her.

Joule toed off her shoes, climbed under the covers, and felt her bones melting again. Something about Kayla and Ivy being here made it okay to let go. She drifted into a hard, deep sleep.

Dusk had almost faded into night by the time her eyes opened. It had been a few hours, but it had been a deep, dreamless, restful sleep—maybe the first since Cage had gone missing. She almost didn't want to admit that she'd been able to do it. It seemed wrong to learn to sleep well without her brother. She didn't want to learn to eat well without him either. But she also knew that if she didn't do those things, she wouldn't have the energy to sustain the effort to get him home.

She recognized that they were reaching that point—where it would be her who would have to sustain the necessary level of fight. Others would start tapping out. They would admit defeat, but she couldn't. *Never.*

She blinked her eyes as she wandered out into the living room. Almost not quite ready for the voice that greeted her.

"You're up." Ivy put her hands on the table, flat on either side of her laptop, popping over to the fridge. With a quick flip of a bottle opener, she put a glass bottle in Joule's hand. "Mexican Coke, they have those in the stores down here."

Pure sugar and caffeine, delivered with fizz. *Exactly what she needed.* Joule smiled. Somehow Ivy had known.

The first big swig crossed her tongue and woke her up. Not normally a soda drinker—which Ivy also knew—she took it as the hit it was intended to be. Her eyes opened wide and Kayla grinned.

"I've been scouring the satellite footage your friend David sent."

Joule had been forwarding them links for the past several days, so she wasn't surprised that Kayla was doing that.

Ivy held up her hands. "I tried! It lasted almost an hour. But Kayla doesn't go cross-eyed and she doesn't miss details like I do."

Like the rest of us do, Joule thought.

Kayla was grinning. She clicked a few buttons, probably rewinding to a marked point. She motioned Joule over and pointed at her screen. "Look what I found."

67

"Where is that?" Joule asked, excitedly leaning over Kayla's laptop.

She set down the soda a little hard and jostled the nice glass bottle, though she did manage to stop it from toppling. "It looks like Cage."

Was it him? Was her brother alive? Joule felt every muscle in her body stop, even her heart. It probably wasn't him. But what if it was?

"Can you get a better resolution?"

"That we can't do." Kayla explained, "It's a satellite image. I've already zoomed it in as far as I can go. This is the resolution we get."

"Show me again?" Joule asked.

He walked like Cage. There was a group of people. Her heart still pounding, she couldn't help asking, "Sarah? Aurora?"

"It looks like only men."

"And boys," Joule filled in. "Though being young it's harder to tell."

"True. A lot of them look young, but I don't see anyone who looks feminine."

Looking at it again, Joule agreed.

Interesting. Still, she didn't like it. If they'd split everyone up it would make it harder to find the three she needed.

With a deep sigh in her soul and a stark admission of her own selfishness, she let the idea roll through her that she would find Cage first. And that she couldn't let that bother her.

After a few minutes of watching the same short clip over and over, Joule re-asked her original question. "Where is that?"

"Here." Kayla had already opened the map and overlaid it on the screen. "It's not that far out of San Antonio."

"Wait! Fuck monkeys!" Joule pulled up her phone scrolling through her messages. "That's very close to the house that the sheriffs served the warrant on."

"But there was nothing there, right?" Ivy asked.

"Nothing *they* could find." Joule felt the correction was necessary. "We can give them this, but they won't do anything with it."

She threw her hands up, exasperated. She didn't mean it like an insult. The Sheriff and even the DEA and ATF were constrained by legal limits.

"We can do this." Kayla said it with utter confidence.

Joule turned to look at her as if to ask *How?* Ivy's look asked *Why?*

"We can get thermal imagers—"

"Can you just buy those?" Joule didn't know.

"I think so. I checked around and it looks like we can rent a couple from our local hardware store."

Joule knew, as she'd been out here for a little while longer, that El Indio didn't have a "local" lot of things. Barely the one grocery store and the one drive thru. There wasn't going to be a local hardware store here.

"Wait," Ivy said, and Joule reacted as if Ivy were throwing a wrench in the whole thing.

Usually, she was more practical as well, but not now, not when her entire remaining family was on the line.

Ivy pressed. "What exactly are we going to do?"

"Well, I say we head out to the houses around here." Kayla waved a finger at the general area on the screen. "And we just check them with a thermal imager."

"So, we're spying on the people inside their own homes?" Ivy asked.

"No," Kayla said, again confident in her answer. "We're not spying. We can't see what they're doing. Not really. We're counting how many people are inside."

"What does that tell us?"

Joule had gotten used to this standard back and forth between Kayla and Ivy over the years. Kayla was the technological innovator usually, and Ivy was the one who tried to troubleshoot it.

But Joule was joining in now. "It tells us if there are too many people."

"What if they're having a party?"

Well, the only way to answer that was to admit that Ivy was right, too. "Okay, we are kind of spying on them."

Kayla wasn't giving in yet. "Let's be honest, think about looking through a thermal imager and seeing a party. You would see everybody in the main room, walking around, going into the kitchen, or onto the balcony. That's not what people being held captive look like."

At that point, Ivy conceded. "And if we find them, then what?"

Joule didn't answer, because she wanted to say, "I carry my gun and we bust in." But she was smart enough to know that she and her lone gun were going to cause more problems than they solved. What if hell broke loose and people got killed?

If she did that, she thought, if she got people killed in the course of saving her brother, she didn't know how she would live with it. But if one of those stray bullets killed Cage? If it was her actions that triggered something that left her brother dead? She knew she wouldn't be able to live with it. So, she made the wiser decision.

"If we see it, we call McQueeny. Maybe we call the ATF or DEA."

Ivy stopped for a moment, crossing her arms, her eyes darting up and to the right as she thought through all the moving parts. "I can live with that. I just don't know how we actually do it."

"We get thermal imagers," Kayla repeated. "I mean, I suppose we call, and we reserve them." She started tapping at her keyboard, likely searching where she could find some.

Ivy reached out a hand as if to make her stop. "I understand that. But the logistics of *doing* it are unclear. We can't just snoop around people's houses with thermal imagers in our hands. What distance do they work at? Can we stand on the street where it's legal, or are we going to have to trespass? And, if we have to trespass—"

They were definitely going to have to trespass, Joule thought, but she let Ivy keep rolling.

"Don't we then need to do it in the dark? Doesn't it seem like these people are out in the dark? So, they won't be there when we are looking, and we'll find nothing."

She pointed to the screen, moving her finger to the time-stamp. 2am. Three nights ago.

Damn, Joule hated that all those points were valid. Why couldn't she just go find her damn brother?

"If we go when we have the best cover, then it's less likely we'll actually find something. Can a thermal imager tell us where people *were*?"

Joule shook her head. She wasn't entirely confident of the answer but when Kayla's expression matched her own, she believed it. *ShitFuckDamn.*

"We'll figure it out," she told Ivy, but she was already heading over to grab her little backpack, reaching for her keys, even as she remembered that Kayla and Ivy had her parked in.

"Let's go find thermal imagers. We'll have to figure it out from there."

She wasn't giving up. This was the best chance they had of finding them today. She was already out the door, hoping that her surrogate moms were following.

68

The plan that Ivy laid out would take over twenty-four hours. Joule was disappointed by the timeframe and trying not to slide into a minor depression.

She had desperately wanted to go out searching tonight. Every day they waited was doing more harm, there was greater likelihood that something went horribly awry, and that Cage, Sarah, and Aurora didn't make it out.

But she had to admit that Kayla and Ivy were right.

As she climbed into the back seat, she immediately texted Amber. She and Brooklyn requested a pick-up ASAP. That alone—that her new friends were ready to roll on no notice at all—settled her anxiety a bit. Luckily, Kayla and Ivy's car was large enough that Joule and the two HST employees could sit across the back seat on the long ride into San Antonio.

Ivy gave directions to Kayla as the rest of them tapped away on their phones until their connections petered out. Then they called where they could. The little, all-female crew made three different stops, picking up a slew of different thermal imagers.

"I can buy my own," Amber offered.

"Only if you want to." Kayla had volunteered to buy all of them, and she was buying a lot.

Gisela and Malcolm had both asked to come out the next night as well when they searched. Kayla's solution had been to buy one for everyone who would be coming along as well as a couple extras for anyone they might add.

"You don't have to cover all of this," Joule told her, hoping that Kayla and Ivy would at least let them split the bills.

Kayla shook her head. "Honestly, I'm pretty sure I can write it off as a business expense."

Joule had almost laughed again. If anybody could, Kayla could.

They bought out three separate stores, taking the two to three that were in stock and renting a large handheld one for three days. Joule had been glad the city was big enough that they could do that. It meant they had several different designs. Kayla pointed out that each version had different pros and cons. And they would take advantage of that.

It was late in the day by the time they'd loaded up what they needed, including an expanded pack of walkie talkies. It would be well past dark by the time they got back to El Indio.

Even Ivy had given up and suggested they drive through somewhere. Across the back seat, all three of the HST workers were grateful just to get a different kind of food this time.

For a moment, despite the somberness of their task, the three had chattered. Joule had felt that maybe she had girl-friends. As long as she ignored that they were getting thermal imagers in an attempt to find a human trafficking ring and return their missing loved ones.

"So tomorrow, how are we going to do this?" Amber asked.

Joule turned to Brooklyn. "Do you have hints?"

"Oh no." Brooklyn's hands went up. "Thermal imaging is for live people with body heat. Dead bodies are cold. My sister doesn't know anything about this."

Joule and Amber must have had interesting expressions on their face. Because Brooklyn simply held up her phone for a minute. "I've been texting her the whole way there and back to see if she knew anything. But she doesn't."

All right, Joule thought. *No help from that quarter*. Though Brooklyn had been on top of it.

Joule would bet good money they could ask Jacob McQueeny, though Katherine was probably the safer bet. She was the one who didn't have to report to any agency.

Joule tucked the thought away in case it came to that. "Well, I think first we practice and see what we can see. How close do we have to get? How much detail will it give us? That kind of thing."

The others were nodding along and then Kayla said, looking up into the rearview mirror, hands always at ten and two on the steering wheel, "Then we have to figure out how to do it without somebody spotting us."

They headed back to Joule's small rental house, sending several of them inside at a time and leaving the others outside to try the equipment. They quickly discovered that two of the units—the small black ones—had smaller screens but were much more sensitive than the four red ones they'd managed to scoop up. Those tended to blur but had larger screens. They worked best if somebody managed to get close.

That might be a problem, Joule thought. They traded places and tried peeking through the bedroom windows and through the walls. They tried the garage and paced off how far away they could correctly guess what the person inside was doing, or how many of them were in the room.

"I don't think we're doing it right," Amber protested at one point. "There has to be a better way to read these."

"I know what we can do," Ivy grinned. "Where's the nearest fire station?"

The three girls turned and looked at her as if to ask what

the fuck she was talking about, but Ivy tipped her imager back and forth in her hands. "Firefighters use these as part of their regular training and they tend to be pretty helpful people. A lot of times you can just knock on the door and ask a question."

An hour and a half later they'd met three firefighters who were manning the El Indio volunteer station.

"You're lucky," one of them had said. "Often the building is empty. But we had a meeting tonight."

They'd found the help they needed, with only a small lie about a school project. They'd wrangled pro tips on settings that made the imagers work better, and even managed to get help with tests. Amber had even gotten asked on a date.

After dropping Amber and Brooklyn off at their apartment, their thermal guns still in hand, Joule suspected that Kayla was going to wind up giving them as gifts to everyone who came along. If her brother was home, and safe, she wouldn't complain. But she sat alone again in the back seat on the way back to the small house, wondering if they would ever find him.

The next day had been interminably long even though they'd left early for San Antonio. The small team had set up a meeting in the city, Kayla and Ivy's SUV leading the way. Amber, Gisela, and Brooklyn were right behind them.

They stood in a nearly empty corner of a warehouse parking lot, not feeling fully comfortable with their planning. The last-minute logistics weren't quite coming together.

"How do we get anywhere near the houses?"

The shiny Buick pulled up. Malcolm climbed out with a bag slung over his shoulder. He offered only the most rote of hellos before adding, "I've been working with the boss—Dr. Murasawa—she basically gave me this drone. I've gotten good with it."

That was a bit of a surprise that he had practiced with the drone . . . and that he was good at it now. Not that he had been spending his time improving his own ways to find his missing family. Joule reminded herself he had lost everyone.

It was Kayla who handed out the walkie talkies. "These are long range. They'll definitely do the job."

"They're pretty small," Amber commented.

"Exactly. If anything happens, try to hide it on you."

Not something they should have to be thinking about. Kayla, as per usual, didn't sugarcoat anything as she'd given the instruction as par for the course.

As she handed them out, Dr. Murasawa and David pulled up, having come from a different direction. They'd all taken off work to do this and Joule felt grateful for the effort. Kayla handed them each a walkie talkie which they accepted and a thermal imager which they didn't.

David leaned into the back of the car. "We brought drones, too." He'd clearly seen the one Malcolm had.

The group—all present at last—convened on the basics.

"We can't all go together. We'll have to split up."

They all agreed, though it was clear they would have to stay in close contact. If anyone found anything, it would need to be reported immediately. Decisions would have to be made.

Joule hoped that they found something. In her heart, a hard, cold kernel of hope lay dormant that they would simply find Cage tonight and she would be able to walk away with her brother. They all climbed back into their cars, Malcolm going with David and Dr. Murasawa, so that no one was alone.

Joule, Ivy, and Kayla climbed back into the SUV and followed the map the short distance to their stopping point. Her fingers flexed, squeezing the thermal imager a little tighter as Kayla parked on the side street.

They all got out, quietly closing the car doors as they snuck around the back of the first house.

69

"There's nothing unusual here." Joule was more than disappointed to report that. In fact, it was the only report they'd been hearing all evening.

The houses in the area had showed all kinds of things. People inside making dinner. One man with more dogs than they could count. A family that looked like they might be too many people in a house . . . but they were just a family with a lot of members. Nothing strange on the heat gun.

No one being held hostage.

It caught Joule for a moment. Would Cage be up and around in his new holding? Making dinner, acting as if he were part of a family? She didn't think so. And she didn't think any of these houses were the right one. If there was one.

Somehow the little team had managed to not get caught out with their heat guns. Mostly they snuck around. One time a man had come out the front door and Amber had apparently told him she was measuring the moisture of native species of plants for her school project. Gisela had commented, "This girl bullshitted the plant species and explained moisture in a way that was . . . so so wrong."

But the man had invited them to bring their "moisture guns" into the yard and check out all the flora. There had been no fauna in the house other than him.

The houses here were far enough apart, scattered on the land, so that they could mostly see inside with relative ease. They didn't have to get too close, which was good, because a lot of the houses had dogs. Big, guard dogs.

Joule had felt her heart race, and she reminded herself that she had nothing against dogs. The Night Hunters weren't dogs.

The walkie talkie crackled, and Gisela's voice came through. Joule, Kayla, and Ivy each held their heads down close to their devices, listening closely to make up for the dropout due to the distance between them. "Are we missing them because they're in a basement somewhere. Cinderblock construction would block these things, right?"

"I don't think the houses around here have basements," Amber mentioned back.

Figuring that was an easy check, Joule pulled her phone out and began a search before she remembered, *no cell service.* Still, she held the phone up into the air once again in case it had miraculously appeared.

It occurred to her then that no one in their group was native to the area. Sarah, Cage, and Aurora certainly weren't from here. Kayla and Ivy were from the same neighborhood that she and Cage were. She didn't know where Gisela, Amber or Brooklyn were from, but she knew that they had moved here with Helio Systems Tech for the job. And Malcolm and Aurora Walker were not from the area either.

Shitballs. Maybe they should have gotten Jacob McQueeny, or at least Kathryn. There were questions that should be answered. But with no service, there was no way to call her now. They kept going. Joule tucked Amber's "school project" idea away in case she, too, got called out. It wouldn't hurt if the neighbors all got the same fake story. They might not check into it if they'd all helped out "the nice kids working on that plant moisture project."

The area wasn't that big. Disappointingly, the houses all checked out. None had any heat signatures indicating extra people. Aside from two different people in their bedrooms—teenagers?—there was not even a single indication of a hostage. And Joule didn't think they had basements.

"Do we come back? Try again tomorrow?" Another voice had tuned in. Dr. Murasawa this time. That meant they had checked all the houses on their list and hadn't found anything of value or even interest either.

"Cage and Aurora were picked up around 2am. It's barely seven. It's just now dark. Do we think they could have gone out this early?" Dr. Murasawa's voice asked when no one had really answered her first question.

They'd picked now specifically because they'd thought this would be a good time to find them at home. Like she said, the runs seemed to be happening in the middle of the night. It matched with when Cage and Aurora disappeared, and Sarah, too. When they thought they'd seen Cage on the satellite image Kayla had found.

"What if we're wrong? What if the runs are happening earlier?" Joule voiced that out loud now, into her walkie talkie. "What if Cage and Aurora were picked up on a *return trip?*"

Amber chimed in. "Could they have left this early? They were coming *back* around two to three a.m.? It would be a lot of hours out in the desert."

Joule didn't get the impression that the health or comfort of the kidnapped was a real concern. She pushed her worries about what was happening to her brother aside in order to stay focused.

"Maybe the schedule just varies," David put in. "Honestly, if I were running a cartel—"

Joule almost laughed. It was a thought she'd had herself a handful of times over the past several days.

"I wouldn't be running at the same time every night and I wouldn't be running in the same direction. I'd have a complex series of paths and exchange points that varied. Different pick-ups and drop-offs. Consistency could get them caught."

That, Joule had not thought about. She had thought more about the treatment of the prisoners than the planning of the business. "It's possible then, that we're not finding the people because they're already out of the house?"

"It's entirely possible," David said back. No one argued the point.

Did they simply wait another day?

There had been so many days that she waited, so many days that her organs ate away at themselves with worry and inaction.

"Well, if we can't find them this way, then how about we get drones up?" Malcolm said.

"What are we looking for?" David asked, but even as he asked it, Joule could hear the soft noises in the background of the drones getting readied.

"We need to reconvene. We have nine people and three drones." Kayla had clearly calculated it and didn't expect to have to explain more to this group. It took a bit of walking to get them all into one point, but she was right. Three sets of eyes on each of the screens was better.

She and Joule grouped with David. Ivy and Amber decided to follow Dr. Murasawa and her drone. Gisela and Brooklyn went with Malcolm, who said to the group, "Definitely people, if we can find them. We need to start with where the original footprint sets end."

The night that Cage and Aurora disappeared, the trail had ended near here. It was the whole reason they were here, just outside of San Antonio. It wasn't even a town, just a cluster of houses far on the outskirts, far more desert than suburb. It didn't even have a name. Anyone watching them on the satellite would see the influx of their cars and think it was either a party or something was up.

They would see the people walking around. But Joule didn't really care.

"We'll have to drive out to start where those footprints ended." And it wouldn't be the easiest drive. They'd brought only the cars that were the biggest, with the broadest wheelbases and the widest tires. The ones best suited for driving in the desert. Even so, they were likely ruining the cars and it was slow going.

Every moment they crawled along hurt. Even when they arrived, Joule wanted to dive in and go, but it took a while to get the three small teams coordinated. The only reason Joule didn't have a fit was because she *knew* they were doing the right thing the right way. *And because it was how Cage would have done it.*

The three drone drivers discussed which direction they would go and what exactly they were looking for. The way David and Dr. Murasawa spoke with Malcolm gave Joule hope that he truly had gotten better at it. They clearly trusted him with the job.

The others, still equipped with their thermal guns—Joule included—held them up and began looking for anything.

She found the faint glow of a snake, not warm blooded, but still retaining a little bit of the day's heat. Another blob of glow darted across the screen. She hadn't seen it with her eyes, but with the more sensitive heat gun, she'd found a small mammal out here making its way.

There were no people.

She aimed her sensor toward the horizon, wondering if it might catch a group. Some little flair on the screen that would tell her someone was out there.

Then, the drones were in the air. The operators following along, eyes on the screens. Two handlers each watching out for snakes and scorpions, things to trip over, and scanning the horizon for anything to investigate.

It was almost two hours later before Malcolm called out over the walkie talkies. "I've got something!"

70

"Footprints!" Gisela announced excitedly over the walkie-talkie. "It's a path. Lots of prints!"

Joule looked to Kayla and David. "What do we do?"

How had they done all this planning and they weren't ready for a find like this?

The three little groups had headed off in different directions. Now Joule wondered, should they double back? Find the others and follow the footprints? Or stay where they were and give themselves more opportunities in case the footprints lead to nothing?

She didn't have the brainwaves to answer it.

Kayla was looking at Joule, but she lifted her walkie talkie to her mouth. She had an answer. Thank God. "I think we all stay where we are until they see *someone* or something that you need more eyes to investigate."

Joule nodded to Kayla, a silent agreement that she understood and that it probably was the best path.

Who knew? What if her brother was a mere five hundred

feet in front of her and they turned around and went the other way?

The hidden ramifications of her decisions haunted her every night. What if they had just gone a little bit further? What if she had just gone out and met Gretchen Mueller and her group earlier? *What if? What if? What if?*

David nodded along, his drone still up in the air under expert control. Even though they had paused to talk about the other team's find, they themselves hadn't found anything like footprints. They had seen a cluster of snakes and Joule had no idea if they were mating or eating or what. They'd seen a large cat with something in its mouth, something smaller and less lucky than the cat.

The three kept moving, heading forward. How long would they stay out? Technically, half of this search endeavor was still on the job for Helio Systems Tech. Would they need to tap out, saying they had to get up early? They needed to get some sleep before attempting to work at least part of a day tomorrow.

Joule didn't know how many working hours Dr. Murasawa would be able to get them out of. Her own drone was being controlled by one of those people—David.

She was trying to think if Malcolm would stay out late with them, or if he even could. Surely his sleep schedule was all fucked up like the rest of theirs. And Kayla and Ivy? Theirs would be too given another good twenty-four hours of this.

"Look," David said as he pointed at the screen showing what his drone captured. The machine itself was just a dot in the sky. Joule could barely keep an eye on it in the dark. They had turned off the lights on the little machine, not wanting it to alert anyone that it was there. Surely, if it passed in front of the moon or ran across a path where someone else was looking up, they would spot it, but they weren't going to make it obvious.

Joule and Kayla gathered in close.

"Footprints."

"We're so far away from the other group, they can't be the same," Kayla said, but Joule was already holding the walkie talkie up.

"We've got footprints too."

"Who's prints look fresher?" Amber asked.

A valid question that Joule hadn't thought of yet. Was she just brain dead? Or did this thing have that many moving parts?

She thought again of what Ivy had told her. *She had a dream team here.* She almost thought if anyone could find Cage it would be them. But the answer wasn't *if* anyone could find her brother it was *that they would* find him.

The teams talked for a little bit, trying to figure it out without Kathryn or Maeve McQueeny here to give them any tracking tips. They tried to remember what they had learned the first time.

"Ours are a little faint. Sand has blown across a few of them, and I can see animal tracks crossing them in two places," Joule said. It wasn't a great indicator of time, but of a greater likelihood that time had passed since the tracks had been left.

Thinking that the tracks the other team was following would be newer, and might lead them to actual people, she opened her mouth.

Then she heard Ivy on the comm. "Keep following your own tracks. We've got enough people we can follow all leads."

Joule thought again that they were doing the right thing, even if it felt as if a fork had been pushed into her stomach and twisted like spaghetti. She could do this. She could do anything if it meant finding Cage.

They kept going.

This path veered, and they followed along, the drone tracking overhead and the three trailing behind. As they got nearer to the footprints, David turned the drone to the left and tracked further away. This trail was out into the open space of the desert.

Joule had no idea what they might be following. Migrants? Hikers? Her brother? There were too many options. Most of them wouldn't lead her to anything good.

"What's that?" David asked, pointing to the screen again.

Something had been left.

"It could be a plastic bag. We've seen plenty of those blowing around. Also, water jugs. Lots of empty bottles out here." As Joule watched, the drone tipped giving the camera a wider view than just what was directly below it.

"It's not moving like something lightweight. There's nothing near it. I'm going down." Using a series of controls as if he were playing a video game, David deftly maneuvered the machine.

Joule watched as the image became clearer and clearer.

"It's definitely not a bag," David said as they got close enough to see. "Is it clothing?"

"Is there something wrapped in it?" Kayla leaned in close, too.

"It's a sweater." Joule grabbed her own phone, then quit, angry that she couldn't take a picture and send it to Malcolm.

"Honestly," Joule said, "It looks like the sweater Aurora was wearing the night she went missing."

David blinked at her. "It *does.*"

The three of them took off running, the drone wobbling in the sky as David lost his very careful control.

The machine had been farther in front of them than she'd estimated, and Joule wasn't prepared for the exertion to her lungs and the buildup of the lactic acid. But she couldn't care. It was ridiculous, there was no way it was Aurora's sweater, but they all ran toward the mystery object anyway.

Eventually, she could see it with her own eyes. She wanted to run even faster, to go and grab it, but it wasn't a person. She couldn't afford to hurt herself for what she now saw was in fact, a pale sweater. The sand had blown over it just a little, a tiny lizard sat on top. As Joule reached down to grab for it, he darted away faster than she could have snagged him. She didn't want him anyway.

Lifting it, she saw it moved oddly, making her brows pull together. Something about the sweater was wrong. Maybe it wasn't Aurora's. Her sweater hadn't looked like this: bumpy and nubby, almost homemade looking. But the sleeves . . . They were manufactured.

Joule held it up stretching the shoulders wide to see it. "I need light," she said to Kayla.

Though they had tried to stay incognito out here, none of the three said anything as Kayla flipped on her phone. Only David kept in touch over the walkie talkie telling everyone else. "We've got it. It's a pale sweater, almost white."

If one of the others responded, Joule didn't hear. "Oh my god. Oh my god."

Kayla held the light. David was still awkwardly keeping the drone afloat, as he held his own walkie talkie out to capture her voice. "This is Aurora's sweater. And I can read it!"

71

"Wait. Put it down." Kayla's hand pushed on Joule's arm where she was holding the sweater out open by the shoulders, trying to read the front of it in the dim light. Kayla had pulled her phone away, but Joule was just moving her head in closer.

The stitches were loose and clumsy, not a nice tight professional stitch. That would have been easier to read—

"Put it down!" Kayla said again.

"I'm trying to read it."

"Think about what we saw on the satellites," Kayla demanded of her, and it took Joule a moment before she folded the sweater and tucked it in close in an attempt to hide it.

It was more than possible that someone already had seen or would later go back through satellite footage of the area. What if they were seen out here?

If someone saw them find the sweater, what would it even mean? The drone dipped precariously as David failed to pay attention to it, his eyes more on the conversation nearby.

"Do you think the cartels have satellite access?" Joule asked.

"It's not that hard to get." David shrugged and righted the

drone. It had to be harder to operate without the lights on it. "One would have to assume that they can access something."

"Do we go back now?" Kayla asked.

"I think we have to. We need to get where we can see this."

"I don't understand how it's a message. It's just a . . ." David said. He seemed to be searching for a polite word. "Poorly knitted sweater."

The arms and back of the top were intact. They had only reknitted the front, an excellent timesaver that Joule appreciated. The machine manufactured pieces also helped disguise what had been done to it. Only a few people would be able to read it, and how many would even think to try?

This was a message just for her.

They'd dropped it along the way, maybe last night, maybe tonight. *It was brilliant*, Joule thought, but said, "I think our best bet is to go back."

She picked up the walkie talkie, ready to tell the others but again Kayla pushed her hands down. "These are great but not secure. I just realized how much information we might be giving away. Someone need only search frequencies to find what we tell each other."

There was a pause, then Kayla instructed, "Tell them we gave up and we're deciding to come back in."

Fuck monkeys. How many times had they been out here saying what they'd found? Was it better that way? Maybe. They needed the McQueenys to tell them what they might have messed up.

Then again, they hadn't really found anything before besides footprints. Still, Kayla's warning about the information they were sharing went straight through her. What if they'd screwed up?

David circled the drone back as they turned around. On the return trek toward the cars, the small machine darted back and forth in front of them as they walked, checking for things they might have missed. This time, though, they didn't go slowly. They weren't scanning the horizon. They had an endpoint and they beelined for it, moving off the straight and narrow only for large rocks and small shrubs.

When the group had gathered back together, Joule motioned to everybody. "Walkie talkies are off?"

Though two of them had to flick the button to make it happen, they all quickly nodded.

"This is Aurora's sweater, right Malcolm?" Joule held it up quickly for him.

"I think so, but it didn't look like that before."

She tried to keep the sweater vertical, out of line of sight from any passing satellite. "Then we need to take this home and get into the light, so we can read it."

"What do you mean, *read* it?"

"I did this when I was in high school. I knit Winnie the Pooh into a sweater in Morse code. Cage remembered. He must have fed the idea to Sarah or Aurora, because he can't knit."

"Aurora can," Malcolm said confidently. "Her work usually looks better than that though."

"But it means they're alive." Joule clutched the sweater close. "If we want, we should all go back to my place. We can figure out what they said."

72

Once again, Cage's fingers itched to hide something in his pocket.

He'd touched the wrapped packs in the bags again. The feel of it was different this time, though. It was harder. The pieces inside didn't quite slide against each other like before—the thing that had made him think perhaps it was some kind of drug patch. Now, it was more like a solid brick with enough plastic wrap on the outside of it to make it feel squishy. It was heavy enough to make the journey into a slog.

He usually put himself on one of the teams that dug a pit for the bag and he rotated the others through that job with him. They weren't being fed enough to do more heavy labor, even though it was required of them.

There hadn't been a chance to talk to Sarah or Aurora about what was going on with the women's group. Was there even a third group somewhere else? Maybe rotating through the house or the caves? There almost had to be. This couldn't be the entire operation. They'd only been able to pass notes to each other, and that had to be saved for the most rudimentary of information.

They had attempted to disguise enough that—if Connor found it—he wouldn't be able to put the pieces together, at least not until the first deed was done.

And they had done it. Aurora had worn her sweater out into the desert, tied it around her waist in the warm evening air, casually putting the new side in. She'd worn it that way through the drop off, then the groups had met up to head back in, Connor leading the way once again.

Cage had noticed that she wasn't wearing it. She'd left it as a message somewhere on the desert floor. Hoping it would reach someone. *Would Connor get mad at her?* Cage wondered. Maybe because of her losing an item of clothing in the desert. Or would they simply not care? She could just go cold or pick a lost item from the pile on the corner of the living room. He'd already used the two T shirts, splinting Terrence's arm.

The arm hadn't festered. But Terrence had.

Cage had no time for him. But the sour grapes the boy constantly expressed made Cage sure he had to watch his back. There was no time to deal with the arrogant, angry kid. It wasn't a position he liked being in and honestly, he had no idea who might be with Terrence, if another coup should be attempted. This one would be against *him*.

No one knew about the sweater, except him, Aurora, and Sarah, unless they'd told someone else on the women's side. He was confident they were smart enough not to do that. So, presumably no one knew about the sweater itself and no one knew of their victory.

There was no doubt in his mind that Joule would find it. What he couldn't predict was *when*. That he had no idea of. She might have already found it. Or she might find it in a month, and everything could be different, the information out of date in ways he couldn't currently fathom.

He simply had to have faith that she would find it in time. She would be looking for him just as they had looked for Sarah.

And their efforts would be even greater now. Would that mean they would find the sweater sooner rather than later? He didn't know and he couldn't bank on it. It was just one move in a chess game.

Once the sweater was in her hands, she would read it. He could only hope it would lead her directly to where they were being kept. Then again, he couldn't be sure. So many *what ifs* crowded his mind. What if she couldn't find it? What if they were moved before Joule and the others figured it out? What if the sweater sat out in the desert rotting in the sun or was blown away by the wind and covered by sand?

There were so many possibilities he didn't like to contemplate. Regardless of how it played out, they had to get on to the next move in the match.

He walked at the end of the line thinking to watch everything to see how it went. If there was a way he could make a move, he would take it. But that was unlikely as Connor stayed so far out front. It seemed his whole point was to be unreachable.

Then, in a move he had not seen coming, Aurora cried out.

For a moment even Cage had the thought that something was truly wrong. Had she stubbed her toe? Been—God forbid —bitten by something?

Very quickly it became clear, and he hoped only for him and Sarah.

"Please! my sweater!" she sounded frantic. "I'm cold and it was . . . I reached for it and . . ."

She'd dropped it last night! Damn, had Connor not even noticed that she hadn't even had it on her at all on this run?

Connor turned around, looking at her coldly, his attitude clear even through the light wind that picked up the desert grit and buffeted them in the cold. He did not care at all.

Still, Aurora played it for all she was worth. "But it's too cold! I can't go out without my sweater. I have to go back and find it."

Cage crept forward as Connor moved toward Aurora. His stance was ready to move, one hand lifted as if to be angry at her. Slowly Cage moved again, and Aurora fought for the lead man's attention.

"I'm sorry! It's just too cold. I can't go out at night without my sweater."

"I'm sure you can find something else!" Sarah snapped harshly, entering the game and showing Cage that they had not yet revealed that they were mother and daughter.

"I don't see any sweaters lying around!" Aurora said, turning to face Sarah, anger glaring on her face.

Well played, he thought as he took two more steps around.

The whole group was moving, shifting like kids on the playground, waiting for a fight to break out. Sarah and Aurora were becoming the middle of the pack as they bickered.

"I *need* to go back and get it. It's special to me," Aurora huffed and said no more. She simply turned to walk away. As though she were just going to walk miles back to find her sweater.

He saw now she'd lost weight. Not good. The sweater game played like it was real though.

Though the group wasn't quite willing to hold her in, they also didn't quite part the seas. She didn't get very far before Connor lunged for her to grab her arm.

Spinning her around to face him, he growled out, "Listen up, bitch. Your sweater doesn't matter. It doesn't matter if you're cold."

He raised the gun in what Cage hoped was only a threat and Cage took two more steps forward.

"If you try to leave, I'll shoot you." It was the hollowness behind the words that convinced Cage he couldn't afford to miss an opportunity like this.

Aurora cowed to the threat, crying out and dropping downward.

The distance was too far, but it was his only chance.

Cage lunged going low. He whacked upward on Connor's arm, not having the control he'd hoped for. He prayed to any god willing to listen and he placed himself between Connor and Aurora just as the gun went off.

73

Joule laid the sweater on the table. So many hands touched it, read it, and tried to figure out what it meant, but she didn't mind.

They'd stopped back at the original parking lot, picking up Malcolm's Buick. Then they'd caravanned all the way back from San Antonio.

They might have to go right back out, Joule thought. But here she had laptops and equipment. Kayla could log into satellite feeds with fast download times, and she was already doing exactly that.

Joule read off the first lines of the sweater again. "Thirteen men, and eleven women."

"Given the footprints, it might be all ages." Amber added in.

Joule read the second line. "C S A all okay."

Even the order of the letters told Joule that Aurora had knitted it, putting herself last.

Her heart had instantly let go of some of the terror she'd carried for the week when she'd first stood in the desert and read that line.

Folding the sweater over with the light on in the back of the

SUV while Kayla drove them home, she had deciphered the whole message for the first time. And promptly broke into tears. It had taken a while to get past line three.

"Here," Joule said now. *How many times had she read it so far?* She didn't think she could count. "Five houses in a rough line. They are in the Westernmost one."

It wasn't exact. He didn't have an address. She was certain he would have given it if he did.

"It says they were taken to this place the first night. And that the bosses stay in the house, but they've been shuffled between there and several caves."

"You are shitting me!" Brooklyn pushed her way forward. "Hold on . . ." She was tapping on her tablet, frantically looking things up. "We just have to find caves, probably near the house, big enough and deep enough to hide ten-plus people."

"Can you even do that?" Malcolm asked.

Joule bust out with near glee. She almost yelled. "She's a hydrospeliogeologist!!"

Everyone stared at her, but Brooklyn didn't even look up.

"She finds caves! She has a P H fucking D in *this*!" She really did have a dream team.

"There are caves in Texas?" Malcolm asked.

Brooklyn looked up. "Yes, but only around this area. It's part of why the hydro plant is getting installed in El Indio. It's why I'm on this project."

"Then we start with where the footprints led," Amber chimed in. "I mean it's possible that they walked through there and to an entirely different area, but . . ." she paused, "they probably lead back to the house or the caves."

"He says the house is at the edge." David pointed. He also could read it.

"It's got to be one of these." Kayla pointed on the satellite image she had pulled up. Joule couldn't match the roofs to the facades.

Had they been there already? Passed by with their thermal guns earlier tonight?

Had they simply just crossed paths at odd times? Or had they been at another location. The desert was so vast and dark that they might have done that and just not seen each other. Had her brother and the others been just beyond the horizon and not realized how close they had been?

She would never know.

But she felt she was finally seeing what the puzzle could look like. She hadn't been this happy since before . . . since before Dr. Brett had died.

Though the others looked to the map and Kayla's pointed out suggestions, or to Brooklyn's hasty red dots on her tablet, Joule's eyes stayed on the sweater—the precious lifeline that she had to her brother. It told her that he was, in fact, still alive, or at least had been when the sweater was knit. There had been no attempt to correct it though. She told herself he'd been alive when it was dropped.

Let the others figure out where the house was, where the caves were. She thought about the sand and how there had been very little of it over the edges of where it lay as if it had just been dropped. The sweater couldn't have been there long. *Cage was still okay.*

"It could be these." Brooklyn was pointing at nothing on Kayla's screen.

Kayla, of course, had the largest laptop available. It could hardly be considered a laptop, and it had a full ten key on the side, but it was wonderful for looking at these images. She marked the spots their resident expert thought there might be caves.

"What about these?" Amber asked, pointing to another cluster of houses.

"It could be that, too."

There were barely fifteen houses in the area. "Is that a line of five? The message says five."

"Agreed." Kayla didn't look up. "I think it's these." She pointed again. "There are two here that could be the farthest west."

"How is your brother with directions?" Dr. Murasawa asked Joule directly.

"Passable?" she answered. West would be west, but he might not have realized there were two western ones to distinguish. That would be totally like Cage. But it meant it could be either of them.

She almost laughed. Almost chuckled as if she wasn't desperately clinging to an abandoned piece of poorly knit clothing she'd found in the desert. Thank God for the drones. Thank God, she thought, for the dream team.

For the first time, the hope that had lived as the cold hard kernel bloomed and was crawling higher in her chest. *They could do this.*

What she told the group was, "We have to do this right away. We have to get back there before they get moved. We already have multiple locations."

It was David who nodded once again citing his *if I ran a cartel* ideas. He weighed invisible ideas between his open palms. "I don't think I would keep my people in the same place very long. But multiple locations means they can stay longer. And moving is a lot of effort . . ."

"Then we need to get there first." She wouldn't allow herself to think that she had gotten so close, and that her brother had slipped through her fingers. He wouldn't. He couldn't.

Joule looked around the group, waiting to see exhausted faces. Waiting for one of them to tell her they needed to get a good night's sleep. When no one spoke, she filled the air.

"Anyone who needs to rest can stay here in one of the beds or go home." They all did have cars.

No one moved.

"We have the thermal imager guns." It was Gisela who offered that and shrugged as if she did this every week. "It's possible we were there at the wrong time."

"We need to check out those caves now, too."

"So, we go back out now?" Joule asked, her heart fluttering at what she saw.

But a few faces moved for "no."

"We need to charge the drones," Dr. Murasawa told her. They had already been plugged in once they all reached the house, but they weren't fully recharged, given the time they'd spent out in the desert.

"I have a charger in my car," Kayla said. "It has enough outlets to plug them all in."

Of course, it did. Joule thought. Kayla would have three prong outlets, too.

"I prefer not to plug them into square wave chargers," Dr. Murasawa said.

Around the table, the crowd nodded. Joule appreciated that they all seemed to understand that the square wave charging would likely shorten the drones' overall lifespan.

As she watched, Dr. Murasawa shook off the idea and started to concede. Drones versus her people was a stupid debate and she was seeing that.

But Kayla was faster. "It's not square wave. And the drive back to San Antionio to park is several hours. Is that enough?" But she didn't wait for all the answers, she probably just assumed they'd calculated it for themselves, or they simply agreed that her numbers were correct.

"It should be." David agreed.

"I'm bringing my laptop." She told them without segue. "I recommend everybody else bring theirs as well. Is everybody charged?"

It was David who held out his tablet. "Um, I could use the charger too."

He'd been using it a good portion of the evening off and on with the drone, downloading screenshots and more.

"I've got you," Kayla said. She even smiled but she did it at the screen she was looking at. "In fact, if you want you can ride with us so you can work on the way."

They all started to move but it was Ivy who stalled them. "We need food. At least snacks with carbs, and Gatorade or caffeine . . . And a restroom break, now and one when we get there."

"Okay, *Mom*," Kayla answered a smile on her face. This time she looked at Ivy and the kind grin was matched with a sparkle that told everyone else this had been teased before.

Joule hoped she would one day find that in her own future partner.

"It's your house, you go first." Gisela swept a hand indicating the short hallway.

Amber piped up. "Yeah, just make sure there's enough toilet paper for all of us!"

It took far too long for everyone to cycle through the lone bathroom. As if sharing it in the mornings wasn't enough. Joule was itching to get back out on the road, wondering if it'd be worth sending the cars off in waves and let the ones who were ready faster get a head start. But if anyone was looking for them on the satellite, they would find them anyway. They were better off sticking together.

Nothing was open in the middle of the night. Not here in the tiny town. There were no drinks to buy. Ivy handed out the remainder of the glass soda bottles and bottled water that she'd already stocked into the fridge.

Bless her, Joule had thought. Ivy was always ready for anything.

Not soon enough, but eventually, they were all back in the

cars, caravanning down the road. Kayla, Ivy, Joule, and David were in the lead car, David tapping away on his iPad.

Joule had been quiet a bit when her phone pinged.

Interesting. "We must have passed the cell tower. I'm getting service for a moment . . . Wait a minute!" Joule looked at the phone again and watched what was happening.

"You either liked what you saw or you're scared." Ivy pointed out as she twisted around in the front seat.

Joule couldn't decide which it was.

Ivy pushed. "Tell me."

"My tracking app just pinged."

74

C age felt the reverberation through his entire body, even though he couldn't quite place where it had started.

Was there heat, searing pain? Just the weird dull throb of everything vibrating quickly at once. Then Connor moved, yanking himself from Cage's hold, twisting and spinning. Trying to get away.

The ringing in Cage's ears suddenly made sense. It was screams from those around him.

In slow motion, he twisted his head, trying to see if everyone was okay.

Aurora was face down, her hands over her head as time expanded and contracted around him. Cage tried to make sense of everything. Next to Aurora, Sarah crouched low, her hand on her mother's back, as she looked up at Cage, clearly wondering what the hell she should do next.

He motioned to her to join him, not even understanding quite what he was doing. He blinked in slow motion, his ears a cacophony of sound, and at the same time nothing.

Connor gained his feet and stepped back. The gun had

gone off, but he didn't see blood. He looked to Connor. His eyes were no longer dead now but enraged.

The gun swung up, aimed at Cage. "You do not get in my way. You piece of shit."

Oh, the irony of this man calling him shit, Cage thought. But Connor, too, had been startled by the incident. The gun wavered.

He was so close Cage could taste it. *Or was that blood?* Had he bitten his tongue? Had he actually been shot, and he hadn't figured it out yet? Maybe it was blood, burbling up through his esophagus. He didn't know. As long as his body responded, he would try.

He went for startling his opponent. Leaping forward at Connor, he aimed low and through his abdomen, toward the man's spine.

He tackled like a football player, taking Connor down. Maybe it was just sheer luck, but Cage would take it.

Sarah had joined him in the thick of it. As soon as Cage felt his shoulder go into Connor's midsection, he heard an *oof* that he wasn't sure was his own or the other man's. Connor's gun arm flailed wildly, and then Cage felt Connor's body take a second hit, only realizing after a moment that it had been Sarah dogpiling onto the man.

She reached for Connor's flailing arm trying to get control of the gun, even as Connor twisted his wrist. Thank God the gun was so big and unwieldy that maybe he couldn't get the end of the barrel aimed the right direction to shoot one of them.

Feet in old shoes appeared in the corner of Cage's vision. Hands, old and gnarled, grasped for Connor's arm, digging in tight, dirty nails breaking the skin.

"No Dodger!" Cage yelled, but nothing came out of his mouth. Or did it? The ringing of his ears was so much he couldn't even hear his own voice inside his skull.

The gun went off again and Dodger stumbled backwards. But this time, Sarah leaped onto Connor's arm. Her knees planted on either side of his elbow, her fists pounded on his wrist until his grip gave up.

Cage was straddling the man's legs in a way that prevented him from sliding out. Then he saw it, the white handle that he'd originally thought was mother of pearl or something lustrous and, as Sarah grabbed it, he saw now it was some kind of resin or plastic.

As Connor tried to roll over and scramble for it again, he accidentally knocked it out of Sarah's hand. The gun tumbled out of both their reach, and a hand came down for it.

"No!" Sarah screamed.

Had he heard that? Or had he just seen her mouth move?

It didn't matter, Cage's muscles tensed, his finger dug into the man's flesh. In his karate classes, he would have been concerned about the pain he was inflicting. Here, he was only concerned about the pain he was not inflicting.

The wind kicked up a bit, cool air swirling around him, reminding him that this was all dark, all in the deep of night, and no one could hear them. As noisy as their screams had been, no one would come to their rescue. If anything, all they had done was scare away the snakes and the large cats—the creatures that might have hurt Connor for them.

Slowly, Cage's eyes blinked closed and then open as his head lifted in time to see Terrence reaching down for the gun as Sarah lunged forward.

75

J oule waited while the line cut out, trying to keep her patience intact. It was difficult to do in the backseat of the SUV with David next to her and spotty cell phone reception.

"You did *what?*" Jacob McQueeny barked out.

She'd explained she hadn't turned the app off. She'd wanted to see if Cage's phone moved. It was stupid.

"I knew that was going to be an issue."

Had he though? Or was he just having an "I told you so" moment? It did tell her something about what was going on though.

"It might be Cage. He did get the sweater to us, maybe he got to his phone?"

"He sent you a sweater knit with morse code. Don't you think he would have gotten a message to you rather than turning on the app?" Jacob asked.

Probably. But he would also use any means possible.

"If you're right, then they know you were at their house."

"Well, they know we were at *all* the houses in the area," she countered. They hadn't found *the house*—which was the problem.

"They know you got closer. That's not good. Delete the app!"

Had she tipped them off? Would they move their people?

She told herself it was done, and she couldn't change it. She could berate herself if it caused problems. "I'm calling Kathryn, too. You can both meet us in San Antonio."

"I'm actually in San Antonio right now. Sitting next to her. I'll tell her. We'll be there. Make sure everyone is armed."

His warning gave her pause.

As she set the phone back in her lap and stared out the window into the dark, repetitive scenery, she realized she should have been tired. The sun would be up in just a few hours and, given all the driving back and forth they had done, they should all be sleepy.

But she was wired. Everyone was. Hope and sports drinks kept them going. No one was willing to be the first to tap out. They arrived in San Antonio to find Kathryn and Jacob already waiting. The siblings had brought Kathryn's car, so they didn't have any official vehicles on them. Maverick County didn't extend quite this far out anyway. Jacob was out of his jurisdiction.

They all piled out and started talking. Jacob didn't like the thermal guns getting used again.

"How else will we see people?"

He countered with "Have you turned your phone off?"

"I uninstalled the app." She'd turned it off but didn't say that.

"It sounds like a good plan to me," Kathryn had inserted to stop their bickering. That was all, no more reprimands, no discussion of what they might do next.

They were close enough to the houses in question. They'd definitely checked these two earlier. They parked far enough away that they figured they might not be seen, Jacob and Kathryn giving instructions where to go. But in the end, they had all agreed it was the best they could do. Not that it was good enough.

They spread out, working in small clusters. The teams surrounded the first house, thermal guns out. Joule quickly found a man sitting on the couch, legs wide. Joule thought she could even tell he was wearing cowboy boots. Something cold hung from his fingertips, a glass, maybe a drink. He ran a hand through his hair and continued to look at the wall across from him.

Two other people roamed the house. Back and forth they moved into the kitchen then into the rooms. Maybe they were cleaning. She couldn't be sure.

Nothing more really came through, and one by one their little team all looked at each other and tapped out. This wasn't the place or, if it was, no one was here right now.

Stealthily, they moved as a unit to the next house. If no one was here, they would head toward the caves Brooklyn had marked. None of them acknowledged how very dangerous this could be if they got caught. But they worked quietly and spotted an older couple already climbing into bed. One was in the bathroom, clearly brushing teeth and then taking medicines.

"Doesn't look like them," Malcolm said. But it was David who countered, "If I was running a cartel—"

"—That's exactly what I would do," Joule finished. "Because obviously, who would suspect a nice middle-aged couple of human trafficking? They can get away with it far longer than anyone else."

But again, they were the only ones in the house.

"Assuming one of these is the right house, that means that the people are still out right now." Amber whispered into the night air after they'd all stepped far enough away to not look like they were doing what they were doing.

Joule asked, "Can we assume that?"

Kayla added, "Actually, we're also assuming that our interpretation of the sweater is correct."

"It's correct," Joule said. "I read it. It's Aurora's sweater. It's a message just like Cage and I sent each other before."

"I don't think she means that," Amber said. "The information was just sparse. We've made interpretations. We've know these two houses here are the western most ones, but we are assuming he knows that and that actually represented what was there."

"I don't understand," Gisela said, and Amber turned to her.

"Well, look around. It's relatively dark. They probably don't get out during the day. Do they recognize that there's a shed behind the other house over there?"

"There is?" Malcolm turned to check.

"Exactly. I saw it on the drive in last time, but I can't even see it now."

"Sounds like a good place to keep people . . ." David suggested.

"I don't think there's enough space. Not at all for the numbers that the sweater told us about. Also," she tipped the imager, "There was no one in it."

For a moment, they all looked at each other, standing in a loose formation.

"We're staying too long. We're still too close to the houses." Jacob began ushering the group away. "If this is one of the houses, and they see us out here, then they'll catch on and we can cause more trouble."

They followed along, but Ivy piped up. "I think we have to make the assumption that we had it right. The bosses should be in one of these two houses. If we don't assume that, then we have to leave this area to find the caves. At least if we make that assumption, we have a starting point."

"Agreed," Joule said. "If they started from here today, they're not back yet. Do we wait?"

"Some of us do." Jacob said. "Two on each house as surveillance. They can call in if the group returns and tell us which house it is."

Kathryn seemed to read her brother's mind. "The rest of us can head out. See if we can find fresh tracks."

"Fresher than what we found earlier?" Joule asked. *Had they been so close? Had they just barely missed her brother?*

Jacob helped set up the teams on either side of the two houses. The team members would stay together, right next to each other, so they couldn't be separated if they were found out. He gave instructions to give three beeps on the walkie talkie for mild trouble, but only one or two if they couldn't get three out. The fewer beeps, the more dire the emergency.

Kathryn handed out satellite phones. One to each group.

"We have walkies," Amber shrugged.

"Not secure," Kayla said at the same time Kathryn answered, "Anyone can tune in to them."

It was clear from the look on his face that Jacob McQueeny didn't like it. But it was also clear that he wasn't in charge. He could be a friend and help, or he could leave. His own sister was clearly deep in the game.

He set Gisela, Amber, Brooklyn, and Ivy on watch, giving them strict instructions that Joule didn't hear all of. She was too busy working out how all the pieces might fit. Then Jacob joined the remaining team to split up again into two search teams.

With the drones fully charged and ready to go, they sent two with one group and one with the other.

"We can't cover as much ground with fewer people," Joule said. "Which paths do we follow?"

"We think the sweater was left there relatively recently, right?" David asked. When they all nodded, he added, "Then that's probably a path they won't repeat for a little while. In fact, the other path also was relatively fresh."

"It had to be," Ivy said. "We saw it. The desert has to eat those things pretty quickly, doesn't it?"

Joule didn't know the answer, but it seemed as good of logic as any.

Kathryn had nodded along, though she didn't have her mother's tracking skills. Like Ivy said before, they either followed what they had, or they did nothing.

"So, we don't follow a path," Joule thought it through.

"Right, we send some toward the caves and the rest into the spaces between the recent paths," David declared.

A short while later, Kayla, David, Kathryn and Joule we're heading out into the desert one more time.

C age scrambled as Sarah leaped to her feet, now tackling Terrence. She managed to get the gun away, but it was clear by the way she held it that she didn't know what she was doing.

Terrence swung wildly at her with his good arm. On the ground, Connor—who'd been accidentally released as Cage tried to help Sarah—scrambled to get up.

Grabbing the gun from Sarah, Cage swung it back toward Connor. Sarah would have to keep his back clear from Terrence ... and any other comers.

Where he faced now, Cage could see Aurora had gained her feet. That was good because everything had turned around. Cage's eyes darted from person to person as they scooted out of the way, not wanting to be in the line of fire. Had Connor purposefully put himself in between Cage and the others or had that been dumb luck?

Putting his hands up casually, Connor offered a soft grin that would have been considered friendly on anyone who didn't have shark eyes. "Hey, man, you don't need to do that. We're good here."

He reached out as if Cage would casually hand the gun back. Cage took a step backwards and braced both hands on the gun. His finger rested inside the trigger guard, ready.

Connor took a step forward. "You're not going to pull that trigger. You may be Terrence now, but you don't have what it takes."

It would be inappropriate to chuckle or offer a sharp comeback, so Cage just stood his ground. "If you come any closer, I will shoot you."

"You don't mean that."

Connor's foot had moved so Cage put a bullet in his shoulder.

His whole body ricocheted back, both men pushed opposite directions by the force of the bullet leaving the chamber and hitting Connor.

The affable expression flipped to that of a monster. His lip curled, his left arm now hanging limp. Shoulder shots were not the easy through-and-through that they appeared on TV. But Connor didn't offer any more words. Instead, he just lunged.

Cage pulled the trigger two more times.

By the time Connor stumbled to Cage's feet, he was on his knees, his right hand now grasping at his chest where red bloomed on that ugly, stupid, wife-beater tank top that he always wore. The black jeans were absorbing the color as the red ran down into them. But there was no escaping that he wasn't going to escape this.

Connor breathed heavily, making sick sucking sounds as he tried to inhale. At least one of the shots must have collapsed a lung. That hurt like a motherfucker. Cage found he didn't care. Whatever he'd hit, it would soon be fatal.

Connor gasped, rolling over, trying to both grasp at his chest and brace himself up from the ground with his one good hand. It didn't hold for long and he fell onto his side, staring up into the night sky.

It was impossible to tell when the light left his eyes because it had never been there in the first place.

Cage's own chest felt like it had been in a vise. He'd not yet figured out if he had been shot or not. But there wasn't time for that.

Terrence snarled at him though Sarah was still holding him off. His bad arm kept him from being too willing to blatantly attack.

"You told everybody you're Terrence," he said, "I suppose you're Connor now, too."

"No," Cage said turning and looking around the group. The gun stayed aimed at the ground, but not held loosely. Three bullets he'd fired. Two from Connor during the fight. There should be only one more. He didn't stop to check.

He turned to see Sarah trying to help with Dodger's wound. It didn't look too bad, but what did he know?

"No one is Connor now. We need to leave."

"I don't understand," one of the teens said. The others mostly didn't speak at all. They just looked frightened or babbled back and forth in rapid fire Spanish that Cage could not understand. No one was translating.

"We're less than an hour from base." He couldn't call it home. "I don't know how much leeway they give Connor for when we get back. But sooner or later, they're going to see that we're not there. They're going to come looking for us."

He didn't have to say it. He could see the change in the eyes around him. They all understood when the others came looking, they would come with guns.

"They have ATVs," one of the younger men who'd been talking in Spanish said. "Three of them. I've seen them."

Fuck, Cage thought. He'd not seen the ATVs come out. But they would make it very easy to run these people down. Between them, they had one bullet and there was no telling the amount of ammo the others had.

They were sitting ducks.

"We need to scatter," Cage told them. They had to get as far away as possible. If their captors got near them, their only hope would be to hide—*where?*—until morning, and pray their captors decided to stop looking.

Were there caves that the runners didn't know about? Would that be enough if they mobilized troops?

Cage looked up at the night sky. The stars overhead would have been beautiful in any other circumstance. He couldn't even read them. But he could see where they were, and he could follow a path. He was pretty sure he knew which direction was West.

It would be a long walk in the heat of the desert. They had only whatever they hadn't drunk or eaten tonight, but Joule would be looking for him and they would make it. Unless any of them encountered someone else looking for them.

All he could do now was hope the pickup teams already had what they were after. They'd gotten their materials while he'd watched through the binoculars. So maybe he didn't have to worry about them until much, much later.

"I don't think we can run." One of the women looked scared. "We have to go back. It's safer. You're Connor now."

Cage shook his head again. "No, I'm not. I'm not going back. If any of you goes back, you kill those of us who leave. We *all* have to escape."

Nobody said anything. He tried again. "You're free now!"

It was clear some of them had been here for too long to even know what to do with that, but they were wasting time standing here.

Sarah had help from one of the other young men as they now tried to tie off Dodger's wound. The whole thing was taking too long. They should have been running as soon as Connor's eyes rolled back.

Three of the teenagers began their rapid fire talk again.

Cage recognized this time that it wasn't Spanish but Portuguese.

"Were going back," the one said.

Cage quickly protested.

The kid held up a hand. "We're going to get the ATVs so they can't follow us."

"That's not safe. What if they catch you?"

"They'll definitely catch us if they get the ATVs."

Cage couldn't argue that as he agreed.

The kid had a plan, though. "If we go back and get the ATVs, we should be able to get there before they realize we're missing. Then we'll ride away."

Cage was thinking they would puncture the tires or find a way to empty the gas tanks. But the vehicles weren't repairable if they weren't even there. Also the boys would get further, faster on the ATVs. It would help make up for heading back into the Wolf's Den.

He looked between them. *Could he trust them?*

If they went back and alerted the men that Connor was dead and the others had defected, it would put Brown Eyes on the trail that much faster. As much as Cage did not like Connor, every step up the ladder seemed to attract a worse person.

There was no time to say no. "Do you promise me? You'll just get the ATVs and get away? If you tell them what we did, I will hunt you down myself."

The English speaker nodded solemnly, quickly translated for his friends, and they too nodded. He had to trust them. Reaching into his pocket, he pulled out the knife he'd originally taken off Terrence. "Take this. Once you run out of gas, slash the tires."

The one handed it to his friend, then took three steps backwards. They watched Cage as if waiting for him to make another move. Then, they turned and bolted back toward the house. They had to get a move on. Cage knew if they waited any longer, if the boys betrayed them, if there was more than ATVs that could come out looking for them, the remaining people didn't have much time to escape.

He motioned to Sarah and Aurora to join him. Sarah tried to stay with Dodger, having tied his shirt tightly around his wound, but the older man waved her away. Two of the younger boys stayed against his side and Cage only now realized they bore an uncanny resemblance to him. A family.

One of the young women darted over to join them, the spell of their separation broken. Dodger's arms linked around her in a relieved hug that in itself almost made all this worthwhile.

Looking at Cage, Dodger pointed to himself, then the kids, then a direction that was relatively northwest.

"Go!" Cage told them. "As fast as you can."

The little girl translated for the man who was her father or her grandfather. Cage couldn't tell.

Then he pushed the gun down into his pocket. Grateful, not for the first time in his life, that he wore cargo pants.

Then he, Sarah, and Aurora linked hands, aimed themselves west, and ran.

77

Thirty minutes and nothing. Then an hour and nothing.

Joule hated that things had gotten slow enough that at one point, Amber had checked in with "All Quiet on the Western Front."

Even the chatter among their little group had ground to almost nothing. They only spoke if David spotted something on the screen that he needed someone to look at. Then a couple of them would lean over, agree or disagree, and keep going.

It wasn't supposed to be like this. They were supposed to find something. They'd gotten the sweater—a huge leap forward—and she'd wanted to maintain that speed so desperately. It simply wasn't happening.

Somebody had to see something, she told herself. If it wasn't tonight, then they would just keep going. She made plans, though she stayed silent. Her inner world was rife with conflict. They could sleep in the cars in shifts. Someone would keep an eye on both the houses. Unless the cartel had moved everybody just before they got here . . . then she made a plan for that, too.

The information Cage had sent couldn't be wrong. She was his twin. She wouldn't have misinterpreted it.

Could she convince everybody to follow her plan? Or at least convince someone to give her a better one?

The sat phone came to life and Kathryn, automatically in charge of her own equipment, held it up so everyone could hear. They'd kept an open line the whole time though no one was talking now.

"Something's going down." Gisela and Brooklyn were on the southern house that was being watched. Amber and Ivy were watching the one more north.

"Are you watching the right place?" Kathryn asked what they were all thinking.

"I don't know yet. But three teenagers just came out of the desert."

"Did you watch them come in?" Joule jumped in close.

"Yeah, we spotted them a little while ago and didn't know what they were or which house they were going to go to. We didn't want to say anything," Brooklyn told them. "But they came here and snuck into the garage."

"I don't think anybody's seen them but us," Gisela added.

Joule, David, Kayla, and Kathryn looked at each other. It certainly sounded suspicious.

"It's not enough people," Joule said.

"I know," Gisela was speaking softly, "But something feels like they're part of the group."

Why would only part of the group come back? But she wasn't the only one who thought it.

"There's no evidence of them splitting up before," Dr. Murasawa added in from the other team.

"Have the search teams found anything?" Ivy asked, though she had to know if they had they would have said so.

Brooklyn started to speak, but Joule didn't catch what she

said as a rough noise cut through the sound, interrupting the conversation. Then another, second, louder version interfered, and at last another.

"What was *that?*" David asked, leaning over to speak directly into the phone.

"They just left on three ATVs from the shed out back!" Brooklyn and Gisela were excited. "They're heading back out into the desert!" "It looks like they're going a different direction than—"

Holy gopher shit. Joule's heart pounded as Brooklyn and Gisela's voices disappeared. Their line went dead.

78

They'd seen nothing and heard nothing. That had to be a good sign, Cage thought.

But their ability to keep going was fading. None of them was hurt per se, but they were at the end of an already long night. They always arrived back at the house exhausted. The work was strenuous and what they were fed wasn't enough.

It hadn't been the kind of food they could stash away in their pockets for an escape either. And they hadn't planned on escaping tonight. In fact, they hadn't actually escaped yet . . .

Had that low quality food been on purpose? Underfeed them so they didn't have the stamina to get away?

He put one foot in front of the other on sheer willpower, lying to Aurora and Sarah that they could keep going. All three of them neglected to comment that the sun would come up and the land would get unbearably hot for three people with almost no water.

Still, the opportunity had presented itself and they were committed.

Even like this, he felt more free than he had since he'd been taken.

A hand tugged at his, slowing him down. It wasn't Aurora who had trouble keeping up, but Sarah. Even given their week in captivity, Sarah's *extra* week seemed to have made it harder for her to exert herself.

Shuffling places, Cage and Aurora put Sarah into the middle, holding hands with a firm grip and pulling her along.

He prayed for everything to work.

He prayed for Joule to find them before Brown Eyes and the others did.

He prayed for the boys to make it to the ATVs and to get away cleanly.

He prayed that they didn't tip off their captors, either by accident or on purpose as to what had actually gone down.

He prayed for Dodger and his kids—or grandkids—to get far enough away.

But Cage didn't quite know who he prayed to, what gods held sway out here in the middle of nowhere.

As the stars faded away in the growing light of the dawn, he watched a streak cross the sky.

Aurora commented, a smidge of wonder in her voice, "A shooting star. It's good luck."

Cage didn't correct her that it was likely a satellite.

79

They all stared at each other, waiting. The other group, and Ivy and Amber watching the other house had to be doing the same—all holding their breath and wondering what had happened to Gisela and Brooklyn.

The line stayed open for the rest of them, but no one spoke.

Then, a voice came across the line. Ivy. "We can see some of what's going on. People just ran out of the house. Just a few, two or three."

There was a pause, her voice was low, and they all leaned in close to hear it.

"I think Gisela and Brooklyn turned the phone off themselves to keep it from making noises and alerting anyone they were there." Another pause. "I think they're okay. If the house empties out and they can get away somewhere safe, they can talk."

Joule's racing heartbeat began to slow but this was not the normal activity of the group—not that she truly knew normal, but this couldn't be it.

The night was still dark. She couldn't see everyone, and she was petrified that, instead of bringing the three missing home, they'd just lost two more.

"Tell us what's happening." Kathryn almost demanded it.

"Men ran out, guns in hand. One tall, skinny, brown hair, brown eyes, brown skin. Angry. The other one came out behind him. Honestly, he didn't look quite right, maybe drunk."

A pause and Joule waited until Ivy could narrate again.

"They ran to the shed first. Looks like they see the ATVs missing."

"Hold on," Ivy took a breath in, and the line was so quiet they could all hear it. The wind picked up, whirring softly past Joule's ear, letting her know the morning was coming. Soon.

"They're coming out of the shed now and running out into the desert."

What even was going on? Joule couldn't make it work.

The first ones left on ATVs and these guys *ran* after them? They wouldn't catch up.

She looked to David then to Kayla, keeping her voice low, hoping not to be loud across the line. "Do you think the group split up? Maybe a few of them came back and got the ATVs?"

"Somebody's on ATVs and somebody is on foot," Kayla said. "I don't know who the good guys and bad guys are in this story right now."

True. The only known good guys were Cage, Aurora, and Sarah.

As far as Joule knew, there were likely more but she didn't know the players. And there were likely bad guys and *very* bad guys, if there was a cartel involved.

"We have to go back in," David said.

"No!" Kayla protested quickly. "We're out here already. We just need to change direction to intercept wherever the group is. They're obviously not back. Or only three of them are." She was talking a mile a minute.

"If they're close to the house, then that's the direction we need to be going," David argued. "But more than that, we need to get back where I can get a connection and start combing satellite photos."

As Joule and Kathryn watched the conversation, it was easy to see the moment Kayla's eyes lit up. "Yes, that's exactly what we need to do!"

"No!" This time it was Joule who uttered it sharply. "How long is it going to take us to get back in the first place? We're going to lose all our advantage."

Kathryn moved the phone closer to her head. Had she heard someone talking? She held up one finger and asked into the device, "Do we have contact with Gisela and Brooklyn yet?"

"Not yet," Ivy answered, Amber had been staying silent. "But I don't see anything. There was no fight. No shots fired. I don't see where they would be damaged. I suspect they're just laying low."

It made sense, and Joule liked an explanation that made sense and kept her friends safe.

Jacob's voice came over the line for the first time. Joule had gotten the impression that he was quiet because he didn't like the plan. He probably liked it less now, but his tone was heavy and brooked no opposition. "As soon as you see them and we get them on the line, we need to reframe who's watching the houses. Two of the watchers have to head back to the car with one sat phone. They'll hook up a hotspot and start searching satellite images and relay information to the searchers in the desert."

But the women on the house were not the people who should be searching those images, Joule thought, *that should be David and Kayla.* Maybe Dr. Murasawa. All the people they'd put into the desert with the drones! Not one of their good image searchers or tech savvy people had been left to watch the houses!

Was there time to send their top people back?

Joule worked it out. She and Kathryn could stay out here, continue the search.

But there likely wasn't enough time. What if they ran into someone? They would need to outnumber them if they could. Sending two of their people back would make that a problem.

They couldn't send David and Kayla back. They were needed here, too. Joule simply had to have faith in whoever got on the computers. Faith that they can follow instructions and do the job.

"We keep the drones and we keep going," Kathryn confirmed with her brother, then she instructed David to make wide sweeps with the drone.

Again, the conversation lulled except for a few moments where they heard that Gisela and Brooklyn were safe.

"I see them!" Amber called out. "They turned off their phone and hid."

"Hi! Sorry for the scare," Gisela told them. "We used the thermal guns, and the house is empty now."

It seemed to take forever, but eventually the four at base camp reported back that Ivy and Amber were watching the houses now and Brooklyn and Gisela were almost into the SUV.

A little while later they were locked in, camped in the backseat and following instructions to start combing the satellite images.

Though Joule's group had listened to all the updates, they'd stayed quiet with nothing to add until Kayla—who was occasionally looking over David's shoulder at the drone images—said, "Go over there. Look . . . check that."

She pointed to one place and then another.

As Joule watched, David grinned. "Footprints."

80

"Looks like three sets," Joule pointed, glad she was looking at the marks with her own eyes now. The sun had come up just enough that she didn't even need the light from her phone if she kept her gaze directly in front of her.

No word had come from Gisela and Brooklyn in the car, but they probably had hours of images to search. Who knew if they'd find anything?

"They aren't large," Kathryn said, looking up at the others.

It was Kayla who caught on first. "You think it might be the three who went back for the ATVs."

"They're aimed in the right direction," Turning, Kathryn pointed back the way they'd come.

"Then we follow them backwards," Joule said, ready to move.

She felt her energy kick up again. It was difficult not to run, but that was a bad idea. The group did pick up their pace though.

They weren't even twenty minutes further along when the marks changed.

"Something happened here." Joules eyes were still aimed straight at the ground. In the dim light she saw a mess indicating people had been down on the ground and wiggling around, then getting up and walking different directions.

"There were more than just the three here." Kathryn stated.

"Do you think this is where they split up?" Joule asked, just as Kayla cut in.

"Guys?"

"It looks like some went that way." David still managed the drone as he pointed to a set of tracks, some smaller, one larger.

The larger set was deeper, the smaller ones tucked right beside it. She was no tracker, but it looked to Joule as if the smaller ones were supporting the larger person in the middle.

"Guys," Kayla said again.

"Still not as many people as Cage told us about." Katherine pointed again. "Three that way, maybe four or five that way."

"Guys!" This time Kayla spoke with a staccato that Joule knew meant business. "There's a body right here."

"What?"

They all turned.

How had they missed that? But there was scrub brush all around. Occasionally rocks. The body had been rolled over facedown. An empty water jug was crushed nearby, so the white of the shirt wasn't shocking in itself. A bag rolled across the sand a few feet away. And the sun wasn't up high enough for them to see more than four feet in front of them.

"Is he actually dead?" David asked, for once stepping back.

Was he squeamish around dead bodies?

"It doesn't look like he's been here very long," Joule said. He didn't look anything like the body that she'd found before.

With David hanging back, the three women gathered around, Kathryn the first to nudge at his hand with the back of her fingers.

When he didn't respond, she pulled back. "I don't have any hand wipes or . . ."

"I have hand sanitizer," Joule volunteered and rummaged in her bag for it.

Kathryn reached around the wrist and checked for a pulse. Apparently finding none she moved the arm back until the body flopped over, revealing red stains down the front of him.

"There was blood on his back, too," Joule told her, "But I didn't recognize it because the sand had blown up into it and stuck."

"When it was wet," Kayla added and they noticed how the sand had clumped along the front of the shirt, too. This had been enough blood to soak through, though. Enough to leave a soaked spot on the desert floor.

"He's not cold," Kathryn said.

"Would it even get cold out here?" Kayla asked.

"At night, yes."

"You have a *body?*" Dr. Murasawa exclaimed through the open line.

"Just found it. In the middle of a scuffle."

"Kathryn." Jacob's voice came over the line next.

"You didn't hear *anything,* Jacob. You can find this one later and call it in then."

"I have to call it in!" he almost yelled it.

Kathryn shot back, "You're not even in jurisdiction!"

Joule held her breath, waiting for the siblings to come to a conclusion. It didn't sound like Kathryn would stop her from tracking farther. Even if Jacob did come out here and turn this into some kind of federal crime scene, Joule could be gone before he got here.

Though, hell. The only agency she hadn't crossed yet was the Rangers, so why not get them involved, too?

The conversation stopped as Gisela's voice popped up. "Hey, guys?"

"Jacob," Kathryn drew out his name, making Joule believe that Kathryn was definitely the older sibling.

"Fine," he replied, giving up.

"Guys?" Gisela's voice came through again.

This time, Joule thought she might listen, "What is it?"

"Three large black SUVs just squealed up in front of the house. People are getting out."

"How many?" Jacob pressed.

"We don't know because we slid down into the footwell so we're not being seen," Brooklyn said, punctuating each word.

That was smart.

"How many doors slammed?" Jacob again. Smart question.

"Hold on." A short wait later she announced, "Five, at least."

So, there were at least five of them. That could not be good.

"Ivy? Amber?" Jacob asked, always the one to check in and make sure his people were still in place. Joule appreciated that.

"All good. Heard the cars but don't see anybody yet," Ivy was nearly whispering from her roughly hidden spot behind the houses with Amber.

"They're going in the front of the house—for God's sakes, Brooklyn! Don't peek!"

Joule could practically hear Gisela winding her fingers into Brooklyn's shirt and pulling her down.

Joule's entire group had stopped where they were, waiting, tense, until Ivy said very, very softly, "They're coming out the back of the house. Do not answer me. No noise . . . They're armed, heavily . . . One of them just got out his phone. He's tapping on it."

Joule wanted to ask if he was calling someone and how could they find out who? Did Jacob or Kathryn know a way to trace the number? Hell, maybe David did.

Ivy spoke again. "He didn't put the phone to his face. He's messaging someone or checking something."

Just then Joule's phone pinged. Frowning, she pulled it out

of her pocket. She must have gone pale, because Kathryn looked at her and asked, "What is it?"

"I didn't think this could happen." Her chest clenched. *She'd made a horrible error.*

Kathryn stepped in close, her presence demanding an answer.

"I didn't delete the tracking app. I just turned it off."

The look on Kathryn's face told Joule exactly what she had just learned. *That wasn't enough.*

Kathryn stared at her and asked, "It just pinged, didn't it?"

81

They walked on, the three of them still hand in hand. They carried their water bottles, though the levels were low.

"Sip," Cage said.

They stopped, drinking ever so slightly, conserving as much water as they could. Each time he drank, he felt it through his entire system. He had to be so dehydrated to feel it that way, but he also wouldn't drink more. He was watching the water level drop and knowing what it meant.

This time when they walked again, Sarah swayed then stumbled forward. With only a glance to each other to communicate, Cage and Aurora quickly moved in, draping Sarah's arms over their own shoulders.

The three of them were closer now, supporting Sarah. The extra effort wasn't good for the two of them. They weren't doing that well without carrying a third. But they weren't going to leave her behind.

They went a little further, the sun still coming up behind them.

Cage realized that, being closer, whatever body heat they had was multiplied. That was also bad. The counter for that was more water, which they absolutely did not have.

He wasn't sure how much longer or further they went. The light was getting a little bit brighter, and his vision was distorting the distance.

Cage was glad now that he was no longer navigating by the stars. All he had to do was keep the sun behind him and continuously step forward into his shadow. It would be the right direction.

But his thoughts swam.

He had walked this distance the first night, not even in a straight line. If they beelined back, they could make it.

Except they'd already gone out tonight and back. They'd dug in the sand. They'd carried heavy bags, and they'd done it on poor rations for a week. So maybe they couldn't make it— even heading straight.

Maybe they shouldn't, he thought. Towns out here were sparse and far between. What if they walked right through the towns and into Mexico?

They shouldn't be able to cross the Rio Grande without noticing, right? But hadn't the Rio Grande gone dry recently?

He did not want to walk all the way into Mexico.

San Antonio was somewhere behind him, but he had no idea what he was closer to.

He was certain he didn't have the navigation skills to figure out where he was starting. Or even if he knew that, which direction San Antonio was. If they headed into the sun, they would likely have to go close—if not through—whatever little cluster of homes the cartel had kept them at.

They wouldn't go back.

He moved his left foot then his right and tried to keep his mouth shut. It was tempting to open and breathe through it.

But he couldn't. He would lose the moisture in his mouth. Though that might cool him, the moisture was precious. The sand would blow in the finest tiniest of grains and he would wind up licking the inside of his own mouth to make it go away. He'd learned that the first night out.

Sarah stumbled again and, over her shoulder, Cage looked to Aurora.

"We'll stop and sit down just for a short while," he announced.

What he wouldn't have given for a phone timer. They didn't have anything digital on them. Of course, no one had worn an actual analog watch, either. Not even Aurora.

His phone and his gun had been taken. He was tempted now to jettison the gun in his pants pocket. What good would it do if he couldn't lift it? It was just a heavy item he was carrying. But then he remembered it was *evidence* and he left it where it was.

Sarah sat down faster than him or Aurora, plopping hard onto the sand. Cage was almost surprised she managed to stay upright.

Though they had never planned it, they only drank with each of them unscrewing the caps of their water bottles, together. They held them up, then drank, then held them up again—as if to monitor that all of them were drinking the same small amounts. That no one was going through theirs too quickly.

He didn't know how long they sat there. He'd thought they would just wait until Sarah was doing better, but there was no *better* for Sarah.

He thought for a moment of the Donner party, trapped in snow and ice. What he wouldn't give for snow and ice right now. But he didn't want to imagine dying twenty miles away from salvation.

He had no idea how long it had been when Aurora nodded at him. They needed to get going.

But this time when they went to pick up Sarah, she didn't move.

———————

82

"They're tracking you," Kathryn told Joule, looking her in the eyes. "And they know now right where the four of us are."

"How is there even a cell signal reaching out here?" Joule was grasping at straws.

"They bounce." Kathryn shrugged. "You'll get a random signal in the middle of the desert sometimes. You walked into one and they found you."

"Unless it's Cage."

"I doubt it's your brother. Any new text messages, any indication that it's actually him?" The same things she'd asked last time.

Desperate not to have been this stupid, Joule scrolled through as much as she could, trying to hold on to whatever little signal she had.

She shook her head at Kathryn. "Why would 'they'—" She held up her fingers in air quotes, "—be tracking *me?*"

"It's what the cartels do. If someone won't comply, they'll get their family members involved."

Joule had an idea that *get their family members involved* was the kindest way that Kathryn could say they intended to kidnap Joule and hold her to make Cage do whatever they wanted.

What had her brother done? And fucking good for him.

"What if I shut the whole phone off?" Joule asked.

"You can. But unless we shut down the entire cartel, they can track you forever on that thing."

Joule was reaching for the power button anyway, but it was David whose hand came out to stay her.

Kayla looked at David, the two of them seeming to share an idea. That was happening more and more. Joule always thought she had a logical mind, but Kayla's put hers to shame. Somehow, Kayla and David had found the same wavelength.

"Leave it on," Kayla said. "We need to throw it away somewhere."

"Well, they'll be able to track it to here," Joule motioned to the ground, and then to the footprints around her. If this was where Cage had gotten away, she didn't want them to find it. If she threw the phone in the direction she'd been going, how far could she throw it? Would it do anything?

It looked like some of the escapees had gone off in that direction. Joule absolutely did not want to get them in trouble. Particularly her brother.

"No," David said. "Don't throw it. We'll make it look like you're walking off in some other direction."

For a moment she froze. Were they asking her to sacrifice herself to the cartel to save them? Maybe she should. Kathryn had specifically told her to delete the app and she had thought that if she just turned it off, it would be okay. That if her brother ever got his phone again, or if she ever needed to track his phone to prosecute someone, she could turn the app back on and get them.

Fucking fuck balls.

But David wasn't looking at her like that. "We need a rubber band, something to tie it."

They all checked pockets, and no one seemed to have anything.

"Wait," Joule was already digging into her backpack. "Ponytail holders!"

"Excellent. Give me the phone." David held out his hand but then told her to take off the case.

The drone was a small, light thing. She worried about her phone being on it even though the phone wasn't that heavy.

It wasn't much but she peeled the casing, watching a paper flutter out of the back. She picked it up, brushed off the sand, and stuck it into her pocket. She had to keep that.

Then she handed the phone over to David. Even as he hairtied it on to the back of the drone, she wondered how far it would get.

"That'll weight it down. It won't get very high." She hated to be negative but she had to.

"I'm guessing that your tracking app doesn't have an altimeter. Because why? But it's probably better if the drone stays low to the ground. Just in case." David finished strapping the phone on top. He set it on the ground and added, "It gets as far as it gets. Even with the extra weight, we should be able to get it relatively far away."

Joule breathed in a little too deeply, the dry air sucking moisture from her lungs, even as it gave her oxygen. Then she watched as David steered her phone away, and all she could think was they had to do it. They couldn't lead the cartel directly to them.

She could only hope that she found her brother before he tried to contact her. Because she wouldn't be on the other end of the line now. Maybe in a couple of hours, the cartel would be.

83

While David was watching the drone fly away, the rest of them kept their eyes on the ground.

The sun getting high enough that they could actually see footprints out in front of them now. Joule figured at least now she'd spot a body. And they wouldn't all stand around like idiots while Kayla tried to get their attention.

David had sent the drone in an arc and then off orthogonal to where they were heading, hoping to make it look as though Joule had simply moved that way. He kept the pace fast enough to put distance between them, but slow enough that it looked like a person moving and not a drone.

Joule was grateful for a brilliant solution, but their group had had only one drone and now—due to her complete ineptitude—it was gone.

There were several sets of footprints going in this direction. They had to choose one set to follow.

A couple of tracks seemed to be clearly a pair. One group was four, another was a cluster that looked bigger. Joule followed one set: three sets of footprints side by side.

"Do we call this in?" she asked.

"Call what in?" the stern voice came over the line, and she should have been smarter.

Kathryn informed him about the tracks they'd chosen to follow, and Ivy and Amber had let them know that the men had come out at the back of the house, armed. They'd looked around then headed back and gotten motorbikes out of a trailer they'd brought.

Gisela and Amber updated everyone that they were staying in the footwell but continuing their work. If they were found it would have to be somebody looking directly into the car.

Joule only hoped they were far enough away from the house that the car didn't attract attention, because it didn't seem that they were in any position to get out of there.

Ivy updated everyone, "I don't see anyone else coming. But I have no idea if that means those men were headed your way or not."

Another voice cut through, "I've got something!"

Joule's heart lifted as Brooklyn explained. "The image is about four hours old."

David nodded, as if that were to be expected. They weren't getting live satellite feeds, just already archived images.

"It looks like a group out in the desert—"

"Do you see Cage or Sarah or Aurora?" Joule interrupted. She couldn't help it even though she knew Brooklyn was looking for the exact same people she was.

"Hold on," Brooklyn rattled off information so Gisela could search the same area and timeframe and Joule swore she could hear the tapping of keys.

"No, I'm looking down on the tops of their heads. I can't identify anyone, but I see people who could be them."

That was the best they could hope for.

"There's a series of images the satellite snagged as it went by. It seemed to go by pretty quickly so they're only in three or four. But it looks like a bit of a standoff—"

"Is one of the guys in a white tank top and black jeans?" Kayla asked, always making connections.

"Possible. He has black hair," Brooklyn added.

"Yes!" Joule almost screamed it. It had to be this group. And he was dead. Whether or not Cage was responsible, the group had scattered after this standoff. He must have been the ringleader.

Jacob growled through the line, probably at the confirmation of the body he wasn't reporting.

"Can you give me coordinates?" Kathryn asked.

"Hold on. I've got another one." This time it was Gisela, "Once we had that starting point Brooklyn found, I went around the area and I've got another image, more recent."

She rattled off coordinates.

"That doesn't mean anything to us. We're out in the middle of nowhere," David said.

Kathryn smiled. "Coordinates are good enough. I've got the satellite phone. It can locate us."

Gisela rattled off the numbers again, and it took a minute to get them into the phone. Kathryn was pointing them in the right direction when Gisela added, "I can only see the tops of their heads. But I think it's Cage and Sarah and Aurora."

84

S arah couldn't get up.

Cage didn't know how long it had been that she hadn't been able to. She was still alive, but he didn't want to lie her down in the sand. Cage and Aurora were giving her more sips of their own water in every effort to save her. They weren't strong enough to carry her, but he imagined that he would be if it became necessary.

Sarah and Aurora faced the direction they were heading, and Cage faced them, into the sun. Someone had to keep watch behind them. He felt his face starting to burn.

In the distance something shimmered. Something cast a shadow against the light, and it moved toward them. Probably a big cat looking for an easy dinner. He pulled the gun from his pocket, then tapped Aurora's arm trying to tell her *Look, someone is coming.*

Friend or foe, he couldn't tell. He wasn't even sure if it was human or some bug that had caught the sun, making him think it was much further away than it was.

He tried to grip the gun tightly, but even lifting it was too much effort. He'd already put fingerprints all over it. So hopefully they could find Connor's from under the mess. Hell, even Dodger and Sarah had touched it.

He had only the one bullet, but he was ready.

Keeping his eyes trained on the moving blob he only heard Aurora saying, "Sarah, we have to go."

He glanced over, concerned that she wasn't even responding. She just stared into the distance. He could see now that it was people approaching at her back.

A faint sound carried to him on the wind, and he had no idea if it was a yell of irritation, or call of friendship.

Aurora kept the bottled waters, letting him focus on what was coming. He didn't like not having it on him, but he had to keep holding the gun.

He wanted to run, but they simply couldn't. They wouldn't leave Sarah, and they couldn't carry her fast enough to make the effort useful.

He watched as the blobs moved and shimmered with the sun behind them. He thought he saw four people. There could be more if some were walking behind others, but he counted at least four . . . or maybe it was two and he had double vision. He blinked to clear his eyes, and then he heard it.

"Cage! *CAGE!*"

Another voice called out "Aurora!" and then "Sarah!"

He dropped the gun into the sand, scrambling to his feet and running.

85

"That's it. The drone is dead," David announced.

They all gathered around Cage and Sarah and Aurora. It seemed impossible, but he felt a million times better for having sports drink. He'd eaten a small nibble of food, too.

They'd managed to get Sarah revived a little bit, though there was no doubt she would need medical treatment. He and Aurora had managed to regain their own feet. But before they stood Sarah up, they had to decide which way did they go?

He might be found, but he wasn't quite saved yet.

"I don't know how far out we are." He told them. "Do we walk all the way back to El Indio?"

"Our cars are back near the house," Kathryn told him.

"That can't be good. They'll know we're gone by now," Aurora added.

"Oh, they already know," Kayla said, never one to pull her punches. "They're already sending people out this way and they're on bikes."

Cage almost put his hand to his forehead. But his skin felt

so hot after so long, that he didn't dare touch any part of him to any other part of him that he didn't have to.

"They'll find us," Kayla added. "I have the satellite phone, we can go where we need to, I just don't know where that is."

"They'll just follow the tracks until they find us."

"There were five of them," Joule told him, still looking at him as if he were a miracle. She'd hugged him long and hard enough to make him need air. But given the direness of the situation they'd quickly slipped into work mode. "How many groups did you split up into?"

He couldn't remember. But it didn't matter, five was enough that the odds of their track being followed by someone was relatively high.

"How fast can they go if they're on bikes?"

"I don't know." None of them did.

Brooklyn's voice came over the line again. "We got a very recent shot. It looks like the bikes found the scuffle."

It had been wild, not only seeing his sister, who had hugged him tight and celebrated that he'd finally been found, but also Kayla, and David. There was a new woman, a redhead, her hair up in a high ponytail. Her clothing was layered perfectly for the desert. She had hung back before introducing herself as Kathryn McQueeny.

Then the voices had come over the phone. Ivy first and then the others. Amber, Brooklyn, and Gisela. Kathryn had handed the phone to Aurora and let her tell Malcolm that she and Sarah were okay. But even at the sound of her father's voice Sarah hadn't responded. Aurora assured him that Sarah was still alive. They just needed to get her to medical treatment now.

First, they had to get out of here before the cartel caught up.

"Hey, you guys." The voice that Cage now recognized as Jacob McQueeny broke in. He had to be related to this Kathryn person, right? "Do you want my help now?"

Kathryn seemed to give in, and it was clear the argument was an old one, at least on today's search for their missing and maybe going back longer. "Yeah, Jacob, of course we want your help."

But even as she said it, Joule and Kayla turned abruptly, looking over their shoulders in the same direction.

That couldn't be good.

Cage thought they must have heard something. He was facing his sister and already aimed the direction that she had her head turned. It was Kayla who held her hand up, motioning for everyone else to stay quiet. But they didn't have to listen for long.

Two dirt bikes appeared in the distance, closing in the space faster than he could have thought possible.

He was stuck, motionless, where he was.

It was David who asked, "Do we run?"

Even Joule looked as if she couldn't decide.

Cage thought, *This is it.*

The men approached fast enough that he could see long barrel guns slung over their shoulders. They weren't here to dick around. He had one bullet, though he could see the gun at his sister's hip—the semi-automatic they'd bought to come out into the desert.

It wasn't enough. They would be mowed down with the room brooms.

They would be lucky if they managed to even wound one of the two.

"What is it?" Jacob was demanding over the open phone line.

"They're here," Kathryn told him. "On bikes. With guns."

86

The grind of the motors on the bikes got louder and louder.

They weren't dampened in any way, made for open desert riding.

As Joule watched, terrified, she saw one of them raise his arm. Before she even processed what was happening, she heard a bullet rip through the air.

But her own gun was already out and raised. As she aimed, she saw that, next to her, Kathryn McQueeny had already leveled two shots. Of course, she had. Every member of her family was in some kind of high-end law enforcement.

Joule squeezed off another, noticing a hand beside her. Her brother leveled a silver-barreled old fashioned six shooter, but he didn't fire.

Another shot came. She couldn't tell from where. She waited for the jolt, for one of her companions to fall, but one of the bikes flew sideways and went down. Somebody had hit a tire.

Yesss!

The owner went tumbling ass over teakettle, and it would

have been funny if he hadn't so quickly stood up and reached for the long gun on his back.

The ringing of the bullets dampened her hearing as the sand swirled up around them. Why was the desert rising up?

She didn't know, but she had to stay alive.

The noise was deafening, another tone came from somewhere over her head. Deep and awe inspiring, it issued a command though she pulled the trigger again because she couldn't quite hear it.

Next to her, Kathryn held out a hand for her to stop, then she turned and waved upward. Only then did Joule make out the sound of a helicopter hovering low, announcing that they were the DEA.

87

They'd arrived at the hospital by way of a second medical-equipped helicopter.

By the time he was taken in, Cage already had an IV in his arm. That was good, because after the DEA had rounded up the two on the bikes, he'd barfed up whatever sports drink he'd been given. Honestly, he'd been surprised he kept it down as long as he did.

The IV felt good, having been mixed with more than one thing. He was probably on antibiotics. Definitely on some kind of nutrition, and possibly on a painkiller. He felt a little too good.

He was entirely aware that his biology might be making massive amounts of endorphins, simply for still being alive. Or it might be a heavy narcotic.

It was only when they put him into a room that he'd noticed the heavy circles under Joule's eyes. Though she smiled incessantly, he could see the toll on her. She'd lost weight. *Well*, he thought, *that made two of them.*

He remembered when the tornado had taken her, and he hadn't been able to find her. He'd had faith that she could survive. But he'd been worried, *so worried*. Would he get to her in time? Or would he be too late?

Joule would have suffered the same fate now.

He knew, despite them being twins, they were different enough that she would have held it together better than he had. At least in the respect that she wouldn't have felt all the horrifying feelings while he was gone. They might be flooding her now, though.

She came into the room, drinking her Gatorade and eating a packet of orange crackers stuffed with peanut butter. She sat down in the chair next to him, she smiled at him, and when he blinked, she was asleep.

Okay, maybe narcotics, he thought.

When he blinked again, the sunlight had changed in the room.

Hell, what had they given him?

This time, a nurse was standing over him—probably what had woken him up—taking his vital signs. She smiled, declaring him all good and then turned to rouse Joule.

Only Joule didn't wake up.

The nurse shook her a little harder. She called out for help from beyond the door. Her tone wasn't panicked, but it panicked Cage. Then she reached over and hit a button, calling for the doctor.

88

"Eat the chili." Kayla held firm.

Joule was glad to be home, or at least at Kayla and Ivy's.

Eventually she'd wound up in the hospital bed on the other side of Cage's room. She remembered hearing Kayla's voice suggesting that she be put there with him. The nurse had responded that they didn't put men and women into the same room. To which Kayla had replied, "She's his twin sister," and then something about a lawsuit.

Joule had been in for two days—treated for dehydration, malnutrition, and general dumbassery on her part. It wouldn't have been excused except for the shittiness of the situation she'd been in the last week.

Kayla and Ivy had stayed with them—one of them sleeping in the room each day, the other going back to the little house and holding down the fort.

Ivy brought food and news that Aurora and Sarah both were doing well. Sarah wasn't out of the woods yet, but they expected a full recovery eventually. She'd told her mother that she'd left the clothing as a trail to find her.

They'd taken a long time to follow it, but they'd done it.

Kayla brought silly videos scrubbed from the internet and a small machine that she had designed. She'd updated Dev for them. And dialed the twins' grandparents, just for a much-needed chat.

Kathryn McQueeny had come through, bringing news. "The DEA got both of the guys who approached us on bikes! They were midway up the chain. It was a good collar." Then she added, "They also nabbed the two who showed up where the tracker led."

"Do I get to have my phone back?" Joule had asked.

"No!" Kathryn had told her in the tone that indicated she'd asked the most ridiculous question ever.

Joule let it go. "DEA got the credit?"

"Yup, it's my sister Lindy's case now."

"I'll bet Jacob's mad." Joule had almost laughed from her hospital bed.

"Nah, Lindy wrote him in on everything. Now the DEA wants him. Poor boy is trying to decide between that and the FBI."

"Good for him. When I get out of here and get a new phone, I'll tell him thank you myself."

Then, the next day Jacob had shown up, and Joule had thrown her arms around him. She'd already learned that the reason the DEA had shown up was because when he and Kathryn had argued about calling in the body—though it had seemed Kathryn had won the argument—Jacob had opened another line and called his sister Lindy. That timing had saved their lives.

If he had waited until they had conceded to needing help, they wouldn't still be here.

He told them there had been bodies found under the shed, too. Though he hadn't said anything about it, Joule had seen how hard that had rocked her brother.

He'd lived in that house off and on for a week.

Of course, not all of the cartel had been caught. Connor's body had been identified as already being wanted. Cage had confessed to killing him. But Sarah and Aurora told basically identical stories, so there was no chance of him being prosecuted. Jacob had recommended therapy for him. Then he'd set his eyes on Joule and said, "You, too, young lady."

Joule had complied. She'd be starting tomorrow. Apparently, after she ate the second damn bowl of chili. "I'm full," she told Kayla.

"That's fine. You don't have to eat it right now, but you have to eat it soon."

"Am I allowed to microwave it?"

Ivy had given her a look that said basically, don't be a smartass. But Kayla had answered the question. "Of course, you can."

The twins were staying now in Kayla and Ivy's house. Joule thought they could stay for maybe two or three more days. *But no more than three,* she told herself. She put a note on her calendar so that she couldn't just keep saying *one more day. One more day.*

She and Cage would move back into their own house. Kayla and Ivy had risked everything they could, taking time off work, coming out into the desert indefinitely, and even putting their own lives on the line.

It would be time for the twins to get out of their hair. Though Kayla and Ivy were serving as surrogate parents, Joule and Cage were adults, and they needed to live in their own home too, she knew.

"I'm going to wrap it and put it in the fridge. Then I'm setting an alarm for two hours. If you haven't come back in two hours," Kayla was telling her, "I'm going to hand you the chili again."

"That's fair," Joule conceded because, as much as she wasn't hungry and as much as she felt she'd eaten until she was stuffed, she still wasn't back to her original weight. She knew she needed the food. She and her brother had had more milkshakes in the past week than she could count. Chili was a welcome change.

The group migrated into the back room, as Cage had requested a silly movie. He'd been doing that a lot—seeking a distraction. Joule hoped his therapist could help him too.

Joule headed upstairs to the guest room she was sharing with Cage. It would be easier, they told Kayla and Ivy, to only worry about one room. In fact, it had been easier to stay in the same place as her brother, so that if she woke up in the middle of the night, she could see him. More than once she'd checked to be sure he was breathing. He might have done the same for her.

Night had fallen around them while they ate dinner and talked, ignoring the ordeal they'd all been through, trying to discuss normal things. Now Joule came up here to grab her ereader. She had no particular interest in the movie, but she was absolutely not going to try to outvote her brother.

She picked the device up off the bed, reaching up to pull the blind on the window. But as she looked down into the street, she saw a series of shadows just beyond the edge of the streetlight.

Low, long, and lean, they moved in a way that made her blood freeze.

ABOUT THE AUTHOR

A.J.'s world is strange place where patterns jump out and catch the eye, little is missed, and most of it can be recalled with a deep breath. In this world, the smell of Florida takes three weeks to fully leave the senses and the air in Dallas is so thick that the planes "sink" to the runways rather than actually landing.

For A.J., reality is always a little bit off from the norm and something usually lurks right under the surface. As a story-teller, A.J. loves irony, the unexpected, and a puzzle where all the pieces fit and make sense. Originally a scientist and a teacher, the writer says research is always a key player in the stories. AJ's motto is "It could happen. It wouldn't. But it could."

A.J. has lived in Florida and Los Angeles among a handful of other places. Recent whims have brought the dark writer to Tennessee, where home is a deceptively normal-looking neighborhood just outside Nashville.

For more information:
www.ReadAJS.com
AJ@ReadAJS.com

www.ingramcontent.com/pod-product-compliance
Lightning Source LLC
Chambersburg PA
CBHW020253030726
47499CB00001B/186